THE PRICE OF POWER

After centuries of persecution, the new races known as Genies rose up to demand their rights, led by a born leader known as Morgan of Alb'ny.

With two Genies at his side—the engineer known as Nebo, and the beautiful Alicia, a genetically bred politician who became his bride, Morgan led them in a great battle and won a resounding victory, assuring a future of dignity and hope for the new breeds of man.

But now that triumph had turned sour. Spared by a rash pledge, Ramon lived on to stir the fires of insurrection. And Alicia, driven by her desire for power, and Nebo, seduced by the lure of pure science, walked the borderline of betrayal.

Faced with the collapse of all his dreams, Morgan turned to the source of all power—the earth itself—to end a dying age and bring a new one to birth.

The majestic sequel to *Pure Blood, Mother Earth* is a fantastic epic of conflict and courage in the far distant future by Mike McQuay, bestselling author of *Jitterbug*.

Bantam Books by Mike McQuay
Ask your bookseller for the titles you have missed

JITTERBUG

LIFEKEEPER

MOTHER EARTH

PURE BLOOD

MOTHER
EARTH

Mike McQuay

BANTAM BOOKS
TORONTO · NEW YORK · LONDON · SYDNEY · AUCKLAND

MOTHER EARTH
A Bantam Book / August 1985

ISBN 0-553-25123-6

Published simultaneously in the United States and Canada

Bantam Books are published by Bantam Books, Inc. Its trademark, consisting of the words "Bantam Books" and the por-
trayal of a rooster, is Registered in U.S. Patent and Trademark
Office and in other countries. Marca Registrada. Bantam
Books, Inc., 666 Fifth Avenue, New York, New York 10103.

PRINTED IN THE UNITED STATES OF AMERICA

O   0 9 8 7 6 5 4 3 2 1

When in the morning I looked upon the light I felt in a moment that I was no stranger in this world, that the inscrutable without name and form had taken me in its arms in the form of my own mother.

—GITANJALI
Rabindranath Tagore

Prelude

The sky rolls perpetual gray above the lush jungles and charging rivers that are the lands of N'ork. It moves swiftly, borne upon hot winds of always summer, to bring the blessing and the curse of steaming rain that frees Nature's growth and condemns those not anchored in the soil to a sentence of daily war with the Earth for lifespace and freedom.

Thus it has been for a millenium. The dim past holds answers—heat-producing energy sources that gradually gave permanent rise to the temperatures, melting the polar ice caps and turning the planet to a tropical rain forest. The humans who made the heat made other things, too. Genies, they were called, genetic mutations bred for specific slave labor who decried the unbalance of the Earth and their own status, and banded together to end human rule for good. Genocidal wars ensued between the two species that culminated in the subordination of all to the Will of Nature.

And so it was for a thousand years, human and Genie living in separated pockets of humanity, carrying on their wildly varied bloodlines, fighting the age-old battles over superiority of species.

But all things, in their time, must change.

Enter Morgan of Siler, bastard son of the Governor of Alb'ny. Denied his birthright by his own brother, Ramon, he vows on the grave of his murdered mother to seek his just vengeance and to create a land where all species can bask in the radiance of freedom without restraint.

He takes to the lush, deadly jungles to hone the edge of his understanding and build a force not seen before in all past history—beast men and humans, dark Mechs from the clock-works city, eyeless seers, and albino eunuchs. . . .

And Alicia.

Alicia, whose brightness outshone the unseen Sun, whose mesmerizing beauty was matched only by her directed mind—a mind that existed for one purpose alone, the attainment of absolute power.

His life force charged with the heated plasma of indignation and justice, Morgan uses Alicia as the key to unlock the doors of power and responsibility, moving his ragged army to the shores of the wild raging Hus River, the essential artery to the heart of N'ork.

Ramon is meanwhile dreaming dark fantasies of his own brand of justice, preparing his incredible armada of humans and half-humans for the rape of the country, to put it under his own control and end the existence of the Genies for good and all.

It is the time of genocide, the time to confront the code of breeding and the cult of Pure Blood. The armies poise on the brink, knowing that change is in the offing. The moment hangs in the air, heavily, like the perpetual cloud cover that calls the tune of their lives. They are all trapped in the whirlpool of absolutes, choosing up sides, waiting for death, hoping for salvation.

And, as always, the difficulty in life is the choice. . . .

Band of three,
Band of three:
Soldier, builder,
Referee.

Band of three,
Band of three.
The perfect mix,
The apogee.

PART ONE

IDEALS

1

Kipsie—The Holy City

Serge, the giant, scrabbled up the small mountain made of the bones of twelve thousand men and flung his arms wide.

"U-Mans!" he called, his huge voice bellowing above the churning of Father Hus below. "Look what Morgan has done for you!"

And the humans of N'ork looked up and cheered while the mammoth Genie took their measure. They jammed onto the beach by the thousands, Southern humans, dressed in simple robes and dragging carts overladen with gifts of genetic fruits and flowers.

Serge watched, overcome with the exultation of it all. His mind, lost to the complexities of war and politics, only comprehended victory, only understood the excitement and riotous colors of it all. And perhaps that was the very best way to view the turn of the wheel of history.

"Serge!" Nebo, the Mech, called from the foot of the bone mountain, his mechanical hands cupped around his mouth. "Come down! We have need of you!"

The giant waved and started down immediately, for Nebo was *his* Mech, the other half of his life force, and was to be obeyed in all things.

The bones rattled around him, shifting and falling, as he climbed down the forty-foot pile. They were Schneck bones mostly, homicidal half-humans who waged the battle of Kipsie. But there were Genie bones, too. And some human.

Serge lost his footing on a slippery, lopsided Schneck skull

3

and tumbled, falling heavily to the ground at Nebo's sleek black feet. The dark man in the brown robes bent to peer into the face of his giant.

"This is no time for a rest," he said, his face without expression, his tones a rumbling melodious bass. "The processional is about to begin."

Serge grunted to a sitting position, the ground indented where he had fallen, and wagged his shaggy head. "The whole world comes here today," he said. "This is the day of all days!"

Nebo watched the giant stand. The Mech was as tall as any human alive, but Serge was twice his size. "The whole world isn't here," he told the Genie. "But we must pretend that it is."

"Pretend?" Serge asked, cocking his head.

"We sell ourselves today," Nebo said. He closed his mechanical fists with a clang, tiny puffs of gray-white smoke bleeding from the small hydraulic valves. "We sell the end of this world. Come. You help carry the dias."

And they moved through the carnival atmosphere of the beach toward the forty-gun wooden ship that had proved the end of the holy city and all that it stood for.

The heat was as hot as always, which was as hot as it could be, and the sky churned its perpetual roiling gray. If heat was the birthright of N'ork, then sweat was its legitimate heir. And they sweat, human and Genie alike. They sweat back to the soil that which they took from it.

And the beach was jammed with the People of N'ork. Human and Genie rubbed shoulders for the first time in peace to celebrate Morgan's victory in the first skirmish of the wars of Pure Blood. It was a manic celebration, bred as much by fear as happiness. For one battle did not a war make, and the worse, by far, was still ahead.

But this was Morgan's day, and it would be celebrated with a clamor that would shake Ibem in his cloud-jammed heaven. Already a scaffolding had been built beside the pile of bones, and bucket upon bucket of Hus river mud was being passed by hand to the top of the scaffolding and dumped upon the bones, ultimately to stand as a lasting memorial to the victory over the Schnecks.

While Southern humans gave huge displays of the juggling ability gleaned from years of living in the greenhouse jungles, Minnies delighted the crowd with living pyramids of

up to fifty of their numbers. There were songfests vying for
attention and the smell of carp roasting over pit fires that took
twelve women to tend.

The crowds grew larger with each passing day. As news of
Ramon Delaga's march of attrition through the South spread,
Southern humans and scattered pockets of Genies rallied to
Kipsie to gather under Morgan's aegis.

The boat was the focus. Called AVENGER by Ramon
when he sent it downriver to destroy Morgan, his half brother,
it was now called VICTORY, the spread-winged eagle of its
masthead the rallying point of Ramon's opposition.

It lay at anchor near the decimated pier from whence ten
thousand Schnecks under the command of Redrick of Firetree
disembarked to do battle with Morgan's small band. The
Schnecks now formed the foundation of a memorial to a new
world.

Redrick of Firetree, the human Schneck commander, was
among the missing.

And all around raged Father Hus, river of life, the unifying artery of N'ork. Though the virulent jungles tried to
smother the flowers of civilization, Father Hus kept them fed
and growing.

Nebo and Serge shoved their way through the jubilant
crowds and climbed up the makeshift gangway that led from
the river bank to the foredeck of VICTORY. Assorted Genies
jammed the deck full, plus Southern human dignitaries come
aboard to view the deck guns or try and plant a verbal seed in
the ear of the new Governor of Alb'ny.

Huge Woofers growled on the deck, or bayed at the gray
skies, the ship's movements unsettling their digestive tracts.
They retched and slobbered down upon those unfortunate
enough to be walking beneath their muzzles, Nebo making his
way through the crowd under an upraised, protective arm.

"Foreman," came a raspy voice from the darkness of a
cabin. Nebo and Serge shoved their way to the wooden door,
the stairs to A Deck forming a slanting roof above their heads.

The cabin was filled with Masurian Mechs of mixed blood,
all standing, crowded in together. Their dark skin was lost to
the shadows of the unlit room, only the white of their eyes
caught the glint of the light coming through the door.

"We've waited for you," the Mech at the door said.

"I have responsibilities in the parade," Nebo said, and

looked past the Mech's head to see who else occupied the small room. "Wait here until I summon you. We will march to the city together."

"Nebo . . ."

"Yes, Pietro?"

"We have heard . . . rumblings among the other Genies about . . . about . . ."

Nebo frowned. He'd been waiting for this. "About the blood-mixing during the victory celebration?"

Pietro nodded his patchy-haired head. "They are calling it the Night of Hemolysis."

Nebo looked at Serge, who stared back with just a hint of understanding. "What of it?" Nebo replied.

Pietro hesitated slightly, then turned to look at the others before answering. "What is . . . our position on the blood-mixing?" he asked.

Serge reached down and wiped the sweat from Nebo's hairless skull.

"I haven't formulated an opinion yet," Nebo said. "When we get through with all the ceremonials, I will dwell on it."

"We await your decision," Pietro said.

Nebo nodded, then walked off. He and Serge climbed the stairs that led to Morgan's cabin.

"The Mechs have a funny way to pick mates," Serge said to Nebo's back as they climbed the stairs.

"They mix the blood very carefully," Nebo said over his shoulder, "always looking to improve the mix. I think Morgan's pronouncement the other night shocked them."

They reached A Deck and stepped aside for a line of squat, muscular miners wrapped in garlands of wild orchids big as a fist.

"Serge hears talk also," the big man said. "Some of the People are unhappy with Morgan."

"Yes," Nebo answered, but his engineer's mind had detected a slight flaw in the design of VICTORY's prow and was already preoccupied in juggling possible solutions.

Just ahead of them, the door to Morgan's cabin burst open and a bundle of clothes came flying out. The bundle hit the wooden rail and burst like a melon on a hard pavement, sending blue, red, and bright white lengths of cloth fluttering away on the river breeze or drifting upon the heads of the already irritated Woofers on the foredeck.

"No!" Morgan screamed. "I won't!"

Serge and Nebo crept quietly up to the door and poked their heads in. The Governor of Alb'ny and hero of the Battle of Kipsie stood hip deep in shirts and bundles of material, his long red hair and beard brushed sleek and untangled, his naked chest glistening with sweat. Beside him, his wife, Alicia of the fox hair and golden eyes stood with her arms folded tightly over the bodice of her pale blue velvet gown.

"You're just being petulant," she said in her calm, Politico's voice. "Put one on."

Morgan snatched up a bright red shirt from the stack on the floor and shook it at her. "I don't like shirts. They make me hot, they bind me up. I've never worn shirts before, and I certainly don't intend to start now."

Alicia sighed, but remained calm. She was a negotiator by nature, a genetic wonder geared for diplomacy. "Many of the Southern kingdoms are offended by the hair on men's chests," she said. "We need their support. You must either wear the shirt or shave your chest."

Morgan put a hand to his chest, his fingers tangling in the curly red hair that matted it. "Do I have to?" he said sadly.

Alicia nodded. "That red one you were brandishing at me should do quite nicely."

Morgan grimaced and bent to the shirt. "Don't stand out there craning like loons," he said loudly. "You'll end up with a stiff neck."

Nebo cleared his throat and entered the cabin, Serge squatting down to look through the doorspace of a chamber he was too large to occupy.

"How go the preparations?" Morgan asked, as he slipped the billowy red shirt over his head.

"Everything's ready," Nebo said. "The Woofers are making a mess of the decks, though."

"Bunch of foolishness if you ask me," Morgan replied.

"You know we need to do this," Alicia said, as she handed Morgan the bandolier containing his sword and pistol. "A display of pomp and strength will do more to cement you in the minds of the South than five years of promises and negotiations."

"I know, I know," Morgan said wearily as he strapped on the leather belt.

"Any word from Nyack or Rockland or Mud Plains?" the Politico asked Nebo.

The Mech shook his head. "Not so much as a messenger."

"We need them," she said. "We must have their support if we're to have any luck at all against Ramon."

"What are you talking about?" Morgan said, drawing his sword. He looked at it carefully in the dull daylight of the open room. "There must be ten thousand people out there. We're already a success."

"There's closer to fifteen," she replied, "and we'll need triple that amount. Exuberance can only carry us so far, my love."

He smiled at her, knowing that she was reminding him that well-planned enterprises had never been his most profound consideration. "You'd think they'd at least send someone to parlay," he said.

"They fear the contact," she replied. "As the largest Provinces, they have the most to lose. They hope to remain neutral and join with the strength when it becomes evident."

"A dangerous game with my brother."

"We need to convince them of that."

Squan, the cat-man, scurried down the promenade and vaulted Serge's massive shoulder to land on all fours in the middle of the cabin. He stood to a half crouch, his nose whiskers twitching madly.

"All are aboard," he purred, then blinked his big yellow eyes several times. "And the Woofers make the decks unclean." He shuddered in revulsion.

"I don't care about the Woofers' mess," Morgan said. "We'll worry about it some other time. If everyone's on board, let's get this thing over with. Nebo, go line them up. Squan, make sure little Marek's out there. He rides with us."

"The Lawgivers will want Ibem on the lead dias," Nebo said.

Morgan looked at Alicia. She answered with a barely perceptible shake of the head.

"No," Morgan told Nebo. "Ibem and the Lawgivers must ride on the second dias."

"They won't . . ." Nebo began.

"See to it," Morgan said. "The parade begins immediately."

The Genies left, closing the door behind them.

"What do you think?" Morgan asked, opening his arms and turning a circle.

"You'll do," Alicia replied, stifling a smile.

"Well, you look beautiful," he said, moving close to fold her in his arms.

"Of course I do," she replied, returning the embrace. "Thanks for wearing the shirt."

"So long as I don't have to do it all the time."

She kissed him gently on the neck. "We'll see," she whispered.

He broke the embrace. Bending, he picked up the clothes remaining on the floor and bundled them into the closet recessed in the wall. "Whoever had this cabin before certainly liked a lot of clothes," he said, shutting the door on the jumble. "How could anyone wear this many?"

"Let me handle the discussion with the Lawgivers," she said. "It will require a delicate hand."

"Be my guest," he replied, and moved to the cabin door. "I'd as soon never deal with them or the little fella."

"The 'little fella' has gotten you this far. Don't forget it."

He threw open the door and stepped onto the deck. Below him, thousands swarmed the beach as the Kipsie Guard cleared a pathway for the processional.

"I'm not forgetting anything," he smiled. "I just see a day when Ibem may prove to be a tree fallen across our road."

Alicia took one last look in the mirror to reassure herself of what she already knew to be true, then joined Morgan at the door. "Any number of obstacles may await us on the road," she said. "We can only deal with them as we encounter them."

He snaked an arm around her slim waist. "Then let me escort you to our first encounter."

A Deck was deserted except for Morgan and Alicia. They swept along it easily, then descended the stairs into the beehive of the foredeck.

A platoon of giants crowded around the gangway. Morgan took his new bride by the hand and led her through the crowd to the giants. The Woofers stood behind the giants, whining and baying, as the Minnies tried to get upon their backs. Nebo stood arguing with Penrad, the eldest of the Lawgivers.

"The God of Heaven and Earth will not take seat behind any person—man or Genie," the old man said, his droopy white mustache bobbing up and down. "What sort of blasphemy is this?"

"This seems to me a display of very bad faith," said Lawgiver Rothman, waving his spindly fingers in the air. "We make a pact of equality, and you put God in the subordinate position at the first opportunity."

"Gentlemen," Alicia said smoothly, and glided unobtrusively in front of Nebo. "Surely you don't think that we're trying to subordinate God."

"What else would you call it?" asked young Lawgiver Dycus, his chubby face drawn hard.

"I'd call it good politics," Alicia said, and smiled at the Lawgivers as if each one of them was the smartest man in the world. "Let me explain."

Morgan moved away from the discussion to check the dias. Ibem was set firmly in the lead pallet, his shiny, stainless steel box of a body bleeping quietly, his small transmitter keeping him netted to his data source buried far beneath the blood-soaked Kipsie ground. A small gold crown was affixed to the top of Ibem's box. It overlapped a corner and was tilted at a jaunty angle.

"How are you this fine, lovely day?" Morgan asked the box.

"WE MISSED A REGULARLY SCHEDULED MAINTENANCE CHECK YESTERDAY," Ibem responded in monotone. "AND I HAVE BEEN IGNORED IN MY REQUEST FOR A PROGRAMMER IN PHYSICAL PROXIMITY AT ALL TIMES."

Morgan grimaced. "Well, you know, we've been pretty busy what with the war and all. . . ."

"THIS UNIT MUST BE PROTECTED AND SERVICED AT ALL TIMES. TO DO LESS IS TO NAIL SHUT THE COFFIN OF HUMANITY."

Morgan nodded, patting the box on the side. "Well, listen," he said. "I'll have a talk with some of the boys and see what I can do."

He wandered back to Alicia.

"Ibem does not need the respect of the South," she told the Lawgivers. "Morgan does. For Ibem to defer to Morgan, just this once, is a sign to all that this is the leader picked by God to defend the Southern Provinces."

"They can share the dias," Penrad said.

Alicia shook her head. "Morgan must stand alone," she said. "That must be the image left in everyone's brain. Look. Your city has been destroyed by those you thought loyal. Your way of life and your lives themselves will be lost next if we don't handle this just right."

She looked at them each in turn and put the right timbre in her voice. "Just once, just for a little while today, let Morgan be God. The life of the South may depend upon it."

The Lawgivers conferred briefly, their harsh whispers lost in the baying of the Bernards. Finally, Rothman spoke for the group.

"Just this once," he said, "we will let Morgan ride in the front dias. But only this once."

"Gentlemen," Alicia said. "You have made the wisest of decisions."

She strode to the lead dias and quickly snatched up Ibem before they could change their minds. Penrad grabbed the box from her and cradled it gently.

"WHAT HAPPENS?" Ibem said. "WHAT IS THIS MOVEMENT?"

"You are simply changing seats, my Lord," Rothman said soothingly to the box.

"WHY?"

Penrad carried the box to the second dias, speaking gently to it the entire time.

"Let's get this over with," Morgan told Alicia as they watched God move away. "Squan! Squan!"

The cat-man came running up, squeezing through a forest of giant knees. He held a small baby in his arms.

"Marek!" Morgan said, taking his child from Squan. "Are you ready to watch your father's triumph?"

With that, he boarded the large litter with the makeshift thrones, Alicia, his wife of less than a week taking the seat beside. They were staring way up into the crowd of wide, giant faces.

"Take us up," Morgan said.

The dias was lifted on the shoulders of six giants, Serge giving the orders from the lead spot. The crowds below cheered when the dias was hoisted into the air.

Morgan turned to look at the corps of Genies that filled the deck. "My friends," he called. "Between cloud and mud we stand. Let us stand tall. Destiny awaits!"

"Go!" Nebo shouted from the deck, and Serge moved the litter to the gangplank and down, a tumultuous greeting offered up from the crowd.

And the parade was met, Morgan, Alicia and Marek on the first dias, Ibem and the three Lawgivers on the second. Behind them, a double row of giants, beating on their huge drums in the strange, syncopated rhythm of their kind. Behind them were fifteen Woofers, all Bernards, with Minnies aboard, several per animal. Hundreds of Mechs followed, with Nebo of the Pure Blood in the lead, and behind them, the remainder of Morgan's Genie army, Genies of such assortment and de- meanor as to astound the view of the Southern humans come to pay them homage.

And for Morgan of Alb'ny, formerly Morgan of Siler, it was the realization of a dream nurtured in the dungeons of Alb'ny through the medium of pain and mud. Morgan of Alb'ny, son of Kings, Genie who passed for human—his hour was at hand. Already his newly won mantle hung upon his shoulders like a rusted steel girder, for as his fame and conquest grew, so grew his responsibilities.

As the procession stepped from the gangplank onto the soil of Kipsie, small children ran before the parade, throwing wild orchids onto the path. The Minnies spread the Woofers out when they reached land, using their telepathic contact to have the Bernards do tricks in unison.

They marched the beach, then took up the road to the city itself. The dead forest leading up to the Kipsie gates held human mutants, victims of the defoliants used by the Law- givers to keep the jungles away from their city. They peeked from behind rotting trunks, and darted from rock to rock, pale- skinned creatures accepted in no world at all.

The roadway was pitted with large craters thanks to the guns on the ship in the harbor. The main city gates were torn asunder. Within, the city itself was no more. Once a monu- ment to the lives of the ancients, it was a city untouched by the ravages of time and the jungle; now it was a still smoldering pile of mortar and beam, the perfect ashes from which to con- struct a new world.

"Many of us made peace with the Genie eons ago," said Notern, prelate of Fishkill, and his words were punctuated by grunts from around the bonfire.

He took a bite from the large applegenic that he held in two hands, its sweet juice mixing with the tobacco stains in his thick, wiry beard. "If we're to be damned for it, I'd as soon some Northers be damned with us also."

Morgan shook his head, watching twin bonfires reflected in the dark man's eyes. "We'll not be damned," he said. "When this is done, the lands of N'ork will belong to all of us."

"Bold words around the campfire," Notern answered, and bit again into the heavy red fruit.

Morgan gazed around the fire and saw the heads bobbing. Fifteen Southern leaders sat in conference with him, plus his own Genie council and young Dycus for the Lawgivers. Alicia hovered somewhere in the dark background, her sweet natural perfume mixing with the smell of frying carp from the campfires stretched out around Kipsie. Her place was to speak when asked, so as to not undermine the charisma of her husband.

"You doubt our righteousness?" he asked, unable to understand anything save his own unflinching devotion to cause.

"It's not your righteousness, Governor," said Trilly of Beacon. "It's your manpower. We're fifteen thousand strong, counting women and small children. Ramon is said to have nearly seven times that amount in seasoned troops. Look what just one of his warships did to our holy city. How can we hope to defeat such as that?"

Trilly sat coiled up on the ground, as if he were ready to spring like a rab at any moment. His face was long and angular, his look condescending.

"And I defeated that ship," Morgan insisted. "It sits moored on the river, its ten thousand warriors sacrificed to the sky."

"They were fools led by a fool," Trilly responded. "You will not be so fortunate next time."

Morgan felt the anger redden his face. The Schnecks may have been fools, but they were the most vicious warriors he had ever seen. "Listen . . ." he began, but stopped when he felt Alicia's hand on his shoulder.

"Gentlemen," she said with authority. "Ramon may have the numbers, but we have the combined wisdom of the ages."

With that, she threw a handful of what looked like yellow dirt onto the fire. It flared high with a roar, driving everyone back in fear and filling the clearing with a putrid odor. All dissipated within seconds, the fire returning to its original dimensions. Only the smell remained.

"A cheap trick," Alicia said. "Sulphur. Nothing special. But we know more, much more, more than the lives of Ramon's hundred thousand can account for."

"Evil science is not our way," said Duchess Clorina of Staatsburg. Clorina was young, still in her teenaged years. She had been the fifth wife of Duke Killough. The old man's heart had given out on his wedding night while discharging his husbandly duties, leaving the youngster in charge.

"Science is neither good nor evil," Alicia returned in her Politico's voice, smooth and non-threatening. "It is what we make it."

Notern spoke up. "Hain't that against our learnin' then?" he asked.

"We've adjusted to changes," Dycus answered with the authority of Ibem. "The new days are here. The new days bring new ways. Nothing of our lives will survive unless we embrace the viper."

Trilly spit loudly into the fire. "Maybe life without our values isn't worth living."

Morgan stood slowly and rounded the fire to look down at the man. His hand rested upon the boar's head hilt of his sword. "You came running down here for help fast enough when you felt Ramon's hot breath down your neck." He drew the sword slowly, its rasp like a whispered scream as it slid from the scabbard. "If you wish to die for your ideals, it would give me the utmost pleasure to make your wishes come true."

The man gulped loudly, his head wagging back and forth like a reed bouncing in a South wind. Morgan sided his weapon and squatted next to the man, putting an arm around his thin shoulders.

"My friend," he said softly. "I'm come to save you, not to kill you. We'll win the war, then you may return triumphant to your city and live by whatever ideals you choose."

"Can that happen?" the man asked.

"I swear it," Morgan said, then addressed everyone. "I want nothing from you except your help in saving yourselves. My kingdom lies to the North; it was given me by the Lawgivers. My only wish beyond that is for peace and freedom for all."

"And what of hemolysis?" came a voice from the darkness. Morgan stood, turning to look beyond the circle of fire-

light, the ruins of Kipsie a jewel of a thousand fire-facets set
firmly in a ring of wood and leaf.

"I speak not to disembodied voices," the Governor of
Alb'ny said. "Show yourself."

A small Genie walked into the light. It was El-tron of the
long, twiglike fingers and large, magnifying eyes. Morgan and
Alicia shared a look. El-tron had been one of Morgan's closest
allies since the black days in the dungeons of Alb'ny.

"Am I free to speak?" he asked.

"We're all free here," Morgan replied.

The Genie turned himself halfway to the fire, keeping its
light from reflecting directly on his sensitive eyes. "There is an
issue that needs resolving," he said, and his voice sounded
strained, his words fighting release. "The night of your victory
over the Schnecks, you had the People mix their blood by mating outside of their species."

"I did," Morgan said.

There were murmurs around the huge fire.

"That was a hateful precedent to many of us," El-tron continued. "I can trace my own line back for nearly twelve hundred years. To mix the blood means an end to the Clan of
Circuitwelder."

"Are we not all of one flesh?" Morgan asked.

"We are of one heart," El-tron responded. "That is not the
same thing. My balance is delicate. Mating outside of my Clan
will breed weakness."

"You don't know that," Morgan said.

"Would you have human mate with Genie?" Duchess
Clorina asked in distaste.

"Ramon Delaga, my half brother and pillager of the South
is a half-breed," Morgan said. "My own son, Marek, is the
result of such a union."

Lawgiver Dycus stood up and moved to Morgan's side,
the firelight sliding up and down his sleek robes in long
streamers. "Preservation of the species is of primary concern to
Ibem," he said. "Such hemolysis is a sin of the worst kind."

"Don't you understand?" Morgan told them all. "Separation of the species is what has led to all the problems we now
face. The species . . . all species must mix and start the new
world, the united world."

"The Schnecks were all half-breed," Notern said, and

threw the carcass of his dinner into the flames. "They were like mad Woofers, insane and deformed."

"Would you force such union?" Trilly asked, his brows knit tight.

"Our statements were in a philosophical vein," Alicia said before Morgan could speak. "The Night of Hemolysis was a symbolic action. While we support the mixing of species, we force no one to perform any action against his will."

"I can speak for myself," Morgan said low, through clenched teeth.

Alicia widened her eyes, trying to glare him to silence.

"This sets poorly," Trilly said, shaking his head.

"I force no one to my protection," Morgan replied.

Dycus turned to Alicia. "This issue of blood-mixing should have been discussed as part of our original deal," he told her.

"Talk to *me!*" Morgan bellowed. "What deal are you speaking of?"

"He's talking of the agreement I made that gave you the Governorship of Alb'ny," Alicia said quietly.

"I'm speaking with the Lawgiver," Morgan said. "Of what did this 'deal' consist?"

The man's chubby face reddened through the beads of sweat that slicked down it. "In return for the Governorship of Alb'ny," he said, "you agreed to acknowledge the religion of Ibem, to help liberate the South, to extend your own rule no farther than the boundaries of Alb'ny, and to honor the wishes of Jerlynn Delaga by not killing her son."

"Ramon," Morgan whispered and looked at Alicia.

"There was no other way," Alicia said quietly, letting her eyes do the pleading.

"He is the murderer of my mother," Morgan said, incredulous. "I am entitled to my just vengeance."

"Not if it includes the taking of Ramon Delaga's life," Dycus said. "Your wife spoke for you. The agreement hinges on this point."

"Alive, he's a danger to all of you," Morgan said.

"His mother had prior claim to the throne," Dycus said. "She would only abandon it for the life of her son."

Morgan stood, alone amidst thousands. He had made a solemn oath of vengeance, an oath that he now had to break. He looked at Alicia again; her face seemed flat and resigned.

Why had she kept this from him? Was his own wife not to be trusted? And in full measure he felt the crush of responsibility and knew just how much of himself could be lost in that crush.

"The audience is over," he said, and strode off, alone, into the night.

2

Germantown

The large man with the golden hair seemed to glide from branch to branch, tree to tree, his white robes floating around him like a suit of cloud fluff.

"You offer no proposal, sir," the man called down in a high, strained voice. "We must have a proposal. Otherwise there can be no discussion. Without discussion, there can be no resolution."

The man dove from his leaf-choked branch, landing nimbly on another ten feet below.

"You will come down here and address me directly," Ramon called through cupped hands. "We cannot conduct a war in this fashion."

"We wish no war with you in any fashion," the man returned. He scurried across the fat branch of a fat oak and bounded from it, using the branch's resilience as a springboard. He catapulted to the next tree, coming down upon a small branch on all fours. He embraced it with arms and legs as it waved up and down under his weight.

"Perhaps we should have one of our archers pluck him from the trees," Count Delmar said from beside Ramon.

"I think not," Ramon said. "Not yet, anyway."

Delmar wiped a line of sweat from his forehead with a lace

handkerchief. "Do *something!*" he said. "I'd like nothing better than to be away from this wretched place before dark. I don't relish spending another night in this damned forest."

Ramon looked back at his army. They were lined out behind him by the thousands, filling the already dense jungle to overflow. Germantown was three days hard march from Father Hus, three days of hacking their way through the immutable superiority of the trees. And it was only through the black arts of the Physicians that they could be there at all. The steam-powered roller they made flattened through the underbrush, while their petroleum kept it from growing back behind and stranding them.

The Physicians themselves sat a distance from the parlay under a canopied tent, fanned by servants of the houses they supposedly served themselves. Pompous and enigmatic, they dressed in everything from hide and feathers to body paint, masks, and leather. Since their knowledge made the war possible at all, they enjoyed a privileged status accorded to few nobles bred. They enjoyed their status to the utmost by demanding concessions and special treatment far in excess of their worth.

"Will you come down and face me?" Ramon called.

"No, sir!" the man in the trees replied. "I will not face you."

"Kill him and be done with it," old Reeder said from his litter. He used a banana leaf to swat away a number of flying bugs that were clinging to his rotted, cancerous nose. He was carried aloft by six young boys, who held him, rags over noses and mouths, a distance from Ramon's group of generals and advisors. From time to time, Count Delmar would turn a covetous gaze toward Councilman Reeder's male stock, only to be glared away by the Councilman himself. In fact, keeping Delmar away from the bearers had become the old man's major occupation when he wasn't worried over his impending death.

"I don't want to just kill him," Ramon said. "He is flaunting the trees at us this far inland, telling us that we can't roust the deep tree dwellers."

"We'll climb up and get them," Senator Murray from Cohoes said. His Physician, Jerico, stood beside him, his pet squirrel running across the contours of his monumental belly.

"That's what they want," Jerico said. "Meeting them in

the trees would be the biggest mistake any of us could ever make."

"I quite agree," Ramon said. "These heathens spend their entire lives in the trees. We'd be no match for any of them there."

"I'll make a deal with you!" the man in the trees called down. "You leave us alone and we'll promise not to add our forces to your brother's army."

"What madness is this?" Murray said. "Your brother's army?"

"Jungle chatter, that's all," Ramon said, then turned to the man in the tree.

"I'll make a deal with *you*!" he called. "You and your citizens come down and surrender to me now, and I'll promise to spare your heathen lives!"

And the trees rang with laughter from uncountable voices. Though the one man was all Ramon could see, the trees were full of people, their voices pelting down like the torrential rains of N'ork. And when Ramon looked closely, he could see their city. Among the thick branches it was, twisted vines here, lean-to branches there, woven tightly together to shelter from the weather. The people of Germantown had truly given themselves over to the forest. They were one with it, breathing its breath, massaging its beating heart.

Ramon turned. His people were searching upwards with fearful eyes, his incredible armada worse than useless in this tangle of nature.

The Green Woman sat on the ground, her back against a tree, removed from the company of the other Physicians. She was already staring at Ramon when he looked at her. A slight smile brightened her face.

He walked toward her, casually, so it would look accidental.

"What do we do, Governor?" Count Delmar asked Ramon's retreating back.

"I dwell upon it," Ramon said, without even turning to the man.

He walked through thick ground clutter to stand near the Green Woman's tree. Though wife she was to him, he didn't think it proper to take counsel openly from her. He stood at her side, facing away, toward the troops who swatted bugs and cursed the trees.

"I'm very jittery," he told the woman. "You must give me something for it."

"I just don't know if I have anything," she said.

"What do you want?" he asked.

"I want you to do the right thing."

"Which is?"

"You know as well as I do that there is only one thing that will finish the tree dwellers for good and all."

He did stare at her this time. Her green face was round and innocent as a baby cat's making its first kill. Her coal black hair wound down under her chin like a hat strap.

"I can't do that," he said.

"You can do anything you want."

"Then, I don't want to do it."

She sighed, shaking her head. "And I don't want to try and find any . . . medicine for your jitters."

"Sometimes I think I could kill you."

She smiled, her green lips pulling tight across white teeth. "Only sometimes?" she said in a little girl voice.

There was a commotion from within the ranks, someone thrashing through the underbrush. Ramon looked toward the confusion. A black-robed group of men was pushing its way through the troops toward him.

The Green Woman was craning her neck around the tree trunk. "Looks like Faf's people," she said. "What are they doing out here?"

"Well, well," Ramon said. "It appears Dixon Faf is among his people. The Programmer has returned."

"Perhaps he'll have news from downriver," the Green Woman said.

"Perhaps," Ramon replied, and moved back toward the clearing where he had been speaking into the trees.

"My husband," the Green Woman called, and Ramon turned to her. She was dangling a chain that was wound around her neck. It had a vial containing white powder attached to it. It swayed seductively in the grasp of her green fingers.

Ramon took a step back toward her. She immediately closed her fist around the vial, shaking her head. He would have glared at her, or ordered her to deliver up her magic potion, but that never worked with the Green Woman. Instead, he turned once again and stalked off.

A short distance away, Dixon Faf approached Ramon. He was surrounded by a contingent of his black-robed abbots, he wearing his own familiar brown robes, his gray beard long and tangled. Behind him, the Lady Jerlynn Delaga rode upon a covered litter, one of her servant women beside her, fanning her with a palm branch.

Faf dropped to walk beside the litter. "You need say nothing," he told her. "Ramon will know of the events of the past days through my interpretation."

"He's not going to like any of it," the woman returned.

"You will have his life, my Lady," the Programmer said. "That was what you asked for. No other considerations were possible."

Jerlynn Delaga's cheeks were flushed from the extreme jungle heat. She felt slightly faint, but didn't know if it was from the heat or from the weight she was going to bear once her son had been informed of the events in Kipsie.

"Behold!" Ramon called to them from his clearing. "Our holy man returns! Let's give him a proper greeting, for we have been too long without the salve of his healing words."

The troops within earshot cheered half-heartedly, and other heads could be seen poking from their hiding places in the trees.

Faf feared the sharp edge he detected on Ramon's words. "Has he been like this long?" he asked Jerlynn.

"He's half-caste," was all she said in return.

The contingent entered the clearing, Ramon immediately moving to embrace the Programmer. "Welcome home!" he said loudly, and Faf realized that it was a show being put on for the people of Germantown, who held their religion more dearly than did Ramon of Alb'ny.

Faf broke the embrace, noticing that Ramon's generals had moved several steps closer. There was to be nothing private about his meeting with the deposed Governor.

Ramon's attention had been drawn to the litter. He moved to it, sliding its mesh curtains. "Mother," he said. "How nice of you to join our little seige."

"I come to offer comfort to my son," Jerlynn said.

"Isn't that thoughtful," Ramon said, turning a full circle. "Do you see what a fine mother I have?"

"I hear you've wed in my absence," Faf told Ramon.

"That I have, holy one," Ramon said. "But that is news we're all aware of. You, on the other hand, perhaps bring something fresh to us."

"That is possible," Faf said, "for I just return from Kipsie."

"Speak up then," Delmar said, fluttering his handkerchief. "The heat oppresses."

Faf looked at Ramon. "Perhaps you would like to speak privately?"

"Nonsense," Ramon said. "There is no news that my faithful followers cannot hear first hand. What of Kipsie? The Lawgivers are well, I trust. The Lord Ibem is still in good hands?"

"There has been a battle, my Lord," Faf said, choosing his words carefully, for they were perhaps the sinews that would keep his head on his shoulders.

"Yes, yes," Ramon said. "Did Redrick engage the farmer?"

"Redrick did much more than that, my Lord. Redrick attacked the holy city itself."

"What?" Ramon said low. "Attacked . . . Kipsie?"

Faf shut his eyes and nodded solemnly.

"Tell me the rest," Ramon said, all the fire gone from his voice. His brown eyes had turned cold as spring water.

"I was in Kipsie, conferring with the Lawgivers," Faf explained, "when Morgan of Siler marched into the city to demand audience. Being from Alb'ny, I was allowed in the meetings."

"They talked to him?" Reeder asked, before losing himself in a coughing fit.

"Yes," Faf said softly, and the jungle had gotten quiet around him. The soldiers were as the trees. The people in the trees stared down, their leathery faces poking through branches like pale coconuts.

"Go on, for heaven's sake," Delmar said.

"What would the farmer want to talk about with the Lawgivers?" Ramon asked.

"He had a letter," Faf said, "supposedly written by your father, Ty'Jorman. The letter declared you to be . . . not of Pure Blood."

Ramon clenched his fists, every muscle of his body tensing. The letter. That damned letter.

Faf continued. "He asked that you be removed from the throne as a half-breed and he, as a Pure-Blood Genie, be declared Governor. During the debate, Redrick arrived at the Kipsie dock. Without preliminary, he opened up on Kipsie with the ship's guns, leveling the city."

"On whose authority did he do that?" Senator Murray asked.

Faf looked at the man, then turned back to Ramon. "I presume that he took that authority upon himself. During the shelling, Morgan of Siler made a bargain with the Lawgivers. They were to declare him rightful ruler of Alb'ny and its possessions, and he would defend them from Redrick and . . ."

"And what?" Ramon demanded.

"And from you, my Lord," Faf said.

"What happened then?" Delmar asked.

"Morgan had a small force, perhaps three thousand, many of them Mechs. He met your Schnecks on the beach and defeated them."

"How badly?" Reeder asked.

"He killed all of them," Faf said, "all ten thousand. The only body not found was Redrick's."

"The boat," Ramon said. "Did Redrick scuttle the boat?"

Faf shook his head. "Morgan of Siler now has the boat, and the legal Governorship of Alb'ny."

Laughter filled the trees. The man in the white robes called down. "Now, maybe you'd like to come up and make a deal with us!" More laughter followed his remark.

Ramon looked calmly into the trees, waving at the man in the white robes. Then he turned to the archer who had been awaiting his command. He nodded.

The man in the blue and white-striped tunic raised his bow and let fly. The arrow caught the man in white squarely in the chest. He fell, holding onto his branch in a last, reflexive action as he died.

Old Reeder tried to laugh, but it turned into a painful cough. "You're not Governor anymore," he managed.

"You think not?" Ramon asked.

Drawing his sword, Ramon walked to Reeder's litter. "The holy city is no more," he said. "The Lawgivers' power is no more. The power belongs to he who can hold it."

With that, he used the flat of his sword and whacked two of the litter bearers on the shin. They went down, dropping the litter. Old Reeder hit the ground hard, with the snap of several bones. The man blanched white, the pain bubbling from his sputtering lips.

"Best hold onto your own power," Ramon said.

As he straightened, he saw the Green Woman on her feet, walking toward him. She held a torch in her right hand and the vial of white powder in the left.

Ramon stretched his lips to a boyish grin and nodded.

"People of the trees!" he called before he could be inundated by his own people's questions. "My forces have destroyed Kipsie!"

"And united the South against you!" an unseen voice returned.

"The way of Ibem is no more. I make the new way. Will you come down and surrender?"

Thousands of voices raised in a single word. "No!"

"Then the people of Germantown have committed mass suicide!" Ramon called and took the torch from the Green Woman.

"What are you doing?" Faf said. "That's insane. The trees are our life, our culture."

"No," Ramon said. "The trees are our sign of subjugation. I, for one, am subjugated no longer."

Ramon carried his torch around the clearing so all could see. "Today the city of Germantown dies forever," he said, and threw the torch into a mass of dry underbrush. He turned to his troops. "Burn the forest!"

So the beliefs and dreams of a thousand years went up in hot, orange fire. The unthinkable had been done, as humans and animals fled blindly from the flames, only to be brought down by Ramon's archers. The rules were gone, the very heart of N'ork put to the torch.

When the future songs would be sung of this day though, that was not what would be remembered. For Ramon, when he consigned Germantown to the flames, drove the rest of the South directly to Morgan of Alb'ny for protection.

3

Last Chance

Ona sat cross legged on the floor of the creaking tree house, pounding the acorn meat to powder between two flat rocks. Beside her, lying naked on a rab fur, three-month-old Ty'Jorman gurgled contentedly, his little eyes rolled up in his head, his tiny fists grabbing handfuls of air.

"Where do you go when you do that?" she asked her son. "What manner of your father's child are you?"

The house creaked loudly, shifting in sections under the pressure of the wind. Ona frowned deeply, hurrying her pounding. It wouldn't be long now.

"I hate it when you do this," she told the child. "Is it sickness? You don't seem sick. Is it visions you see?"

She lifted the top rock, satisfied that the nuts were powdered enough. Picking up the bottom rock, she dumped the powder onto the rest in the tightly wound basket of vine. Then she took the water crock and poured it over the contents of the basket to wash off the acrid taste of the nut, leaving the good-tasting nutrients in the basket.

Her finger went into the wet paste, then to her mouth, tasting. She nodded, putting her finger into the paste again. This went to the mouth of Ty'Jorman.

Even in his reverie, he sucked greedily on her finger. Ona smiled, standing.

"You know when the food's here, don't you?" she said, though the child couldn't answer. She bent, picking up the basket. Then she carried it to the wooden table which sat right next to the huge branch poking through the living area. "I hope your brother's getting enough to eat."

The wind roared again, shifting the large branch with a loud groan that nearly knocked the table on its side. Ona frowned in response and hurriedly began patting the paste into large, flat cakes that she would bake over the fire later.

"Ona!" came Grodin's voice from the base of the tree. "Are you tyin' down, woman?"

Ona just went on with her housework, figuring the old man would climb up and see for himself anyway.

"Ona!"

Ona sighed settling into the splat-splat rhythm of her caking.

A moment later Grodin filled the doorspace, the large, scarred Breeder dressed in britches and boots, sweat slicking his gray-haired chest and craggy face. The headless carcass of a large snake was wrapped around his shoulder like a length of rope.

"Why didn't you answer me, woman?" he demanded. "The rain will be here any second."

"Hello," Ona said from faraway, and dipped her hand into the paste, feeling the right amount for another cake.

The old man grunted, easing the dead snake from his arm to drop heavily on the creaking floor. "We've got to tie down," he said, and moved to the table, working around the woman to lash it to the branch.

Finishing with the table, he began stacking the few rough chairs that sat around, lashing them as a unit to the window sill.

"We'll have meat tonight," he said, indicating the snake.

"Ty'Jorman's dreaming again," she said.

Grodin crossed the floor to pick up the child. It was off in another world someplace. He just stared at it, as if it was some new kind of bug he had never seen. When the baby was off like this, it was impossible to bring him back unless the baby was ready to come back. Grodin had tried many times.

"I wonder if his brother does this?" he asked.

Thunder crashed loudly nearby, rumbling the sky for several seconds, and total darkness descended in the middle of the afternoon.

Gordin pulled the child close to his sweat-slick breast. "Put up your stuff, woman," he said. "The Pain is here."

Lightning flashed in the clearing beneath the tree, bringing to life for a brief instant the tree city of Last Chance, once Morgan's base camp before the war.

Ona still contentedly pattied her meal.

Grodin moved to her, grabbed her wrist. "Put it up!" he demanded.

Hatred flared quickly in her eyes, disappearing just as quickly. Without a word, she moved around the now-rocking floor to secure her utensils.

Then the rain hit.

It fell, not in drops, but in large, blinding sheets, ravaging everything beneath it. It was the water of Ibem, the hardships of sin that man was forced to endure.

It was the Pain.

The rain tore through the house in blinding torrents, filling the floor knee deep, quicker than it could leak back through the large holes. Grodin, huddling the child, climbed onto the large branch, pulling Ona up after him. They sat close together, clinging to one another and the rough bark of the branch. The maelstrom never even stirred the baby.

Below, in the yard, the water had already climbed several feet up the tree trunks, flooding the jungle and drowning everything not able to get to higher ground. It washed through the land in deadly currents, pulling everything southward, toward the Great Sea. The rain was N'ork's fickle ruler, the whimsical power of life and death over all.

"I went to the roadway today!" he called over the noise of the rain.

"Why?"

"News! I wanted news of the war!"

"For what reason?"

He just glared at her, at the glint of meanness in her eyes, at the long dark hair that was matted by rain to her pale face.

"I met a messenger from Ramon name of Maio," he said, "who was on his way back to the Provinces to check on local matters. He had news."

"Should I be interested?" she replied.

"Morgan has been declared legal ruler of Alb'ny by the Lawgivers."

"I don't believe it."

"It has been discovered that Morgan is a Pure Blood Genie."

"Impossible."

"His father was one, his mother also. Ramon is not of the Pure Blood. He has been stripped of office by the Lawgivers."

Ona laughed without humor. "And how says Ramon Delaga?"

Grodin lowered his eyes. The water was climbing up the tree trunk. "The war goes on," he answered.

"You're telling me that the children I had by the farmer are half-breed," Ona said, her eyes daggers.

"I'm repeating what I heard on the roadway."

She clenched a fist in front of his face, shaking, fingers white from the pressure. "I don't believe that," she said angrily, "and I won't believe it. The thief who stole my child is not a Genie. It's unthinkable."

"It was his child, too," Grodin said.

"I know how things are," Ona said. "And I know how they will be."

Reaching out, she snatched Ty'Jorman from Grodin's arms and held the baby close. "My babies are human," she said. "They are."

Grodin thought not to waste his words on the woman. Though she refused to understand, there were many things that were becoming clear to him about his former friend and pupil. There were things coming clear to him about himself also.

The storm kept up its fury until the afternoon darkness turned to evening darkness, leaving behind a mass of destruction and a hot, steamy jungle.

4

The Land of the Grunts

Galen sat on the small rise that overlooked the city of Gimlock and watched Lili, his life-mate, shed her skin. It was a tedious and private process that involved a great deal of copious sweating and personal embarrassment, not aided by the fact that occasional help was sometimes needed.

She lay in the bushes ten yards below his vantage point, groaning and crying with the strain. It sounded like she was in pain, but Galen had been through this process over five hundred times with her and knew that it was mostly the vulnerability of it that brought the tears to all of her eyes.

"Are you well?" he called, just to reassure himself.

"Yesss," she moaned back. "Please don't trouble yourself."

"No trouble, my love," he replied, then returned to his quiet meditations.

The dermis of a Grunt was over an inch thick, the epidermal layer a sleek, hard coating that was undergrown about once a year and peeled away. This armored, outer skin gave Galen and his people a shiny, polished look that had earned them the nickname, Shiners; but they had been designed as unkillable fighters a millenium before, and their warrior name, Grunt, was the one that stuck.

As Lili peeled away the shell of her left leg, Galen turned his attention to the city that lay far below. Something had been going on down there since his pilgrimage to the hilltop the day before. Messengers had been traveling in and out of town and there had been more than one meeting in the square. So much attention was being paid the meetings that the daily land clear-

29

ing was suffering for it, and Galen knew that something quite important was in the works.

He had wondered what had been going on, but patience had been a virtue he had learned hundreds of years ago.

Obviously, it could wait no longer, for a contingent was even then climbing the hillside to seek his advice. They were being careful to mount the blind side, away from the place of shedding, so as not to interrupt or humiliate Lili.

"Something commands my attention," he called to his mate. "There are those who come to speak with me."

"Spare me their eyes," Lili groaned in return.

"Fear not."

He turned his body to watch them draw nearer, leaving his left hand palm out in Lili's direction to keep a loose eye on her. He blinked his hand and opened the third eye, monoscopically switching between his mate and the intruders.

They mounted the hill slowly, speaking animatedly among themselves. Their squat, naked bodies shone dully in the overcast haze, their colors shifting to blend with the waving grasses of the hill. They were like great, human reptiles, the thick pads of their faces drawn in concern. They hadn't moved close enough yet to be recognizable, but judging from the size of their horns, all classes were represented, from the oldest to the youngest.

Lili yelped, then sighed deeply, and Galen could see that she had cleared the left leg, the new armor beneath still glistening with lubrication.

Galen smiled when he saw who comprised the delegation. A more varied group he hadn't seen since the monumental decision several hundred years before to stop eating the flesh of animals. There was Gert, who was called Longnose. Gert was the oldest and hence had the longest nose, since noses never stop growing. With him were Mama Spire, the last woman to give birth in Gimlock, and the young lovers, Marta and Gregore, both barely over a hundred and thought to be the only Grunts still actually involved in the physical art of lovemaking.

"No farther, please," Galen said, when they had approached the crest of the hill. "This is a private moment."

"We understand," Longnose said, bowing his head slightly. "And we beg your indulgence. We would not interrupt unless this was a most grievous matter."

"I know that," Galen said. "Please feel free to speak."

Mama Spire spoke first, her hands grasping the two long, twisting horns of flesh gristle that protruded from her temple. "Our outpost watches have been all reporting in since yesterday with news."

"I saw them," Galen replied.

Mama Spire continued. "They bring news of unrest and turmoil on the outside."

Galen scratched his own horn. "Unrest is not unknown to the land of humans," he said.

"This is different," Gregore spoke up. "A Genie has formed alliances with many human and Genie tribes. He wishes a consolidated state."

Lili groaned loudly, and everyone politely pretended they didn't hear.

"Not only that," Marta said, "but his aim is to homogenize all the species."

"Homogenize . . . how?" Galen asked.

"Physical homogenization," Longnose said, a fire in his eyes that Galen hadn't seen since *he* was young. "He forces his followers to engage in acts of sex outside of their own species."

"That's unthinkable," Galen said, and in the three hundred years since he had governed Gimlock, nothing of such consequence had ever occurred. "I had no idea that the world of men had come to such degradation. I grieve over such insanity."

"We have fears," Gregore said. "Suppose this leader, this Morgan, is to have his way. With control of the land of men comes expansion. What should happen if this blood-mixing should find its way to Gimlock?"

Galen shuddered. The Grunts were a species apart, bearing only marginal relationship to their human models. They took great pride in their separateness, their uniqueness. Blood-mixing meant the destruction of the species. Even given the nature of their life eternal, death would be more welcome to a Grunt than hemolysis.

"We cannot allow that," Galen said at length. "We must call a halt to it before it reaches our valley."

"The citizens are in agreement," Mama Spire said. "But how will we do it?"

"We will go to this Morgan," Galen said, "and we will show him the error of his ways. If we should fail to convince him to give up this insane path, we will have to use our natural resources to destroy him."

With that, he brought his fist to pound once on the boulder upon which he sat, and had sat upon over five hundred times previously. A large crack appeared on the huge rock, splitting it in twain.

5

Victory—The Captain's Cabin

Little Marek, naked, scurried up the half-open closet door and perched, catlike on its upper edge.

"Come down from there," Alicia said, stamping her foot and holding her arms out. "You're going to fall and hurt yourself."

"Leave him alone," Morgan said from the starboard bunk. "He's just testing his wings."

She flared around to him. "It's not his wings, it's his head I'm worried about," she said angrily. "And you should be, too."

She turned back to the baby and held her arms out, but the child, giggling, flung himself from the door and grabbed the large kerosene lamp that hung by a gold chain from the ceiling. He swung on the light, his tiny laugh sounding like the squawk of a baby racoon.

"Honestly," Alicia said, hands on her hips.

"Marek," Morgan said from his reclining position on the bunk, and held his arm out stiff.

Marek swung out on the lamp several times to gauge his distance, then jumped off at the peak of the arc, grabbing Morgan's arm and swinging on it.

Man and child laughed.

"You're a fool," Alicia said. "You're both fools."

Morgan frowned, staring at her. "I guess I'm fulfilling the role that you've cast me in," he said, pulling the baby down to lie beside him.

"Don't start in on that again."

He sat up. "It's not bad enough that you made a bargain in my name that I would have never agreed to, but I had to find out about it, like a . . . fool, in front of all those people."

She lowered her eyes. "I'm not proud of that," she said. "Ever since it happened, I'd been searching for a way to tell you."

"Well, you certainly picked the worst way."

"I'm sure no one noticed," she said, smoothing her soft, brocaded gown. "They were all in a state of conniption over your revelations on the subject of blood-mixing."

"What's that supposed to mean?" he said, swinging his legs over the edge of the bunk and standing. "I've never made any secret about my feelings on this matter. Part of the reason all of us are here is to help end the suffering carried on in the name of racial purity."

"Through forced hemolysis?"

He grabbed her by the shoulders. "If that's what it takes," he said low, then let his arms drop to his side. "I don't mean that."

He walked across the cabin and stared out the starboard porthole, watched his people gathering for the trek southward to N'ork City. It had been decided that Morgan would travel slowly to the South, liberating Southern cities as he went, taking their entire populations with him to the Jewel of the East, there to make a stand against Ramon.

"I don't want to force anyone to anything," he said, not turning to her. The baby scrabbled up his leg and arm to sit on his shoulder. "But where does the equality start? Where does it stop? We're fighting a war over this issue. How far do I push in the opposite direction?"

He turned around, sitting on the bed, just glancing at her for a second. "It's funny. I just assumed that everyone would come around to my way of thinking. That we would all, I don't know . . . feel, the same about this. The only way to stop the cult of Pure Blood is to mix all blood."

"Not through force," Alicia said.

"Force?" Morgan said. "We're *killing* the other side."

"Can't we accept our differences and our equality at the same time?" Alicia asked softly, trying to slip into her negotiator mode.

"If we don't change that which we're fighting about, are we not simply replacing an inherent evil with the same thing?"

"As do most wars."

"I mean, if we mix all the blood, then racial purity and all that goes with it will no longer be an issue. We will have accomplished, in a very clear sense, exactly what we set out to accomplish." The baby climbed upon his head, pulling his long red hair. "Ouch!"

He pulled Marek down and rolled him around on the bunk.

"I don't know how much of this I can accept myself," Alicia said. "It smacks of the kind of tyranny that can tear a kingdom apart. If people don't want to do it, you'll have to make them, and the more you make them, the more they won't want to do it. Besides, you promised the Lawgivers you only intended to rule Alb'ny and leave everyone else alone."

"Your job isn't to accept or reject anything," Morgan said. "You do what I tell you to do."

"If you believe that, you'd better open your eyes because you're asleep and dreaming."

"If you don't like it," Morgan said, "there's always Masuria."

She stared hard at him. "You're not being rational."

"I know what you want," Morgan told her. He stood and took off the shirt she had asked him to wear that morning. "You'll say anything to get the power, you've already proven that. You don't care about any of this. You're just afraid that everyone won't go along with my ideas, and you won't get your power fix." He balled up the shirt and threw it on the floor in disgust. "You're a great one to talk about right and wrong."

There was a knock on the door.

"Go away!" Alicia shouted.

"Come in!" Morgan shouted.

There was a moment of silence, then the knock came again. The new Governor of Alb'ny and his Lady stared at one another. Finally, Morgan walked to the door and pulled it open. Nebo stood there, his face contorted in anger.

"You've given away my lab space," he said.

"Just a part of it," Morgan replied. "We needed room for Ibem's holy food."

Nebo shook his fists in front of him. "You promised me that section of the hold for development and testing."

Alicia walked up beside Morgan. She had never seen such a range of feelings run through a Mech, and she had lived around them for years. "It was unavoidable," she said. "You still retain a great deal of the hold. More, I should think, than you would actually use."

"I've already made plans for that space," Nebo said.

"Change them," Morgan said, angry. "There's no other choice."

Nebo shook his head, walking inside the cabin. "You don't understand," he said. "I *need* that space."

"Why?" Alicia asked.

The Mech began to talk, his eyes staring, almost transfixed, into the distance. It frightened Alicia to see him this way. "I've found a way to . . . liberate the total energy of the atom. It's quite exciting. The possibilities are . . ."

"Sorry," Morgan said, cutting him off. "I'm really not interested in whatever that is. Work on the bombs and that microwave thing. We don't have the time or the . . . space to work on anything new."

Nebo looked at him, his face an unreadable blank. "I have another request to make. When we get downriver to Rockland, we'll be near a source of an element that I need in my work. Can we stay there long enough for me to secure some?"

"I told you we don't have time for any new projects," Morgan said. "We just need to beef up the old ones."

"I can't *not* work on new things," the Mech said. "It's the nature of my species."

"Well, we'll have to change that, won't we?" Morgan said, getting right up in the black man's face. "We're fighting a war here. I don't have time for a lot of nonsense."

"So be it," Nebo said in his melodious voice. Without another word, he turned and stalked from the cabin.

"I don't like that," Alicia said. "It never does well to deny a Mech."

"He'll get over it," Morgan said, but really wasn't nearly so sure as he pretended. "Once we sail, Nebo will come around."

"That will be your problem," Alicia said.

"My problem," Morgan repeated, and walked back to the bunk.

"I won't be sailing with you." She turned and moved toward the closet.

Moving to her, he took her arms again, spinning her around to face him. "Where will you be?"

"I'm taking to the roads," she said. "I go to prepare for your arrival in N'ork City."

"So soon? You could do that farther downriver."

She jerked herself free of his hold. "Don't do that anymore," she said. "Go grab some of the freewomen you've been eyeing in the camps."

"Why are you going?" he demanded.

"Will you give me an armed escort?"

"Why now?" he shouted.

"There is animosity between us," she said, "points of honor. We both must think if we choose to pursue life further in one another's company."

"You're my wife," Morgan said.

She fixed her deep golden eyes upon him, and they were colder than anything ever got in the lands of N'ork. "A formality, sir, I think neither of us should examine too closely. Will you give me an armed escort?"

"No!"

She nodded. "All right, I'll go alone."

He shook his hands in the air. "I'll give you the escort," he said, then his own eyes softened. "You mean to leave me."

"Not yet," she returned, and the hardness was still there. "We've both worked too hard to throw it all away without a fight. A little time will tell for both of us. You once told me that your ideals were more important than the campaign or my help. Perhaps I'm the same way. I want . . . no, need, the power more than I need to breathe, but it's going to have to feel right. We'll both think on it."

"I'm not going to change," he said.

She shook her head. "I didn't ask you to. Just so long as you don't ask me to stay if I don't like the direction of it."

They locked gazes, Morgan realizing that Alicia would hold to her own council no matter what he did or said. "Fair enough," he said. "When will you leave?"

She turned back to the closet and began taking clothes from it. "As soon as possible," she said.

Wordlessly, Morgan turned from her and walked back to stare down at the bunk. Little Marek was lying upon it, vibrating. His eyes were rolled back in his head.

"He's doing it again," Morgan said.

Outside the cabin, Nebo stood, hyperventilating, leaning against the rail. He had barely been able to contain himself with Morgan. It was opening up to him, every bit, every part of it; and with a whole army of Mechs to help him, he could have his fingers on all knowledge to the parameters and beyond.

Except for Morgan and the war.

They had helped before, had given him access to things and people and materials. But now he had all he needed—except time. He didn't have the time because of the war to do what he needed to do. Emotionally, it was leaving him frustrated and disoriented. Physically it was killing him.

All the years he had spent in the dungeons of Alb'ny had passed as a long night. He had had nothing, so there had been no loss. Now, with knowledge in his grasp, his inability to exercise it was tearing him and the other Mechs to pieces.

He walked the deck oblivious to the activity around him. The ship was being stocked with equipment and provisions while on shore the Southerners worked quickly, lashing together the logs that would form the huge rafts upon which many of them would travel the wide river behind VICTORY.

Nebo took the stairs down to the foredeck, shoving his way through its milling crowds to the hold where Ibem's support equipment was being loaded onboard.

The silver-robed Repairmen had taken total control of the loading, wide berth being given to them by the faithful, who viewed them as demi-gods. Nebo watched as one of the mammoth black boxes was being hauled up with block and tackle. The boxes contained complex chains of fuel and electrical generators to keep the computer operative, what Morgan called "Ibem food."

Nebo studied the Repairmen. He had heard that they were a sub-Mech species that was bred in Kipsie itself. Their genetic orientation was based solely on keeping the machine alive the way it had always been kept alive. Their skin had a slight brownish tinge to it, and the Mech concluded that they could have, in fact, been lower-form Mechs. Keeping the computer alive for a thousand years, though, would take more than repair knowledge. It would take either a great many spare parts, or microcircuitry production capabilities. Curious, Nebo walked to the foredeck rail and looked at the dock.

There were several more of the bulky generator packages lined up on the pier, and behind them, something else. Two huge refrigeration units the size of small houses sat humming on the dock, ready to be loaded.

Kipsie was shutting down. As a city, it no longer existed. The Lawgivers were packing up, and Nebo reflected that it was probably N'ork City where they intended to next set up shop. That being the case, they would take everything concerning Ibem with them on the trip. The refrigerator units could only be one thing—spare parts. When the ancients created the religion, they stocked it with enough spare parts to keep it active at least this long and probably a lot longer.

The Mech felt a warm glow spread through him when he thought of all those intricate microchips and pre-printed circuits, manufacturing that he would never have been able to duplicate. Such engineering was meant to be used, and not just to keep some silly analog computer operative. Nebo was beginning to have plans, and, he figured, what Morgan of Alb'ny didn't know certainly wouldn't hurt him.

6

i

CASTLE ALB'NY

Sir Martin of Rochester sat up slowly, the ache in his head a wild and impassioned thing in marked contrast to the overall stupor that had taken control of the rest of his body. His eyes were shut as if they had been pasted that way, and judging from the sticky consistency of the inside of his mouth, that was what had been used as the glue.

His hands went to his head, to make sure it was still normal size. A horrible smell caused him to breathe through his pasty mouth. Where in the world was he?

Against their will, his eyes reluctantly opened. His head seared, as if the pain were a physical thing that slipped through the eye sockets.

The kennels. He was in the damned kennels! But how did he . . . then he saw the two naked women asleep on either side of him and he remembered.

A half-filled wine crock was still balanced between his legs. He slowly picked it up and brought it to his lips, gulping down several mouthfuls. It tasted fetid, horrible. He drank some more, then threw the crock to splatter on the straw-strewn mud floor of the empty building.

He looked at the women again. Yes, it had been quite a night and, he reflected with a half-smile, the kennels had been the perfect place to end it.

The young woman with the large breasts on his right side stirred slightly and changed position. Her nipples were bright pink, iridescent, undarkened by motherhood. He reached out and kneaded the breast closest to him. Through the haze of sleep she reached for him, taking his penis in her hand and bringing it to full throttle within seconds.

"Remarkable," he said, unable to understand how his equipment could still work so well when he felt so bad. He briefly considered rolling over on top of her right then, but his stomach conveniently heaved and reminded him of the impossibility of it. Besides, he had all the time—and all the women—in the world.

Removing the gentle fingers from his privates, he stood shakily, letting his head acclimate itself slowly to the change of perspective.

"Ladies," he said with a smile, for Sir Marty was indeed a genial fellow. "I'll never forget whatever it was we did last night."

The other woman, whom he vaguely remembered as being the young one's mother, responded by rolling onto her back and snoring loudly.

There was a water trough for the Woofers against the far wall. He walked to it and began splashing himself. The kennels were made of ill-fitting wood slats, open across the entire front of the long room to the castle courtyard. Things were just beginning to stir, as early morning light crept over the high walls, bringing the day's heat up to full measure.

After he had splashed himself, Sir Martin dunked his entire head into the trough, holding it under until his breath gave out. It didn't help much. There were no Woofers in the kennels; they were all off to war with Ramon.

"I don't know whether this is a blessing or a curse, my Lord," Martin groaned, and though he'd always had a penchant for overabundant enjoyment of life's pleasures, his indulgence had been without boundary since Ramon had left Castle Alb'ny and the entire Province in his care.

His head somewhat clearer, he picked several pieces of straw from his chest hair and looked around for his clothes. "Today's the day," he said with conviction, as he retrieved his dirty britches from where they hung on a stall divider. "Today we get down to work and get this place cleared out. I've got responsibilities."

That said and acknowledged, he put on his pants and walked down the steep incline in front of the kennels and into the courtyard.

The castle, looking like a huge mud hill, glowed dully in the morning light. A high wall ringed the castle all around, barracks and the kennels being built up against it. Everything sloped toward the center of the courtyard and the large conduits that carried away the incredible rains.

Ragged people slept all around the courtyard in the wall's shadow. Those in the light were already awakening. It was a mixed group of hangers-on, the dregs that set up shop in a military compound, then stay after the army has moved on to drain whatever they can from the local economy: whores and their keepers, wandering musicians and pickpockets, beggars, purveyors of the sacred and the profane. Martin needed to roust them off the castle grounds, but he hated to send people out into the jungle when they were so happy. Besides, he had made a vow to sample every whore who didn't have a rash, and he still had a long way to go, last night's debacle notwithstanding.

Patches of green seemed to be showing up around the edges of the wall. Undergrowth? In the courtyard? What was going on?

"Sir Martin!" came a voice from across the dusty yard. It was Feral, the head gardener. The little bald man with the apple-red nose came charging full speed across the yard to intercept the acting Governor.

The little man was breathing heavily when he reached Martin's side.

"My Lord, I . . . I . . ."

"There, there, my man," Martin said, putting an arm around him. "Wait a second to catch your breath."

The man put up a hand, swallowing hard. After several long breaths, he was able to speak. "You must come up on the wall with me," he said. "You must see."

"I'm not much on heights," Sir Martin said, raising an eyebrow. He had been brought up on the river, his father a rich merchant. Climbing had always been a frightening endeavor to him, one that he avoided at all costs.

"Please, my Lord. Just this once."

Martin thought about it, then remembered the vow he had taken minutes earlier to straighten everything out. "Oh, all right," he said, twirling a hand in the air.

They moved to the wall and started up the narrow stone steps. Martin hugged the wall as they climbed, refusing to acknowledge that the stairs had another side to them.

"Do I see undergrowth around the wall?" he asked the gopherlike man's back.

"You do, indeed, my Lord," Feral said. "And there is more, much more. By the way, a messenger from Ramon is waiting to speak to you in the Governor's chambers."

"Oh?" Martin said, brightening. "Who is it?"

"Sir Perkins, my Lord."

"What a good fellow," Martin said. "We'll have to speak at length about the war. See that he has plenty of wine, would you?"

"Yes, my Lord."

They reached the top of the high wall, and Sir Martin looked in horror at the outer courtyard. It was covered with vines and fast growing algae. Young saplings grew rapidly, and ivy totally buried the outer battlements of piled up ancient carriages.

"How did this happen?" Martin asked, incredulous.

"The jungle, my Lord. It encroaches."

"But that courtyard was clear two weeks ago!"

"It has not been kept up. Look down the wall."

Sir Martin looked. Ivy had climbed the wall, was nearing

its summit. The jungle was trying to bury them completely.

"And there," Feral said, pointing to the barracks. They were covered with a thick layer of blue-green algae. The little man shook his head. "That since yesterday."

"Yesterday," Martin repeated. He looked at the outer courtyard again. It had been absolutely cleared the last time he looked, had been Alb'ny's pride and joy. Now it was choked with new jungle. "We must do something!"

"I've been telling you that for weeks," Feral said. "Now what do you propose to do?"

"Me?" Martin said. "You're the gardener."

"The Governor usually used anyone handy to keep the yard cleaned . . . the Castle Guard, the citizenry."

"Well, let's do that."

"Yes," Feral said. "I have tried. But no one will listen to me. They enjoy their pleasures too much. They became fat from catering to the troops and now don't want to return to work. No one even plants the fields. They all want to be merchants."

"Nothing wrong with merchants," Martin said indignantly.

"No, my Lord," Feral said. "But the jungle must be cleared away from the castle or we will lose it."

"Well then, do something!"

"No one will listen to me," Feral said loudly, running short of patience. "You must take command of this situation. Use your authority to make them work."

"Me?" Sir Martin put a hand to his chest. "I want these people to look up to me, not hate me. It's your job. You take care of it. I must attend to important matters of state with Sir Perkins."

Feral watched the man leave, moving slowly down the stairs, his back against the wall, hugging it. Before Sir Martin had reached the courtyard, the gardener had made his decision. Hurrying to his room off the supply shed, he threw his belongings into a cheesecloth and left the castle, taking the West road toward Delmar. Perhaps he could have a job there.

Sir Martin hurried to the castle, no door guards on duty. In fact, he saw no Castle Guard anywhere. They were getting very lax. He'd have to speak to someone soon.

Sir Perkins was nearly asleep on a leather couch in the Governor's waiting room, the place of candles, his spider web armor tossed to the floor, his undersuit of white cotton torn and dirty. Several night candles still flickered, bringing the rows of tapestries on the walls to jumping shadowy life.

"Perky!" Sir Martin said. "You've missed the wine of Alb'ny."

Sir Perkins sat up slowly. "What's going on around here? Everything seems to be falling to pieces."

Sir Martin poured them both a crock of wine. "No one will work. I push and prod them all day long, but it's as if some vast mutiny had taken place. Life was never like this on the river."

Sir Perkins laughed. "On the river you were the same wastrel you are now. Your father bought you a place in Ramon's retinue to make a man out of you. It seems he wasted his plastic."

Sir Martin took a drink and frowned deeply. "I fear I am not cut out to be a leader of men. I want to be liked, not feared. I want the men to drink with me because I'm a good fellow and the women to bed me because of their heart's palpitations."

Sir Perkins laughed again and took to his wine. "I can't blame you for that, old friend."

"That's the spirit! Come. We'll get drunk before breakfast and talk of the war."

And while Sir Perkins told him all that had been happening, the jungle crept ever nearer to the rasping throat of the Province of Alb'ny.

ii

KIPSIE

Alicia, the Politico, picked her way through the ruins of the holy city. The perpetual cloud cover was turning a darker gray, signaling the descent of night. She walked carefully through the nightmare landscape of twisted steel and jagged concrete—the death, finally, of the Old World and its ideals.

Though Ibem traveled with them, it was clear to almost all that his power to rule was at an end. That was why he rode in the second dias at the parade, and the Lawgivers, unless they were total fools, knew it, too.

Alicia walked slowly, disturbed. Her breech of honesty with Morgan had been more serious than she would have liked to believe. And it had been her fault. She had wanted to cut a deal with the Lawgivers so badly, she took a responsibility upon herself that she didn't merit, then compounded it by keeping it from her husband.

If only he wouldn't be so hardheaded, none of it would have happened. Yet even that knowledge paled under the lapse of trust that she had committed. The knowledge had changed him, she could feel it. She was a genetic empath, tied completely to the feelings of others. Now she could sense a lack of trust in Morgan toward her—and the knowledge was tearing her to pieces. Like it or not, she loved the red-haired man, loved him with a heart that had known nothing but calculation. And love, she had discovered, was beyond rational calculation.

That frightened her.

She passed an occasional citizen trying to beat the night and sift through the wreckage for personal items before it became too dark to retrieve them. There would be no searching in the morning, for VICTORY sailed at first light and its fleet of barges with it.

Alicia's path was a different one. With the debarkation of the fleet, she and her party would take to the Southern road and make their way to N'ork City. There she would use her Genie's skill to convince them of Morgan's quest and prepare for the final defense of the South.

She walked through an alleyway, high, jagged walls of stone and glass rising on either side of her. A tree had been blown from the ground and was balanced like a bridge between two walls. There, sitting atop the horizontal trunk, was the man she had been searching for.

Hitching up her ankle-length blue gown, she gingerly climbed a large pile of rubble that was piled against the wall. A hand, half-eaten by small scavengers, was sticking through the rubble with clenched fist.

She made the top of the wall that no longer connected up to anything, and traversed it until she reached the log.

"The balance is delicate," the old man with no eyes said just before she put a foot onto the wide trunk. "It must be walked carefully and with great precision."

Alicia stepped onto the log, ignoring the twenty-foot dropoff to the ground. "I think, Master Twiddle," she said, "that you are speaking about something other than this wooden bridge."

The old man smiled, turning his smooth face in her direction. Where eyes would be was smooth, flat skin, but still he somehow saw her. "There are layers and layers," he said softly, then cackled in a shrill voice. "You try and change a world, but there are always others—waiting, just waiting." He slapped his knees and rocked back and forth, the tree trunk shifting with him.

Alicia sat down beside him, dangling her legs over the edge and swinging them back and forth. "What others?" she asked.

He motioned out toward the dead forest that surrounded the city. "They're out there," he said, "hiding in the forest. The cast-off children of Kipsie."

"The deformed ones? We saw some of them when we first came. They're the victims of the defoliants."

"The castaways," Twiddle said, nodding. "Yes, the castaways. They, also, will have their day."

The sky was darkening by degrees. Alicia sat on the log and watched the ruins slowly shadow into amorphous lumps. "We'll need to go back soon," she said.

"Do you fear the dark?" he asked. "I'll protect you. There have been fires, too, you know. Great fires."

"Where?"

"To the North," Twiddle said casually. He pulled his tattered robe up his calf and scratched his leg. "The spawn of Rensselaer has set to burning the woods. The rains have put out much of the fires, but many villages were destroyed, many good minds burned with them."

Alicia tucked up her knees, resting her chin on them. So, Ramon had taken to burning interior villages. It was a terrible thing, but good news for Morgan. "Will there be refugees?"

Twiddle nodded. "They are making their way here now. It may be necessary to delay the departure."

"You know I travel to N'ork City?"

"I will travel with you."

She chuckled. "That was my next question. Do you mind?"

"It is my destiny," he replied. "But there is something else on your mind."

She nodded, her face bouncing up and down on her knees. "Morgan wishes to force hemolysis on the People," she said. "Everything I know, everything I believe, tells me this is wrong. I believe it to be a grave error. You must help me, give me some sort of . . . sign. What should I do? If this is folly I wish no part of it."

"Everything is folly," Twiddle said. "All turns to dust. What are desires except dust dancing in the light?"

"I can only live in the here and now."

"But you ask me of the future."

She tightened her jaw and persisted. "How will this all end? Is it my folly to pursue Morgan's?"

The old man covered his empty eye places with the palms of his hands. He rocked back and forth, moaning slightly. And the images came, strong, stronger than ever. It was the matrix, the focus of history and its images exploded in his brain like a flash of lightning.

A forest, dank and steamy, settled into a deep pit. The pit, alive, coursing with life, teeming with it. Minds, minds, minds in collision. Fire in the night.

Innocents like animals held the key, jungle babies pure and unafraid, leading, leading, leading through twisted, burning mist. A vision of a clearing . . . and the needle of Cleopatra. A pool of life holding the harbingers of death.

It throbbed in his head, brighter than any color, more vivid than life. The fires of fear, burning away the boundaries of reality to reveal the band of three. All the answers in the pool of life, a woman of Nature's colors, shining brighter than the fire . . . and pain!

The pain tore through his chest white hot, flashing his vision, burning his brain. He shook, pulling away from the vision forcibly. He took a labored breath, his robes soaked through with sweat.

He removed his hands from his face and turned to Alicia. "Woman, cleave to your husband," was all he said, and he couldn't be persuaded to say anything else.

iii

ROCKLAND

Redrick of Firetree leaned on his cane, the bough of a hickory nut tree wound all around with snakeskin, and listened to the story of the man from Nyack. They sat beneath the twisting branches of a Dutch elm, the large array of insect life that inhabited that most fragile of trees moving through it, taking its lifeblood in ancient patterns, oblivious to the human activity at its base.

The trees all around Redrick were alive, the citizens of Rockland preparing for the evacuation that would soon reach their harbor. Rockland was a beautiful place, many of the ancient buildings that rested in its branches were still well intact, their stone surfaces nestled comfortably near the clouds. Steel girders, merged organically with growing wood, spanned the thick trees, creating paths and connecting bridges between them. Rockland was a spider web of a city, an intricate labyrinth of readjusted ancient artistry and the wisdom of Nature.

Redrick would take great pleasure in destroying it.

"You say you are the only survivor of the massacre of Hudson, Sir Benford?" Crispet of Nyack asked Redrick.

"If there are others I haven't seen them," Redrick replied, and hoped that the man wouldn't question him too closely about something he had only heard about.

"How did this come to be?" Crispet asked.

The man had sparse gray hair and a face splashed heavily with light freckles. He had a jovial look about him, but there was something dark and inquisitive about his eyes. Redrick determined to be careful around this one.

"I was downriver fishing," Redrick said, idly scratching his deathshead face with the curve of the hook that served as his right hand. "I made my way back when I heard the cannon fire, but when I arrived, it was already too late."

Crispet seemed concerned. "Did Ramon really slaughter all of them?"

"Those that the cannons didn't get first," Redrick said, fighting to keep the note of pride out of his voice. "The destruction was total."

"Look," came a small voice. "Uncle Benford looks like a frog!"

Two small children, a boy and a girl of no more than six years, ran up to Redrick, hugging his arms. The way he sat on his rock, leaning on the cane, he did, indeed, resemble a squatting frog.

Redrick laughed, putting an arm around the long-haired children in matching white robes. "My adopted family," he said. "When I wandered South after the massacre, I somehow ended up here."

Moira, the children's mother walked up, a bundle of clothes balanced on her shoulder. She was fair and altogether fragile looking, but Redrick had seen her moving lithely through the smallest branches of her tree house too many times. Her fragileness, if it existed at all, was not physical. "Don't bother Uncle Benford while he's talking, children," Moira said, smiling graciously.

"These fine people took me in as if I were a member of their family," Redrick said.

"You are," Moira said. "You are part of our family now."

Redrick stood, leaning heavily on the cane. "They're far too kind to a man who's too broken up even to take to the trees anymore."

Crispet drew his brows together, and Redrick thought if the man were any more sincere, he'd crack his face. "Your injuries . . ." he began politely.

"Very old, I'm afraid," Redrick said. "Not worth talking about." He slapped his thigh. "My bad hip keeps me from climbing."

Crispet nodded, tightening his lips. After a few seconds, he spoke again. "Is it . . . is it difficult to stay out of the trees?"

Redrick wanted to laugh in the man's face, to spit back the disgust he felt for all of them. Instead, he replied, "It's the hardest thing I can imagine."

Citizens were moving past them in large numbers, dropping from the trees like ripe apples and carrying their belongings down the wide stone path to the river, there to await the arrival of Morgan's fleet. The river was close, its rumbling surge a constant song playing in all their ears.

"This is all very exciting," Moira said. "And a little frightening."

Crispet nodded again. "The world is changing," he said. "We're here to witness it, to . . . live it."

"Mr. Crispet has just come downriver from Kipsie," Redrick said, trying to move the topic back to the holy city.

"Is that right?" Moira said, eyes wide. "My husband's up there now, helping with the organization."

Crispet smiled, eyes twinkling. It was obvious that he, too, was caught up in the excitement. "I went up to see the destruction and to hear the red-haired man."

"I've heard he's like a demon," Moira said, picking up the

little girl and settling her on the shoulder opposite the clothes bundle.

"Not quite a demon," Crispet laughed. "More like a wizard. He's fearless, and he talks of large things, great things. He draws all to him like a magnet—human and Genie alike."

"He came to power so quickly," Redrick said. "What exactly happened up there?"

Crispet was still sitting, while Redrick and Moira stood. He leaned back onto his elbows to keep from craning his neck to look at them. "I've just heard rumors . . ."

"Then tell us rumors," Redrick said quickly, almost impatiently.

The man's eyes flashed for just a second, then he answered, "We've heard that a deal was made with the Lawgivers for the throne of Alb'ny."

"What sort of deal?"

"The story goes," Crispet said, "that Dixon Faf, the Programmer of Alb'ny, was present at the negotiations between the red-haired man and the Lawgivers."

Redrick nodded. He had seen Faf on shore just before he had to abandon ship.

"They say there was a letter that proved Ramon of Alb'ny was a half-breed, making his rule illegal under the Laws of Ibem. The throne was offered to Jerlynn, as a Pure Blood human, but she turned it down through Faf and left the way clear for Morgan as Ty'Jorman's only other heir."

"Why would she do that?" Redrick asked.

Crispet shrugged wide. "How should I know?" The man stood up slowly, picking up his bundle as he did. "Well," he said. "I've rested long enough."

"Where to now?" Moira asked.

"Back to Nyack to await the evacuation, same as you," he said. "These are historical times."

"Yes, they are," Redrick said, and waved his good hand. "See you in Nyack."

"Then on to N'ork City!" Crispet said, thrusting a fist in the air. "Luck with rain!"

"Same to you!" Moira called, she and the children waving as Crispet disappeared into crowds moving through the dense green forest toward the beach.

"Can I give you a hand with anything?" Redrick asked when Crispet was gone.

"You just rest here," Moira said, setting the girl back on the ground. "There's hardly anything to be done. Come on, children."

With that she walked off, the boy and girl toddling happily after. He sat back on his boulder, watching the gentle sway of her hips beneath the white robes she wore. As his fingers slid up and down the snakeskin of the cane, he thought about his information and the new position he'd hold in Ramon's army once it arrived at this nest of vermin.

7

The Beach—North of Tivoli

The bonfires were high, fed by the trunks of trees hundreds of years old, trees cleared by Ramon Delaga's formidable army so they would have a humanlike camp for the night. The bonfires, and there were nearly a hundred, sent flames licking up to fifty feet in the air in an attempt to dispel the night. They lit the wide-spreading camp nearly to daylight, but it was a daylight that Ramon Delaga should have been loath to own.

Riches of plastic and gold glowed like groundstars in the flickering light, plunder piled high near the fire, lest the thieves try and steal from one another. They were riches paid for with the flesh of the South. Probably fifty thousand had already died for Ramon's booty, and that was a slow beginning. Had Germantown not been put to the torch, the booty and the body count would have been far higher. But then, Germantown couldn't have been helped.

Father Hus charged Southward just on the edge of the

firelight, and upon it, lapping gently at anchor, Ramon's armada. Four strong ships of wood and steel, each decking forty big guns, awaited the real daylight. There had been a fifth ship, but that was now in the hands of the farmer.

Nearly one hundred thousand camped around the fires. They laughed and sang of their victories—and their profits. For the journey thus far had indeed been profitable. Five Southern cities had been sacked—five cities rich in treasure and defenseless citizenry, five cities poor in protection. It was a soldier's vacation, take without give, thievery without retribution. Their excesses had been legendary, their brutality well beyond animalistic. The army had already become violent hedonists without restraint, an army of the dead, and Ramon encouraged it to insure their loyalty. They had all, as the Green Woman put it, "become addicted to the terrible darkness of the human heart." And addiction was something the Green Woman knew a great deal about.

Food was plentiful. The torching of the Germantown forest had driven beasts into the open. Meat of snake and rab was most bountiful, as was canine pack meat from the ancestors of the Woofers. Ground birds were oft seen on the fires, and many of the larger insects were being roasted on sticks and eaten that way.

In the center of camp sat a huge tent. It was made of light blue canvas. It rose to a peak in the center where the trunk of an oak tree stood as its support beam. Within, Ramon of Alb'ny gave a feast.

Here, also, a fire burned. Set near the oak post, it burned hot and bright, venting through a hole at the top of the beam. A giant rab roasted on a spit that took four Castle Guard to turn. The tent floor was a mush of piled carpets. Seating was upon cushions that made a circle around the fire. Low, individual tables were set before the cushions, so the guests could eat while reclining. The rab was nearly cooked, its pungent, slightly gamey smell filling the large tent, mixing with the smoke of a multitude of candles to thicken the atmosphere to a warm haze.

Ramon sat upon a raised cushion just outside the circle. Beside him sat the Green Woman, her dark hair piled high atop her head and studded all over with ancient copper coins that had been found in the ruins of Catskill. She wore a wisp of a gown, her green flesh showing boldly through the transparent fabric. A small leather case sat beside her, from whence she extracted the potions that were part of her hold on Ramon.

The cushions were occupied by Ramon's generals and their Physicians, plus several soldiers who had distinguished themselves in the few skirmishes fought in the Southern cities. Jerlynn Delaga, and Faf, the Programmer, were conspicuously absent from the proceedings.

Ramon, giddy, stared into his wine crock. He wore his blue jumper, the webbed armor discarded in a trunk. He was just on the edge of cognizance, yet felt confident and in control. The Green Woman knew just how to treat him.

He lay back, his head overhanging the cushion until he was staring into an upside down fire. "My friends!" he called. "Was there ever a quest as righteous as ours?"

"No, my Lord!" the voices returned. And applause rumbled through the tent like distant thunder.

"Will we kill the Genie, my friends?" he called.

Senator Murray, commander of the GAMECOCK, stepped forward, raising his drink. "We will empty them from the lands of N'ork like the rain empties from the clouds."

Ramon rolled onto his stomach and stared at the man. "But the rain returns to the clouds."

The man's face went sour. "I confuse my metaphor," he grumbled and took a drink. Then he started again. "We will drain them from the land as . . ."

"As Murray drains the Governor's wine!" Delmar laughed, and everyone joined in. Murray frowned deeply, turning a circle to glare around him.

"The rab is done!" one of the Guard called.

Ramon rolled off the cushion and stood shakily. "The meat of the South," he said, and staggered, nearly falling headlong into the fire. "We will eat their choicest meat and leave the carcass for the scavengers. Come! Fill your bellies on the plenty of the South, for when we get done we will have drained the Southerners also from the land."

Everyone was on his feet, hurrying to the rab, for they had not eaten since early that morning. Ramon nodded wildly, swinging his arms around as if he were some sort of celestial band director. They pulled huge hunks off the beast, laughing and drinking while they stuffed it into their mouths.

Ramon continued to stagger, feeling lightheaded standing up. "Where's Reeder?" he said. "The old man dishonors me."

"He lies abed, my Lord," Delmar said, his arms around two of the Councilman's litter bearers. "You broke four of his bones when you tumbled him from his pallet."

Ramon hooted loudly. "So, the old sot has brittle bones," he said. "I thought them as mushy as his brain!"

Everyone laughed except a young man of tender years, dressed in pure white robes, who stepped forward. "The Councilman is well loved in Watervliet," he said. "Though you think him foolish, our people honor him as their greatest leader."

"And who might you be?" Ramon asked, his words slurred somewhat.

It became suddenly quiet in the tent.

"My name also is Reeder," the young man said politely. "I am oldest son of the Councilman. I appear tonight to ask for your official apology to one who has been wronged by you without reason."

Ramon's face took on a mock posture of sadness. "Have I wronged your dear father?" he asked in an exaggerated whine.

Pack, Ramon's Physician before the Green Woman, stepped forward, his ancient gray suit and tie dusted white from the march. "Do not mock the boy," he whispered to Ramon. "We need his support if the old man dies."

Ramon ignored the Physician for, truly, his mind was altered beyond the normal scope of his thinking. With a wicked gleam in his eye, he walked to the young Reeder and put an arm around his shoulder.

"You seem to be a fine young man," Ramon said.

"I'm surprised that you could tell," Reeder replied.

"Doesn't he seem like a fine specimen, Count Delmar," Ramon continued.

Delmar moved around the fire to stand closer, his two litter boys still in hand. He brushed a long strand of hair from his face and looked Reeder up and down shamelessly. "Oh my, yes," he said clinically. "A fine, healthy lad." He jammed a hand between Reeder's legs, the young man jumping away. "Stop!"

"A fine lad," Delmar beamed, cocking an eyebrow to the amusement of the guests.

"I won't stand for these indignities!" Reeder said loudly.

"Then sit down!" Ramon screamed, and pushed the young man to the ground.

Hatred flashed across Reeder's face, and he tried to scrabble to his feet, the Castle Guard upon him before he got halfway up.

"Now, boy," Ramon said, as the Guard dragged Reeder to stand before him. "Perhaps it is you who should apologize to me."

"I'd die first," Reeder said.

"That won't be necessary," Ramon said. "But I think the least you could do would be to let us see what such a fine young man looks like without his robes on."

Reeder's face blanched white. "You wouldn't."

Ramon smiled, then pointed to one of the serving women he had brought from the castle. "Marlene," he said. "Come here and help us with Prince Reeder."

Pack moved over to the Green Woman. "You've got to stop this," he whispered.

"What makes you think I could do anything," she said, craning her neck to get a look as Marlene used a long knife to cut away Reeder's garments, exposing him to the derision of the guests.

"We need our allies to hold together if we're to have any hope of winning the war," Pack said low.

"I don't control Ramon," the woman said casually.

"You control his every move," Pack said, teeth clenched. "We can't afford to lose Watervliet."

"You worry too much," she answered. "Let Ramon have his fun."

And Pack was struck, for the very first time, with the notion that the Green Woman didn't care if they won the war or not.

"That's right," Ramon said. "Get it all."

Marlene finished slicing through the robe, the Guard pulling it from Reeder's pale white body. The young man stood, breathing heavily, his eyes closed tightly in embarrassment. A tear slid from the corner of his left eye.

"Don't cry," Ramon said. "You don't have anything to be ashamed of. Marlene, help the boy have a better time."

The woman reached out and took Reeder's manhood in her hands, stroking gently, bringing him to pulsating life.

"That's better!" Ramon said, and the assembled applauded politely.

"P-please, no," the boy sobbed. "Don't."

"He's still unhappy," Ramon said. "Maybe it's because his robes got torn." He picked up the clothes and tossed them into the fire. "There, you don't have to look at them anymore."

Young Reeder broke down, crying loudly.

Ramon shook his head. "Still unhappy," he said. "Well, let's cover you up so you won't be embarrassed anymore. Some dirt and ashes ought to do it."

He picked up a handful of dirt and threw it on the man. "Doesn't stick very well," he said. "I've got it." Walking to the rab, he rubbed a hand across it, coming away with grease.

"Try this," he said, and rubbed grease across the boy's chest. "The dirt should stick now. Come on, everybody, let's help the lad out. Don't be shy. Everybody. A handful of grease and a handful of dirt."

Pack watched as the guests lined up to humiliate the heir apparent to the throne of Watervliet. He blamed it all, every bit of it, on the Green Woman. She cared for nothing save the fire—the fire in the forest, the fire in men's souls. She was a catalyst, and trouble was the chemical reaction she lived on. She enflamed the other Physicians to thoughts and deeds beyond their ken, thereby destroying the delicate balance between leadership and science.

If Ramon and Alb'ny were to be saved, the Green Woman would have to be dealt with. And Pack realized that this responsibility would have to fall to him.

He was ready for it.

Dixon Faf lurched, again and again, his large body totally engulfing the small woman beneath him. Jerlynn Delaga whimpered softly, encouraging with her hands, pale legs wrapped around the holy man's waist.

"Yes," he called. "Yes."

His words, whispered harshly, filled the darkness of his cabin aboard VIPER, his sweat dripped in salty gobs upon Jerlynn. He had dreamt of this moment day after day during his long mission to Kipsie. When he was sick with the fever, it was the image of Jerlynn that eased him through the chills and the burning sweats.

He looked down at her. Her eyes, soft and glazed, held his fiercely. "Ibem help him," she cried low. "I do love you so."

"My Lady," he wailed, the spasms upon him. "Oh, my Lady."

He fell upon her, thinking at the last second to roll off lest he smother her. They lay like that, side by side, for several minutes before speaking.

As they touched, the feelings flowed back and forth between the two of them, strengthening the bonds that held them prisoners of each other's will. As the world fell apart around them, they each had the stability of the other as a solid anchor. Their love was strong, the strongest thing in either's life. It gave them the courage they needed to continue; it gave them the tenderness they needed to live—enough reason for anyone to go on.

"I feared for so long you'd never come back for me," she whispered, afraid in retrospect of what might have been heard on deck. "It's been horrible. Ramon's been . . ."

"Inhuman?" Faf helped.

She buried her face in his shoulder and cried. "He consorts with the heathens. He seems so lost."

"He burned the sacred forests," Faf said, stroking her, trying to calm her. "He *is* lost. His tainted blood has taken control of him and now it threatens us all."

"It's the blood," she said. "The blood."

"Our only hope is to help Morgan of Siler."

"The bastard," Jerlynn spat.

"Shhh." He pulled her close, held her to him. "He's the only chance we've got to salvage anything worthwhile from our lives. Ramon would burn us all to the ground. The blood has made him crazy."

"And that woman."

"Yes, yes. The woman."

Jerlynn sat up, folding her arms delicately across her breasts. "Do we now conspire against Alb'ny?"

"Morgan is the future of Alb'ny now," Faf said. "You traded Ramon's life for the life of Alb'ny. The lives and spirits of the people of my Province are what I fight for now." He sat up and gently moved her arms so he could gaze at her. "We conspire *for* Alb'ny, not against her."

He bent to kiss her small, upturned breasts.

"Wait," she said, taking his head in her hands and forcing him to look at her eyes.

"Yes, my love?"

"We are doing the right thing, aren't we?"

He stared at her, wishing that his own mind was pristine

enough to not realize that they had already taken their first and greatest steps against Ramon, and that rightness and wrongness were no longer issues. Survival was the key now.

"Yes," he said at great length. "We are doing the right thing."

She sighed gratefully, happy to lose herself within the righteousness of the Programmer's ideals. It reminded her of the good times with Ty'Jorman.

Reaching out gingerly, she took his penis in her fingers, marvelling at the tremendous girth it could reach in a matter of seconds. This is what she needed tonight—action beyond thought, reaction beyond control.

Jerlynn Delaga, for the first time, was allowing for the possibility of her own death, and wondering therein if she were really so much different than Morgan's mother, the Genie who died for her son.

Ramon stood near the dying fire, watching the remnants of his victory dinner waste away to embers along with the flames.

Young Reeder, his face set in contorted hatred, was tied spread-eagle near the front entrance, his soot and dirt-smeared body still straining against his bonds. Most of the guests were either unconscious or nearly so, their clothes strewn around the wreckage of Ramon's quarters. It had been quite an evening: mass sex, a duel to the death between two of the honored warriors, and assorted grotesque behavior as the Physicians took turns commanding the actions of those present.

Through it all, the Green Woman sat aloof on her cushion, a cat smile turning the corners of her emerald lips. Pack, for his part, partook of neither food nor drink, claiming to be on a fast for religious reasons. He sat apart from the revel, his back against the yielding material of the tent.

"Clear this fungus out," the Green Woman told Ramon. "I tire."

He turned to her, a look of confusion straining his features. There was blood on the carpet, and dead among the sleepers.

"What went on here?" he asked.

"You should know," the Green Woman smiled. "You were more often than not in the middle of it."

He put gentle fingers to his temple, massaging. "It's not

that I don't remember," he said, "it's just that I don't exactly know what it is that happened."

"She did it," Pack said quietly.

Ramon turned to him. "Pack," he said, friendly. "You seem all right."

"She put something in the wine," Pack said.

Ramon turned to the Green Woman. "Something . . . in the wine?"

She cast a withering glance at the Physician. "Just a little feast-making powder I conjured up," she said, looking at Pack the entire time. "Nothing to be alarmed about."

"You could be alarmed about the young prince," Pack said, and Ramon looked at Reeder as if he'd never seen him before.

"Untie him, will you?" he said, and turned away from the young man. "Give him something of mine to wear, whatever he wants."

"I want nothing from you!" Reeder yelled.

Pack hurried over to untie him. "Don't blame the governor," he said as he worked on the bonds on Reeder's hands. "It's the woman, all the woman."

Ramon was looking at his wife. "You shouldn't have done that without asking me first," he said. "What are the other soldiers going to say when they find that their heroes were killed here tonight?"

"We'll tell them that it happened in a drunken stupor," the Green Woman replied. "The soldiers will love us more than ever."

"That's not the point," Ramon said.

"I don't want to hear the point," she said, standing. "You don't control my actions. I do as I please."

Ramon's head was throbbing. He massaged harder. "We have a war to win," he said.

"If you don't like it," she said, "I'll be gone in the morning."

He shut his eyes to hold back the pain. "I didn't mean that, I . . ."

"Then swallow it down whole and shit it out," she said, and walked off the cushion and right out the front of the tent.

"Please!" he shouted after her, but he knew he wouldn't see her until the morning, after she had spent the rest of the night trying her best to dishonor him with commoners.

"Take a robe . . . something," Pack told Reeder.

The young man stood up, eyes flashing. "I go to my people as I am," he said proudly. "Better to show them the hospitality of the ex-Governor of Alb'ny."

Ramon would have responded, but his head hurt too much. Silently he turned to watch the prince leave.

"Mark me," Pack said. "The woman will prove your undoing."

"Not now," Ramon said, his brain already filled with pain and conjecture as to his wife's unfaithfulness. "We'll talk of it another time."

"My Lord . . ." Pack began, but was interrupted by the sound of approaching soldiers without.

The entry guard poked his head in the flap, his eyes going wide at the scene that greeted him. "Some of the men want to show you a prisoner," he said.

"Prisoner?"

"They say he's a special one."

Ramon walked back to his cushion, sinking heavily onto it. "All right," he said. "Bid them enter."

Seconds later, a contingent of Castle Guard in blue and white-striped tunics entered with what appeared to be a eunuch dressed in a loincloth with the musculature of a man and the facial features of a woman.

"We found this one near the perimeter," one of the Guard said.

"A Genie?" Ramon asked.

"A strange one," the man replied, and pushed the man to the front of the group. "His name's Harrison."

Ramon stood and walked to the man who looked like a woman. "Do we speak the same language?" he asked.

"Yes, my Lord," the man said in a high-pitched, somewhat breathless voice. He kept his head lowered.

"What were you doing near my camp?"

"I came to try and steal food," Harrison answered without hesitation.

"A bold thief you are, too!" Ramon said, angry.

"That's what makes him special," a Guard with a long, tangled beard said. "He can't tell lies."

"You can't lie?" Ramon asked, incredulous.

"My kind were bred as observers," Harrison said in that same voice. "I have the gift of clear understanding, a good memory of everything I see, and an . . . inability to distort the clear truth."

"Nonsense," Ramon said. "Anyone can lie."

The man shook his head. "I would pass out from intense pain before a lie could pass my lips. Just the consideration of such things makes my head throb."

"Give me your sword," Ramon said to the bearded Guard.

The man drew his blade and passed it, hilt first, to Ramon.

"Now," Ramon said, and lifted the point of the blade to the man's throat. "I want you to tell me there are no clouds in the sky tonight."

The man grimaced. "I cannot, my Lord."

Ramon tightened his lips and pushed the point deeper, drawing blood. "Tell me!"

Harrison choked, sputtering, his mouth moving wordlessly.

Ramon put a hand behind the man's head to hold it steady against the sword. "Say it, or so help me God, you're dead where you stand."

The man tried to speak, but instead he began convulsing, his eyes rolling up in his head. He dropped to the carpet, vibrating madly.

Ramon stared down at the Genie. "Extraordinary," he said. "The perfect spy."

"What should we do with him?" the Guard asked, as he took back his sword.

"Nurse him back to health," Ramon replied, his face settled in contentment. "I feel that I will have need of him." He gestured around the room. "As a reward, if you see anything here that interests you, it's yours for the taking."

The Guard picked up the still-convulsing man and carried him out, several of the serving girls heaped on for good measure.

Ramon turned to Pack. "No one is to know of this," he said.

"No one, my Lord?" Pack said.

"No one."

"Yes, my Lord," Pack said, a large smile upon his lips.

PART TWO
LOYALTIES

8

Rockland

In ancient times a large stone bridge had spanned Father Hus at Rockland. The bridge had been washed away long ago. All that remained of it were the remnants of support pilings that pushed jaggedly up through the turbulent waters and the beginning and end segments that stood like waving sisters upon opposite shores. On the Rockland side, the ruins of the bridge were kept meticulously clean of growth, the only part of the city where that was done. It jutted out from the bank, forming a perfect pier, and it was here that VICTORY was anchored, her gangplank hinged down to kiss the natural dock.

Morgan stood on the upper deck with Jella, the young and swarthy Prelate of Rockland. The city's rulers were always on the young side, and they took most of their advice from a council of elders, all over eighty plantings old. The young and old worked together in graceful cooperation, fusing the vigor of youth with the wisdom of age.

"Have you seen Moira and the children?" Jella called through cupped hands.

Far below, amidst the evacuating crowd, a man in brown-and-green forest robes waved back. Around him a confusion of melancholy endings and exciting beginnings swirled an emotional tapestry as the city prepared for abandonment.

"The children have already taken their places on the raft!" the man called up. "Moira is seeing that everyone is away from the city!"

Jella waved back, turning to Morgan with a wide smile on

his heavily bearded face. "I have never been away from my
wife so long," he said.

Morgan put a hand on his shoulder. "Hopefully your last
separation," he said, but his mind was on Alicia. They had
parted in Kipsie with animosity between them, spoken and
unspoken, and he wondered if there would ever be a mending
between them. He missed her, too, just as Jella missed the
wife he had spoken of often during their journey downriver.
But there was more than love between them. There were responsibility and ideology and emotional differences that right
now seemed far larger than mere love could overcome.

He forced his mind away from the gold of her eyes, but
couldn't force away the melancholy. He thought of Ona, sad
Ona who didn't understand. He thought of Grodin, friend of
his life, now bitter enemy. They would walk through the fire
for one another, yet something nebulous and insubstantial had
come between them. It hurt him more than he could bear to
think that ideologies were more important than feelings, that a
wall of thought could separate those who truly loved one another.

Below, thousands surged around the ship, loading supplies and building more barges, adding, always adding, to his
group of nomads. Upon the dock, working around the feet of
those coming and going from the ship, a group of young boys
were pulling vines of ivy from around the bridge.

"What are they doing down there?" Morgan asked.
"There will be scant need of that now."

Jella nodded, his usual genial face settling to something a
bit darker. "The bridge is sacred to us," he said. "When a boy
reaches the age of ten years, it becomes his responsibility to
keep the bridge cleared. At age thirteen he jumps from the
bridge and swims the river from support to support."

The man gestured across the river. Morgan followed his
arm, taking in the pillars of stone that dotted the charging waters all the way across. A possible swim, but a treacherous one.

"It is the way of manhood of our people," Jella said.

"How do they get back?" Morgan asked.

The man smiled again, his good humor returning. "They
must bring back a fish," he said. "You see, the waters below us
are the fishes' graveyard. Fishing boats come through here
with their nets out and get them snared in the old bridge pilings. They cut off the nets and go on, but the nets stay woven

through the supports, catching fish whether there is anyone to take them away or not. There are always thousands of fish in various stages of death and dying. Our young men must save a fish from the net and bring it back as an act of goodwill."

"What happens to the fish then?"

The man looked surprised. "We . . . let it go," he said. "We eat only fruit in Rockland."

"A proud tradition," Morgan said.

"A dead tradition," Jella responded.

"Maybe when this is over . . ."

The man shook his head. "Things can never be the same again." He took a breath and smiled. "We'll make new traditions."

"Traditions of brotherhood," Morgan said.

"You are a man wise beyond your years," Jella told him.

"Don't believe it," Morgan replied, and put a leg up on the wooden rail, the material of his white britches strained across his thigh. "I'm just a dreamer with a sword."

Jella turned to stare out at the milling crowds. "When enough people share the dream," he said, "it is what we call reality."

Morgan hugged the man close, tugging on his beard when he released him. "Perhaps you are the one who is wise beyond his years."

Jella shook his head. "I just appreciate dreamers," he said, and both men laughed.

There was a commotion on the beach, a large, vocal crowd assembling near the gangplank.

"Something wrong," Jella said.

Morgan jumped up on the upper deck rail, holding a support beam and leaning way out to get a look. He still couldn't see. "I'm going down," he said, turning to Jella.

The Prelate opened his mouth to speak, but as he did, Morgan released his hold on the beam and dropped the fifteen feet to the main deck. He hit in a crouch, then rolled backwards, jumping to his feet.

He scurried across the deck, jumping on the rail again at the gangway to avoid the crush of the Rockland elders and their retinue who were at that moment pushing onto the deck. They were harmonizing a song of farewell in the high, chirping voice that Southern N'orkers used for singing.

They looked up in astonishment as Morgan vaulted over

their heads from his position on the rail, turned a flip, and landed on his feet farther down the gangplank.

He hurried to the dock, past the young boys who sorrowfully cleared it, and pushed his way into the turmoil.

A large, jeering crowd had gathered. They were angry, their fists in the air, their voices filled with hate. Morgan shoved his way through them to arrive at the center of the controversy.

Three Schneck warriors with drawn swords stood back to back, the angry mob just out of their range pelting them with rocks. The half-breed human/Genies were tattered and bloody, their dull eyes glazed with fear, their lopsided heads bruised and swollen even more out of shape.

"Stop!" Morgan said, striding up to stand beside the Schnecks. He looked in horror at the faces that surrounded him. They were faces strained ugly with hatred, etched deeply with the lines of deep-rooted anger.

They stopped the stoning, their shouts diminishing from the inside of the circle outward. Morgan walked around the Schnecks, staring out at the faces of his people. He knew their look and he grieved for it.

Abruptly, he turned to the Schnecks. "Why have you come here?" he asked.

The Schnecks straightened from their defensive crouch, sword points lowering. One with dirty blond hair that sat in patches all over his grayish skull spoke up in the slurred voice that characterized the Northern half-breeds.

"We run," he said, and a line of dried blood stretched from lips to chin. "From the b-big fight, we run."

"You were at the battle of Kipsie?" Morgan asked, and the crowd chattered loudly for a minute.

The Schneck gulped, nodding slowly. "Our people died and we run. We can't run anymore."

"Why are you here?" Morgan asked again.

The Schneck looked around, eyes darting, before answering. "We heard about you," he said. "We heard the red-haired man looked at all as b-brothers. We thought that maybe even Schnecks could be brothers, too."

"There are many Genies with me," Morgan said. "I have heard that Schnecks wish to kill all Genies."

One of the other Schnecks, with eyes of different sizes and skull holes instead of ears spoke up. "Schnecks live to kill Genies," he said, and the crowd started yelling again. Morgan glared them to silence.

"Why?" Morgan asked.

"Because then the humans won't hate us," he said, and cast his eyes downward. He began crying softly. "We only wish to live, as all creatures wish to live. We didn't ask to be this way."

He looked up at Morgan, his eyes filled with tears that flowed down his face, mixing with the patches of blood. "Please not to hate us," he said softly. "We didn't ask to be ugly. We didn't ask to be . . . s-stupid."

Morgan walked to the deformed half-man and took him in his arms. "You are as welcome here as the breeze," he said, holding the man tightly. "You are as beautiful as the breath of morning."

He released the Schneck and turned to the crowd. "Is this the lesson that you've learned from all we've been through?" he demanded. "Do we wish to take the hatred of bigotry with us into exile like extra baggage? So be it." He stood up straight. "Pick up your rocks and stone me, too. For I swear to you I'd rather die here with my brothers than share the burden of this hypocrisy."

One by one, the citizens of Rockland dropped their rocks to the ground and walked quietly into the passing lifestream.

Redrick watched what used to be his boat sitting at anchor in the Rockland harbor. The hate seethed within him, for no matter what he set himself to accomplish, the red-haired farmer was always there to take it away from him. He looked at the hook that was once his right hand, another present from the farmer, and it was all he could do to keep himself from charging down the beach and killing the bastard right then.

"You seem deep in contemplation," came a voice, making him jump.

He whirled around to see Moira standing there, bathed in the soft light of morning, a garland of wild flowers woven into her golden hair.

Her eyes were wide in surprise. "I didn't mean to startle you," she said.

He shook his head, his vibrating hook dropping to his side. "Quite all right," he said. "A glimpse of your beauty is worth any shock."

She smiled sweetly. "Thank you," she said. "Jella, my husband, is with the ship today. I wanted to look pretty for him."

"You are of a beauty that any man would wish to possess," Redrick said.

"Sir Benford," she said, startled at his familiarity. "You make me blush."

He locked eyes with her. "And my lady, you make the blood rush through my veins in a fever."

Moira, unable to ascertain the look in his eyes, changed the subject. "Why have you not gone down to the beach yet?"

Redrick laughed, taking several steps toward her. "The beach, I fear, would be the worst place for me to go."

"Your cane!" she said, pointing. "You're walking without your cane."

He looked at the wood in his hand, then threw it to the ground. "It only served to keep me out of the trees," he said, and walked closer, within reaching distance.

"Who are you?" she said, backing up, but bumping into a fat oak.

"I am the man for whom you wore the flowers in your hair," he said, and lunged quickly at her, knocking her to the ground.

There was no one around; everyone was down on the beach. The sounds of Moira's screams were lost in the trees and the low-hanging clouds, and when Jella found her dishonored and mutilated body later that day, all trace of Sir Benford of Catskill had completely disappeared.

9

THE OUTSKIRTS OF ROCKLAND

Galen the Grunt squatted in the highest branches of the tall
elm and watched the strange ritual being performed on the
Rockland beach a half mile distant.

The lower half of his body was gray-brown with dark bark
grooves, the upper half several shades of green to match the
slick, pointy leaves that hung near him. He watched the spectacle of the beach intently, watched the mixture of humans and
Genies who moved around upon it in disorganized confusion—
a terrible waste of time and energy. They were stacking up rot
wood in a huge pile, while many of the humans stood nearby,
openly weeping.

There was a tapping on the tree trunk, a question in
Morse language that he picked up through the sensory radar of
his bristly body hair around his horns. He glanced down to see
Gregore, the youngest, staring up at him. They were too far
away from the proceedings to be heard, so he called to the man
with words.

"Why don't you come up and see?" he said to the Grunt
whose body had the black-dirt tinge. The others sat in shadow,
taking on its proportion. They were nearly invisible, even to
Galen, and he knew where they were.

Gregore reached out to touch horns with his mate, Marta,
before climbing, Galen smiling at the tenderness of their physical relationship. The two lovers were the pride of the clan,
their joy with one another a plane of sentience that all could
share.

The young Grunt came up the tree, stabbing hand and
footholds right into the trunk. He probably could have used
the holes that Galen had already made, but that way he

couldn't show Marta his own prowess as a climber. In a moment he joined Galen on the limb, his body changing color to match his new surroundings.

"They're pale as the beach," Gregore said as he stared out at the confusion below. "Are they like us?"

"No," Galen smiled with his deep, wrinkled mouth. "They're that color all the time. Have you ever seen the like of what you see now?"

"Never," Gregore said, pulling off a leaf that had gotten speared by his curling left horn. "So many possibilities."

"And all unique," Galen replied. "That's what we're here to protect."

"What is that cloth they wrap around their bodies?"

"It's called clothes. They wear them for protection from the elements and for modesty."

"Modesty?"

Galen had been watching a tree snake winding its way across the branch to wrap around his leg. "It's a difficult concept to understand," he said, as the small snake slithered up past his knee. "We'll probably have to do it too when we meet with them."

"They seem so fragile," Gregore said, almost sadly.

"They are," Galen said, and he passed the fat pad of his hand near the snake's head. It struck, trying to bite, but its fangs got no farther than his shiny, epidermal armor. "Do you know what they're doing down there?"

"Some sort of ritual," Gregore said, his eyes fixing on a long processional that was winding its way from the city down to the stack of wood. "But what kind?"

Galen pulled the snake from him, gently setting it back on the branch to slide quickly away. "It's a burial," he said.

Gregore looked puzzled. "A what?"

"Someone has died. They will burn the body upon that altar of wood."

Gregore's face went slack. "Death," he said, shaking his head. "I've never . . . seen it in . . . creatures like us." He looked down at Marta, the concept of eternity without her unthinkable. He then turned back to Galen. "Have you ever seen it?"

The ruler of Gimlock nodded solemnly. "I saw too much of it in the old days," he said softly. "I've even seen our own kind pass away."

Gregore turned his face from the scene. "It's unthinkable," he said, voice hoarse. "I can't stand the . . ."

"You'll see much more of it before we're through," Galen told him. "A hundred years is old enough to know death."

There was the sound of distant chanting as the body of Jella's wife, Moira was raised high in the air and set upon the pyre. Then, with much wailing, torches were put to the wood. Gregore forced himself to watch. He would try to understand this thing called death. He would try to accept it as part of this world. "Will we go to them now?" he asked.

Galen barely shook his head. "Not yet," he said. "We will follow at a distance and study them. Farther downriver we will make the acquaintance of Morgan of Alb'ny."

"Look," Gregore said, pointing with his open palm, his third eye watching below.

"I've been watching them," Galen said, and he, also, scrutinized the procession with his third eye. It was a single-file line of robed people picking their way carefully through the thick jungle. The one in front was using a handheld beam of laser light to cut a pathway for them.

"Dark people," Gregore said.

"They're called Mechs," Galen said. "Although only the one in front is of Pure Blood. The others are of mixed breed. I have often wondered if that kind survived the wars."

"Are they friendly?"

Galen looked at Gregore, his eyes clanging as he blinked. "They are the single most dangerous species on the planet," he said.

Below, Nebo and his contingent of Mechs passed within twenty feet of Galen's tree, but never knew he was there. They were busy following a trail dictated by the clicking machine in Nebo's mechanical hands.

Surrounding the Mechs in a loose circle were a number of giants, prepared to defend them against anything that might come. The largest number of Mechs and Genies were still on the beach, attending the funeral to cover the activities of Nebo's group.

Pietro, tall and bent like a praying mantis, walked beside Nebo. He held the laser box out in front of him. Its muzzle was deeply charred and partially melted due to the wide beam that Nebo was forcing him to use. He stared at Nebo, who intently watched the needle on the small counter that was attached to the length of pipe he held in his metal hands.

"Stop," Nebo said, and the procession halted immediately. The Mech turned a semicircle, slowly rotating the pipe in all directions. He stopped turning, pointing to the northeast. "This way. Use it sparingly."

"As you wish," Pietro said, and flashed the light beam in the direction of Nebo's pipe. A second later, a steaming, charred tunnel appeared in the dense jungle—a circular hole, large enough for them to walk through.

"How's the charge?" Nebo asked.

"Nearly depleted," Pietro said. "Such a wide beam drains it quickly."

Nebo strode into the vaporized area, a large tree, its trunk cut in half, falling across his path. He climbed over it and continued walking. "We have no choice," he told Pietro. "We have to hurry. It was just lucky that the funeral held up our departure long enough for us to make this side trip."

"What are we looking for?" Pietro asked as he climbed over the fallen trunk.

"When I was very young," Nebo said over his shoulder, "and lived in Master Thulow's house, I was taught of the seven shrines—seven refining plants within a reachable distance of N'ork. In these seven plants, an element called Plutonium was extracted from Uranium and made into fuel pellets for nuclear reactors. One of the shrines was located just outside of Rockland."

"I've heard of this nuclear," Pietro said, respect in his tone. "It *is* the power of the Sun."

"It will soon be ours," Nebo said, and his liquid brown eyes seemed hot as lava when he turned to stare at his disciple. "The ultimate power of creation and destruction will be in our hands. Listen."

He turned a knob on the counter. A loud, fast clicking noise issued from the box. "The ionization tube I carry is filled with helium at low pressure that reacts to the gamma rays given off by uranium. They form electrons that create a negative pulse in the tube—that's the sound you hear. And judging from the frequency of the pulses, we're very near the heart of the deposit."

"Why did we sneak off to do this?" Al-ke-do, Pietro's bloodmate, asked from behind.

"Because it needed to be done," Nebo responded, "and it had to be done, and this was the only way to get it done. We will have this power. It opens new worlds for us."

They walked in silence for several moments, Nebo occasionally altering course by degrees, Pietro burning a new pathway with each change. Finally, the box gave way in a shower of sparks and a melted front end.

"That's it," Pietro said sadly, dropping the now useless pile of junk on the ground. "Our greatest triumph is no more."

"What matter?" Nebo said. "The triumph is in the understanding, not the making. And besides, our greatest triumph stands before us. Behold, the nuclear tree."

He opened his arms wide, his counter eaten up by a solid barrage of sound. Directly in front of them grew a giant dogwood tree, far larger than the runt of the forest they were used to. It stretched out high and spindly, large pink buds blooming in profusion.

The remnants of an ancient building grew with the tree. It had been a warehouse of thick metal walls bolstered by concrete. The limbs of the dogwood bowed under and around the weight of the still-thick walls. And large brown rocks were scattered among the branches and within the bark of the tree. They were balanced everywhere, the tree growing up to cradle them to itself, waiting—for Nebo.

"Serge!" Nebo called, a slight edge to his voice. "Pull down the tree."

Serge and the other giants moved to the dogwood, leaning all their weight against it. They began pushing. They strained with the exertion, the tree crying under their hands as it gave way. It snapped with a loud crack, shaking wildly. Stone and rock and concrete rained down along with floating pink blossoms. The giants ran, covering their heads with their arms, as the tree leaned over at a forty-five degree angle.

"Enough!" Nebo shouted, running to pick up a brown rock the size of a small applegenic. He carried it proudly back to Pietro and the others.

They gathered around solemnly, their devotion and love total for Nebo. They watched his barely contained excitement and knew that their lives had changed somehow, though none of them had any idea of the direction of that change. They were content to let knowledge lead them where it would. It was their nature.

"The color is caused by oxidation," Nebo said clinically. "Watch."

He set the rock on the ground, then leaned over and pushed against it with his metal hands. After a moment, a small chunk broke off. Nebo picked it up. Within, it was bright white, blinding white.

"You want to see why we came out here?" he asked. "Do you want to have just a small idea?"

He set to work with the rock, scraping it into small pieces onto the hard, charred ground. Within minutes, he had ground much of it to a fine powder. Then, satisfied, he stood back and watched.

All was silence, as Mechs and giants crowded around the white uranium powder. It seemed to hiss, almost to glow. Then, all at once, magically, it burst into flame—a large, hot, blue-white fire.

"It *is* the power of the Sun," Pietro said, and he knelt upon the ground.

ii

LAST CHANCE

Grodin stopped walking the old rab trail and listened for the sound of thunder. Dropping the hooked rope of dead beaver that rested on his right shoulder, he traced with his fingertips the scar that ran from temple to jawbone on his swarthy face. It throbbed painfully, usually the sign of approaching rain, but he didn't feel it in the air or hear it in the wind.

Grunting, he bent carefully and picked up his bundle, using it to balance a similar catch on his left shoulder. Several days before, he had noticed the creek that ran through the ancient tree city was not running as swiftly as usual. Then it slowed down to nearly a trickle. He made the trek upstream to find out what happened and found the beavers industriously damming it up to make themselves a pond.

He trapped and killed the animals, then destroyed the dam. They could make a stew with the meat, and he had an idea to sew a cloak of beaver skin for Ona to try and take her mind off her all-consuming hatred of Morgan.

He moved down the trail again, picking up his pace without realizing it. He had felt apprehensive all day. Something in the woman had changed of late. Instead of throwing off the mantle of her hatred, she seemed content in it, as if she had come to some unholy decision about it. His scar had throbbed since he had left early that morning, and he was beginning to feel that, perhaps, it had nothing to do with the weather.

He walked the trail for another hour, stopping occasionally to rest his aching shoulders. The jungle was malevolent around him. It hissed and cawed to him, and he became convinced that something was desperately wrong. Finally, he could stand it no longer.

With a violent jerk of his arms, he dropped his bundles to the ground and ran. He ran swiftly, belying his stretch of years and reached Last Chance nearly exhausted just as the perpetual gray of the sky was beginning to darken to the cover of night.

"Ona!" he screamed when he reached the clearing. "Where are you!"

There was no response.

He looked slowly around, taking in the tree-house city that sat in a natural bowl. The overflow creek was running strong again, the waterfall that still churned Nebo's water turbines screaming frothy white down the rock face of the bowl.

"Ona!"

No response.

He hurried to their tree, climbing the metal rungs inlaid in the bark. The porch creaked under his weight as he climbed upon it to hurry in the front door.

She was gone. He quickly searched the house, then ran back to the porch, leaning upon it, letting his eyes rove the deserted city once more.

There was only one place for Ona to go and he knew it: Ramon. She was returning to Ramon, who she once served, to try and gain her vengeance upon Morgan for taking one of their sons with him on his quest.

The old man would have cried if there were time, but with darkness descending, time was something he had lost back on the trail.

His own feelings about Morgan and his blood-mixing were still vague, uncertain. But his feelings about Ramon were strong. He would have to stop Ona. He could not be even an unwilling party to her insane treachery.

Several acorn pancakes lay upon the wooden table, Ona's dinner present for Grodin. He stuffed them in his britches and scurried down the tree. He knew which trail she'd take, but he also knew she had nearly a ten-hour start on him. He ran into the jungle. It would be dark within minutes, but he'd get as far as he could before the sponge of the jungle soaked them both up for the night.

iii

THE WESTERN ROAD—EAST OF DELMAR

"My child and I are obliged," Ona said, as she slid off the back of the Woofer, holding onto its tight ringlets of Poodle hair to ease her fall. Little Ty'Jorman, giggling, jumped off after her and latched onto her shoulder, perching there.

"A pleasure, ma'am," the grizzled farmer with the floppy straw hat said. "In these troubled times, us simple folk have got to stick together."

Ona paid no attention to the man's words, but smiled up at him anyway. The Woofer panted heavily, the man on his back craning his neck to find water.

"Thanks again," Ona said, and moved to the cart the animal was pulling to retrieve her bundle.

The man turned once to her, his emotions strong as he saw his own possessions loaded into the cart. "That's a mighty unusual child you've got there," he said idly.

She pulled her burlap sack out of the wagon with a jerk, and turned to face the man whose name she never thought to ask. "What do you mean by that?" she snapped.

His eyes narrowed, and he looked at the large crowds flowing past them on the dirt roadway. "I don't mean anything by it, I . . ."

"He's perfectly normal," she said, lips tightened to a bloodless slash. "A normal, healthy baby."

The man opened his mouth to speak, but thought better of it. "Yes, ma'am," he mumbled at last, then gave a loving pat to the Woofer's rump. "C'mon, Chuck."

Chuck, still panting, walked slowly off, the man on his back turning to stare at Ona as they moved into the scores of refugees. The rickety wooden wagon creaked loudly behind, its wheels bumping into all the holes and grooves on the road.

Ona turned from them, and they were totally gone from her mind. What remained was that she had made great time after she had reached the Western road. The war was bringing turmoil at home. Every place she passed on the road had the same story: encroaching jungle due to lack of manpower.

The roads were full of people with their belongings. Totally homeless, they walked the roads looking for a new place to settle but finding none. The desperation in their eyes increased with each unhappy step. They deserted Delmar in droves, filling the road in both directions.

It was a great break for Ona, providing not only the safety of numbers, but several Woofer rides out of pity for a woman alone and her baby. She wasn't sure if Grodin would try and find her, but she was sure that she had distanced him by a long stretch if he was searching.

Moving into the flow, she walked, solid jungle walling up the roadway on either side. There seemed to be many eyes peering through the curtain of forest at them, the creatures of the dark curious as to why so many humans were on the road.

A road gang sat lined up beside the road, their backs against the line of trees, their legs chained together, their guardians idly toying with the big, black whips they used to keep the workers in line. They were scarred and grimy, and the mass migrations were a break for them, too, because the crowds not only were too thick to allow them to do their job of road clearing, but the thousands of feet tramping the hard-packed ground were actually doing the job for them.

Ona saw them, but didn't see them, her eyes straining for the thing she sought. She remembered the place from past trips down the road with Morgan when they were foraging for information. It would be around here somewhere.

A farmer stood by the roadside selling tomatoes, and Ona might have walked right past him had he not gotten involved in an altercation that commanded her attention. A man in bright red knickers with white stockings and a black vest over his bare chest began rousting the farmer.

"Move on!" the man said. "You're killing my business."

"You don't own this highway," the farmer said. "I have as much right to be here as you do."

The man picked up a tomato and smashed it on the farmer's head, juicy pulp running in rivulets down the man's slack face.

"Get the point?" the man said.

The farmer nodded, quickly gathering up his baskets and hurrying off, the man grabbing a large tomato and eating it as the farmer left.

Ona watched the exchange, then saw behind the man. A sign hung tacked on a tree that read: QUICKEST ROUTE TO THE RIVER, with an arrow pointing into the jungle.

Ona broke from the crowd and approached the man. He was very large with a sneering, gnarled face. His eyes roved up and down Ona's body as she neared him. "Whatcha need, miss?" he asked in a gutteral voice, red juice dripping from the corners of his mouth.

"I want to get to the river," she said. "I must get to the river."

He grunted, throwing the half-eaten fruit into the jungle. He wiped his mouth on the back of his arm. "You got gold or plastic?" he asked.

"Barter," she said.

He grunted again. "Come on."

She followed him down a narrow pathway into the thicket, the sounds from the road disappearing quickly behind. It was almost night, and darkness was already thick in the wood. She had to follow within touching distance just to be able to see the man at all.

A minute later they arrived at a small clearing that was paved with rocks. A shack sat in the middle of the clearing, and behind that, a long white concrete slab rose from the ground and into the trees at a forty-five degree angle, disappearing in the distance. She could see several people laboriously climbing the slab.

"Name's Firust," he said, opening the ill-fitting shack door. "What's yours?"

"What difference does it make?" she said.

He shrugged and ushered her into the dark room. After lighting several fat candles, he took a seat behind a makeshift desk formed of long planks glued together.

"I don't do charity work," he said.

"I told you I have barter."

"Let's see it."

Setting Ty'Jorman onto the desk top, she reached down into her bag and rooted around. The baby, meanwhile, had jumped off the desk and was busily trying to scrabble back up.

Ona pulled a silver candlestick out of the bag and held it proudly up. "What do you think?"

The man tore his incredulous eyes from the infant and looked, his gaze widening in satisfaction. He nodded and reached for the candlestick.

"That's the remnants of an ancient roadway," he said, jerking his head in the direction of the slab. "If you climb on up, you got a straight walk through the treetops to the Southeast. Take you right to the river without going through Alb'ny."

"Is it safe?"

"Not entirely. I just collect for the road and set up boats on the other side, that's all."

"You have boats?"

He held the candlestick in his hands, turning it round and round. "Sure," he said, and put his prize behind the desk. "I gotta couple barges."

"What would it cost me to get a boat downriver?"

Ty'Jorman clawed his way back up on the desk, and was just about to throw himself at Firust, when his mother picked him up and put him back on her shoulder.

"Now why would a sweet little thing like you want to go downriver?"

"How much?"

The man sighed and scratched his head. "Hasn't anybody told you there's a war going on?"

"I must go to Ramon Delaga."

The man laughed. "You just don't want to go downriver, you want me to take you smack in the middle of everything. I'd have to be crazy to do that."

Ona dropped the whole sack on the desk, dumping it in the process. More candlesticks fell out, and jewelry, and porcelain plates wrapped in cloth.

"It's all yours if you take me to Ramon," she said.

He looked at the stuff, worth more than six months of his usual drudgery, and understood that for him, too, the war was a good thing. He scratched again, the lice giving him fits.

"You really want to go bad," he said.

"Will you take me?"

"Well, this is almost enough," he said, and stared hard at her.

She knew the look in his eyes. Ramon's knights had taught her what that look meant a long time ago. With Grodin somewhere behind her, she really didn't have time to worry about it. "I've done it for others," she said. "I could do it for you. After we reach our destination."

He shook his head. "Now," he said, "and as often as I want until we get there."

She looked around the orange, flickering room, thinking of Morgan and how he had driven her to this. She thought of her baby being raised by him, being degraded by association with Genies. Her eyes finally rested on the ceiling and the beams that cut across the slanting roof for support.

She held the baby out to him. "Could you . . ." She motioned upward with her eyes.

Firust took the child from her without a word and lifted it up to one of the beams where it gurgled happily and swung on the wooden support.

"If that ain't the damndest thing," he said, watching Ty'Jorman on the beam.

"Come on," she said, uncinching the rope from around her middle and lifting her coarse shift up over her head. "Let's get it over with."

10

The South Road—Pleasantville Checkpoint
One Day North of N'ork City

Alicia sat with Twiddle and her communications Minnie in the private box atop her mover and watched the faces of the citizens who occupied the trees all around them. They were hollow faces, faces in limbo. Caught in the vortex between their

old lives and what they wanted in N'ork City, they waited at
Pleasantville, waited for the papers that would let them
through the gates and on the road to the Jewel of the East.
Many of them had been waiting for years, their lives caught in
stasis, refugees filling the trees, holding their breath as it
were—and holding. For most of them it was the end of the
road.

And the trees were crowded now, homeless people from
farther north grasping for a new breath of life. They were sys-
tematically turned away at the checkpoint, the shanty tree
houses of Pleasantville filling to overflow.

The mover ground patiently through the undertow of refugees. As wide as the roadway with wheels taller than a full-
grown man, the mover was a wooden skeletal framework that
stretched nearly to the tops of the trees. Powered by a steam
engine that also provided energy for the large calliope on the
rear, the mover was impressive and audacious, qualities that
Alicia hoped would get them through the gates from which so
many others had been turned away.

Alicia carried with her an entourage of twenty, fifteen of
whom were genetic neuters who formed the core of her personal staff. Bald albinos, they dressed in long red robes to high-
light the pink of their eyes. Proud and stoic, they hung onto
the framework of the mover and silently watched over their
mistress. There were also two Mechs, one to drive the con-
traption and one to play the calliope, plus three of Morgan's
Genies to feed the boiler and act as bodyguards.

With the steam pipe music in her ears and a gentle breeze
moving through the open front cutaway of the box, Alicia sat
half asleep. Through lidded eyes she watched Merit, her
driver, sitting closer to the front of the machine under a striped
canopy, yelling at people to clear the dust-heavy road. Twiddle
snored lightly beside her, his unlined face the picture of innocence.

She was glad to be away from Morgan and on the road,
doing what she did best. It was more difficult than she had
thought to share command with him. She knew what was
best—why wouldn't he listen to her? Her whole life had been
geared to command. Every part of her was bred and crossbred
to rule, and rule well. Then Morgan blusters in with his moods
and his hemolysis and expects that everything should be
turned over to him.

"You've gotten this far, haven't you?" Twiddle asked from beside her.

"I thought you were asleep," she said, turning to him.

"Your brain was screaming at me," he replied.

"Look at me," she said, and took his hand, placing the fingertips on her face. "I was born with make-up on. My lips are too red, my cheeks always blushing. The skin over my ever-so-dark eyelashes is light blue."

"What does this mean?" he asked, lightly tracing the curves of her face with his hand.

"Mean? Do you realize if I messed my hair up, then shook my head, it would all go back in perfect place. I was *born* with holes in my ears for earrings. It means that every part of me was designed to look and act just right so that people will accept my inborn knowledge and authority."

"So why haven't you gotten it before now?" he asked, taking his hand away.

"I haven't had the breaks," she said.

"Leaders don't blame outside forces for their problems."

"What are you trying to say, that I'm not fit for command?"

"I'm trying to get you to remember the rhyme that brought us here to begin with." Twiddle stopped talking, putting his fingertips to the place where his eyes might have been. He recited.

Band of three,
Band of three:
Soldier, builder,
Referee.

Band of three,
Band of three.
The perfect mix,
The apogee.

She frowned. "Maybe I'm not as fit to rule a world as I think," she said.

"Or maybe," he returned, "the world is too large and complex for one person to rule. You and Morgan . . . yes, and the Mech, your fates are intertwined. The band of three: the fighter, the engineer, the . . . negotiator. You are as one person whether you accept it or not. One life . . . to glorify, or to lose."

"What do you . . ." she began, but Merit called back from the controls.

"The checkpoint!" he yelled. "It's just ahead!"

Alicia put her hand on the old man's, squeezing. "Thanks for the talk," she said. "Now we'll see."

Twiddle smiled. "I have every confidence in you."

She leaned forward, staring through the cutout. Past Merit's back she could see the gate. It was tall and made of interlocking fingers of rusted ornamental iron fashioned to look like a miniature version of a tall, cement building, N'ork City's symbol. It cracked in the middle and opened in two pieces. Swarming around the gate were thirty or forty N'ork City regular army. They carried crossbows and were dressed in bright white uniforms that covered them from head to toe, leaving only mouth and eye holes in the hood.

"Odd," Alicia said. "Those gates only span the width of the roadway. What's to keep people from simply going around through the forest?"

Twiddle was leaning back, his head resting on the seat back. He knit his brow for a second. "I see glass balls," he said.

"Yes," she replied. "The jungle all around here is set with clear glass globes sitting atop wooden poles. They look ornamental."

"The woods are set with traps," he said. "Each globe represents one life that was lost on that spot."

"Those gates don't look as if they've been opened very much," Merit called back over his shoulder. They had come to a stop on the road, waiting behind a long line of refugees to speak with the gatekeepers. Each group of refugees was being turned away.

"We shall see about that," Alicia said, and stood, opening the door to her box and walking out onto the scaffolding itself.

"Prepare," she called down to the neuters, who responded with smiles and waves. Then she walked up to stand beside Merit.

"I hope your plan works," he said to her, his hands on the stick controls, both feet locked solidly on the brakes.

Alicia stooped to get under Merit's canopy. She patted

him on the back. "There are always other plans," she said. "Don't worry about it."

He smiled, his skin light enough to contain very little Mech blood. That's why she used him as her driver. He didn't have the creative aptitude of most of the Mechs. "You're sure of yourself."

"It's my job," she winked, moving under the canopy to walk back to her box. She wasn't any more sure than Merit that her plan would work, but confidence was part of the game.

A peach tree hung, heavy laden, against the side of the mover. Alicia plucked a large one and bit into it, the juices lubricating her slightly dry mouth. She stood outside as they moved slowly along the line, finally reentering the box as they pulled up to the gate. The stage was set.

From the shadows, she watched the N'orkers walk around her mover, looking it up and down and scratching their heads. One of them wearing goggles over his eyes put his hands on his hips and stared up at Merit.

"Name and business," he called up.

Merit stood and announced loudly. "Her Lady, Alicia of Alb'ny, Consort of Morgan, Governor of Alb'ny and its Provinces and Commander-in-Chief of the armies of the South, demands immediate access to this roadway so that she may confer with His Highness King Willow of N'ork City on the morrow."

"Is that so?" the man called back, then looked down the length of the mover. "This thing can back up, can't it?"

"This machine has no need to back up," Merit replied. "It is going forward."

The man pulled a large blue cloth from inside his suit and blew his nose loudly. "Well, we'll pass along your request to the proper authorities in N'ork City and see what they say. In the meantime, you'll have to back that thing up and find a place to put it so it doesn't block the roadway. Okay. Next!"

"Sir. We will not back up," Merit said, voice shaking slightly.

The man's brows narrowed in concern and he shouldered his crossbow, aiming at Merit. "That would be a very counterproductive thing to do," he said with quiet intensity. "I haven't gotten to kill anyone all day. You wouldn't want me to spoil that, would you? Now back it up . . . right now!"

It was then that Alicia stepped from the box, her gown shiny purple embroidered with diamonds. She shone radiantly in the dying grays of late afternoon. She still carried her peach, taking a casual bite from time to time.

"What is the meaning of this delay?" she asked angrily. "You are endangering important matters of state."

The man's grip loosened somewhat on the bow, his face slackening. "You're going to have to wait," he said, "until we get confirmation from N'ork City."

She took a last bite from the peach and let it drop, falling at the guard's feet to bounce against his boots. "Judging from the rust on your gates," she said, "that confirmation never comes."

"We don't have many visitors," he said. "Now back the machine up." He tightened his resolve and his grip on the bow.

"You are handling this all wrong," Alicia told him, then called down to one of the neuters. "Jalap-po! Get all of their names!"

The neuter moved out of the scaffolding and approached the soldiers, asking names. The one pointing the crossbow watched in consternation.

"What's your name?" Alicia asked him. "When the heads are taken, yours will fit nicely on the tallest pike."

"Are you trying to frighten me?" the man asked loudly, a false laugh on his tongue. Alicia knew she was getting to him.

"No sir," Alicia answered quickly, businesslike. "But we of Alb'ny believe in paying all our debts . . . with interest. At this exact moment in time, you are holding a head of state hostage, an act of war under any circumstances. You, at this second, are negotiating for the lives of everyone in your beloved city, because when my husband marches down this road a hundred thousand strong, he's not going to understand how someone of your position could be the cause for war between N'ork City and every Province between here and the land of the Schnecks."

"I'm only trying to do my job. Can't we . . ."

"Do you want to see the kind of trouble you're getting ready to unleash? Do you?"

"Please, I . . ." The crossbow was shaking in his hands.

"Opel!" she called. "Aaron! Come up here!"

Two of the neuters quickly scaled the height of the tall

machine. "Give of yourselves for me, so that we may show the gravity of this endeavor." She pointed to the edge of the mover. "Jump!" she said.

Without a word, without hesitation, the neuters dove headfirst from the top of the scaffolding, crumpling to the ground with a thud and a rising cloud of dust. They lay still on the road, the dust settling back on top of them.

The crossbow fell from the man's hands as he watched, open mouthed, while several of the other neuters picked up the bodies and placed them back within the framework of the mover.

"Now, gatekeeper," Alicia said, her tone harsh. "In what positive direction do we take our little standoff?"

The man tried to speak, but the words got caught in his throat. He coughed loudly, spoke again. "Open the gates," he said.

They slid the long bolt from the metal studs. It took ten men to push the rusted gates open, the metal complaining loudly the whole time.

Merit started through immediately as soon as the gates opened, Alicia smiling with her hands on her hips. The refugees in the trees began cheering the first time they had ever seen the open gate.

"Come on in!" Alicia called to them, and waved her arms wide. "Everybody come in!"

The road was immediately jammed with people who dropped from the trees like leaves in a wind storm. The gatekeepers tried to stop their entry, but it was like trying to hold back a flood. Cheering throngs followed Alicia into the inner sanctum of N'ork.

As soon as they were well clear of the gates, the "bodies" of Opel and Aaron, the dead neuters, climbed the scaffolding and waved happily to the appreciative crowds. They had been practicing their "death dive" for three years and were overjoyed that it worked so well the very first time they got to use it.

11

The Genetic Fish
South Father Hus

The Schnecks and Minnies squealed as Serge, laughing, dunked Morgan into the river again and again by his ankles. They moved swiftly with Father Hus, the distant bank blurring past Morgan's vision as he came up for air. The gangplank was down, nearly dragging the water, and they were all tied to it, trying to fish.

Morgan struggled his head out of the water for a second, gasping in a lungful of air, then went back under, wrestling with the monstrous bluefish that one of the Schnecks had hooked but was unable to bring in. It was a good four feet long and probably several hundred years old—it was crafty.

Morgan would go under, grabbing it close to him, its tail flapping madly in his face. Then it would cease its struggle, going dead in the water. Just as Morgan would have Serge pull him and his prize out of the river, the thing would struggle frantically, slipping from his grasp. The battle had see-sawed back and forth for thirty minutes, neither combatant willing to give in.

Morgan's face was red with tail-lash welts and he had drunk so much river water he had silt for blood.

"Sock him!" one of the Schnecks yelled, and the Minnies picked up the chant, telepathically sharing it with all the other Minnies on the ship, who picked it up and infected the passengers and crew with it.

Within minutes the rails were crowded with spectators,

all shaking their fists and chanting. "Sock him! Sock him!"

Morgan heard the chant as he was ducking out for air, and when he went under, instead of grabbing hold of the monster with the gaping mouth that had put Morgan's manhood in jeopardy more than once, he got eye to eye with it.

The thing stared at him, full of meanness. Old bluebelly had ruled the river for a long time, his gene-altered heritage his claim to kingship.

Pure Blood, Morgan thought, and it made him so angry, he hauled off and punched the creature right between the eyes, knocking him out cold.

When Serge hauled him out this time, he dragged his prize out with him, all to the delight of the spectators on deck. The Minnies immediately swarmed the creature, measuring its size against their own. Morgan lay panting against the forty-five-degree angle of the gangway, his hands gingerly touching the raw spots on his red face.

"Take it up!" he called, and the gangway was laboriously hauled back onto the ship, Minnies falling everywhere, dangling by the ropes that had lashed them down to begin with.

Morgan had his breath by the time they were pulled back on deck, and he climbed aboard laughing, accepting the congratulations and the teasing of his people. The Minnies crowded around him, giggling and pulling on him like children, and the children crowded the Minnies—kindred spirits in boundless exuberance.

And the decks were crowded with life, all manner of life, rubbing shoulders in peace and brotherhood. And as Morgan walked through them, joking and making small talk, he was struck with the sadness that even this would have to soon have its reckoning. Would that they could simply sail off down the Hus and into the Great Sea, and never have to settle anything with anyone. It was a hollow wish, and he knew it while he was wishing it. Freedom, he had learned, went hand in hand with the responsibility of maintaining it.

VICTORY moved swiftly with the current. Drawn out behind, nearly from bank to bank, was Morgan's fleet of skiffs and barges and rafts. His army had swelled to immense proportions thanks in large measure to Ramon's torching of Germantown. Genies were also showing up. From parts unknown they made the trek to the river, joining the fleet as it passed by. The

word was spread, and not a Province of N'ork was untouched
by the war.

"Need a lift through the crowd?" Serge asked, offering his
shoulder to Morgan.

Morgan waved off the big man, smiling at the warmth in
his eyes. "I like it," he said.

The giant shrugged. "U-mans," he said, which was his
general response to all behavior he didn't understand. Waving,
he lumbered off, undoubtedly in search of Nebo.

Morgan moved aft, running hands through his long hair to
wring some of the water out of it. His bare chest glistened with
water and already-forming sweat from the unending humidity.
He moved mindlessly, filling his time with routine and motion
to keep from dwelling on Alicia.

Jella, the Prelate of Rockland, stood with his two children
at the aft rail, the small ones waving to friends on the Rockland
barges. In a world of death, the death of Moira, Jella's wife,
had been the hardest to take. A woman beloved by all and of a
passion for life and love equalled by none, her demise had
been a cause for serious mourning among all the People, the
nature of her passing an open valve of fuel on the smoldering
blaze of their anger.

Morgan joined them at the rail, watching the thousands
upon thousands who followed behind, their rafts bouncing on
the wake created by VICTORY.

"I haven't seen you for a few days," Morgan said, leaning
down to rest his elbows on the rail.

Jella answered without turning to him. "The children and
I have been . . . checking around, looking for clues."

"The entire country is in flight," Morgan said. "It will be
difficult to find anything or anyone until all this settles down."

"That's my problem, isn't it?" Jella said.

"It's all of our problem," Morgan said, remembering
something that Alicia had once told him. "You have a responsibility to your people."

"I have a responsibility to myself," Jella said. "I intend to
take that bastard's hook and tear out his own insides with it the
way he gutted Moira."

"Did you say hook?" Morgan replied.

"I found out," Jella said, finally turning to look at Morgan.
Gone were the laughing eyes and jovial spirit, replaced by a

smoldering of the spirit that was worse than death. "He is a thin man, all gristle and bone. He wears a hook where a right hand should be."

"Redrick," Morgan whispered.

Jella grabbed him by the arms. "You know him?"

"Was me cut off his hand," Morgan said. "It should have been his head. He led the forces against us at Kipsie. He must have holed up at Rockland to rest and spy on us."

"We've got to go back!"

Morgan shook his head. "We can't stop now."

"Morgan . . ."

"I'm sorry," Morgan said, "truly sorry. But we all have to make sacrifices."

"I have a duty to seek vengeance," Jella said. "All else pales in comparison to that."

"Would Moira have felt that way?" Morgan asked.

Jella stared at him, his lower lip quivering. Silently, he took the children by the hand and walked off into the crowds. Morgan turned to watch him leave, only to be confronted by Dycus the Lawgiver carrying Ibem under his arm.

"We have a major problem," he said. "We will talk now."

Morgan stared at him for a long moment. Dealing with the Lawgivers had always been Alicia's forte. Morgan had never developed any sort of rapport with them. He had, in fact, been studiously avoiding them since Alicia took the South road to N'ork City.

"Can it wait?" he asked finally.

The man just stared at him. Then, pulling his umbrella off the crook of his arm, he brandished it like a sword, pointing it at Morgan's chest. "God cannot wait," he said, and his face held such stupefaction that Morgan couldn't help but agree.

"So what seems to be the problem?"

"Not here. We'll show you."

Dycus turned, wandering into the crowd with Ibem tucked in the crook of his arm like a baby. Morgan followed him past a line of bellowed air vents, then down the stairs into the dark hold.

Below the waterline, the ship's hold was cool, a respite from perpetual summer. Very little light shone amidst the creaking of the boards, fire being used sparingly to avoid a tragedy.

The narrow passages were filled with sleeping cat-men,

curled up in impossible positions, many with their legs in the
air. As they were jostled to allow the Lawgiver passage, cat
eyes opened sleepily, only to slowly sink back to blissful
slumber as soon as the men passed.

"The Repairmen have been checking parts inventory,"
Dycus said over his shoulder. "Something isn't right."

"LOSS OF PARTS IS A MORTAL SIN," Ibem said.
"LOSS OF PARTS IS TO BE GRAVELY PUNISHED, BY
DEATH OR WORSE."

"Worse?" Morgan said, while apologizing to a cat-man for
stepping on his arm.

They moved into a bustle of shadowy activity in the large
section of the hold that had been set aside for Ibem's personal
entourage and life support. The slightly rocking room was
filled with silver-robed Repairmen wearing helmets with attached lights, much like the equipment his men had worn
when working the Masurian shale mines.

The back two-thirds of the room was filled with the huge
storage batteries that gave Ibem his breath. The section in
front of them was taken up with the large parts cabinets. Sleeping and eating space filled the rest of the room.

The cabinets were open, Repairmen moving through
them like army ants, large clipboards tucked in their arms.
They wrote furiously on the clipboards with long quills. Dycus
walked Morgan right up to one of the Repairmen.

"Tell him," he said.

The man frowned deeply, then looked at his clipboard before speaking. "Equipment is missing," he said.

"Maybe you just misplaced it," Morgan returned.

"A great deal of equipment is missing," the man returned
without inflection. "We inventoried before putting this stuff on
board, and have just inventoried again. Enough microcircuits
and transistors and wiring and cathode tubes and synthesizers
are missing to build a great many computers."

"More Ibems!" Morgan said. "Heaven protect us."

"What's that supposed to mean?" Dycus said.

"Nothing," Morgan sighed, waving his hand. "Are you trying to tell me that someone on board ship is stealing your
equipment?"

"Precisely," the Repairman said. "I don't know how they
do it, but we're missing close to a third of our inventory."

Morgan shook his head. "Well, I don't know who would . . ."

"You know as well as we do who took it," Dycus said angrily. "It was that heathen Mech and his half-breed cohorts."

Morgan took the man by the front of the robe, nearly dislodging Ibem. "That 'heathen Mech' helped save all of your hides back at Kipsie, my fine friend. I suggest you not make accusations without proof to back them up."

Dycus jerked away from Morgan, cradling Ibem to his chest and moving off several paces. "You dare to profane the living embodiment of the God who made Heaven and Earth. You're no better than the black Mech."

"And you're no better than the stench of hypocrisy that we fight against," Morgan returned, walking to the door. "I'll try to find your missing equipment for you. In the meantime, stay out of my way and keep your accusations to yourself or I'll personally throw every one of you overboard along with your God."

He moved out of the room, slamming the door behind him. He regretted his actions immediately, knowing that Alicia would have handled the situation with delicacy and tact. They needed the people of Ibem. He'd have to try and find a way to make it up to them.

He stood in the hall for a moment, thinking, then turned in the direction of Nebo's rooms. The thing that bothered him the most was that Dycus was undoubtedly right—no one save Nebo would have any use for the Ibem equipment.

He walked to the door. "KEEP OUT" was printed on it. He turned the knob. The door was locked. He banged on it angrily.

"Open up!" he yelled. "Come on."

The door opened a crack. One of Nebo's Masurians poked his head out. "Yes?" he said.

"Open up," Morgan said.

"What do you need?"

Backing up a pace, Morgan brought up a booted leg and kicked the door open, sending the Mech sprawling on the floor. He walked in, stepping over the Genie.

This room was well lighted by electric bulbs. Nebo was seated on a high stool, bent over a gaggle of electronic gear. Several Mechs were huddled around him like honey bees protecting their queen.

"You certainly know how to make an entrance," Nebo said, and all the other Mechs stared suspiciously.

"Why did you take the Lawgivers' equipment?" Morgan demanded, walking up to the table.

"I needed it," Nebo answered, as if that explained everything.

"It wasn't yours."

"Their Ibem is dead," the Mech answered. "You and Alicia have killed it. The equipment is no longer of any use to them. They just don't realize it yet."

Nebo picked up a small, machine-tooled device that he had been using a screwdriver on, and held it up, twisting it this way and that.

"We need them for this campaign," Morgan said.

"I've got all I need," Nebo said. "I won't take any more of their parts."

"That's not the point! Why didn't you come to me with this first? This is still my expedition."

Nebo turned his eyes from his device to look at Morgan. "Would you have let me have the equipment?"

"No," Morgan said. "I probably wouldn't have."

The Mech shrugged. "That's why I didn't ask."

"I've got to tell those people something," Morgan said. "They know that you did it."

"Tell them it won't happen anymore."

"They'll want it back."

The Mech put down his device. "I can't stop you from coming in here and taking everything back by force, but you should consider the fact that what I'm working on is probably a great deal more important than what they can do for you."

Morgan had thought of that, and realized that he should have handled the Lawgivers more diplomatically to begin with. He knew the nature of Nebo's addiction to technology; it had helped get them that far. If he had to make a choice, he'd go with the Mech every time.

"Please don't take anything else," Morgan said. "I'll try to think of some way to put them off for a time. Maybe we can promise to give it all back after this is finished."

"Why not?" Nebo said, and immediately turned back to his work.

Morgan stared at him for a moment, understanding that Nebo's genetic quest for knowledge put him beyond the ken of all others alive. The thought frightened him a bit.

He walked to the door. "Meet with me later," he said. "I want a full report on the work that is so 'important.'"

He left, the Mechs listening to his footsteps receding down the hall.

"Relock the door, Pietro," Nebo said. "We may have to think about bracing it to avoid other such intrusions."

"What are you going to tell him about your work?" Laila, a female Mech, asked, and all of them watched him carefully, hanging on his words, his gestures. He was their god, a deity a lot more powerful than Ibem.

"Very little," Nebo said. "We tell him only of the direct work that he ordered. Nothing is to ever be mentioned of the reactor or any related activity. He wouldn't like it."

"Are we really finished taking from the Lawgivers?" Pietro asked, as he rejoined the group by the table.

Nebo turned to the wall, to the removable hole they had cut through to sneak into the Ibem room at night. "We probably have enough micros," he said, "but we'll need one of those storage battery cabinets."

"Maybe we can just hook to the cabinet through the wall," Laila said. "We won't have to take it, then."

Nebo widened his eyes. "Perhaps you're right," he said, and all the Mechs got excited, hugging Laila and congratulating her.

"And now, children," Nebo said. "Gather around. I want to show you something."

They all crowded in close, Nebo holding up his small machine. "This is a triggering device," he said, "that we can use for the liberation of total energy."

The room got very quiet, all the Mechs mesmerized by the spectacle of infinite possibilities. Nebo set the device on the table. Folding his hands in front of him, he stared at the thing.

"The humans appreciate power more than anything," he said, his eyes glazed. "We will show them power beyond the limits of power, freedom beyond the constraints of the world. We will show them their future."

With that, the Mechs all got quietly to their knees and bowed their heads, all of them reaching out to touch the hem of Nebo's brown robe.

12

The Orchards of Rhinecliff

Ramon sat atop an applegenic as large as he was, wishing that he could give himself a 'dorphin injection without anyone seeing it. The tensions were just upon him, that little jagged edge that always accompanied the dissolution of the drug from his body. It wasn't bad yet, but it would get that way if he didn't get the injection soon. Oh, if he could only sneak off.

Once, several weeks earlier, he had tried to do without the drug when the Green Woman was insisting that she take the base ingredients from his own neck glands. He had refused, saying that he didn't need it. Within hours, the sweating began, followed by the chills and alternating hot flashes. He shook uncontrollably, his insides like broken glass. And all the while, time hung heavy like stocks around his neck. The minutes crept, the hours dragged themselves, half dead, across the flat field of total boredom that was his conscious mind.

Halfway through the night, he was on his knees, begging the Green Woman to inject him, all the while cursing her for the hell she had made for him. Of all things, he feared that living death more than any.

The orchard spread wide around him. Monstrous trees laden heavy with the huge fruit that bent the branches, making them sway and crack in the wind. The bright red applegenics were so heavy that they usually took the whole branch with them when they fell, leaving neat row upon row of scarred trees, applegenics with branches lying between the rows.

Ramon sat with his fellows: rulers and knights of obligation. Some took the low branches of trees out of fear of the large, toothy worms that enjoyed the applegenics and an occasional arm when they could get it, but most used the fruit to sit upon, their unhappy faces mirroring the consternation of their hearts.

"Everything from Rhinecliff to Glasco, and as far east and west as you can defend, will go to Daedlous Nef for the province of Troy." Ramon spoke quietly, forcing everyone to crane to hear him.

Nef spoke up. He was the third ruler of Troy to hold office since the beginning of the expedition. "I should like to keep these orchards intact, my Lord," he said, knowing the answer before he asked the question.

"Why do you persist?" Ramon asked, and he was getting more and more irritable. "This area, as with all the other areas, will be burned to the ground."

"That renders it useless to me," the young man in the white britches and blouse said. "The ruler of charred earth commands nothing but ashes."

Ramon wore his blue cotton jumper. His armor had gone back into the trunk after the razing of Germantown had changed all their lives. "This is the only way," he sighed. Removing a dagger from his belt, he stuck it into the large fruit upon which he sat, watching the juice leak out and down the side of the thing.

"Don't you understand," he continued, looking at Nef. "It will all grow back soon enough. All except where you don't want it to grow. Besides, if we don't burn it, the rightful owners may want it back!"

Everyone laughed, Count Delmar reaching out to slap Nef on the back.

Nef wasn't laughing. "I believe that decision should be mine to make, not yours, if this is, in fact, my land."

"It is your land," Ramon said, getting an idea. Taking the syringe from his leather pouch, he quickly injected it into the applegenic, then used the knife to cut that hunk out. He took a bite of his 'dorphined applegenic. "But while I'm in charge of this expedition, my word is supreme, and I want the forest burned."

"That goes against my nature. I . . ."

"To hell with your nature," Ramon said, taking a bite of the fruit. He could already feel the 'dorphins rushing into his bloodstream, calming him, fuzzing out the boredom and the pain. "If I were to concern myself with every little quirk of every soldier's nature, we'd still be sitting at my castle in Alb'ny. You're new to my command. For that I will forgive your outbreak this one time."

"I am the leader of an entire Province!" Nef said.

"Sit down, son," Ramon said, low and menacing, "before I knock you down."

A blue-and-white tunic was moving toward him through the field of bright red and dark green. It looked good, a nice contrast. All at once it turned into one of his perimeter guards, installed for security reasons at this meeting.

The man snapped a brisk salute, his eyes wide open like drain holes. "Sir," the man began, "a contingent of Physicians is asking admittance to the meeting."

"Tell them we'll see them later," Ramon said.

"One is your . . . the Ladyship," the man said. "She's very insistent."

"She is," Ramon said, weaving slightly as the 'dorphins took complete effect. "Tell her to wait. If she doesn't, detain her."

All of those present applauded and laughed, all of them knowing too well how the Physicians usually had say over them.

Ramon sat smiling, sitting out the rush as the drug settled him into a different plane of consciousness. The pain was gone now, the irritability melting away. It was comfortable there in the orchard, a place to tarry if it weren't for the responsibilities. The day was calm, the gray sky still. The air smelled sweet. There had been no rain since Germantown, a sure sign that Ibem was pleased with the turn the war had taken. He was doing the right thing.

He turned and watched the retreat of the blue-and-white tunic. "Are there messengers?" he called out. "We expect messengers from upriver and down."

"We will send them to you when they arrive," the man replied, nearly tripping over a branch when he turned to answer.

"You exclude the Physicians," Senator Murray said with his usual subtlety. "Why?" The man was hanging from a branch by his elbows, his feet dangling several feet off the ground.

"The Physicians have done much for us," Ramon said, but

he couldn't get the Green Woman's ways out of his mind. "But we are the rulers of N'ork, not they. It is our place to make decisions."

"Hear, hear," Delmar said, standing and applauding, his frilly sleeves flouncing with the movements. The others joined in. "We have felt in their clutches for a long time."

"Perhaps that time has passed," Ramon said, and the words felt good coming from his mouth. But then, it was always easier to speak against the Physicians when his wife wasn't around. Everything got all confused when he was with her. "We wish no alienation, only proper perspective."

"They've been practically demanding a section of N'ork City for themselves," someone spoke up.

"Aye," came another voice. "And Genies to help them with their experiments."

"Those experiments we must watch out for," Ramon said, standing and addressing them. "We've seen what their experiments have done to others. It would never do well to have them turned on us."

More applause followed that remark. Ramon hadn't intended to go this far, but his support was surprising, as if the same thoughts had been going through everyone's mind. The real reason he had excluded the Physicians was to get even with the Green Woman for cuckolding him with a commoner of barest rank. He had killed the man when he had found out who it was, but that didn't alleviate the humiliation.

"Jerico had moved me out of my cabin onboard GAMECOCK," Murray said sadly. He lost his delicate balance and fell to the ground. He worked his way to a sitting position. "He says he needs the room more than I."

A liege lord whose name Ramon didn't remember spoke up. "I think they play us for the fools. They taunt us with their black arts."

"So they do," Ramon said, thinking of the drug that even now surged through his body. "We are all victims of their sorcery."

Count Delmar stood and moved beside Ramon. "My mother, the Countess, used to say that consorting with pigs meant eating their slop. Would that we soon walk from the pigpen."

A large man dressed in brown leather strode into the orchard. "My Lord," he said, sinking to one knee before Ramon.

"Maio," Ramon said, patting the man on the head. "How go things at home?"

The man stood, a small leather hat twisted up in his hands. He seemed nervous, highly agitated. "I have met with the representatives you all sent back to your Provinces," he said.

"And?" Delmar demanded loudly. "What was said?"

"The jungle encroaches," Maio said, his face leathery as his clothes, his frown etched deep. "There is insufficient manpower to hold back the jungle. Smaller Provinces are already lost. There is no planting. The people flee, but . . . to where?"

Silence fell upon the group. Ramon watched them all, but they wouldn't meet his eyes. "Give me the good news," he told Maio.

The man simply stared at him.

"We've failed," said a man farther down the orchard row. He stepped into the aisle, his fringed leather jacket and britches flapping as he walked. It was President Wilke of Sand Lake, a small settlement on the East road. Beside him stood Sir Ike of Averill Park, a tenant of Wilke's who owed allegiance to the President, not Ramon.

"We conquer the South," Ramon said. "Where's the failure?"

"We conquer dead earth," Sir Ike said, his spider-web armor gleaming in the dull light. "They've taken or hidden their booty, and leave us only the empty trees, which we, in turn destroy."

"And now we lose our homes," Wilke said, looking at Maio, who nodded grimly in turn.

"Our booty isn't lost," Ramon said. "It has simply moved farther South. We'll get it all when we take the Jewel of the East."

"The taking won't be so easy now," Sir Ike said. "Have you forgotten that an army awaits us?"

"What would you have me do?" Ramon asked, and it was only the 'dorphins that kept him from flying into a rage.

"Disband this ill-conceived venture," President Wilke said. "Let us return home and try to salvage our lives."

"And what will you eat?" Delmar asked.

"We can still hunt," Ike said. "We'll clear land and hunt until we can bring in another harvest."

"And live just like the Southerners we kill," Ramon said,

disgust strong in his tone. "Once again you want to quit so close to our goal. Within weeks the Jewel of the East will be ours. That time won't mean so much if your homes are already overrun. We can gut N'ork City and return triumphant, with an army of slaves to clear your land if you want. Just a matter of weeks."

"The soldiers complain," Murray said. "They expected a campaign of forty days. Ty'Jorman died nearly a year and a half past. The people grow weary."

"We are within reach of it!" Ramon shouted. "Are you so foolish and stupid as to not understand that? We take the entire country as we move through it."

"What good if we can't keep our own homes clear of the jungle?" Wilke asked, taking his cathide hat off and scratching his bald head.

Count Delmar spoke to the group. "We have nothing to lose at this point," he said. "We'll take N'ork City as easily as we've taken everything else. Then we'll have it all. What harm in that?"

"Ask that question of the Schnecks who died at Kipsie," Ike said.

Delmar drew his sword. "I, also, am better than any ten thousand Schnecks," he said. "Would you like to try me?"

"No," Ramon said, staying Delmar's sword arm. "We must end dissension right here and stand together. I ask only a few more weeks. We have a large and unstoppable force. Failure is impossible." He took Delmar's sword arm and thrust it high in the air. "Join me in harmony. I ask little and give much. Join me!"

"And what of our troops?" Wilke asked.

"We will give them a diversion of some kind," Ramon said. "Find them some Genies to kill or something."

"They won't take well to the loss of their homes," Ike said.

"Then we won't tell them," Ramon said, and turned to Maio. "Does anyone else know of this?"

"No, my Lord," Maio replied. "And they won't hear it from me."

"And the Physicians?" Murray asked.

"I will attend to the Physicians," Ramon said. "I have a plan. Will you join me? Will you?"

They drew their swords and moved to Ramon, raising them in the air beside Delmar's blade.

"We will triumph!" Ramon said.

"At what price?" came a voice from behind.

They all turned to see young Reeder, Prince of Watervliet, standing before them, his face twisted in deadly rage. "At what price does this triumph come?" he repeated. "And for whose glory?"

"You will take a more civil tone with me," Ramon said.

"I take nothing with you," Reeder said, "except, perhaps, an oath of vengeance. My father has died from the injuries sustained when you knocked him down. The rule has fallen to me."

"The rule belongs to whomever I appoint on the field of battle," Ramon said. "This campaign is under my domination."

"Not anymore," Reeder said, his young face strained old with hatred. "Not anymore."

Turning quickly, the new Councilman stalked away, and it was loud to Ramon because fifteen thousand troops stalked with him. This was the Green Woman's fault, every bit of it. He tried to force his mind away from the place of addiction he held for her; he tried to force his feelings into submission. But it was so difficult, so very difficult.

13

i

THE JUNGLE—SOUTHEAST OF DELMAR

Grodin lay on the hard concrete that was the ancient roadway and watched the fire show that danced through the heavens above him. The roadway, treacherous but passable, stretched in uneven chunks across a cushion of tall-growing trees fifty feet in the air. Wide enough for two wagons to pass side by side, it was limited to foot traffic because of its uneven nature. The old man reclined on a straight, even stretch that traveled unbroken for a quarter of a mile, giving him good visibility in either direction should any two or four-legged night creatures decide he was worthy of a close look.

He lay on his back staring straight up, the hot humid air tracing a fiery latticework of lightning across the entire sky, displaying what most N'orkers referred to as the Necklace of Heaven. His scar wasn't throbbing, so he took no precautions for rain, but instead enjoyed the rumbling, popping show overhead.

He was worn out from his breakneck attempt at catching up to Ona. Drained now of all energy, he knew for the first time in his life that he was truly not the man of his memories. The roadway, even in the dark, was passable. He would have continued, but his strength gave out at that spot.

Exhaustion became his tormentor, his old man's body its own worst enemy. And with the exhaustion, he cancelled out all bodily functions save one—he was forced to think.

His small cookfire was burning down, its remaining embers like a glowing treasure chest of sparkling rubies. Beside the fire lay the bones of the squirrel he had eaten for supper. He wouldn't have had the strength to catch it himself. A huge hawk had snatched the thing from a tree top, but had lost its hold while trying to fly away with its prize, dropping the creature right at the old man's feet. That Grodin took the action as a divine message was not surprising; he barely had the strength to skin it after it was handed to him.

And he lay there, feeling he wouldn't have the ability to rise if necessary. He thought about his position, his feelings— and he felt shame.

He had always prided himself on his system of judging men, not on their appearances, but by what they were like beneath the appearances. He knew how people fell into patterns of judgment based purely on personal bigotries, and had always felt himself beyond that. All men were his brothers. Conversely, Genies were not men, so not deserving of consideration on any level. They were bred, just like his Woofers, bred for work like pack animals.

And that philosophy had served him well throughout his life, until Morgan of Siler had the insensitivity to expect the pack animals to be treated as men. That situation was intolerable to his long-held ideals, and so he put it behind him. Then everything fell apart. Morgan, it seemed, was a Genie himself.

A pack animal. He knew Morgan, knew him as the most honorable, most honest *man* he had ever met.

Grodin had loved the man-animal, more than he thought possible. And then he knew he had been wrong. In his righteousness, in his pride, he had been just as bigoted and harmful as the rest of them—worse, perhaps, because he thought himself better.

The tears rolled from his eyes, softening the hard-baked leather of his face. "Oh, lad," he sobbed, "I'm so sorry. If you be animal, then men should bow to animals."

He struggled on his elbows to a sitting position, realizing that Morgan would have no one bow, that he wished only for all to walk erect proudly together.

Once sitting, he shakily rose to his feet, his legs numb and weak. He rolled up his pack and put it under his arm. Ona still had a good jump on him. He'd have to make up a whole lot of time if he were to catch her.

Grunting once, he wiped the sweat and the tears from his face and hobbled off into the night.

ii

NYACK

There was no beach in Nyack, the tree city going all the way up to the waterline. Instead, a wide path had been cleared from the Nyack pier straight through the middle of town, a thoroughfare kept cleared by the citizens in lieu of taxation. Covered with close fitting flat rocks, it gave the appearance of a street in the ancient sense. Unfortunately, every time it rained, the rocks were washed away and construction had to begin anew. It was called the Boulevard and was a major attraction of that area of the country.

Galen and ten of his Grunts walked the wide street, studying the various life forms that thrived and moved along the cobbled stone. Excitement hung in the air like the charged humidity of a thunderstorm, and not the least of it was because of the presence of Grunts in Nyack, a spectacle not witnessed for a millenium.

Small human and Genie children ran circles around the Grunts who were not so much taller than they were. They laughed and waved at the squat creatures with the shiny grayish skin that took on the coloration of the objects they passed.

All around, people prepared for evacuation. Bundles were dropped from trees to waiting arms; transients slept on the street; mothers searched for their babies; human and Genie rubbed shoulders in easy harmony as they filled the clearing with the echoing clop of hammers and axes constructing barges.

There were smells and colors the like of which none save the oldest had ever witnessed, and Galen was drawn to smile more than once at the childlike awe with which Gregore and Marta greeted each new sensation. It made him feel old for once, made him realize how much lay dormant and abandoned in his own mind.

The lovers moved up close to Galen again, their heads leaning together so that their horns touched. Their mouths were stretched wide across their flat faces as they moved their nutra-sticks across their hard tongues.

"What is this concoction called again?" Marta asked. "We find its sensations a pleasure."

"The humans call it candy," Galen answered, a slight smile stretching the scales of his face. "Be careful. Too much of it is dangerous."

"That figures," Gregore said, taking the red and white-striped stick from his mouth to study it. "All such pleasure has pain connected with it."

Marta slapped him on the arm. "What's that supposed to mean?" she said.

His eyes irised wide in surprise. "I . . . I didn't mean you, my nectar. I was merely generalizing."

She frowned deeply for a second, then laughed. Pushing away from him, she scurried to the back of the group, Gregore hurrying to catch her.

Galen shook his head, old Longnose joining him at the head of the line. "We have perhaps kept to our own counsel for too long," he told Galen.

"Perhaps," Galen responded, and he turned for a second to watch Lili, trying to remember when they were like Marta and Gregore. "Our senses haven't had stimulation like this for a long, long time. Maybe there is more than the cerebral."

"When does the red-haired man arrive?" Gert asked, and

he tugged on the coarse robe that Galen had forced them all to don.

"Feel the tension," Galen replied. "It charges the air itself. He must arrive soon."

They continued walking, taking in every step of the shaded two-mile promenade. From every store front and tree house and stoop eyes watched them, most in curiosity, some with darker motives; for the strangers were unlike all, human or Genie. Their roots were somewhere separate from the tree of man.

A group of three human men and a bent planter Genie emerged from the treeline to stand in their path. They held wine crocks, their gait staggered by their indulgence. A tall one with sparse brown hair and brushed leather clothes had a crossbow strapped to his back. The humans blocked their movement. They giggled like children and kept looking at one another.

"You will excuse us," Galen said. "We cannot move past you."

"They tell me youse Shiners," the tall one said.

"We have been called such," Galen replied.

"You're awful small," the man continued.

"We are of a dense molecular structure," Gert, the Longnose, said.

"You don't look so tough to me."

Galen was beginning to remember why his people had cloistered themselves away. "That is an opinion you are most entitled to."

The man slid the crossbow slowly off his shoulder, the glint of cruelty in his eyes. He pointed the bow at Galen, a bolt already locked in it. "What do you think would happen if I were to shoot you with this thing, small fry?"

Galen held his head up and met the man's eyes fiercely. "It would be interpreted as a hostile act, human. I suggest you let us pass now, for we have no quarrel with you."

"Well, maybe I've got a quarrel with you," the man said, and dropped his crock to splatter on the stones beneath his feet. The other humans backed slowly away from him, giving him all the street.

"You're being very foolish," Gert said. "You are not a match for such as us."

"You don't think so?" the man said, and walked right up to them. Reaching out a hand he made to slap Galen with it, but the Grunt caught his arm in mid-swing and levered it to push him to the ground.

Galen turned to the group. "We will continue now," he said. "Make no contact with these humans."

The man jumped to his feet, shouldering the bow, the stock fit snugly on his shoulder. "Stop right there," he said low.

Galen ignored him and walked on.

"Stop!" the man shouted, and Galen turned to him.

"This is your last warning, human. Walk on."

"You get no more warnings," the man said through clenched teeth, and loosed his bolt.

The bow string sang, the arrow blurring to Galen, its force splintering it on contact with the Grunt's skin. It dropped in pieces to the ground.

Reflexively, Galen held out his arm and opened his third eye, the quiet rage that seethed within him leaving his control with the battle met.

The man saw the eye, was caught by it. It swirled him down, down into a vortex black as night and eternal as the stars. Within seconds he lay shaking upon the ground, whimpering like a baby, the wine he had drunk gurgling back out of his mouth.

Galen pulled his hand away as soon as he was able. He immediately buried his face in his hands, repentant for his action.

"You couldn't help it," Longnose said, putting an arm around him. "None of us could."

"He didn't know what he was doing," Galen said, and Lili was there, comforting him also.

"We're here on a mission," she reminded him.

He nodded slowly, then walked to the fallen man. The others were gathered round, but they backed off at Galen's approach.

He bent to the man, then looked up at their inquisitive faces. "You must nurse him now," he said. "With some luck, maybe in a few years . . ."

He left the sentence unspoken. Standing, he moved his people silently down the roadway. No one else bothered them during their stay in Nyack.

iii

ABOARD GRAYCLOUD

No light shone through the nightcover of Heaven as Newcomb Reeder stared out at the long stretch of beach that was the Rhinecliff encampment. GRAYCLOUD lapped gently beneath his feet as Father Hus moved swiftly past it, hurrying southward to mingle with the salty kiss of the Great Sea.

His people moved silently in single-file lines, silhouettes against the backdrop of dying campfires. They moved provisions and arms on board GRAYCLOUD in preparation for an early departure.

The young Prince, now Councilman, turned from the foredeck rail and walked resolutely back to the masthead, the giant ax that symbolized the Province that had been hewn by his father from the impossible tangle of jungle that had been Watervliet.

There, beneath the bite of the ax, the body of the Councilman lay in state. His armor of command was set on a form next to him for, truly, of late years he could not have fit himself into it. He had been a warrior lean and proud when the gout claimed him, his girth increasing after years off his feet. Then the sickness came and wasted away what the gout had increased. It took the enterprise of man, however, to fell the great leader.

Tied to the masthead base was Dunbar, the Physician, his leather face mask and black eyeglasses presenting a total blank in the dark, dark night.

"You're a fool," he hissed at Reeder as the young leader stood staring at his father's body in the flickering torchlight of the main deck.

"You're not under the protection of your band of magicians now," Reeder said, not even looking at the man. "Best relearn the meaning of a civil tongue."

The Physician laughed dryly. "Come now, young Lord. Untie me and forget this foolishness. It is yet not too late to untangle the knot you so ingloriously tied."

Reeder, the torchlight sliding up and down his armor, walked to stand before the man. "You dare speak to me of glory after the perversion you and your kind have visited upon us?"

"We've done nothing but bring progress to these lands."

"The disease of progress," Reeder replied. "I would slit your throat and toss you into the river if I didn't fear I'd have some need of your black arts."

Dunbar laughed again. "Even in your hatred you need me."

Reeder stared sullenly at him, his expression never changing. "For the moment," he said.

There was silence between them for a time, then Dunbar said, "You do your people an injustice. Do you return home, sadder but wiser, with nothing to show for the rape of the coffers and the land? Ramon keeps charge of the booty. I'll venture you intend to leave here without it."

Reeder returned to the body, kissing the pallid lips of his father. "You think my strain of blood so weak?" he said. "I will not return to Watervliet empty-handed. These boats are nothing more than barges, able to move only as swiftly as the current. We sail ahead, taking Southern booty as we go. Ramon, saddled with a larger army and himself a prisoner of the current, will not be able to catch us. When we've got our share, we'll abandon the boat and take the Northern road home."

"And what happens when Ramon returns to Alb'ny?"

"He must defeat the red-haired man first," Reeder said. "I no longer know if he can accomplish that."

Sir Kelvin, knight banneret, and old Reeder's most trusted retainer, clomped heavily across the deck to stand before the new Councilman. "All are aboard, sir," he said, standing at attention.

Reeder nodded. "How many?"

"We've a core of five thousand whose loyalty to Watervliet is unquestioned. The mercenaries and liege lords we thought best not to trust with this."

"Good," Reeder said. "Have any suspicions been aroused?"

The dark man shook his head. "We told perimeter guards that we were simply preparing early for departure at your orders. They had no reason to not accept that."

"You're all fools," Dunbar said. "Idiots and pirates!"

Sir Kelvin's hand went to his sword. "Should I silence this one?" he asked gleefully.

"No," Reeder said, "unless he tries to shout. Then cut his throat with my compliments."

"A pleasure," Kelvin said, smiling.

"Have we any surgeons?"

"We kidnapped three, sir," Kelvin said. "That should do us. We also swiped two tentmakers for the return trip."

"Good man!" Reeder said, taking Kelvin by the arms. "I don't know what I'd do without you."

The man locked arms with Reeder. "All the love and loyalty that was your father's to command, I now pledge to you."

"For our Province and our God."

"Amen!"

Reeder broke from the man, a large smile on his face. "Help me with the anchor," he said.

Sir Kelvin nodded and the men hurried to the turnbuckle. Amidships, the gangway was already being raised. Straining, Reeder and Kelvin laboriously turned the take-up wheel, the boat moving out of its mooring as soon as the anchor drew out of the river silt. A bell clanged in the wheelhouse, the vessel's captain steering them into the current.

Once in motion, those on deck began cheering loudly, the wheelhouse bell clanging continuously. On shore, soldiers were waking up with the commotion and running to the waterline to watch GRAYCLOUD's departure.

And they drifted into the bite of the current, soon turning a bend and leaving Rhinecliff far behind. Newcomb Reeder stayed on deck for a long time, staring down at the dark waters. He would now be known as a freebooter and pirate, though had it not been for his sense of responsibility to his people, he would have been remembered as the executioner of the Governor of Alb'ny.

14

South Mud Plains
The Shore of N'ork City

Alicia's arrival in Mud Plains was much heralded, partly due to rumor and partly due to the neuters she sent ahead to stir things up. When she and her small army of refugees rolled into the tree-house city, they were greeted by cheering citizens and garlands of wild orchids.

Much of the area was clear of trees, the land being partly underwater. It was a marshy environ, well-suited to the harvesting of rice which, it turned out, was the chief occupation of the citizens of Mud Plains. The rice they grew was exported across the water to N'ork City for subsistence barter items in return. It seemed to be a good system.

They rolled through the mud, the mover's huge wheels grinding easily, and came to a stop before a delegation who stood in the middle of the roadway. They all wore platformed shoes that kept them just above the mud level. Alicia came out of her box atop the mover and walked to the edge to look down at them.

"Greetings!" said a chubby man with bright red cheeks and a long pipe of briar jammed between his lips. He was stuffed into earthen britches and shortcoat that were far too small. He wore a tiny hat of the same material as his suit. It was tied around his chin to keep it upon his bald head. Beside him stood a woman and five step-ladder children arranged according to size, and all stuffed into similarly ill-fitting clothes.

"I am Alicia of Alb'ny," Alicia called down, "wife of the Governor."

110

The man pulled the tiny hat from his head and placed it over his heart. "I am Ritta Rem, Foreman of Mud Plains, and this is my unworthy family." The woman and children bowed low. "We welcome our great visitor from the North. How may we be of service to you?"

"We seek passage across the water to the Jewel of the East," Alicia called back down.

"Most assuredly," the man said. "Deary me, you certainly will have passage. A delegation from King Willow is even now bringing the royal barge to greet you. This is an exciting day for Mud Plains, an historical day!"

"Where must we go to meet the royal barge?"

The man put a finger to his lips, then half turned without moving his feet. He started to point down the road, then started to point in another direction. Then he scratched his head and put his little hat back on. "Perhaps I could just show you," he said.

"Certainly!" Alicia said. "You and your family climb aboard."

Rem and his family sloshed through the deep mud, climbing aboard the mover to the cheers of his people. He waved happily, puffing himself up and striking heroic poses. Foreman Rem climbed to the top to share Alicia's box, while the children played within the structure of the mover or bothered the neuters with a million questions.

When he was snugly seated between Alicia and Twiddle, they got underway, the Foreman occasionally leaning through the cutout to give directions to Merit and wave to the appreciative crowd.

"Oh, this is exciting," Rem kept saying, and he'd puff furiously on his pipe until he filled the box with blue-white smoke. "You don't know what you've done to my standing in the community. No siree, no siree."

"Many people have come with me this far," Alicia said, smiling at the happy innocence she felt from the man.

"Yes, yes, they certainly have. Most assuredly." The Foreman was a vigorous nodder, and he was having a fit of it then. "Go around it! Around it!" he yelled through the cutout, nodding and puffing after he said it.

"Can I leave them here?" she asked.

"Here? Here? Deary me." The man thought for a minute, neither nodding nor puffing, the act of intellect such an all-consuming chore. Finally he said, "Of course. We grow rice here. Lots of rice. But we sell it all, every bit, every crumb. We have many rice fields and have room for many more. We'll set them up with fields and help them out until they get on their feet. Wonderful thing, rice."

"Excellent," Alicia said, and, leaning over, she kissed Rem lightly on the cheek, his round face turning the same bright red as his cheeks.

He wiggled his eyebrows at her. "Besides, more people means more constituents. I like constituents almost as much as I like rice."

"Then this is your lucky day," Twiddle said.

Rem nodded and puffed until they feared he'd shake his head loose. "Indeed it is," he'd say. "Indeed it is."

"My Lady," Merit called from the driver's canopy. "We've arrived at the shore."

Despite herself, Alicia felt a rushing of her blood, her own sense of excitement piqued by the nearness to the power of N'ork. She climbed out of the box and walked to the very front of the machine. They were on a long stretch of beach, the waters of the Great Sea breaking in waves against their wheels. As far as she could see was water, broken slightly by what appeared to be large trees on the horizon.

"That's it all right," Rem said from beside her, and he was pointing his pipe stem at the distant trees. "Don't look like too much from here, though."

"There," Merit pointed, and Alicia picked it up, too. A large boat at full sail was moving toward them.

"It will be a while before they reach us," Alicia said. "Shall we have tea?"

"What a civilized idea," Rem said, nodding and puffing. "Tea on the beach. Splendid."

So they climbed to the beach and built a fire, Rem stretching out his tea break for a long time so that more of his constituents could come by and see just who he could have tea with when he chose.

At length Alicia addressed those who had come through the Pleasantville gates with her. "My friends," she said. "I must travel now on a journey meant only for me. But the door does not close for you. In his infinite compassion and wisdom, Ritta Rem, Foreman of Mud Plains, has offered all of you a place to stay and land to work for as long as you want."

The refugees cheered Ritta Rem, who responded by sticking his chest out and popping several buttons on his tiny jacket.

It was while the crowds were cheering that the royal barge slid up to the beach, oars weighed, red and white-checked sail being furled. Upon its mast proudly waved its large pennant, bright red applegenic on a field of sea blue.

A group of loinclothed, bronze-skinned sailors dove from the decks, using a long coil of rope to drag the flat-bottomed barge upon the beach. Ornate it was, with flowing balusters, the entire prow intricately carved to resemble a pigeon in flight.

The gangway was a flight of wooden stairs lowered right onto the beach. A small honor guard came down the gangway first: four large, well-groomed men dressed in billowy blue trousers with a bright red tunic overlay. Big gold buttons in double rows clasped the tunic in front, and large curved swords of gleaming silver hung on leather straps from their sides. They wore silver helmets that closely hugged their skulls. Following the honor guard was a scribe dressed in plain gray robes that hung loosely on his thin frame. Behind him, a man descended in opulent red robes that opened in front to expose a body stocking of deepest blue. The robes were satin, fixed with thin veins of blue velvet and fringed all around with rab fur. He wore shiny brown leather hip boots and a small beret inset with rubies. His face was long and severe, his eyes bold and piercing.

Alicia moved toward the small party, determined to meet it halfway. When she reached them, the honor guard immediately formed a defensive ring around her and the dignitary in the red robes.

"I am Alicia of Alb'ny," she said, and offered her hand.

The man pursed his lips, taking the hand after a moment and shaking it coldly. "I am called Telemay," he said, his tones dry. The scribe began writing furiously on parchment, his quill inkwell attached to the side of the thing. "I am liaison to King Willow in matters of state. You certainly make a dramatic entrance."

Alicia smiled, looking around at the still-cheering crowds. "It was my intention," she replied. "It takes an amount of doing to shake the tree of N'ork City."

Telemay arched an eyebrow. "And now that you have shaken our tree, whatever can we do for you?"

Rem had moved up to stand just outside the ring of the guard. "Greetings, Your Excellency," he said, waving. "This is a proud day for N'ork, a very exciting day."

Telemay glanced at the man, then turned his gaze on Alicia.

"My business is with King Willow," she said. "With all due respect, I would prefer to speak with him."

"I have already told you that I am his liaison in matters of state. You must speak with me first."

Alicia looked at him and recognized a man unshakably convinced of his own righteousness and supremacy, though she also felt his genuine concern. She decided to try the truth on him. "You do realize there's a war going on?"

"Your Excellency!" Rem shouted, waving again, his pipe bobbing in his mouth.

"That has nothing to do with us," Telemay said as he looked with annoyance at Rem.

"When a couple of hundred thousand people come floating down the Hus and into your city it will have everything to do with you."

"You will go back and tell them not to come. We don't want them."

Alicia laughed despite herself. "That would be like asking the rain to stay away," she said. "It is truly an inevitable occurrence. Just as with these people . . ." She gestured toward the large crowd of refugees. "We sit at the doorstep of destiny and, like it or not, you and yours are sitting there with us."

Rem was jumping up and down. "Your Excellency! Your Excellency!"

Telemay's face went dark, and he turned to Ritta Rem. "Silence, you silly man!" he screamed, and Alicia knew that she had rung the proper bell. Telemay was arrogant, but not stupid. A good beginning. He turned to stare deeply at her. "We will discuss this on the boat in greater privacy."

"Perhaps while we're underway for N'ork City," Alicia added.

The man sighed, his features noticeably settling. "As you wish," he said, and turned immediately, walking back to the ship. "You bring an entourage of two only. Come aboard straightaway."

Alicia turned to find Twiddle, and the man was standing beside her. The honor guard walked off with the scribe trailing behind, writing furiously as he walked. Rem stood with a silly grin on his face.

"He spoke to me," the Foreman said proudly. "Did you see? Ambassador Telemay spoke to me."

"Congratulations," Alicia said, then spotted her Minnie atop the machine, staring down in wonder at the goings-on. "Biddy! Come with me!"

Biddy climbed down the mover, running up to Alicia and Twiddle at the gangway stairs. Alicia picked her up, holding her like a child. The neuters and Genies were left in charge of the mover and given instructions to return to Morgan if Alicia wasn't back in two days.

They got underway immediately, the muscled sailors taking to the galley to pull the oars, the sail left tightly furled. Telemay and his people had disappeared below without leaving word behind, so Alicia stood on deck with Biddy and Twiddle, tasting the salt air and watching the treeline of N'ork City loom ever larger before them.

Her thoughts turned involuntarily to Morgan, and it made her angry that she would think of him at a time like this. Her negotiator skills twirled in full motion, her heritage taking center stage for the first time in her life. And all she could think about was the farmer. "Damn him," she muttered.

"Time will tell," Twiddle said. "Nothing is what it seems."

The trees of N'ork City grew closer. Odd they were, straight up and without branches. And tall, so incredibly tall.

"It gets more impressive," came a voice beside her. Telemay had joined her by the foredeck rails, bright red and blue balusters, the spokes carved in the image of chubby fish. "I don't know whether I hope you're lying to me or not."

"I'm not," she said.

"Oh, I believe you," he returned. "That's why we're here right now. I hate to be wrong, but in this case, perhaps being taken in by a liar wouldn't be so bad."

"I'm not lying. The end of the world is at hand."

He nodded, turning to stare at the trees.

"How much have you heard?" she asked him.

"We've heard many things," Telemay replied, "probably much of it fantasy."

"Ramon Delaga comes to take your city," Alicia said flatly. "Morgan comes to protect you."

"At what price?"

"That is a matter for discussion," Alicia said.

"Perhaps we lose no matter who wins," Telemay said.

"No," Alicia answered, and of this she was certain. "Morgan of Alb'ny wishes nothing from you. Your city holds not his fascination. Only the defeat of his brother matters."

"And what of hemolysis?"

"You *have* heard many things."

"We receive news from all over," Telemay said. "Why must you fight in our city?"

"There is nowhere else. It is the prize Ramon seeks. It is the place to dig in for a last stand. Together, we may defeat the armies of the North."

"Together," he said, and something was hidden behind his eyes. After a time, he said, "Our city, I fear, may not be what you expect."

But Alicia's eyes were already riveted to the spectacle of N'ork City up close. They had arrived. The first thing was the trees. They weren't trees at all, but the monstrous shells of ancient buildings poking up out of the rolling waves. They were covered with thick vines and plants of bright flowers, some reaching hundreds of feet in the air—ivy-covered monoliths spraying straight up from the dark, turbulent waters.

Holes were cut through for windows, the tree/buildings serving as dwellings for the city. People climbed the vines, waving at the royal barge as it made its way into the stone forest. They rowed small skiffs through the streets of water and dove happily from different heights into the waves. Flocks of brilliant white gulls flapped from building to building, dipping to the waves in search of dinner, as the gray pigeons of the region perched in the vines, warbling their love of life to anyone who might hear.

Suspension bridges connected many of the buildings, bright red and yellow flowers wound through the support ropes. They were well into the city now, totally surrounded by its atmosphere. An air of peace and well-being lay like a fluffy white cloud over everything.

"It's beautiful," Alicia said, and her voice was nearly a whisper.

"Yes," Telemay replied. "It is."

"Hello, hello, hello, hello," came a chorus of many voices, chirping voices, from below.

Alicia leaned over the rail to see a school of dolp-men

swimming happily beside them, gilled kelp-farming Genies who lived in the water, half man, half fish.

"Hello to you," Alicia called down to them, and a sleek blue dolp-man sprang from the waves head high with Alicia. It gyrated in the air, spraying water upon her, laughing with her as it plunged headlong back into the blue-green ocean that was the land of N'ork City.

Biddy giggled, pointing, and happily established light contact with the dolp-men, talking gibberish in their clicking voice.

"Expect nothing from King Willow," Telemay said. "When you deal with him, though, treat him with the utmost respect."

"My forte," Alicia replied.

"The palace," the man said, pointing.

She had expected the King to reside in one of the taller structures, but quite the opposite was true. The palace rose to no more than three stories above the waves, and from the seaside angle, seemed no different than any of the other buildings.

"The closer to the waterline, the higher the station," Telemay replied, answering her unspoken question. "The higher one goes, the more climbing. King Willow resides atop this building."

"Why not right on the waterline?" she asked.

Telemay smiled at her ignorance. "We must allow for seasonal rise and fall of the waters," he said.

A movable dock that floated with the roll of the waves was attached to the palace. Several attendants wearing blue shorts and tight red cotton shirts hauled the barge to dock and tied it down, the sailors hurrying on deck to lower the gangway.

The visitors were led onto the dock, an attendant taking each of their hands to help them across the slowly rolling pier. A small fixed platform was attached to the building and led to a doorspace, which they entered.

Candles were set within, dimly lighting cavernous darkness. The rooms were empty down here, mud caking the occasionally subterranean floors and walls. The smell of incense wafted strongly through the place, probably to cover up the dankness of the mildewed interior.

They were led up a long flight of stairs to the rooms above the water, Alicia holding Biddy's hand to walk her up. Softly and richly furnished, the inner palace had the look of off-handed elegance that was the mark of true wealth. The candles blew bright up here and many window spaces were hacked through the vines to let nature's light in.

"These are the retainers' and servants' quarters," Telemay said, as they skirted several of the rooms to mount another staircase.

"I see very few guards," Alicia said innocently, as she turned her head this way and that to take everything in. Telemay's ignoring of the question was so pointed that it set her to wondering about several things.

They climbed richly carpeted stairs through another set of rooms reserved for honored visitors and guests, and finally climbed up to the roof of the structure.

The King's quarters occupied half of the roof, the other half open space filled with gardens and a large hedge maze. Young women in gauzy robes laughed lightly through a game of blindman's buff, while several middle-aged men occupied a nearby table, playing cards and watching the girls.

"You will wait here," Telemay said, and walked to the structure that took up half the roof. It was white stone and rose nearly two stories on its own. Large white pillars supported the front of the sloping roof. A stainless steel Ibem shrine held a place of honor near the door.

Biddy took up a position near the retaining wall and watched the young women with undisguised envy, for Minnies loved few things in life more than a game. Meanwhile Twiddle, inexplicably, wandered to the table of men with sure steps and determination. Alicia drifted over to join him.

"Honored sirs," Twiddle said to them. "I am Twiddle of the second sight."

"Is that right?" one of the men said without looking up from his game. "We're, uh, friends of King Willow."

"Yes," Twiddle said. "I know."

The men stopped playing for a moment and stared at the eyeless man. "Who's your friend?" a man with a blond beard asked.

"My name is Alicia of Alb'ny," she said, her eyes drifting from Twiddle to the men.

"That's to the North, ain't it?" the blond man asked.

"Yes," Alicia said. "North."

"Long way from home," one of the others said, and played a red card.

"Not so very far," Twiddle said, a smile playing on his withered lips.

"What brings you all the way down here?" the blond man asked.

"Destiny," Twiddle answered, and the men went back to their game.

"My Lady," Telemay called from the structure. He was waving her over to him. She hurried to the door. Telemay opened it wide. "The King will see you now."

Alicia moved into the place, several gangly boys running past her to the roof. They were giggling loudly. King Willow occupied a throne toward the back of a large room. It was made of gold. Stained glass in blue filled all the windows, casting a haze over everything. The room was wide open, its floor carpeted in red.

"Come forward," the King said, and his voice quivered in range from tenor to soprano.

Alicia moved to face him. He was a boy of no more than fifteen years. His childish face was smeared dirty. He wore old, torn canvas trousers and held a wine crock in his hands.

"You're a handsome wench," he said to her. "Come give us a kiss."

"Your Majesty," Alicia said. "I come on a mission of grave importance."

King Willow took a long drink. "You think I'm too young for you," he said, pouting.

"Your Majesty?"

"I'm not good enough to kiss because I'm too young."

Alicia turned to stare at Telemay who stood by the door, his face a blank.

"I have news for you from my husband, Morgan of Alb'ny, of the gravest importance."

"I'll bet he's not young like me," Willow said, and threw his wine on the floor. "I'll bet you'd kiss him right now."

Alicia took a deep breath and walked to the boy. Leaning forward, she kissed him lightly on the cheek.

"That's not a kiss," he said.

"Your Majesty," she said. "You really must hear what I have to say."

"I've had women before," he said, "if you think I'm not experienced. I've had hundreds of women, isn't that right, Telly?"

Telemay bowed slightly. "Hundreds," he said.

"Your kingdom is in grave danger," Alicia said. "You must muster your army and prepare to defend yourself."

"Army?" Willow said, his young eyes widening.

"You have no army," she said, finally understanding.

The boy stood up, putting an open hand to his chest. "What need of an army when they have me? Will you kiss me now? You are truly a walking work of art. I will have you in my bed immediately."

Alicia turned to Telemay. "You have no army?"

"We've never had need of one before," the liaison said.

"No defensive capabilities?"

"None that I know of."

"Will you come to my bed now?" Willow said. "I promise you'll enjoy it. All the others do, don't they, Telly?"

"All of them, Your Highness."

"What do you say?" Willow asked, his face alight with childish expectation.

"He can't make the decisions," she said to Telemay. "He can't run the government."

Telemay smiled slightly.

"Will you bed me or not?" Willow said angrily. "I'm a King not to be kept waiting."

She turned quickly to him, wanting to scream, yet acquiescing to her better judgment. Moving closer to him, she whispered something quickly in his ear. His eyes went wide and he slumped down on his throne, his young lips sputtering. Turning, she walked back to Telemay.

"There is really very little time," she said.

"It had to happen this way," he said. "Kingship is an honorary position, one convenient for dinners and pomp. The King has nothing to do with the operation of the city. I will now take you to the real power."

He opened the door and pointed to the tableful of men playing cards. Twiddle was now sitting with them, talking animatedly.

"The merchants of N'ork City," Telemay said. "They've been scrutinizing you since your arrival. They are the power and glory of our forest."

Alicia nodded. "Thank you, Telemay," she said. "You are a real diplomat." She began to walk toward the men.

"Wait," he said, and she stopped, turning to him. "What did you tell His Majesty to make him leave you alone?"

She smiled, winking at the severe-faced man. "I told him I was a man wearing a dress," she said, and resolutely walked to the merchants' table without a backward glance.

15

Nyack

Serge sat on the foredeck by the wooden spread-winged eagle and lathered his face with rab fat soap while Lannie, the giantess who had been his most frequent companion, sharpened the shiny silver dagger to a fine edge on a whetstone.

Serge watched the female with his usual interest. Giants had very low genetic sex drives, traditionally taking many years before picking a mate. But Lannie had been following close behind Serge since Masuria and it was a foregone conclusion on everyone's part that they would eventually mate. Both had thought of it; neither had spoken of it, since that was not the way of the large people. Rather, an innate understanding built up over a period of time, culminating in a quite natural and not unexpected mating that would bind them for life. And among the giants, Serge was considered a real prize, being the symby-partner of the only Pure Blood Mech in all of N'ork.

The foredeck was filled with giants, the men in loincloths, the women in loosely draped, brightly colored robes. They watched the activity on the Nyack road as a group, the way they handled everything. The sky was dark for the middle of the afternoon and thunder rumbled lightly, rippling the dark overhang of cloud with gentle echo. Humans and Genies crowded the wide boulevard that ran right up to the long dock, and the processional seemed rather more orderly than what they had experienced in other cities, owing to the pre-preparation that had gone on here.

The big news, on ship and on land, was that a contingent of Grunts occupied Nyack, Grunts thought even more rare than Mechs. The talk on the deck, though, was not of Grunts or even of the war. The foredeck flowed with talk of hemolysis.

"There is to be a Genie meeting about this," Lannie said, testing the blade on the light hair of her arm. Satisfied, she walked up to Serge and studied his face, as if looking for the best place to start shaving. "El-tron will be leading the discussion."

"Serge has heard of such things," he replied, sputtering lather from around his lips. "It saddens me to think that El-tron would have forgotten so quickly how much Morgan has done for him."

"El-tron loves Morgan as you do," Lannie replied, going to work on his left cheek. "But he worries for the fate of all the People."

"I trust my life to Morgan as to no other," Serge replied. "He will not harm . . . ouch!"

The knife had nicked his cheek, a small trickle of blood turning the bright white lather pink. "Sorry," she said, wiping away the line of blood. "You cannot trust Morgan more than you do Nebo."

"Nebo doesn't count," Serge said, and he watched a flock of large blackbirds flapping down close to the river. "He is a part of me."

"The Mechs discuss the blood-mixing, too. Suppose they go against Morgan on this point?"

Serge focused his eyes on her. She looked at him innocently, long brown hair falling into her face, red lips parted just slightly. "Nebo and Morgan have been themselves like Mech and giant since the beginning," he said. "They would not go against one another."

"Who rules who?"

"What do you mean?"

"You said they were as giant and Mech. If that is so, which one rules?"

Serge sat quietly as she shaved his upper lip, splattering

the lather right onto the deck, then dipping the blade into a bucketful of water.

"They understand one another," he said when she finished the lip.

"Suppose the Mechs vote to go against Morgan on this issue?"

"Why are you so concerned about this?" he asked angrily. "It could obviously not affect us either way."

"It couldn't affect you," she said, her eyes involuntarily drifting to his lap. "But it would be possible that it could affect me."

"No!" he said loudly. "You speak foolishness."

"See?" she responded. "See how you react when you even dream of it? That's how the others feel."

"Morgan is good," he said. "Morgan wants only what is best for all the People. I love him without restraint."

"Then if he and Nebo split over this issue, you would follow Morgan?"

"I didn't say that!"

"Then what are you saying?"

He stood up, pushing her arm away. "It shall never come to pass," he said, bending to splash water from the bucket onto his face. "Serge will have no more shaving today."

"Please," Lannie said, laying a hand on his arm. "I meant not to offend you."

He smiled, his half-shaved face looking lopsided, and patted her hand. "Lannie just makes me think too much, that's all," he said, and rolled his eyes.

She smiled shyly back, not saying the words of love that were on her mind.

"Serge!" came a voice from the rail on A deck. The big man turned to see a dark robe and mechanical hands grasping the railing above him.

"Ho, Nebo!" he answered, waving at the Mech.

"I have need of you," the Mech's melodious voice rang down.

"Coming," Serge said, and turned to the female. "Serge could never stay angry with Lannie."

She put a hand to her mouth, hiding her smile. "You'd better hurry" was all she said.

He turned from her and walked to the rail. Ignoring the

stairs amidships, he simply hoisted his leg up high, catching the lip of the next deck. With a long stretch, he caught the bottom rail with his hands and pulled himself up. Nebo was waiting for him.

"I have some heavy equipment that needs to be moved around in the lab," he said.

The giant nodded. "I will do it right away."

"You have my thanks."

All at once, Morgan was hurrying along the deck toward them. "Have you heard?" he said before he even got there. "Have you heard the news?"

"There's news?" Serge said, eyes wide, for he wasn't exactly sure what constituted news.

Morgan smiled at him through the tangle of his beard. "There are Grunts in Nyack, Grunts in my city, and the talk is that they've already demonstrated their abilities."

"Grunts can be extremely dangerous and unpredictable," Nebo said, his face a mask.

"Can you imagine them fighting for us?" Morgan said, his own eyes dancing. "A small, unbeatable army?"

"They follow nothing save their own path," Nebo said.

"Well, we're going to find out if the paths can intersect," Morgan replied, rubbing his hands together. "Serge, I want you to go down and ferret them out and invite them to a feast tonight in the officers' mess."

"I've already given Serge a task," Nebo said.

"This is more important," Morgan said. "I'll give him back to you in a while."

"I've already given him a task," Nebo repeated.

"Serge," Morgan said. "Go into the city and find the Grunts. I think their leader's name is Galen."

The giant turned to the rail, putting his leg over it to climb down.

"No!" Nebo said. "Serge. Do what I told you."

Serge stopped halfway over the rail, confusion making his face a battlefield.

"What's wrong with you?" Morgan asked Nebo. "Why cross me on this?"

"Grunts and Mechs are natural enemies," Nebo said.

"Not in my army," Morgan replied. "Serge. Get them."

The giant looked to Nebo, his face now drawn in sadness. The Mech looked at him, then at Morgan. He sighed.

"Oh, all right," he said low. "You'll get them aboard anyway. Go ahead, Serge."

With relief, the giant hurried over the rail before either of them changed their minds. And he realized that Lannie was just trying to show him something that he had been too stupid to recognize on his own.

He climbed to the deck and hurried to the gangway, wondering what he would do if Morgan and Nebo ever had a permanent rift.

For the occasion of Morgan's dinner, Nebo had fixed the officers' mess with vacuum tube lights from his lab that bathed the double cabin-length room in brightness all the way up to the corners. He had also provided a large turning blade called a fan that circulated air through the stuffy room. Both devices were hooked up to a small generator that chugged steadily by the unguarded door.

The gathering provided an interesting sampling of N'ork life. Galen the Grunt was there, accompanied by the elder called Longnose. Nebo, also, was in attendance, for Morgan most certainly wanted to see how the breeds mixed in polite fashion. Morgan took the head of the table, flanked on his left by Jella, Prelate of Rockland, and on his right by Diitmar D'an, Premier of Nyack, and the oldest human any of them had ever seen. Beside D'an, gnarled Notern of Fishkill sweated liberally despite the air for he had a problem with the confinement of enclosed places. Across from him, Duchess Clorina of Staatsburg tried desperately to retain her teenaged composure amidst the wild variance of life surrounding her on all sides. The Duchess had let it be known that she was looking for a proper match for herself despite the inconvenience of the war. Notern was the object of her attentions this night, though on other nights there were others.

Morgan, inexplicably, had invited several beast-men also, among them, Squan the whiskered cat and Melon of the long, doglike snout. Beast-men did not seem to have the trouble getting along that man and beast actually had, and perhaps it was for this reason Morgan chose to include dog and cat among the guests—as an example to Galen and Nebo.

He thought about Grodin, wondered what his old mentor would say about such a gathering. And, as always, his heart was blunted with the loss of one so dear. He worked hard to think about something besides the craggy-faced old man, but it was no use. Present or not, Grodin was the ghost at the feast. And no matter who spoke, it was Grodin's gutteral laugh Morgan would hear.

"I have personally supervised over two hundred plantings," D'an said proudly, his watery blue eyes alert and young, "and I've probably got a crag on my face for every one of them."

"Much character shows in your wrinkles," Clorina said, but she didn't mean it, for she had already decided privately that she would rather be dead than live with the outward signs of old age.

"And you, good Morgan," Galen said. "How many plantings have you seen?"

"Mid-fifties," Morgan replied as he chewed casually on a nectarine, a meatless meal being decided upon so as not to offend.

"And what's that by the ancient countings?" Gert the Longnose asked.

"Twenty-six years," Morgan returned.

"Doesn't it seem stuffy in here?" Notern asked, turning this way and that.

"Perhaps some air by the door," Morgan said, pointing, and he was proud of his diplomacy in the face of such differences.

The burly man jumped up like a child, his chair falling over loudly, and hurried quickly to the open door, drawing in deep gasps of air.

The Minnies were serving, and one hurried over to right the chair. He noticed the Prelate's crock empty, another Minnie hurrying immediately through the kitchen door with the jug to refill it.

Galen brought long strands of boiled marsh weed up to his mouth, his hand covering defensively as he ate, a genetic trait of his kind. "In our society," he said to Morgan, "one is not ready for the responsibility of decision-making until he reaches his two hundreth year."

"Would that my kind had that luxury," Morgan returned, knowing what it was that the Grunt was saying.

Gert picked up his wine and held it under his truly magnificent snoot. He snorted loudly, then quickly drank, his eyes darting back and forth as he did. "Does it frighten you sometimes to think of the world in the hands of someone of your tender years?"

"How could it?" Morgan replied. "My kind was made without fear of any kind."

"What he's getting at," Nebo said, his mechanical hands picking through the plums, carefully closing on one to keep from accidentally crushing it, "is that he's engineered as a fighter and leader of . . . what, men?"

Everyone at the table, except the men, laughed.

"He is doing," Nebo continued, "what he was born to do. Just as the rest of us are."

"And we follow him," Jella said, "because he is our friend, our salvation, and the instrument of our retribution."

"Retribution," Galen said, leaning back in the specially built chair that made him as tall as the others, "is not a game for tender years. When you plant thorns, you can never expect to gather roses."

"What is that supposed to mean?" Notern said, coming back into the room.

"Your condition is called claustrophobia," Galen told him. "You've lived too long in the trees."

"What condition?" the man replied, and sat down, his face immediately breaking out in sweat. Clorina reached across the table and fondled his hand.

The Grunts shared a somewhat disappointed glance. "So you travel downriver to N'ork City," Galen said.

"We protect the South from Ramon's expansion," Morgan replied.

"Just so," Galen said.

Clorina cleared her throat, determined to be a part of the discussion. "And what brings our shy brothers to the river?" she asked.

"I am not your brother," Galen replied, surprised at the look of pain that washed across her face. "But if I were, I would be proud to have a sister like you." He noticed her brighten, and was happy to see that he hadn't fractured the frail creature.

"I'm interested in an answer to that question," Nebo said.

Galen clanged his eyelids and stared with distaste at the Mech, the root cause of the dissolution of the Old World. "The country is in upheaval," he said. "That affects even Grunts. It was time for us to show ourselves again."

"Does that mean you've come to fight?" Morgan asked, sitting up straight.

"If necessary."

"Will you fight for us?"

The room hushed to silence, the only sound the chugging of the generator and the muffled chatter of the Minnies through the kitchen door.

"That is a difficult question to answer directly," Galen said at length.

"Why?" Morgan asked. "You side either with my brother or me in this conflict. As you said, the country is in upheaval."

"There is the question of hemolysis," Gert the Longnose said.

"That word again," Notern said, and stumbled once more to the doorspace.

"Do you believe in the forced mixing of the blood?" Galen asked Morgan, then watched his face turn dark.

"I believe the scourge of prejudice can be eradicated from our lands in one generation," Morgan said.

"By forcibly mixing the blood," Galen said.

Morgan just stared at him.

"Will that not dilute the capabilities and intelligence of all?" Gert said, incredulous.

"Define capabilities," Morgan said. "Define intelligence. Then tell me what's important about them."

"What about you, Mech?" Galen asked. "How would you like your blood thinned by . . . a human for instance?"

"Please!" Duchess Clorina said, standing abruptly. "These are not matters to be discussed in the presence of a lady."

"A thousand pardons," Galen said, nodding his horns in her direction. "I am unskilled in the . . . niceties of your society."

"I accept your apology," the Duchess said. Sitting, she tugged at the scooping bodice of her elegant red gown.

"I am a scientific explorer," Nebo said, "not a philosopher."

The table Minnie looked over everyone's plates and noticed that no one was eating any longer. Within seconds, a troop of the small people came charging through the door. They jumped, giggling, upon the table and began scooping up dishes and tossing them in perfect cooperation to one another.

"You explored enough to destroy the ancients," Gert said. "Is that the manner of exploration you speak of here?"

"And each of you, so proud of your age," Nebo said, "probably killed hundreds with your own hands."

"Thousands," Galen said without remorse. "We were locked in conflict to the death."

"As we are here," Morgan said. "Will you join us downriver?"

"We will go downriver with you," Galen said. "Whether we join you or not is a matter as yet undecided."

"And what if you choose not to join us?" Nebo said.

Galen looked sadly at the Minnies who were bounding gracefully across the long table. "It is our own convictions that compel us," he said. "Choice compels choice."

El-tron stood upon the Speech Rock at the waterline terminus of Nyack Boulevard. In the flickering light of the torches he saw hundreds of Genies and men discussing his points among themselves. He had been nervous, and was still shaking, but the strength of his resolve had taken him through this time of personal crisis.

Several giants who had been standing at the back of the group moved through the crowd to stand before the large-eyed Genie. Even upon the rock, they still towered over him.

"Morgan was your friend," Lannie, Serge's mate, said. "How can you preach against him now?"

"I love Morgan as I love myself," El-tron answered. "I preach not against him, but against the folly of the blood-mixing."

"Are they not the same thing?" the giantess persisted.

"No. I organize here for one reason only. It is time for the People to have a voice in this. If we show a solid block of strength and numbers, asking him to divert from this suicidal path, I'm sure he will listen and hear our voice."

There was a smattering of applause from the crowd, and it made the Genie feel better. This meeting had been the most difficult procedure of his life, but the issues were far larger than his comfort. He didn't want to be in this position, but there was no one else.

His strength came partly from the fact that several of the females had turned up pregnant because of the Night of He-

molysis, and it brought bad memories flooding to the tiny
Mech. Morgan's loyalists were already referring to them as the
First Children, and the thought chilled El-tron's blood.

"Suppose he doesn't listen," Lannie said.

"What?"

"What if Morgan doesn't hear your voice because he follows his own?"

"That won't happen," El-tron said confidently. "It can't
happen."

And the giantess turned from the meeting and walked uncertainly back to VICTORY to find Serge.

16

The Ruins of Rockland

Count Delmar and Ramon stood side by side, leaning against
VIPER's A deck railing, and watching the destruction of the
empty city. The big guns pounded the distant tree city, blew it
to splinters for no other reason than it would make a good show
for the troops.

"There's much discontent among the lesser nobles," Delmar said, his face not betraying what his feelings held. "The
loss of young Reeder . . ."

"I know," Ramon said. "We are but three ships now, and
questioning loyalties. Has everyone forgotten why we're
here?"

"What difference?" the Count asked, and the sweat
dripped from the ringlets of his hair. "The question becomes
what to do?"

Ramon turned to him. "You are a good friend and true."

Delmar returned his gaze, not speaking while they
awaited the thunderous ovation of another volley from the port

guns to die down. Below them, soldiers gathered fruit from the Rockland orchards, while hundreds fished from makeshift skiffs tied by long tethers to the big boats.

"True I am," Delmar said when the echoes had died away. "But even my loyalty has its limitations."

"What are you getting at?"

"You and I must put our heads together and rethink the direction of this campaign if it is not to float away like so much driftwood on the current."

On the starboard side, the guns were turned to water level and blasted, raising huge water sprays and thousands of shocked and dead fish, which were quickly gathered for the evening's meal.

"You're speaking of the Physicians," Ramon said, and knew he was thinking of the Green Woman.

"Among other things," Delmar answered, taking the diplomatic road. "Our discipline must become stricter, our ways of dealing with dissension more . . . severe."

"You've apparently given this a great deal of thought."

"Our army is almost nearly conscript," Delmar replied. "They're tiring. They want to go home. If we don't take a hard stand I fear we will begin to see mass desertions."

Ramon turned back to the rail, sweat soaking the blue jumper he hadn't changed for three days. There was a time when he would have killed Delmar for even thinking that mistakes had been made, but the loss of Reeder jarred him in a very fundamental way. He had made mistakes, bad mistakes, and if he was going to recapture the spirit of their crusade, he'd have to change his thinking.

The Green Woman was at the heart of his concerns. His wife, the sliding lustful snake he had married while mentally altered by magic potions. Her hand still tightly clamped his beating heart and held it in a deathgrip, but he wasn't so much overcome by the fear of that deathgrip as he once was. For power was a drug far stronger than any she had given him, and a sex more potent and satisfying than the pounding, screaming agony that emanated from her bed. In short, he feared the loss of power more than he feared the loss of her.

"You are right, fair Delmar," he said at last. "I have strayed from the path."

"Oh no, my Lord, I didn't mean . . ."

Ramon put up a hand. "Fear not," he said. "It is time,

once more, to take command of this expedition. I think it right that you be made second-in-command with full power of leadership over the troops. We will think upon this and plan out the details. And your loyalty will be amply rewarded in these matters."

Delmar went down on one knee, unsheathing his sword and holding it out in front of him. "My blade and my life I pledge to you, my Lord."

"Rise up, my equal," Ramon said. "There will be no more bowing between us."

Delmar, in red velvet shortcoat and knickers with pale blue stockings, stood and embraced Ramon, his perfume nearly overpowering. "We shall prevail," he said.

"My Lord!" came a voice from the stairs amidships. It was Pack with Harrison, the Truthteller, right behind.

Ramon waved them over, the Physician taking Harrison by the arm and dragging him along in his haste.

The little man was out of breath when he reached Ramon. "I have just attended a secret Physicians' meeting," he said. "The Green Woman didn't want me admitted, but I still have many old friends among the wizards and they insisted. As per your instructions, I was able to sneak Harrison in as my apprentice."

"Excellent," Ramon said. "We'll talk in my chambers."

The four moved along A Deck until they came to the door with the coiled snake painted upon it. Ramon gave them entrance, then bolted the locks behind.

"I want to know everything that was talked about," Ramon said, throwing himself on his bed, the others taking chairs around the small but elegant cabin.

"First," Pack said, reaching into the pocket of his gray shortcoat, "a small present."

He produced a small vial full of clear liquid, holding it up by two fingers. Ramon sat up immediately.

"'Dorphins?"

Pack nodded, smiling. "Harrison was able to get a look at her calculations and commit them to memory. I had to play with the dosages, but I've finally got it right." He tossed the vial to Ramon, who nearly fell out of bed catching it.

Ramon turned to Delmar. "Part of my wife's attraction," he said.

"I understand," the Count said. Delmar was one with so many vices he'd never think of condemning someone else's.

Ramon turned back to the Physician. "You can make more of this?"

Pack's grin threatened to split his face in twain. "As much as I want, any time I want."

"Good." He looked at Harrison, nodding. "You've done well."

The young man with the woman's face shrugged. "It really wasn't anything."

"The meeting," Delmar said. "What happened there?"

"There were about twenty of us," Pack said. "The Green Woman was obviously in total charge."

"Is that right?" Ramon asked the Truthteller.

The young man looked blank. "The Green Woman made all the suggestions, and loudly condemned any who disagreed. All of her ideas were adopted."

Ramon nodded and lay back down, sticking the vial under his goose down pillow. "Go on," he told Pack.

"She called for solidarity," the Physician said. "She said it was time the Physicians stood together and demanded a say in the operation of the war and of the government."

"No!" Delmar said.

They all looked to Harrison, who said, "The Green Woman told us, 'We provide the power, we also should wield it.'"

"Preposterous," Delmar said. "My Physician was in attendance?"

Harrison said, "Scab of the hunched back shared the dias with the Green Woman."

"Treasonous," the Count said.

Pack continued. "She also said the Physicians should make a list of demands concerning their own sovereignty and refuse to work for us unless those demands are met. She said they could work together on their own projects and use them to threaten the power to make you back down."

"I feared this," Ramon said. "Her mouth grows larger each day."

"Is this absolutely correct?" Delmar asked Harrison.

"Pack speaks true," Harrison said.

"How do they expect to make this work?" Delmar asked.

Pack looked at Harrison. "You'd better tell him."

The young Genie closed his eyes tightly, pressing his hands to his temples. "Ramon is the lock that bars our way," he said in a faraway voice. "And I hold the key that opens the lock. He is of weak mind, and I control him in all things."

"Bitch!" Ramon spat, jumping to his feet. "And she did this in front of my own loyal Physician!"

"She thinks her hold on you that strong," Delmar said.

"And that you'd believe her word above mine," Pack added.

"She believes in the power of the 'dorphins," Ramon said, his voice rumbling like the thunder.

"What do we do?" Delmar asked.

"Nothing for the moment," Ramon said, his eyes drifting to his pillow and the freedom that lay beneath it. "But the reckoning comes soon." He clenched a fist before his face. "We can handle the Physicians, and *I* can handle my darling wife."

Firust steered the barge from the back with the large rudder while Ona sat fore with Ty'Jorman huddled to her bosom. They were beginning to see scattered pockets of soldiers on the banks foraging for food. The fleet could not be far ahead.

"You're lucky to have found me," the man called hoarsely to her. "Not many would have been brave enough to take you past that mountain of bones on the Kipsie shore."

"You've been well paid," she said, not even looking at him, keeping her eyes on the always-moving, always-fresh river of life.

"Paid?" he said. "A sackful of junk and a few tumbles on the boards isn't fair compensation for the risks I take."

"You should have paid me," she said bitterly. "I am the consort of Kings."

"Ha! You seemed to enjoy the girth of my "king" well enough."

She turned dull eyes to him. "Don't flatter yourself. You're less than forgettable."

He suddenly veered the barge toward the shallows of the Western shore and made his way toward her, unbuttoning his filthy knickers. "We'll see just how forgettable I am," he said angrily.

She looked at him, putting her mind in a far more pleasant place, and suffered his indignities for the last time.

*　　*　　*

In late afternoon, the prevailing breezes took a stiff turn from the West, and Ramon took the opportunity to gather food while he was burning Rockland. He sent swift runners with jungle experience out several miles due West of the demolished city to set the forest ablaze. When the first plumes of smoke could be seen rising against the darkening sky, everyone went down to the beach to help with the hunt.

Thousands lined the beaches in all directions armed with sword and lance, and waited. Ramon had a large seat put out for himself on the beach. Delmar stood beside him on his right. On his left, a pouting Green Woman stood at his insistence.

"You could have at least had a seat made for me," she said. "After all, I am the power just as you are."

"Not quite the same," Ramon answered, and he kept his eyes from her, for surely in the looking lay folly. "Besides, there was time for the construction of only one chair."

She put a gentle hand on his arm. "Perhaps if you'd share it with me, I could mix up a little something extra for you."

"No, thank you," Ramon answered casually.

She tightened her grip, nails digging into the flesh of his forearm. "Perhaps if you don't, I won't mix up anything for you."

Ramon stared up at her through already hazy eyes. Pack had done his work well. "Suit yourself, my love."

He once again turned his eyes from her, forcing his mind to remember how much damage she had already done.

"Well, I don't have to stand here," she said. "I'm going up to the cabin."

She turned to go, but his hand flashed out and grabbed her wrist, squeezing tightly. "Why don't you stay with me?" he asked.

"Let go of me," she whispered harshly, trying to jerk her hand free.

"Promise to stay," he said, his voice still light, "or I'll have you tied down."

She stopped struggling. "I know not the nature of your game," she said. "But for now I'll play."

"Good," he relaxed his grip. "The excitement should start up any minute now."

They waited, the column of smoke now rising quickly to

join the clouds. After a time, the fire-starters came trudging from the woods, and everyone prepared for the animals.

There were several moments of silence, then birds in large profusion came flapping toward the river. Thousands of birds, filling the sky over the beach. Then animals—wild cats and coons and possum—scurrying across the beach to be stung by the wrath of Ramon. Suddenly a man came charging across the beach among the animals. He was screaming loudly.

"My Lord! Don't kill me! My Lord!"

"Hold!" Ramon said, and he noticed the hook on the wild man's hand.

"That's Redrick," Delmar said, incredulous. "I'll be damned."

Rabs were pouring from the jungle, and the strange man-beasts with heads like bulls, but who ran on two legs. Thousands of animals confused the beach, turning back upon themselves to escape the arrows, only to be greeted by the wall of flame that was moving swiftly through the forest, raising flames a hundred feet in the air. And the crackle was loud as trees, hundreds of years old, fell under the relentless push of the fire. The temple of Ibem became his funerary.

Somehow in the confusion Redrick found Ramon of Alb'ny. The man was filthy and gaunt, his face smeared with soot. He was panting heavily, falling to his knees and hugging Ramon's legs.

"Oh, my Lord . . ."

Ramon kicked him away to roll on the ground. Standing, he drew his sword, the point sticking against the man's neck. "The hero of Kipsie," he said low.

"Please," Redrick pleaded.

"Trying to escape me?" Ramon asked.

"No, my Lord," Redrick gasped. "I've been waiting here for you. But when the shelling started, I went farther into the jungle to escape the slaughter."

"Fine," Ramon said. "Now give me one good reason why I shouldn't kill you right now."

"I-I have information for you."

"What sort of information?" Delmar asked, kneeling to get closer to the man.

Redrick turned to him, taking the front of his shortcoat in his dirty hands. "Oh please, you must listen. I've been living among the heathen, learning of their plans."

Delmar turned and looked up at Ramon. "It couldn't hurt to hear what he has to say."

Ramon nodded, sheathing his sword. "So be it, Knight of Firetree. You've just purchased yourself a little more breath."

"Thank you," Redrick said, standing shakily. "Thank you."

The sky had darkened to night, and the killing, lit by the huge flames of the burning forest, continued unabated on the Rockland sand. It was hot on the beach, and air was hard to come by.

"What happened at Kipsie?" Delmar asked.

"They were waiting for us," Redrick said. "There must have been fifty thousand of them. We were overrun on the beach; we had no chance. And before I could scuttle the ship, Darlow, the coward from Troy, and all his men deserted, leaving me alone on the boat. I tried to get away with it, but we ran aground."

"You say they were waiting for you," Ramon said. "How could they know you were coming?"

"Someone told them."

"Who?" Delmar demanded, his face bright in the flickering orange light of the fires.

"Your Programmer," Redrick said, his eyes wild. "Dixon Faf!"

"What!" Ramon moved up to the man, taking him by the hair and bending his head back. "You'd better know whereof you speak."

"I swear, my Lord. I saw him myself on the beach with the red-haired bastard. Then later, in Rockland, I found out the whole story."

"Tell!" Ramon demanded, still holding Redrick's hair.

Redrick's lips moved silently at first, then the story came pouring out. "He came to Kipsie with a letter that said you were not of Pure Blood and asked that you be taken from the throne."

"Traitor," Ramon said.

"There's more," Redrick said. "There was a wedding. Morgan of Siler married a Genie called Alicia. . . ."

The Green Woman gave out a strangled cry, and Ramon jerked to face her. Her eyes were wide and darting.

"What is it?" he demanded.

"Nothing," she said, but he had never seen her so shaken. "It's nothing."

He turned back to Redrick. "Yes?"

"The Genie convinced the Lawgivers that Morgan, being of pure Genie blood, was more qualified to rule than you. The Lawgivers said that Jerlynn, your mother, had prior claim. Faf relinquished that claim in her name, leaving the way clear for Morgan's appointment and acceptance by the Southern kingdoms."

Ramon released the man. "My own mother," he said low, and turned to the Green Woman. "You're all of a kind, all of you." The fire crackled all around them, reflecting wildly in Ramon's eyes. He looked hard at Delmar. "You'll probably find them in his cabin. Arrest them, both of them. See to it yourself. Lock them in the hold."

Firust's barge bumped up to the shore amidst the conflagration of Rockland. Men ran crazily through the shallows, trying to catch the creatures who had eluded the arrows and pikes on the beach. The fire roared all around, silhouettes darting through its hot light in tangled confusion.

Holding Ty'Jorman close, Ona made to step off the barge as several swarthy soldiers ran up to her.

"Look at this one," one of the men said, and grabbed her arm. "No pocks, no scars."

"Leave me alone! I seek Ramon of Alb'ny with important news."

"She seeks Ramon of Alb'ny," one of the other men said, imitating the woman's voice.

Hands were pulling on her insistently now, trying to force her from the boat. Firust walked up behind her. "So this is what you wanted to hurry to." He laughed. "Better you would have stayed upriver, pleasuring me."

The men all around her laughed, jerking her this way and that.

"You must take me to Ramon!"

"Sure we will," one of the men said. "Just come along quietly. We'll take you right there . . . by way of the sand dunes!"

They all laughed then, Firust the loudest. With a quick motion, she jerked away from the men and turned to the boatman. Reaching out, she pulled his short sword from his belt and gutted him with it. He fell slowly backwards, making a wheezing sound like air escaping a bladder.

The men grabbed her, holding her above their heads. She lost her grip on Ty'Jorman, but the child's natural ability held him to her.

As they moved off through the bright, jumping darkness, she saw Ramon standing with a group near his ship.

"Ramon!" she screamed. "Ramon! Ramon!"

Ramon Delaga heard a voice screaming his name, and turned to see the woman being carried off by his men.

"Wait!" he called. "Bring her here."

Reluctantly, they brought Ona across the beach to him. They set her and the child before Ramon, then hurried off, lest they be in trouble of some sort.

He stood, looking down at her. "Do I know you?"

She stared up at him fiercely. "You should know," she said. "I served you once in many ways."

Redrick pushed his way up next to Ramon. He looked at the woman, then at his hook, and he thought of the hand that Morgan had taken in defense of her virtue so long ago.

"It's Morgan's woman," he said huskily, and raised his hooked hand to her. "I'll handle this creature."

Ramon stayed his arm, then looked to Ty'Jorman. "The child?"

"Morgan's," she said.

Ramon took a long breath, his insides hot as the fire that jumped all around him. "And you come to me?"

"Morgan the bastard has taken my other child," she said, her own anger stronger than ever. "He has gone off with Genies and heathens. I want you to get my child back."

"Go on."

"Use me and the baby as hostages," she said. "I'll help you in all that you do. When he knows you've got this one, he'll come for him. You can take him then. I ask only that I be given the other baby back."

He stared hard at her for a moment, thinking of the duplicity of all women. Taking her under the chin, he said, "My dear, I think we may be able to do business."

And with that, he took the baby from her and cradled it in his arms, tickling it on the stomach with a grimy forefinger.

PART THREE

VILLAINIES

17

i

Grodin squatted on the bank and strained his eyes across the river. His arms rested loosely upon his knees and, even after a night's sleep, his body ached in a very deep and fundamental way from the abuse he had forced upon it in his haste to catch up with Ona.

And it was all for naught. Several hundred yards distant, and on the opposing bank, Ramon's people were breaking camp for the next leg of their downriver journey. Beyond them, the forest lay in smoldering, charred ruins that left an acrid smell in the air and a thin haze over everything as far as he could see. It had been the same all the way downriver— huge, burned out sections of life-giving jungle that stretched for miles and miles.

Even now, the fire continued to burn downriver unabated; but through the haze, thunder crashed and lightning brightened the surreal landscape often enough that it seemed Ibem would once again step in and quench the raging blasphemy.

Grodin had arrived downriver minutes too late. He had drifted in his raft into the tangle of fishing skiffs just as Ona killed the boatman and was herself carried off into the hunt. He had gone ashore, but could do nothing to save the child before Ramon got hold of him.

He stood slowly, every muscle aching. His scar throbbed horribly, and this time it *was* because of approaching rain. But Grodin, as always, was prepared. He had found rain shelter before making camp the previous night.

143

Moving slowly, he hobbled past the flood plain to the tree-line, responsibility a muscle that throbbed far worse than anything physical. He had inadvertently caused all this. In feeding his own bigotry, he had unintentionally fanned Ona's, and he was too forthright a man not to take that seriously.

Upon entering the forest, he walked the overgrown rab river path until he found the tree that he had slashed with his short sword. Groaning loudly, he climbed the gnarled oak thirty feet into the air to the spot where the rusted ancient carriage was tangled in twisting limbs.

The machine was upside down like some dead animal. He slithered through the window space, huddling on the inside roof, a pleasant enough cave after he had torn out what remained of the machine's insides and chased out the small denizens of the jungle who would return to their lair after the human had moved on.

He hung his pack and weapons on the remnants of the steering mechanism and waited. Thunder rumbled continuously, the lightning flashes brighter and brighter. But when the rain came, it fell without warning or fanfare. Angry, pulsating sheets of water rifled mercilessly through the jungle, settling the haze and dousing the remnants of Ramon's war of attrition against the very thing that gave them all life.

It was a monstrous rain, its fury venting in flashing skies and deep, screaming rumbles. It cowered all: men, Genies, and animals. It sat on the cutting edge of ferocity, capable in a second of drowning all in its breathless covering. If it was the voice of God, then God was angry. And if they survived it, it was only through His mercy. Such was the nature of all their lives.

Grodin lay back and listened to the pounding on the carriage. He knew what he must do, and knew what he would do, and in that knowledge he fell asleep again, a deep dreamless sleep—a sleep of peace in the middle of Nature's rage.

ii

FATHER HUS—SOUTH OF NYACK

Newcomb Reeder stood on GRAYCLOUD's main deck and listened to the sound of rain upriver, hoping it wouldn't hit them for a while yet. They had business to attend to first.

"They're making for the bank on the starboard side," Sir Kelvin said, his right arm pointing out over the bow, his left resting on the big fore gun. He had a large, white handkerchief tied around his face.

Reeder, his outfit black, his face painted bright colors to mask his identity, turned aft and yelled through cupped hands up to the wheelhouse. "Hard starboard! Let's cut her off!"

"Aye, Captain," came the distant reply.

Reeder moved to the rail, watching as they closed the distance between them and the large raft that floated ever nearer the West bank. The raft looked to contain over a hundred people and their possessions. Stragglers they were, late leavers from Nyack. Reeder had already waylaid several such transports, finding them well-laden with booty. Though pirating wasn't an honorable profession, there would be no greater dishonor than returning home empty-handed.

GRAYCLOUD was coming about, sluggishly responding to rudder turns. They were slaves to the current. It was only the ship's design that helped them catch the rafts at all.

"We got her," Kelvin said through his mask. "She'll never make it."

"Gunners on deck!" Reeder called, and his faithful from Watervliet, all in masks, hurried out to man the deck guns on the port side.

The gunners yelled and laughed, and young Reeder couldn't help but think that getting away from Ramon was the best thing any of them ever did. They would burn no trees, commit no heresy. They would live as they had always lived—proudly, in the heritage of his father.

They caught up to the raft with inexorable slowness, everything happening in slow motion as they cut the craft off from a berth on the West bank. Reeder walked to the port rail and looked down at a hundred fearful, upturned faces.

"Good morning, ladies and gentlemen," he called down cheerily. "As you can see, you've come under the bite of our cannon. There is no possibility of escape. We're going to throw lines down to you. If you cooperate, there will be no trouble. I wish no blood on my hands."

The lines were thrown over, seamen jumping overboard to surround the raft and prepare for its unloading.

"We wish only your valuables, any gems you might have, or gold or Old World relics. Your lives and your food and your raft you may keep. You may, in fact, continue downriver at your own pace, there to join the red-haired man if you wish. If you do not cooperate, none of you will survive. The choice is entirely up to you."

Loud, crashing thunder punctuated his words, and the need for haste became a concern for everyone. There was no chance for argument, as the rain moved closer in, threatening to wash them all away.

As the booty was hurriedly lifted by rope up to the main deck, everyone, including the victims, helped with its transfer. All the while, large flocks of birds flapped downriver, trying to escape the conflagration.

And they loaded GRAYCLOUD down, everyone hurrying to shore after. Councilman Reeder, observing his own rules of hospitality, invited the vanquished to share dry space on GRAYCLOUD until the rains abated, an invitation that was cheerfully accepted.

So that day, combatants from both sides shared the common enemy of the rain and had a feast in the bowels of the ship. And when it was over, they were set unharmed back on their raft, a number of the Southerners deciding to stay on to serve Reeder under his freebooter's aegis.

iii

VIPER'S LOWER BILGE HOLD

The single candle Delmar left them did precious little to dispel the dampness and gloom of the makeshift brig deep in the bottom hold of VIPER. The yellow glow reflected on the black stagnant pool beneath the planks Faf had set for them as a makeshift floor, and it caught the drippings from above as small bright diamonds, valuable for a second before plopping into the muck below. The smell of pine tar was nearly overpowering.

"I think it's raining," Faf said, and he walked carefully across a plank to rejoin Jerlynn upon the large pile of lumber where they were resting.

"What difference?" the woman said, her voice devoid of all emotion.

Faf laughed uneasily. "I wouldn't want to drown here."

He hoisted himself up onto the boards, putting a large

arm around her. She sighed, enjoying his closeness, and snuggled into his protection. "We're going to die anyway," she said.

"Shhh," he said, and kissed her forehead. "Don't be foolish. We're just being punished, that's all."

"I fell asleep before," she replied. "I was back in the Forest of Kings, and they were hanging Zenna of Siler. Except it wasn't Zenna of Siler anymore. It was me. And I remembered that day, remembered how she looked at me as they killed her. I think I knew, even then I knew." She began sobbing lightly.

"Dreams are just dreams," Faf said. "You're Ramon's mother, for Ibem's sake. Don't fret about it. You'll see, things will work out."

She looked at him then, knowing that he was trying to keep her spirits up.

"I don't want you to feel guilty about this," she said.

"What do you mean?"

"We betrayed Ramon," she replied. "We both did what we thought was right. I made my own choices as did you. I don't blame you for anything. If we are to . . ."

"Shhh. Don't say it."

"Whatever happens, know that I don't regret a single action." She took his face in her hands and kissed him deeply. "I love you, and I share your fate willingly. Our time together has been too short, but you've given me a lifetime of feelings that I'd never known before."

"Oh, my Lady," he said, his own voice strained. "The coat of the traitor fits us ill, but I, also, regret nothing. Our love has made me a whole person."

They embraced then, lying up on the boards and fiercely clinging to one another. And they lost all sense of the here and now there in the timeless darkness of the creaking hold.

iv

CASTLE ALB'NY

"You can't go now!" Sir Martin said, as Sir Perkins pushed his small skiff off the vine growing steps of the castle and into the water that lay several feet deep in the courtyard. "We need all the help we can get."

"Sorry, Marty," the knight returned. "I've stayed too long already. I'm expected back at the front."

He drifted away, using the long pike to force his way through the water, turning into his work so he wouldn't have to look at the face of his friend.

Martin of Rochester stood on the stairs, watching Perky's departure. Around him, jungle choked what was once the largest defoliated section of N'ork. The outer courtyards were lost, barely discernible from the aged jungle around them. The walls were covered with ivy, the barracks and kennels completely lost in the twisting tangle of Ibem. Vines and shrubs that were threatening the inner courtyard had clogged up the drain, the recent rain leaving the yard under deep water upon which the jungle now floated undaunted in its never-ending attempt at total conquest.

Sir Martin wore a loincloth without shirt, his longsword in his hand dulled by hacking away at an enemy far more dangerous and patient than any he had ever known. The muscles in his arms ached from the strain, and still the vines came.

"You'll not get this castle," he said, and walked down several more steps into the dark waters, pulling and hacking at the vines on the stairs that seemed to grow before his eyes.

Around him, loyal Castle Guard floated on logs or stood waist deep in the muck, hacking the jungle from the mud walls of the castle. But there were precious few left to help. The whores were gone, and with them the vendors and minstrels and gamblers. Most of the remaining Guard were gone, along with the good times. And, for the first time, Sir Martin understood the loneliness of responsibility and the price one pays for station.

His sword rose and fell, his blade clanging upon the stone of the stairs, raising sparks. He had been given a duty, and his place in the world depended upon the discharge of that duty. There was no one to blame, for blame would rest squarely upon his own shoulders. His world, his future were his alone to control or lose—and he knew it.

He tried to walk back up the stairs, but a vine had already tangled around his leg and tripped him, knocking him back into the muck.

"Damn you!" he screamed, hacking into the water to free his leg.

The pressure eased with a jerk, and he was free. Breathing heavily, he crawled up several steps and lay back, his head raised to watch the inch-by-inch siege.

"You'll never take this castle," he said low, then yelled, "Never!"

18

N'ork City—The Tree of Decisions

Alicia had never seen the climbing goats before. Large as Woofers they were, except in place of soft fur and pliant flesh, they were a mass of bristlelike hair and rippling gristle. But they were Genies, altered before common memory, and they had the mind to do exactly what they were called upon to do— climb the stairs of the huge structural trees that made up N'ork City.

Alicia's strategy meeting with the merchants was to take place on the upper levels of one of the large trees: It was called the Tree of Decisions by the inhabitants and, Alicia was told, it was not only the second tallest tree in the water forest, but one of the few unoccupied ones.

Alicia stood slightly in the stirrups, trying to ease the pressure in her lower back as her goat slowly made its way along flight after flight of perpetual steps. Biddy, the Minnie seamstress, sat in front of Alicia, her natural psitronics keeping her in a state of lethargic commune with the goat. Twiddle stayed at the palace for fear the journey would be too strenuous for him.

It seemed as if they had been climbing for hours. It was dark in the stairwell, and the tall candles set on the landing of every flight did little to help the darkness.

"Is it true about the destruction of Kipsie?" Telemay asked from the goat behind.

"Kipsie is no more," Alicia said. "Would you entertain a notion to allow the Lawgivers to resettle here?"

"A difficult question," Telemay returned above the clopping of hoofs on the stone stairs. "It depends upon the wishes of the five families, and upon the degree of authority contemplated by the Lawgivers. We are Ibem-fearing people, but our balance of power is quite delicate."

"The five families?" Alicia asked.

"Five merchant families rule N'ork City in a very loose confederation. King Willow's position is the hub of that five-spoked wheel. They use the King as a clearing house for visitors and disputes, a unifying banner under which the five may interact when necessary."

Alicia turned in the saddle to look at the severe-faced man. He seemed strained and tired, as unhappy with the climb as the Politico.

"I take it the five families haven't always gotten along as well as they do now," she said.

"Our history is a bloody one," Telemay replied, "but we live in a land of plenty and there is enough to go around. The families have learned to appreciate that."

"I perceive you to be an honest man."

He seemed surprised at the pronouncement. "Why so?"

She smiled back at him. "You are unattracted to either my beauty or the riches of the world. Such a man has higher concerns to occupy his mind."

Telemay sighed. "Peace, unfortunately, is my addiction. I am obsessed with the quiescence of things. I think, perhaps, in my distant kinship, there is the same blood that runs through your veins."

"Then my sympathies go with you."

"Thank you. I fear my little world is about to collapse around my ears."

"Quite possibly."

"Ah, finally. We're here."

The stairs terminated in a long, well-lit hallway. The hall was opulently furnished, and occupied by a profusion of young men dressed in wildly varying styles of clothing.

"Bodyguards," Telemay said low, as they dismounted, the goats immediately going to a trough at the stair end of the hall to eat. Biddy reluctantly said goodbye to their conveyance and climbed upon Alicia's shoulders.

"All for me?" Alicia asked. "I don't feel that dangerous."

"Old family charters," Telemay said as he directed her down the hall toward sliding glass doors. "They're allowed ten each when meeting at the Tree of Decisions, and they bring them along by habit. We'll be alone on the balcony."

The young men, who had filled the hall with cigarette smoke and loud talk, hushed to silence as Alicia walked by, their eyes silently dissecting her as she passed. It was something she was used to and would have, in fact, been disappointed with any other reaction.

They stepped out upon the balcony and into the light. The men she had seen at the palace were seated in rocking chairs at a distance from one another. They were dressed much nicer now, though, each in a style reflected by the tastes of the men in the hall.

"Gentlemen," Telemay said. "May I formally introduce Alicia of Alb'ny."

The men all stood politely, and Alicia had the feeling they were taking part in some long prescribed family interaction ritual.

She shook the hand of each of them in turn, having to go to each one, probably another interaction ritual. She remembered them from the previous meeting. G'vanni she went to first, the one who was most interested in her as a woman. He was lean and impeccable in a tight-fitting, one-piece green robe tied to billowy pants at the crotch. His hair was short and black, slicked straight back with oil. He had dark eyes and a thin mustache. His eyes burned with pride when she picked him above the others.

Next was Mister Chang, a small man with pale, nearly yellow skin. He was the oldest of the group, standing quietly in black silk robes and soft slippers. He watched her through heavily lidded eyes, and the long-stemmed pipe with the small bowl that he occasionally drew upon could possibly have been the reason for that.

Schmid was next, and they called him Bruno. He was a large, boisterous man with yellow hair and beard. He wore a rab vest over his bare chest, and his pants were wool.

"Looks and brains," he said loudly when they shook hands. "Bah!" He had been drinking heavily while awaiting her arrival, the proof of it wetting his vest and chest.

Waterson stood quietly with his hands behind his back.

His clothes were quiet and informal, cotton shirt and pants, but he wore a profusion of gold chains around his neck and jewelry upon his hands. He had no left eye, but instead wore a large diamond in the empty socket that caught and sparkled the light whenever he turned just right.

And finally, Sahara. A tall, dark man who seemed withdrawn from the rest of the group. He was dressed in brightly colored cotton robes and sandals and wore his hair in long ringlets. The light of tremendous intelligence shone through the liquid brown of his eyes.

"Are you of Mech blood?" she asked when they shook hands.

"No," he replied, and didn't say anything more.

Alicia walked to the rail and looked out over the city. She had never been so high without her balloon before. All around was the forest of N'ork City, limbless trees growing right out of the waves. There appeared to be hundreds of them, all of varying heights. Her view was totally unobstructed, and could have gone on forever had the cloud cover not hampered it.

A number of boats with large sails of many colors moved in and out of the harbor city, all sailing to faraway lands. The boats were nearly uncountable, so great was the commerce of the forest.

G'vanni was at her elbow, his body pressing imperceptibly against her. She moved slightly, but he was there again. "We have the most beautiful forest in the world," he said. "Don't you agree?"

"I do indeed," she replied, and walked several paces away from him, noticing a tree even larger than the one they stood upon in the distance. "What is that?"

G'vanni followed her, moving up behind and looking over her shoulder. "That is our holy place," he said.

Bruno laughed. "It's holy because it's the biggest," he said, and took a drink from his wine crock. "Our families fought over it for centuries and finally made it holy so we'd leave it alone."

Mister Chang joined them at the rail. "We call it the lonely sister," he said, and his pipe smoke had a sickly sweet odor. "Our legends tell us that it once had a twin of the same size right beside her. "We don't know what happened to the other."

"Chopped down, perhaps," Sahara replied, "by the ax of Ibem."

"Do you wish to chop us down, Lady Alicia?" Mister Chang asked.

"I wish only that such beauty may be preserved," Alicia said, and the low rolling Northern sky thundered, a small flash of lightning darting from a position below them to dance on the waters. She moved farther around the rail, drawn to what appeared from above to be a hole in the ocean, a cavity that dug into the fabric of the water itself. "Whatever is it?"

"It is the Central Forest," Waterson said. "Some simply call it the Pit."

"It's beneath the waters?"

The man with the diamond eye nodded. "The water rose slowly," he said, "over a period of centuries. As it rose, our fathers built a wall around the forest, for it was used as a repository for all the strange and unique variations of animals and man-beasts that have been bred and cross-bred through the ages. The more the waters rose, the taller the wall became until it is as you see it now."

"Wavelength, wavelength!" Biddy squeaked from Alicia's shoulders.

"She wants to know how tall the wall is," Alicia said.

"Well over a hundred feet," Bruno said. "In fact we just finished a new layer of bricks a month ago."

"How much area does that cover?"

"Eight hundred forty acres," G'vanni said proudly. "And we still put the weird animals down there."

"Flip-flop?" Biddy asked, excited for some reason by the existence of the Pit.

"She's asking if anything ever comes out of the Central Forest."

"Never," Sahara said.

She turned from the rail to find G'vanni staring intently at her. The fire that smoldered in his eyes was nearly embarrassing. She felt his desire and all it did was remind her of what she had left behind. Morgan continued to creep into her thoughts whether she wanted him to or not, and it affected her judgment. She couldn't read past her own emotions to get at what was inside the merchants. That's why she had spent so much time admiring the city; she was trying to clear her head.

"My husband arrives here soon," she said, for it was the simplest way to approach the question.

"Why?" Waterson asked.

"To rally the South against Ramon of Alb'ny."

"Gentlemen and Lady," Telemay said. "Let us sit and have some wine together. We'll talk casually."

Alicia nodded, taking a chair beside G'vanni. He poured her wine in a glass crock, and she drank it down, thirsty from her long ride up the stairs. She handed the crock to Biddy but only let her drink a sip.

"Why must you rally the South in our city?" Mister Chang asked. "Could you not fight on a more . . . neutral ground?"

"No," she replied. "Ramon intends to have your city regardless. We will have the best strategic position to defend in N'ork City, so the fight will come here anyway."

"Others have come before you," Sahara said. "We have always found ways to work around or with them."

"Ramon intends to loot your city," Alicia said. "He has a hundred thousand men to back him up."

"That many," Mister Chang said, shaking his head and clucking. He lit his pipe and drew long upon it.

"You have no army," Alicia said. "You are at his mercy."

"We are at the mercy of any army," Waterson said, leaning back with his hands behind his head.

"How have you survived this long without defense?"

The merchants looked at one another, Bruno Schmid answering finally. "The families each have a small force that we use to keep order and protect our holdings. It's always been enough before."

"How do we know that you're telling the truth?" Waterson asked.

Alicia watched G'vanni pour her another crock of wine. He smiled, handing it to her and taking one for himself. "If you didn't know most of this already," Alicia said, "I doubt if I would be up here now."

All the men laughed, nodding to one another. "It's quite true," Bruno said, drinking himself. "We are aware of the situation."

"Am I also to assume that you are ready to work with us?" Alicia asked.

"If certain conditions are met," Waterson said warily. "We must have your absolute promise that you want nothing from our city other than our gratitude and monetary reparations for your losses sustained in our defense. We are a rich people and can pay for ourselves."

"What more could I ask?" Alicia replied, draining her glass, G'vanni hurrying to pour her another. She thought it odd that he would be trying to get her drunk, especially considering alcohol had no effect on her system. She finally decided that he wanted her drunk for personal reasons. "Morgan wishes nothing from you. His kingdom lies far to the North and he will be returning there after the campaign, grateful to you for letting him make use of your city."

"You will swear," Waterson said.

"I swear and pledge to you our fealty," Alicia said. "We exist for your defense and nothing more. I am incapable of breaking a promise, which you also probably know already. So my word is a tree with deep-set roots. May I send word to my husband that he may enter your city in peace?"

"How will you send word?" Sahara asked.

Alicia smiled, pulling Biddy down onto her lap. "My friend is in mental contact with others of her kind in Morgan's army. She will send the word for me."

The merchants all looked at one another, nodding in secret, prearranged ways. Sahara, looking troubled, stood and walked to the rail to look out over his domain.

"We have a deal," Waterson said at last, though not a word had been exchanged among the merchants.

"Good," Alicia said, and bent her head to be face to face with the Minnie. "Polarize Charl. Latch-in Morgan rachet, no time delay. Positive coupling coefficient. All positive. All go!"

The Minnie squealed and closed her eyes, concentrating hard while everyone watched, spellbound. Then she shook her little head, and hugged Alicia's neck.

"It's done," Alicia said. "He'll be here within a day."

"We'll celebrate tonight at the palace," Telemay said, standing. "I must say, this went smoother than I suspected."

"We are fortunate to have Morgan of Alb'ny to look after us," Mister Chang said. "We are in no position to deal."

Alicia rose, Biddy climbing back upon her shoulders. "I think I should be returning to the palace now," she said.

"Would you like to come to my section of the forest?" G'vanni asked. "I could show you how my people live."

"Not just now," Alicia returned. "I would like to get some rest."

"Perhaps another time."

"Undoubtedly."

And they said their goodbyes, Alicia taking one last look at the forest of N'ork City before going out with the King's man. The merchants watched her leave, then shrugged at one another.

"Do you think she suspects?" Bruno said.

"No," Mister Chang returned. "The woman is not as perceptive as we originally thought."

"Perhaps I kept her mind occupied," G'vanni said.

They laughed. "Doesn't matter," Waterson said, rocking his chair back and forth. "Tomorrow we will begin to take care of our Northern . . . problems. And we will start with the woman's bastard husband."

19

Duplicity

Morgan stood on A Deck fore of the wheelhouse, watching the trees of N'ork City rise with the morning. It was a breathtaking sight, a living testimony to the wonderment of the land. Sleek green trees reached to the clouds while the waves crashed against their bases and the boiling tapestry of heaven rumbled majestically to the infinite—dark, throbbing green against the backdrop of turbulent blues and grays.

He stood alone by choice, wanting to savor his moment as the city reached out a grasping hand for him to take. Already he could see people poking their heads from among the branches and waving, a reception of small boats forming an honor line along his route.

He wore his white britches with the high leather boots Grodin had given him so long ago. And he wore a billowy red shirt, one that he thought Alicia might like. He had missed her terribly, and had determined they could straighten out their problems once they were together again.

His problem was one of trust. Not sure of her inbred loyalties, he reacted mostly to his fears of her. It was stupid and he knew it. She was his wife. She loved him. With that knowledge he could overcome any insecurity. He wasn't going to let groundless fears bury his love the way they had done with Grodin.

Below him, the deck was alive with activity, as giants turned the large wheel that operated the propeller the Mechs had engineered. As they lost the Hus current, it would be necessary to power the ship somehow. Behind, the Southerners had tied their rafts and barges together and were being towed by VICTORY toward the promised land.

The rails were jammed with People and humans, all waving and staring in awe at the beautiful tree city. As Morgan watched the giants, Serge caught his attention and waved.

"Just like in the dungeon!" Serge called from the wheel, and it was heartening that they had put their servitude far enough behind them that they could laugh about it.

It was the hope of new beginnings that was dawning with the morning light, the daybreak of possibilities, and the realization that there was no problem too great to be overcome. Morgan had never felt better.

He heard footsteps and turned to see Galen standing beside him, the small, stocky Genie looking up at him with steely eyes.

"Do I interrupt your meditations?" he asked.

Morgan shook his head. "My feelings are too great to keep to myself anyway."

"You cut an imposing figure."

Morgan nodded. "You're a strange one," he said. "I can never tell whose side you're on."

"The implications of this venture are far too great to consider lightly," the Grunt said, his hands resting on his horns. "The only 'side' is my own, for though we intersect on our life paths, all of us are truly alone."

They had reached the beginning of the reception line, the small boats lining the watery path into N'ork City filled with cheering citizens bejeweled with orchids.

"Isn't it glorious?" Morgan said, and they were passing the stone trees on both sides, the people above throwing handfuls of flower petals to float down upon them in poetic imitation of all the good things that rain brings.

Galen looked from one side to the other, then turned his attention to Morgan. "Something is terribly wrong," he said casually.

Alicia stood on the roof of Willow's palace, listening to the distant cheers of the people, knowing that Morgan had entered the city. But something didn't set right. The palace was fixed up, a long tableful of food set upon the roof. Telemay ran around in a fit, making sure the palace staff was properly prepared to deal with visiting royalty. King Willow was even cleaned up and in a suit of gold satin with ruffled blouse. He played badminton with his coterie of young girls and teen-aged boys. But there were no representatives of the five families present. Alicia had been watching diligently for them, but not so much as a small skiff had docked at the palace.

She slapped the rail. Biddy. Just to set her mind at ease, she'd get Biddy to contact Charl or Ratif and make sure everything was all right onboard.

The Minnie had been in their quarters sewing when Alicia had come up to the roof. Crossing the span of concrete, she took the stairs down and hurried to the luxurious suite of rooms that Telemay had given her.

"Biddy!" she called, looking around the finely crafted interior. "I need you! Biddy!"

The Minnie was nowhere to be found. Alicia searched the suite, then the rest of the palace, the King's staff hurrying around to comply with the search. Telemay was nearly frantic when he caught up with Alicia in a hall.

"Where is she?" Alicia demanded.

"My Lady . . ." he sputtered, eyes wide. She could read his eyes, read the dark thoughts that flowed through his brain.

"Where are the families?" she asked. "Why aren't they here?"

His mouth moved, but no words came out. Then, a scream from Alicia's chambers.

They hurried back to the suite to find one of Willow's young girls standing in horror in the middle of the room, her diaphanous blue gown stained with the blood that dripped from her hands.

Alicia took her by the arms. "Where?" she asked.

The girl's eyes seemed lost, her head shaking slowly back and forth.

Alicia shook her violently. "Where?"

"B-Bed," the girl managed, and put her bloody hands to her hair, streaking the blond.

Alicia ran to the bed, falling on her knees. Biddy was there, half pulled out from under by the girl. Her eyes were staring wide. Her head had nearly been taken off by one smooth stroke of a sword.

Alicia stood, her brain a stampede of darting thoughts. "A trap," she said, then louder. "It's a trap!"

"There!" Galen said pointing over the bow. "There it is!"

A large boat, brightly painted, slid silently across their path a hundred yards distant. It was wide and flat, rising to half decks on either end. It must have had two hundred oars in the water. Two large catapults were set on the main deck.

"It can't be," Morgan said, temporarily stunned.

"They'll be much more maneuverable than you," Galen said. "Of course, you've got the numbers."

The flowers stopped falling. Morgan looked up; archers were filling the tree spaces.

"We can't turn around in here," he said, jerking back and forth. "Why, Alicia? Why?"

"It may end here," Galen said.

Morgan looked at him. "Don't take odds on that," he said low, his voice a coiled spring. Then he jumped upon the rail. "Gunners on deck! We're under attack!"

A rain of arrows fell, cutting down many on deck, sending the others scurrying in all directions. Rocks fell with the rain, a hail of death from above, and Morgan thought of the people on the rafts.

He ran A Deck aft, Galen lumbering behind. The giants were still gallantly trying to turn the prop. "Serge!" he called down. "Get your people below! Cut the rafts loose. They only want me!"

Serge waved up, an arrow catching him in the forearm. He

jerked it out, face contorted, and hurried to free the rafts.

"Armor and shields!" Morgan called to the lower deck. "Get protection, but get out here!"

The other boat cut across their path again, much closer this time. As it passed, it let fly a fusillade of arrows and fireballs from the catapults.

"Down!" Morgan called, and the living fell upon the bodies already littering the deck. Fireballs bounced into their midst, and screaming filled the air as the main deck caught fire.

The arrows flew, Morgan swiping at them with wide arcs of his blade while they bounced off Galen, who stood calmly watching the conflagration. Armored troops began appearing on deck carrying guns and ammo for the cannons.

"Work on the fire!" Morgan called.

Men armed with swords began jumping from the buildings onto VICTORY's flat top above Morgan's head. Smoke filled the decks, choking up visibility.

And there were men upon him, suicide troops whose sole duty it was to kill the red-haired man. They swung down from above, attacking Morgan and Galen on the narrow aisle of A Deck.

Morgan swung around a pillar, kicking two of them off the deck. He charged five others, driving them back with a ferocious volley.

"Excellent," Galen said, moving his head an inch to avoid a swinging blade. "Your reflexes are most phenomenal."

"Fire cannons when ready!" Morgan called down, and he thrust hard, his blade going through one red and blue-suited assailant to gut the one behind.

Putting a booted foot on the dead man's chest, he jerked his blade free and decapitated another N'orker, the man's head bouncing into the fray on the main deck.

Deck cannons fired, tearing into the stone trees on either side at point-blank range, sending concrete and citizens flying in every direction.

Galen reached out his hand and deflected a large boulder that would have gotten his head. "Did you practice to move so well, or is it natural with you?"

"Natural," Morgan said, fending off three of them at once. "It's my talent."

"I haven't seen the like of your skill outside of my own kind."

Deck cannon fired again, taking a heavy toll on the stone trees. The rain of arrows and rocks had lessened, Morgan figuring they were nearing the end of the gauntlet. The N'orker boat passed in front of them again—more arrows and fireballs, and the bodies were two deep on the main deck. The other Grunts had wandered out amidst the carnage and were watching the activity around them with amused interest, easily protecting themselves when in danger.

Morgan drove back his assailants, then rushed past Galen, putting the Grunt between him and the N'orkers. He headed fore.

"Where are you going?" Galen asked, watching the N'orkers as their blades slid off his stomach. He put up a hand and they went screaming over the rail.

"To stop that ship!" Morgan called, and dove over the wheelhouse rail to somersault onto the main deck.

He jumped a wall of fire and made it to the big gun that pointed out over the bow. A dead Miner lay clutching one of the large shells. Morgan pried it from him and shoved it into the magazine. He heard Genies behind him putting out the fire.

The big boat passed in front again. This time, Morgan couldn't miss them. Tripping the lever, the gun screamed, exploding on the ship's deck no more than twenty yards distant. One of the catapults toppled, the boat listing badly as its own fireballs set it aflame. It slid behind the trees.

"Hard a'starboard!" Morgan screamed up to the wheelhouse. "Give it everything!"

Four men pulled on the wheel, trying to come around wide. They hit a tree with much crashing of boards, but came out of it half-turned down the avenue behind the other boat.

They recovered and pursued. The lead boat was spewing a tremendous cloud of black smoke into the morning sky. The rowers pulled furiously, but the tiller mate couldn't see to steer through the smoke and ran them head-on into one of the trees.

Morgan charged back toward A Deck. Leaping high, he caught hold of the rail and hoisted himself up near the wheelhouse.

"Bring us alongside!" he screamed through the cutout,

then turned to his men below. "Close quarters! Swords and pistols! Grapple them to us!"

They cheered up at him, their fighting spirit high as the tide of battle shifted in their favor. Black smoke filled the avenue, and VICTORY plunged into its curtain.

Galen was beside him again. "You really are quite good at this," he said. "Do you swim well?"

"Like a fish," Morgan replied, and they were bumping up against the other ship, shearing its starboard oars in half. The red-haired man jumped the rail again, then ran the main deck to dive across to the other boat ahead of his men.

He rolled into a crowd. The fighting was vicious as his own people yelled with the bloodlust. Galen watched the battle with interest, moving casually down the stairs to the main deck rail where the other Grunts joined him.

"He's really good," Longnose said.

"Too good," Galen replied. "I had hoped that he wouldn't have the talent to make this crusade work, but now I'm beginning to change my opinion."

Galen judged the distance separating the two ships, then looked at the rail he leaned upon. Stiffening his hand, he chopped through a section of it, then moved a bit farther along the line to chop out another section. Then he pulled the whole thing off the side of the ship. He laid it like a ladder between the two ships and climbed upon it, walking easily across the span while admiring Morgan's prowess.

The battle was nearly over when he got there. The fight knocked out of them, most of the N'orkers were diving from their burning deck to the churning waters and, presumably, home.

Galen found Morgan engaged with four men in green robes with black hair. He noticed that several different camps of humans seemed to be represented in this ill-conceived venture and wondered what the significance of that was. He easily ducked several thrusting blades and watched as Morgan took an arm of one N'orker and sliced through the jugular of another, the other two jumping ship.

"How many have you killed today?" he asked.

"I take no pleasure from the body count," Morgan returned, and the anger still had him pumped up like a bladder.

"A true warrior," Galen said, shaking his head. "You have my respect and admiration."

Morgan turned, pulling a N'orker off Squan and throwing him into the ocean. "Do I have your support?" he asked.

Galen simply turned and walked away, Morgan forgetting immediately about him for he had something deeper and more painful to occupy his thoughts. This had to be Alicia's doing. She was too good at reading feelings to not know what was going to happen when she led them into the trap.

She was a Politico.

She didn't make mistakes—until she underestimated him.

20

The Iron Hand

The Nyack boulevard was perfect for Count Delmar. He rode the long street upon a gold chariot pulled by six of Troy's pure white Woofers. Thousands of soldiers jammed the street, scratching for booty or just a crock of wine. Behind the chariot stumbled a chain line of severely beaten men, each of whom had a sign printed "DESERTER" strung around his neck. The large crowd was encouraged to jeer at or physically assault the deserters, and, truth be told, the crowd needed very little encouragement.

Interestingly enough, the deserters weren't really deserters. The idea had come to Delmar just before they reached Nyack. He convinced Ramon to let the city stand until they were ready to leave, then he went and rounded up several "deserters" from among the faithful crew, beating them until they were willing to admit to anything. Not that there weren't any real deserters, Delmar simply had neither the time nor the inclination to hunt them down. He consoled himself with the supposition that his little play was a "significant symbolic gesture."

And his point was made.

Lines of men parted for him as he rode proudly, regally behind his Woofers. In the deserter line behind, several of the men had died and were simply dragging the ground.

"Within three days we will have captured N'ork City!" he called to those he passed. "The traitors in our midst have been caught and we are once again strong and whole!"

The traitors he referred to were Faf and Jerlynn, and Delmar found it exceedingly easy to blame them for all the ills that had befallen the expedition. Whether the problem be fish or fowl, deserter or shaman, Dixon Faf and Jerlynn Delaga got the blame. And why not? Who deserved it more?

"In three days we'll be rich!" he called to the crowds. "What will you do with your wealth? Think of all the pink, chubby flesh awaiting you in the Jewel of the East!"

He passed a group of Physicians in hides and feathers strolling the boulevard and talking. He pointed to them as he rode by. "Disperse!" he called. "There will be no fraternization among the Physicians until further notice."

Unstrung bolts of brightly colored material came floating down from one of the treehouses, falling on the crowds, who hacked them up in pieces to take back as souvenirs.

"You don't control us!" one of the Physicians called back at him. "We can talk if we so choose."

Angry beyond words, Delmar pulled up his mounts, jumping from the chariot. Without further talk, he drew his longsword and slew the man on the spot, much to the amusement of the crowds, who didn't care for Physicians anyway.

"He's forbidden meetings among the Physicians," the Green Woman said. She stood naked, washing herself at the large basin in Ramon's cabin. She turned to face him full, soapsuds greasing her body slick.

"He has my full authority to do as he feels best," Ramon said. He refused to look at her, refused to fall into the swirling vortex at the peak of his resolve.

"How can we help you with the war effort if we can't meet?" she asked, keeping her voice soft, trying to charm him where grit wouldn't work. She read conflicting emotions within him, and that frightened her.

"We fight in a matter of days," he replied. "There is nothing more the Physicians can do for us. They are most needed with their individual rulers."

She rinsed with a sponge and walked to the bunk where he lay, facing the wall. Scooting his leg aside, she sat beside him, putting a hand casually on his thigh. "Do you use us up, then discard us?"

"Think what you will," he said, pushing her hand away lest it creep to the erection that was pushing insistently against his britches.

"Why won't you let me touch you?"

He flared around to her, unfair anger keeping his resolve firm. "Because I don't want you to touch me! Do I need a reason?"

"I'm your wife!" she said loudly. "Have you forgotten?"

"Wife!" he laughed out the word. "Think you that Pack is qualified to perform marriage ceremonies? Our marriage was a joke, a silly mockery designed to pass the time, nothing more."

She stood up, her eyes narrowing. "What are you saying?"

He met her eyes, and she could see the 'dorphined haze upon them and knew that he was getting his drugs from somewhere else. "I'm saying that what happened upon the foredeck of this ship was no marriage ceremony. I'm saying that you're my whore and nothing else, and that I tire even of that!"

He turned from her, his insides heaving. His arms longed to hold her, his loins pistoned with his need. But he couldn't give in. He couldn't lose all just to try and hold onto that which couldn't be held. His addiction for her was addiction for a dream. She was transparent, ethereal. She would melt under his embrace, leaving him only the poverty of his own spirit.

"How can you say that to me?" she said in a tiny voice. "I love you more than life itself."

The ache was in the pit of his stomach, in the solar plexus where all the neural ganglia met. "You love pain," he said, nearly hissing the words. "And I will be quit of pain."

"Ramon . . ."

"Be silent!" He screamed the words, tightening into a ball and covering his ears with his hands. He hummed inside his head, filled his brain with the sound of his own voice so he could listen to no others. He felt a hand touch him once, but he was numb from the grief and the drugs, and managed to jerk away from it without the message traveling all the way to his heart. When he finally turned around a long time later, she was gone.

The Green Woman stood upon the main deck and watched as the body of Lupus Loam was carried down the street by a cadre of soldiers, the Physicians fearful to be around even the dead body of one of their own.

She watched alone, for no one dared approach her, so well Delmar had done his job. She had decisions to make if she were to save her life, the fate of Lupus not being one she wished to share.

That big, shiny applegenic of control had been so close, just within reach; but it seemed she'd not be plucking it this time. She felt her control slipping away as she felt the change in Ramon's feelings.

Count Delmar, dragging a line of dead soldiers, made his way back to the ship. He stopped on the dock and looked up. There by the rail was the Green Woman. He smiled to think that she had no power over him.

Ramon had done well resisting her to this point, but he trusted not the vagaries of the flesh. Perhaps he should take the matter of the Green Woman upon himself while favor still smiled upon him. It was a risk of acceptable proportions.

He felt eyes on him and looked to his left to see a swarthy old man whom he didn't recognize smiling at the corpses lining the ground behind. He caught the man's eyes and saw a look of cold humor and calculation that made him shiver. Shaking it off, he turned the chariot to make one more pass down the boulevard while the bodies were still recognizable.

21

King Willow's Palace

VICTORY limped to the dock of Willow's palace under Telemay's guidance. The brave and grief stricken man had gone out into the thick of battle and presented himself to Morgan after the defeat of the families' barge. With N'ork City already on its back, diplomacy would have to be the order of the day.

The Southerners' rafts and barges closed ranks and poled their way behind, using the stone trees to push off of.

Morgan stood on deck as the bodies of his fallen were stacked and consecrated in the manner of the Genie. The surrounding trees were filled with people whose faces were as stony as the concrete bark. They were frightened faces of people unused to the cadence of the war drum, and they watched their city fill to overflow with thousands upon thousands of war-torn refugees, rugged frontier people who could take whatever they chose whenever they wanted.

At that exact moment, Morgan was unconcerned with the citizens of N'ork. Whatever fate awaited them was well deserved; whatever evil visited them was called upon by the darkness of their own souls.

Many of his own people were dead or near dead. His initial count showed nearly five hundred lost, including ancient Diitmar D'an from Nyack and his loyal beast-man, Melon of the long snout. VICTORY was taking a great deal of water from where she had banged up against the trees while giving chase to the barge, and was listing badly to port.

Jella walked up beside him as he stood by the foredeck gun watching the palace loom closer. "Where will we burn the bodies?" he asked.

"Wherever the N'orkers here burn them," Morgan answered, his brain still shrouded by the fog of anger.

"I've heard tales that they prefer watery graves in N'ork City."

"We'll work it out," Morgan said. "How many Mechs among the dead?"

Jella scratched his head. "That's a funny thing," he said. "I don't think I saw any."

"I thought not," Morgan said. "I saw none in the fighting."

"Why so?"

"That's what I'd like to know."

Jella turned him around so they could be eye to eye. "How did all this happen?"

"We were played for the fool," Morgan said bitterly. "And now we will see who the fool really is."

"I think maybe these water-dwellers should be taught a lesson in proper manners," Jella said, comfortable now in anger. "Perhaps the taste of their own blood wouldn't set so well on their tongues."

"They want an occupation army, that's what they shall have."

"And now that they've lost the battle, they think to parlay. My children are on this boat and would have gone down with it."

Morgan's hands involuntarily balled into fists. "They have already spoken—loudly." He turned back to face the palace.

Telemay, in his best red robes, moved before them in a small boat rowed by his honor guard. He slid into the dock first, then got out and helped direct the warship into the lock. VICTORY creaked in, her tilt at twenty degrees, smoke still curling from small, smoldering fires. Within minutes, all the lanes around the palace were filled with rafts and barges, a waterway paved in flesh.

"Will you come down and meet with us?" Telemay called from the dock. "There is much to be discussed."

"It seems our discussion has already taken place," Morgan called back.

"Please!" the old man said. "Despite what happened, there are many among us who wish to help you in any way we can."

"We will need to bivouac our troops," Morgan said. "This

area should do nicely. Evacuate your people from all the surrounding trees. I am taking them over."

Telemay stared up for a moment, then turned to one of his
people. "See to it," he said.

"But your grace," the man said, "the families own the
surrounding buildings. We don't have the authority . . ."

"Do it," Telemay repeated, then called up to Morgan.
"You have your trees."

Notern of Fishkill moved across the deck to Morgan with
old Penrad hurrying to catch him from behind.

"We're going to lose the ship," he said. "We're gashed in
four different places down there with no way to fix what's broken."

"How long?" Morgan asked.

The man brushed wild hair from his face. "We might stay
afloat for a day, probably less."

"Water threatens Ibem," Penrad said. "It creeps toward
the hold."

Morgan ignored him. "What of the magazine?"

"We must act soon," Notern said.

"All right," Morgan returned. "I want a contingent from
each raft. Ten men or Genies should do. They are to travel to
the closest trees and move their citizens into them as quickly
as possible then get back here and unload the ship as follows:
the magazine first, ammo and weapons stores, then Nebo's lab
and equipment. Then dismantle the deck guns and put them
on different rafts—we'll mount them atop these trees."

"What about Ibem?" Penrad said loudly. "Surely you
meant for Ibem to be first."

"After everything else is done," Morgan said, "we'll concern ourselves with the machine, not before."

"This is unheard of!" Penrad said. "The people will never
stand for it." He looked at Notern. "Prelate. You will certainly
take care of God first."

"Will God protect our ammunition, Your Eminence?"
Notern asked, and stalked away.

The old man turned, lips sputtering, to Jella, who turned
away, having already consigned Ibem to the ashes of his wife's
pyre.

"You cannot abandon God in your hour of need," Penrad
said to Morgan.

Morgan stared at him with hate-filled eyes. "Yours is the

God of Ramon and the N'ork Citians," he said. "Ibem is not my God."

The old man's face hardened like drought ground. "If you think you're going to run over me without a fight," he said, index finger wagging in Morgan's face, "you're dead wrong. I am not without power, even among your own."

"Don't threaten me, old man," Morgan warned, pushing Penrad's hand away. "You'll be preaching your sermons from the floor of Father Hus."

"You don't scare me, heathen. Our faith has been a rock for a thousand years. You cannot kill it in a day."

Morgan stared at him, trying to wish him away. But it didn't work. He leaned over the rail and called to Telemay, "I'm coming down!"

Telemay waved back in response.

"Lower the gangway!" Jella called amidships, and several giants stopped tending to their wounded to lower the plank.

Morgan brushed past Penrad and moved along the deck, Jella hurrying to catch up. "I want to see Nebo as soon as he's finished supervising the unloading of his equipment."

"Aye."

Morgan pointed over the side. "They have a pulley for unloading boats," he said. "See if we can use it to hoist the dead up to the roof of the palace."

"The roof?" Jella said.

"We'll build our pyre there. If this is their most honored place, then I want my dead offered up from here."

"Aye, sir," Jella said, and it was to his discredit that he secretly relished the pain of those around him, for it made his own pain seem less by comparison. He moved to the hold in search of the Mech.

Morgan strode down the gangway alone, his ensanguined blade still held tightly. He adamantly refused any offers of a retinue, since he wanted to show the N'orkers he had no fear of them.

Telemay was waiting for him on the swaying wooden dock. The man looked apologetic but not broken. He met Morgan's gaze fiercely, as an equal, and the Governor found himself satisfied with the liaison before an exchange had been made between them.

"We have much to discuss," the old man said. "There is more at work here then you know. I only ask you hear me out before judging our people too harshly."

"I came down to talk," Morgan said. "And talk we will, but I make no promises. Are you the ruler of this place?"

"No," Telemay said hollowly.

"Then I will speak with him."

The old man sighed, knowing better than to try and dissuade this wild man before the man had seen Willow. "As you wish," he said.

"As I wish," Morgan repeated, and started down the lapping dock. And there, by the entry of the palace, stood Alicia, and he was struck by a wave of conflicting emotions. She looked fit, and he realized he was hoping that she had been beaten or killed rather than have betrayed him. He was happy and sorrowful that she should be standing thus, and he had no idea of which emotion was the most important.

"I'm sorry," she said when he stopped before her.

"Tell that to our dead," Morgan said, pointing back to the ship. The anger was bubbling up and he did nothing to stem it. "Did you think me so easily defeated?"

She stiffened, eyes widening, mouth tightening. She could feel his mistrust of her, huge and overpowering. "Take care when you begin to throw the accusations," she said. "My loyalty needs no defense."

"No defense!" He grabbed her arms tightly. "You think me so stupid that I didn't know what you were doing? You don't like the way I run things, that's plain enough . . ."

"Let go of me!" she screamed, losing her composure and jerking in his grasp.

He tightened his hold. "You'll hear me, bitch, for I've already tasted your lesson." He met her eyes, the curtains to both their souls pulled tightly closed. "Your plan was simple enough. Sell me out, using my head to barter your position, then run things the way you want."

Telemay had moved toward them, but stopped when he heard the angry exchange. Penrad saw the King's man from the deck and hurried down the gangway to catch him.

"If you believe that," she said, finally freeing herself, "I want you to draw your sword and kill me right here, right now."

"I wouldn't dull my blade on you," he said, turning from her, for he truly could not have done her harm.

She walked around to get in front of him. "Well, let me tell you something. If I wanted to take away your precious command, I wouldn't need any cheap tricks to do it. I could just talk you into the ground. It wouldn't even take long."

He brought his fist up, then let it drop to his side. "I'll hear your story, but it had best be the story of all time."

Now it was she who turned from him. "Go to hell," she said in her diplomat's casual voice. "I'll not defend myself to the likes of you."

"Because there's no defense against treachery."

"As you will . . . Governor," she said. "I've a mind to let you try life on your own anyway. Best we part ways now so I don't get dragged down with you."

Penrad moved up next to Telemay. "You, sir, appear to be of some authority here."

"Yes . . . yes," Telemay said, wishing the man would be quiet so he could catch the gist of Morgan's discussion.

"You think I'd allow you around me after all you've done?" Morgan told her. "You're already the past, but you will tell me who was behind this little ambush before you go. Was it King Willow?"

Alicia merely stared at him, too proud to defend herself.

"No!" Telemay said, moving away from Penrad to join Morgan. "It wasn't the King. Can't we discuss this somewhere more private?"

"Does another trap await me?" Morgan asked him.

"Oh, heavens no," Telemay said. "Please, come up to the King's chambers. I'm sure we can work this out."

"All right," Morgan said. "I'll go with you." He pointed at Alicia. "But she doesn't come. That woman no longer represents the Governor of Alb'ny. She is to be treated as a nonperson by all who deal with me."

He walked off, ignoring Alicia. Telemay shared a look with the woman, whose face remained calm and placid despite the knifeblade of sorrow that was plunged deep into her abdomen. She nodded slightly, and Telemay hurried after Morgan, Penrad hobbling behind.

"Who attacked me?" Morgan asked as he climbed the dark stairs, his voice echoing hollowly through the stairwell.

"It was the families," Telemay said, "the merchant families that rule N'ork City."

"I am Lawgiver Penrad," the old man said, "from Kipsie."

"I am Telemay," the liaison said. "I am pleased to make your acquaintance."

"The God who made the heavens and the Earth resides within yonder ship," Penrad said. "You will make arrangements for a suitable temple in which to house Him."

"I was also fooled by the families," Telemay said to Morgan. "No one in the palace knew."

"Why did they do it?" Morgan asked.

"I believe they think your war to be personal in nature. If they killed you, they thought Ramon could then be placated."

Penrad tugged upon Telemay's satin robes. "Ibem will now triumphantly enter N'ork City and install himself in a large temple here."

"Don't know if we have any free temples at the moment," Telemay said.

"This place here would be appropriate," Penrad said. "Yes, I think we will move in here."

"This is the royal palace, Your Eminence," Telemay said.

"Splendid," Penrad said. "I'll see to the unpacking."

"I wouldn't do that . . . quite yet," Telemay said. "The suggestion will have to be . . . voted upon. But don't worry, you'll be hearing from us very soon."

"I will not be put off," Penrad said. "If I have to go personally to every tree in this forest and rouse the citizens against you, I'll do it. You cannot deny me on this, or so help me God, you'll have a civil war on your hands along with everything else. Do I make myself clear?"

Telemay stopped walking on the second landing while Morgan continued upward. He turned to look at the old man with the cold eyes. "That's the way of it then?" he asked.

"It is," Penrad said.

The liaison nodded slowly. "The palace is at your disposal," he said. "Take whatever you need."

"Splendid," Penrad said again, his mouth wrinkling into a smile. "I think an exterior room for me, with a view. Ibem shall have the entire first floor." He wandered off to inspect the building.

Morgan made the roof, walking immediately to the end of

the tree to look at the dock. VICTORY, tilted even more to port, was nearly as tall as the building. Jella had gotten hold of a Mech, and was using him to crank the mechanical pulley around to the main deck. Bodies were being loaded onto skiffs, ready to be hauled to the roof.

A whole group of young people was playing croquet on a stretch of ground on the roof. It was the perfect spot for the pyre.

"Come on over here!" he called to them.

The game stopped, everyone freezing to stare at the stranger. No one moved.

"The families used every available bit of manpower to attack you," Telemay said, joining Morgan on the roof. "There will be no more threats to your people."

"I said come over here!" Morgan called.

A youngster stalked out of the group and walked toward Morgan with his hands on his hips. He wore a tight gold satin suit with white stockings. He looked trussed up for baking in his frilly blouse. "You have no right to order these people around," he said. "Stop it before I have you arrested."

"Your Grace," Telemay said. "This is Morgan of Alb'ny."

"I don't care if he's Mr. Squirrel from the tree house," Willow said. "He will do as I say."

Morgan looked at Telemay. "This is your King?"

"Excuse him, he's very young."

"I think I'm beginning to understand the situation," Morgan said, and turned to the boy. "Son. Best get your friends over here before I embarrass you in front of them."

"Get off this roof right now or I will thrash you severely!" the boy said, and punched Morgan in the stomach.

Without a word, Morgan lifted King Willow high over his head and carried him to the end of the building, throwing him off to plunge three stories to the water below. "Now come on over here," he said quietly to the others, who hurried to oblige him.

The first pallet of bodies was swinging a graceful arc from boat to stone tree. Morgan had Willow's friends help unload the bodies and drag them to the playing field.

"I will speak with these families," Morgan said while directing the activities of the children. "Arrange it, and tell them I won't do them any harm for now. What is the food situation here? Do you store any quantities?"

"No," Telemay said, recoiling from the sight of a pallet-load of arms. Willow's friends were sobbing and gagging, the young girls' pretty bright robes covered with gore. "We fish. We grow fruit on our trees. We barter with the ships that come in from far away. There's never been any need to live but day to day."

"There is no army besides what I faced today?"

"No army."

"What about weapons stores? What kind and how much?"

The old man shrugged. "I'm not privvy to that sort of information," he said. "Each individual family jealously guards such knowledge."

"Your citizens are in charge of getting food for my army," Morgan said, moving slightly so the skiff could swing past him, back to the ship. "I want it understood. This city is now under my control, and I will defend it as I feel best. There is no longer any authority here save martial law, no opinions save mine."

"Your wife promised you'd leave us in peace," Telemay said, "after defeating Ramon."

"My wife promised me it was safe to enter your city," Morgan returned, and walked toward the King's quarters, anxious to check out his new home.

He strode through the big doors. The place was marble, double thick to stand against the storms, with sculpted pillars and stained-glass windows. There was a pool and a banquet hall complete with lounges and cushions. It was even comfortable up there with a good sea breeze pushing salty air through the double tiers of tall, open windows.

He moved into the large bedroom and threw himself on the big bed, sinking to almost disappear in duck feathered mattress. Glancing around, he thought about security. He had never needed protection before, but now things were different. With all the windows, the palace would be a difficult building to defend unless they simply kept people off the roof entirely.

"You sent for me?" came a voice from the doorway.

Morgan sat up to see Nebo standing before him. He rolled to the edge of the bed and stood. "I didn't see you in the battle today," Morgan said.

"I really must return to the ship," Nebo answered. "We're in danger of losing the lab."

"Where were you and your people?"

"We didn't come up for the battle," Nebo replied.

"Just like that," Morgan said. "You didn't come up for the battle."

"That's right."

"Why?"

The Mech shrugged. "It wasn't opportune."

"What's that supposed to mean? We desperately needed your light beams and microwaves."

Nebo cupped his hands together with a clang. "We were involved in experimentation which we felt was of greater importance than what was going on outside."

"What experimentation?"

"It would be beyond your understanding."

Morgan walked to him, circling slowly. "Perhaps you're right. Because right now my understanding extends no further than the fact that five hundred of the People died while you hid down in your lab."

"You know my allegiance is not yours alone."

"Ah, I've been waiting for this. The Great God Science calls and Nebo must obey." Morgan rounded the man, then stood face to face with him. "It won't work anymore," he said. "You will be mine until the end of the campaign—then you can bloody well do whatever you want."

"You'll have to explain that."

"Certainly. There will be no more experimentation of any kind. The Mechs will become engaged in trying to manufacture more rifles and ammunition. Whatever experimental weapons you have, bring them up to specs so we can use them. If you can't, abandon them."

"Is that all?"

"No. From now on, my representatives will always be present while Mechs work, just so we don't have any more problems like what happened today."

Nebo just stared, his face betraying no emotion. The two, once so close, were as distant as the stretches of the Great Sea. Morgan wanted to reach out to him, to remind him of why they were there, but it couldn't be done. Nebo existed in some other place right now that couldn't be reached from where Morgan stood.

"Is that all?" the Mech asked again.

Morgan put an arm on his shoulder. "I watched those chil-

dren out there today on the roof," he said. "They're so . . .
innocent. We were that way not long ago. What's happened?
What's happened to us?"

"Life is a growing process," Nebo said.

"What I'm doing isn't growing," Morgan said, and rubbed
a hand across his face. He stared at Nebo a moment before
speaking again. "You'd never betray me, would you?"

"I'd never betray you," the Mech said, but refused to
meet Morgan's eyes.

Morgan, despite Nebo's assurance, felt no better. Something was slipping away from him and he not only couldn't hold
it, but wasn't even sure what he was losing. "Help with the
unloading," he said.

Nebo turned without another word and walked out. Morgan was just a little late with his ultimatum, for he had just
taken steps, with the help of his Mechs, to insure himself
safety and tranquility while working on his energy liberation.
As he walked past the makeshift funeral pyre, he thought what
a good thing it was that not all Mechs were of Pure Blood, for
the ones with human taint were better able to think ahead, to
plan ahead.

And now, everything was arranged.

22

The Bowels of Viper

Ramon sat in the soft candlelight of the windowless room. He
had fixed up part of the storage hold to accommodate Ona and
the child, and had done an extra nice job of it. If he were going
to construct a gilded cage, he could do it as well as the next
person.

He had found paint for the walls in Nyack, along with

artwork: the peculiar-colored mud renderings of the region.
Some curtains added color and suggested windows that
weren't really behind them. The table and chairs were polished wood. The bed was of brass with three quarter posts
gleaming in the light.

Ona sat on a rocking chair beside the bed with Ty'Jorman
(how he hated that name), her eyes playing cat-and-mouse
games with the ex-Governor. For once in his life, Ramon had
seen to everything. The stateroom he had made was courtly
enough to turn Ona's head, for though he knew her to be his
prisoner, she need never know—a prisoner by choice and
willingness—the easiest to confine. While the woman contained herself from within, Ramon made her secure without.
Attempting to reach Ona would be a most difficult passage indeed. He had fully a hundred men per twelve-hour shift whose
only job was to see that no one reached Ona to spirit her or the
baby away. That, coupled with the fact that there was only one
way in or out, made Ramon feel that he had finally taken steps
to rid himself of the farmer once and for all.

"How will you get him here?" she asked, her face waxed
soft by contentment.

"You will see for yourself momentarily," he replied and
drank from the gold cup before him. He had tarried here long,
the hidden stateroom like a secret library where he could remove himself from his troubles. He felt good here, strong
again. "Is everything to your satisfaction?"

"You've been more than kind."

"I will send you down a woman servant later," he said, and
drank again. "She will see to you properly."

She blushed slightly, lowering her eyes. "I've never been
treated so well before."

"You've never been my *guest* before."

There was a light tapping on the wooden door. Ramon,
who had his back to the door, said, "Come," without even
turning to see who entered. "Come sit at table with me."

Ona watched Redrick of Firetree enter, with Harrison the
Truthteller, just behind. They immediately sat at Ramon's right
and left hand.

Ramon nodded to them each in turn, smiling at Redrick's
glances at Ona and his puzzlement at her treatment. The man's
hand was gone because of her, and most likely, his mind. He,
at least, wore the mantle of insanity most graciously—his mad

skull-like face and leering eyes, his thin skeletal body like a praying mantis. He was never still. He was forever looking, looking for something that wasn't there to see. Ramon would be happy to get rid of him again.

"Gentlemen," he said. "Have a drink."

He shoved crocks from the center of the table toward each of them.

"I can't drink," Harrison said. "It alters my perception."

Ramon nodded and poured for Redrick instead.

"Funny that we're all here," he said to the man from Firetree. "A lot of what is today germinated within us a long time ago."

Redrick looked at the woman again, and this time he stared, his hatred unconcealable. "Why don't you kill her and the little bastard?" he asked, quite concerned.

"Because, my dear fellow, I'm going to kill the farmer instead." Ramon's eyes twinkled. How he loved this part. "And you, trusted friend, are going to help me."

"Hmmp," Redrick grunted and tilted his cup back full. He drained the wine, then slammed the crock loudly on the table. "Nothing more I can do now."

Ramon refilled his glass. "You underestimate yourself," he said. "There is much you can do—everything, in fact."

Redrick drank again, but his fire was gone. He narrowed his eyes and stared at Ramon. "How so?"

Ramon sat back and folded his hands over his stomach. He kept his eyes on the madman. "My sources tell me Morgan occupies N'ork City," he said. "Tomorrow, with the morning light, you and the Truthteller are going to enter the city under the white flag and find him."

"Morgan!" Redrick said. "They'll kill me!"

Ramon put a hand on his shoulder. "But you will have died for your Governor. Aren't you prepared for that?"

"Of course, my Lord, but . . ."

"Good," Ramon said. "Then it's settled. I have written a message for you to give to the red-haired man. Harrison will be there to report the truth of the meeting to me, and its outcome. Your return passage will be under Morgan's guidance."

"Will there be anything about me in the message?" Redrick asked, his eyes fearful. "Anything to . . . protect me?"

"Of course," Ramon said. "I'll want you back here in one piece . . . and Harrison, too. If you have the opportunity while you're there, snoop around a bit. See what there is to see."

Ramon patted the man on the back. "You're my best man," he said. "Take care of yourself. Now you'd better go get ready. Someone will come to you with instructions and the note."

Redrick stood shakily. So soon back to the fray; he could hardly stand it. He walked in a daze to the door.

"Oh, and Redrick," Ramon said, holding up a finger. "The Truthteller is important to the mission. You are to protect his life as if it were your own."

Redrick nodded, staring in confusion at the boy with the girl's face who smiled back at him. He moved once again to the door.

"Redrick," Ramon said. "Don't come back without him."

The Green Woman stood leaning against the wooden viper that was Ramon's masthead. She stared out at the lines of campfire that dotted the shore. South of Nyack they were, at anchor, awaiting she knew not what. N'ork City was in striking distance, but still they lay at anchor.

Ramon was ready for war, mentally ready, she could tell. There was every indication that he would be successful, too. Unfortunately, she had come to accept the fact that he would be successful without her.

The campfires sparkled up and down the uninhabited beach like dew drops on maple leaves—or like snake venom on white fangs. Most of the soldiers preferred the beach at night to the confinement of the ship, which may have said more for the control of Nature than any of them would care to admit.

Ramon, for his part, never left the safety net of the ship now. An environment he could control, the ship had turned itself into an instrument of protection for the Governor—a defensive womb of wood and iron. He even protected himself from her.

She leaned against the viperwood, its surface solid and reassuring, and thought about what might have been. What had she done wrong? Wasn't it right, if one was to accept the horror of war as a bedmate, to make love to it fully and completely? She had done no more than make love to the horror the way she had made love to Ramon. In the totality of the doing one appreciates the essence of the idea—that's purity. Humans, she reflected, were an incomplete lot, satisfied with less than complete emotions. Then she thought of Alicia, playing the same game on the other side, and wondered if her methods were any more successful.

"I wonder if your blood is as green as your skin?" came a voice from behind.

She turned slowly to see the burly unknown figure who stood before her, a faceless hulk in the dark night. "So, you've come," she said calmly.

The foredeck was vacant, save for the Green Woman and her assailant. He had her trapped between the masthead and the rail. He drew a short sword from his scabbard and took a slow step toward her.

She recognized lust and played upon it. "You could love me instead of kill me, you know," she said.

He came closer, impossible to get around in any direction. The rail was against her back, but she'd have to turn and climb. He was too close. "A right tempting proposition," the dark, gruff voice replied. "But if I loved you, they'd kill me, and it ain't worth that."

"Love me and let me go overboard."

"He wants to see the body."

"Who?"

"No more questions."

He came in close, his smell rancid, his breath sour with wine. He was close enough now. Her hand closed on the powder she carried in the folds of her gown. When he rose up to strike, she held it, palm out, and blew it into his face.

The man gasped, his hand going to his throat. The sword clattered to the deck as he backed up, scrabbling at his neck with both hands, as the silica dust clogged his lungs and breathing passages.

He fell to the deck, flopping like a grounded fish for a moment before finally heaving one last time and lying still.

The Green Woman looked around, making sure the man had no back-up. Then she picked up the short sword and immediately climbed the rail.

It was time to move on.

Ramon watched Ona as she put the sleeping baby in the small crib that Ramon had had constructed for him. Motherhood had done wonders for her. She had filled out some and looked appealing. No less appealing was the role she played in his imagination.

"What was living with him like?" he asked.

She looked at Ramon for a moment, then walked away from the crib to sit on the brass bed. "Like living with an animal," she returned. "He worked on pure instinct. It was all that motivated him."

"Did he ever speak of me?"

"Constantly."

Ramon smiled. It made him feel good that he was never far from the farmer's thoughts. He stood up from table, feeling the effects of the wine and the 'dorphins he had taken earlier. Walking to the bed, he sat beside her, the natural give of the mattress sliding their bodies together. The tension was electric as lightning. They both felt it.

"Did you make love with him often?"

"Quite often at first," she said, resting a hand on his thigh. "Later, not at all."

He placed his hand over hers. "Did you enjoy it with him?"

She looked in his eyes and lived the reality that she chose to live at that moment. "Occasionally," she said.

He slid her hand to his crotch, pressing it against the ever-growing erection. His free hand went to her face, her breasts. She tilted her head back, moaning softly.

"Could he bring you great pleasure?" he asked huskily.

"Not like you, my Lord," she groaned, going to her back on the bed.

He slid out of his britches and lay atop her, pushing himself insistently against her still-clothed loins while she cried softly, like a child. And as he took her clothes off, he reflected that it had been a long time since love hadn't been a vicious game for him. His heights of passion with the Green Woman had their price, and as he slid between Ona's legs, it was a soothing balm for his wounded heart.

Little Ty'Jorman lay in his crib, hearing without understanding the animal noises that came to him from nearby. His brain was white with fire and longing, and he saw a big room with tall white pillars where his longing ended.

Compelled to movement, he pulled himself up and scurried over the edge of the crib, his vision in complete control of his young body. He slid down the legs of the thing and hit the floor on all fours.

Beside him, two bodies pounded up and down on the large bed. He crawled under the bed, the mattress forming a bulging roof above his head. Feeling the direction, he came out the other side, barely connected to the world in which he moved. He stood on tiny legs and made his way across the floor, crawling under the table and chairs that blocked his movement to the door.

He finally reached the door, his brain afire. He had to keep moving, to go on. The door was closed, the knob out of reach, its turning too complex for his ability anyway. Little fingers began to pry, pulling at the door crack in a futile effort at escape.

He pulled and pulled until finally, exhausted, sleep overtook him again there on the floor. Later, that's where Ona and Ramon found him, eyes rolled back, little fingers torn and bloody.

23

Arming the Stone Forest

Morgan leaned over the roof of the tall, long tree and watched the cannon swaying on the pulley ropes a hundred feet below.

"Take it easy," he said, moving his upraised hand up and ever up as the team of Genies strained upon the thick ropes that hoisted the heavy barrel up the thirty exposed stories of the building. "Easy . . . don't bang the tree."

They used a series of pulleys upon each high building, taking the guns up by degrees, transferring them from rig to rig. Wheeled carriages, called mules, had been built for each gun, so they could be moved around the roof to wherever the action was.

A squad of riflemen prepared firing stations for themselves up near the placement. Each of them would be instructed in the operation of the cannon in case of emergency. There would be forty such stations throughout N'ork City to correspond with the guns on the ship. These would be the main batteries of Morgan's defense, each gun tree a command post housing rafters and infantry and gunners, all under a post commander who was answerable to a block general who was answerable to Morgan. The interior staircase of the tree was for the pack goats, who carried ammo boxes and shells for the big guns continually up the stairs.

Galen stood beside Morgan, watching the man who was watching the cannon. "You cannot ignore the positive aspects of selective breeding," the Grunt said. "It enables a species to be brought to its creative peak."

"You don't know that," Morgan replied, just flicking his eyes in Galen's direction. "Easy . . . easy. You can't say you've found the perfect mix until you've tried everything."

"You're speaking as the sophists, who say that you cannot make assertions of fact about anything until you've seen all examples of that thing," the Grunt said. "My friend, from the dawn of time selective breeding has improved the quality of the line. It's an undeniable fact."

The gun reached the top of the building, Morgan and the Grunt swinging it over the edge of the roof. "Slide the mule over here," Morgan said, and two Miners wheeled the sturdy wooden placement under the gun. "Okay, down gently."

The giants let out the pulley rope an inch at a time, Morgan guiding the gun down by easy pressure until it rested in the mule. It needed only to be bolted down.

"Good work!" Morgan smiled at the Genies. "Get the pulleys down and move your team to the next tree on your list."

The defensive preparations were coming along well, despite the problems encountered. Morgan's biggest boost was the fact that Ramon had not yet attacked, giving him time to set up. For some unknown reason, his brother lay at anchor not far to the North.

"You know," he said to Galen, "there's something that you don't seem to understand about my feelings."

"Which is?"

Morgan bent to the towel that he had left on the ground, wiping the sweat from his face and bare chest. "You say selective breeding improves the line, correct?"

Galen nodded suspiciously, never enjoying short lifers' attempts at intellectual conversation.

"What do you mean by improve?"

"I don't follow you."

Morgan tossed the towel back on the ground. "To improve something is to make it better. What's been better about our lives because of selective breeding?"

"One must only look at the alternative to understand that."

"And I suppose you mean by 'alternative' that unselective cultures are intellectually inferior by their very nature?"

Galen rubbed his horns lightly. "Inferior in every way. I've seen your Schnecks."

"All right," Morgan said. "Now suppose I accept your definition. Suppose I say, yes, you're right and mixed breeding is intellectually and physically and even emotionally inferior— what does that mean?"

Galen took his horns with both hands, holding tight. "Well, I don't suppose it *means* anything in itself."

"Good," Morgan said. "Now let's look at it from another angle. With selective breeding, we have superior species who must assert their superiority by keeping those who are not as they are, inferior. Now you've said that once given this superiority, it means nothing in itself. It only takes on meaning when compared to species of less superiority. It leads to comparisons, and class systems, and discrimination and hypocrisy. What I want to know is: What's the point of this superiority? So what if it makes the species smarter or even better? What good is that?"

"The species can reach its fullest potential."

"And what will you have then, a world like the one that destroyed itself before ours? You see, I don't even intend to argue with your reasoning about superiority. To me, the problems brought on by your racial purity far outweigh the dubious merits of total fulfillment—and that's if you're even right about the superiority you speak of."

"Then you and I have nothing to discuss," Galen said.

"We have plenty to discuss," Morgan replied, as he

watched the giants meticulously tearing down the pulley. "Let's discuss you joining me in Ramon's defeat, so we can have room for even further debate."

Galen made a clicking sound down deep in his neckless throat that sounded suspiciously like laughter. "We are at opposite ends of the most important issue our cultures will ever have to deal with, and you ask me to help you defeat one who holds my own ideals."

"There's more at stake here than hemolysis," Morgan said.

"Not to me," Galen said. "I would never, could never, practice the kind of blood-mixing you promote. I believe in the identity and individuality of my species—*my species*—and I would die before letting me or mine degrade themselves that way."

"Then I will ask you to simply stay out of it," Morgan replied. He noticed Notern waiting just outside the conversation, trying to get his attention.

"You are a brave and devout Genie," Galen said. "I could grow to like you a great deal. But you know I cannot stay on the outside of this controversy." With that, the Grunt turned and walked away, going through the door leading to the interior stairs. "When next we meet, decisions will have to be made," he said.

"We can end the hatred in one generation," Morgan called after him, but Galen was already gone.

Morgan walked to the edge of the roof again, looking out over the forest. The colors were vibrant and beautiful, the air crisp, nearly cool. Below, the waterways were filled with rafts and skiffs, fishing and carrying equipment. In the distance, he could see more of his guns being raised up the sides of the mighty trees as the People worked frantically on their flat tops. And beyond the stone forest, the Great Sea stretched to infinity, wooden boats with colored sails somehow challenging its might to join the other small pockets of like creatures in a kind of lifeline. There was something that connected all of them together, something good and something bad. He just couldn't quite put his finger on it.

"We've got trouble," Notern said from beside him.

"I fear the Grunts will take Ramon's side," Morgan said, still watching out over the Great Sea. "They will be difficult to defeat, perhaps impossible."

Notern put his booted foot upon the retaining wall. He wore fur loincloth and vest. "The Mechs are gone," he said.

Morgan looked at him then. "Gone? Where?"

"No one knows," the man replied, and spit over the wall. "They've gone and taken their lab with them. They even managed to get away with one of Ibem's food storage places."

"This doesn't make sense," Morgan said. "They couldn't have gone far."

"I think they're still in the city. They simply set up their own residence."

"What about the weapons stores?"

"They didn't take the weapons."

"Frederick!" Morgan called to one of the giants who packed up the equipment. "Come over here."

The big man ambled over slowly to them, his face set hard.

"You wish me to do something?" the giant asked when he arrived.

"Where's Nebo?" Morgan asked. "Where are the other Mechs?"

"They are in their own place, red hair."

"Where?"

The Genie shook his shaggy head. "The Mechs don't want you to know."

"I'm asking you to tell me!" Morgan said loudly.

The giant looked incredulous. "My Mech said no!" he replied in the same tone of voice.

"I don't care about that. Where are they?"

"My Mech said no," Frederick said again, and turning, walked away.

"Find them," Morgan said.

"It's a big forest," Notern said.

"We need them."

"I'll put some of my men on it."

Morgan turned from the view and sat upon the retaining wall. "Do the merchants await me?" he asked.

"They are in the Tree of Decisions," Notern said, pointing to a tree far taller than those surrounding it. "They will parlay at your convenience."

Morgan stood, moving to his wings. Picking up the bulky wingpack, he slid his shoulders through the retaining straps and snugged it up with the buckle, bright red wings scalloping out on either side of his back. "How goes the questioning about Alicia?"

"It has been difficult to work through the grief of the Minnies," Notern said. "They have been most inconsolable over the death of Biddy."

"Have you gotten anything?"

The man nodded. "Her signal to you to enter the city was genuine and genuinely felt," he said. "She was present at all negotiations, and was killed from behind sometime later, apparently to keep her from relaying any new information to you. Many of them felt her death struggle—there was no understanding connected to it."

Morgan felt a twinge of sadness. "It's difficult to believe Alicia to be a part of that."

Notern shrugged and looked away. "You know her better than I do?" was all he said.

"Do I?" Morgan asked and ran to the retaining wall. Jumping upon it, he dove off the wall without hesitation, firing the jetpack from the controls on his straps.

There was a jerk, then acceleration, and Morgan was flying under his own power. He had learned to use the pseudo-wings while in Masuria and had fallen in love with flying, even using himself as test vehicle when Nebo broke through with the jetpack. He loved the feel of the scenery rushing headlong toward him, his side vision blurring shapes and colors into runny lines. It was the only sort of movement that even partway kept up with his reflexes.

He dipped his right arm and banked mammoth stone trees of uneven heights rising all around him. Citizens watched through their cutouts in the trees and shouted to one another, still unused to Masurian fliers. Life rushed past him as he moved, free and untethered, a streak of lightning in a sluggish world.

Morgan pulled up, climbing. He had decided to take a circle of the city and study his preparations before heading to the Tree of Decisions. He got up high, then made a wide turn. Below, the People were working hard, working together to save their way of life. It was as he had dreamed in the dungeons— or was it? Galen acted as if it were he, Morgan, who was trying to destroy their lives. What did it all mean? There was a key somewhere, something he could touch in the fringe areas of his consciousness, but whenever he really thought about it, it slipped quickly away.

There were so many questions: Alicia, now Nebo and Galen, and Grodin before them. He now operated blind, totally distant from the gauge of friendship that used to be the measure of his feelings. He operated on principle now, real emotion a companion he no longer shared the road with. Was that the curse of leadership or the balm of ego? The question would remain unanswered, for only the distance of time could sort through the miasma of circumstance to arrive at Truth. In the meantime, he had cast his lot.

Alicia. She had disappeared when he rejected her at Willow's palace. He loved her still, desperately, but couldn't be sure of her allegiance. She also lived by principles that could be stronger—genetically stronger—than her loyalty to him. Was this, then, reality? Principles fighting principles without regard to the pliant flesh and blood that formed the principles? Or did the flesh and blood form the principles at all? Where did they come from? What of Morgan's own mind and heart formed the core of his beliefs? Was he the product of his upbringing and style of life, or was he simply playing out his role in some monstrous game begun a thousand years before? He remembered the ancient rhyme:

Band of three,
Band of three:
Soldier, builder,
Referee.

Band of three,
Band of three.
The perfect mix,
The apogee.

The perfect mix, the words said. Mix. As if life were some monstrous stew waiting to be stirred to the appropriate taste. How free were any of them?

He skirted the stone forest, coming at it wide, then zeroed in on the Tree of Decisions, and swooped down to land on its balcony. The merchants awaited him there.

He slipped out of the harness, setting the wings to lean against the retaining wall. He introduced himself to each one in turn, unsuccessfully watching their stoic faces for some sign of their inner feelings.

"First off," he said. "Don't try to kill me here. It would just make things more difficult and complicated all the way around."

"It's too late for that," Waterson of the diamond eye said. "You're more use to us alive now."

"And you are to me," Morgan replied. "You control the commerce and citizens here. I'll need all the help I can get to save you."

"We have a request," Mister Chang said, lighting his long-stemmed pipe to billows of gray-white smoke. He puffed contentedly for a moment before continuing. "We've appointed a spokesman for our group, the better to reach agreements with the ruling body. We honorably request the use of the spokesman."

Morgan thought about that. "Why not?" he said.

"Good," G'vanni said, and stood, disappearing into the interior of the tree. A moment later he returned with the spokesman.

"Alicia," Morgan said, his voice catching in his throat.

She nodded curtly, looking lovely in a long green gown made from the same material as G'vanni's suit. "I hope there are no objections to my speaking for the merchants."

He took a deep breath, trying to calm himself. "You really want to do this?"

"I wouldn't be here otherwise," she said, but he knew her well enough to know that she had been affected, too.

He looked at the merchants. They watched him expectantly. They were in the perfect position and knew it.

"I'll put it all right out front," Morgan said, hoisting himself up to sit on the wall. "I want whatever information you may have on Ramon's invasion, and I want you to help me to the fullest extent of your abilities in the preparation and consummation of this battle. In return, I promise to not raze your city after this is all over. Is that clear enough?"

"It's clear, but unacceptable," Alicia said.

Morgan stared at her, and Alicia seemed to be looking right through him. "What more is there?"

"If we help you now," she said, "you promise to not hurt us later. That hardly seems fair by any standards."

"Neither was attacking me after offering your hospitality," Morgan replied, bowing from the waist.

"We have much to offer of a positive nature," Alicia said, "but we won't give it without equally positive promises from your end."

"Such as?"

"Return of the merchants' power right now so that they may hold some semblance of order among their own citizens. Perhaps then there will be a city left for you to leave behind."

He could barely stand it. There she was, so controlled, so *in* control, while he sat quaking like a frightened child. "Why should I care what happens to any of you?" he asked.

"We also ask that civilian control share in the decision-making with military control." She fixed him with her gold-flecked eyes, but spared him the indignity of flirting with him as she did with everyone else. "We don't wish to vie for power; we simply want to know what's going on as it happens."

"I don't mind informing through a third party," he said, "but I won't share in the decision-making process. You know that already."

"Am I to infer from this that you have accepted our first point, the reestablishing of local power among the merchants?"

He knew her tricks, and hated to see them being used upon him. "Alicia . . ."

"We, of course, want the absolute assurance that you will not try to form a ruling military government after the war is over. N'ork City *must* be autonomous." She walked around the patio, all eyes following her every movement. She was his wife, damnit!

"Stop this foolishness," he said to her. "Stop it right now!"

"I assure you, Governor," Waterson said. "This is not foolishness to us."

"Nor is it to me," Alicia said in slow, measured tones. "I fight for the freedom of these people."

"And maybe a share of their leadership?" he returned.

"Whatever my compensation on this end," she replied coldly, "it is no concern of yours."

And he realized she was right. He had thrown her out,

and now she was casting about for a way to survive. The decisions had all been his. What did he expect? He had rejected her out of genetic imperatives, and now she was doing the only thing she could do.

"Are there any other conditions?" he asked.

"We will wish these things in writing," she said, "in the manner of the merchants."

"Done," Morgan said sadly. "You have your concessions, if you swear loyalty to me for the duration of the war."

"You have my word on that," Alicia returned.

Morgan nodded. Despite what had happened, he still had faith in her sense of honor. "If you wish, I'll let each of you command a tree and its defenses," he said. "That way, we'll all have a stake in your city's salvation."

"A bargain," Mister Chang said. "I feel we have a bargain."

"We'll drink to it," Bruno Schmid said, and the crock was passed around.

Sahara, the tall dark one who looked like a Mech, stepped apart from the group and spoke: "I, for one, would like to apologize for our untoward attack on you and your forces. It was ill-conceived at best, and was a reflection of our fears alone. We mourn your dead along with our own. We all lost many who were close to us in the fighting."

"The lesson was expensive for all of us," Morgan said, tilting the crock to drink. He passed it on when finished. "I only hope we have profited from it."

"Hear, hear," Mister Chang said through half-lidded eyes.

Alicia walked close to Morgan. "I must speak with you," she said.

"What of your new . . . partners?" Morgan asked.

"It's important," she said urgently.

He nodded and drifted from the group, looking out over the forest from the eagle's nest. She stood right behind him. He could feel her presence without seeing her.

"Regardless of how you feel about me you must listen," she said low. "I've been getting some news of Ramon."

He turned to face her, wanting to grab her up in his arms and hold tight, but still not trusting her, not trusting her genetics.

"Have you heard that he has taken a wife?" she asked.

He nodded. "Weird tales have reached me," he said,

taken by the seriousness of her expression. "Stories about Ramon and a Physician with green skin."

"Those aren't stories," she said. "The woman is a Politico."

"How do you know?"

She searched his face with frightened eyes. "She's my sister."

"What?"

She raised a hand to quiet him. "She's dangerous, capable of anything."

"I don't understand."

"Listen to me," she said slowly. "Listen carefully. The goal of my addiction, the ultimate end of my need for power, is all tied up with control. My desire is for control; my method is benign. I feel that total control can only be gained through the positive disposition of power."

He nodded. "What makes the most people happy . . ."

"Try satisfied."

"What makes the most people satisfied for the longest period of time will bring you the most control with the least strain."

"Right. But there's another side to the coin of control."

He looked at her in disbelief. "Villainy," he said.

She nodded. "Control can be gained and held by dark forces, too. Total villainy, total horror—absolutes of untamed power. It can get you to the same place of control."

"The difference is merely philosophical," he said.

"Right." She glanced back at the merchants, who were still passing the crock around, happy to be free of their folly. "She's totally committed to her philosophy, Morgan. She can do . . . anything. Whatever her twisted imagination can conceive of, her body will try to bring to life. She's an expert on death, drugs, poisons, weapons, sex, and human nature. If she conspires with Ramon, or has anything to do with this campaign, it will be far worse than either of us could possibly imagine."

And Morgan shook his head, unable to figure how things could possibly be worse than they already were.

24

ABOARD VIPER

Grodin walked quickly up the gangway, and was immediately challenged by several burly men in the uniform of the Castle Guard, the tunic overlay of blue-and-white stripes.

"Going somewhere, old man?" a one-eyed man with a pock-marked face asked.

Grodin nodded. It was as he had suspected. These were not regular Alb'ny Guard, but bullies recruited from the ranks to protect Ramon. As such, they did not recognize the Governor's Breeder.

"I'm to be a replacement," he said, resting a hand on the hilt of his sword.

The men laughed, Grodin nodding pleasantly along with them, patient in his age.

"A bit long in the tooth, ain't you?" said a man with a narrow rat face, whose tunic was too large and drooped off his shoulders. "Only them that's toughest gets to guard the Governor."

"What kind of authorization you got to be here?" the first man asked.

"My name is Gabil Hays Duncan," Grodin said, bowing from the waist with a flourish. "I have been trusted retainer to the Nef family in Troy for 100 plantings. As a reward they have given me the spot on your staff that was vacated by the untimely passing of Junior Hendry Hallison Wycuff, who was dragged to death behind the carriage of Count Delmar."

"The deserter," the narrow-faced man said.

"Quite so."

"What would make an old man like you want to take on a service like this?" someone else asked.

"Is there not a pension connected with this work?" Grodin asked.

There were grunts of affirmation, and Grodin smiled at his own research.

"You are right," Grodin said. "I am old. I'll need that pension to live, if I'm to get any older."

The burly, pock-marked man stepped back a pace and drew his longsword. Everyone else backed away, leaving only Grodin to face him. "Unfortunately, old man," he said, "there is more to the job than pension."

"I suspected as much," Grodin replied, rasping his own sword slowly out of the scabbard. "Now don't hurt me."

The big man smiled and lunged. Grodin sidestepped easily, kicking the man's rump as he passed him. The others laughed loudly.

"You make quite a target," Grodin said, moving more into the center of the deck.

The big man turned, his pocks standing out bright red in his anger. "No quarter," he said, and attacked.

He was mad, swinging wildly with his sword, trying no more to test the man but to kill him. Grodin had no trouble with him, anger always an easy emotion to play off of. He kept to defense, letting the big man wear himself down with flurries. When the Guard finally tired, the "old man" took the offensive, driving him all the way back to the rail where he had no escape.

The big man tried to defend himself, but Grodin was too quick, breaching his defenses to nick him here and there with his blade, nicks that could have been gashes had he wished it—and everyone realized it.

He drove the big man to the wooden deck, his sword clattering uselessly by his feet.

"Enough," the man coughed, hugging his wounds. "Enough."

The man with the narrow face came up to take Grodin by the arm. "Come on," he said. "We'll get you a uniform and assign you your duty."

"Will you show me around the ship?" Grodin asked, walking off with the man.

"Of course," said rat face. "We'll do that first thing."

ii

A TREE NEAR WILLOW'S PALACE

Galen squatted in the corner of the large, empty room and stared at the other Grunts, faces blank, dermis blending with the light blue and silt of the walls. Beside him, waves lapped gently against the window that opened out at the waterline. In the distance, Willow's palace could be seen. Humans and Genies hurried in and out, scurrying on this mission or that, for the palace was the command post, the nerve center of the Genie war. It existed in marked contrast to the quiet, contemplative atmosphere of Galen's tree.

Lili sat beside Galen, her head tilting in his direction so her horns could be in his closest proximity. She already knew what her mate had to discuss, and it grieved her in its inevitability. It was dark in the room, the only light filtering from the open window, and she watched the glow of her people's eyes—the light of gentle intelligence, won through centuries of meditative thought.

"We have, I fear, a sad duty to perform here today," Galen said, after he had sufficiently lived with his ideas. He spoke without preamble to minds whose powers were the equal of his own. There was no need for rhetoric or explanation, no point to be served by emotional pleadings.

Galen stood, himself turning to the window. A small boat filled with fishermen and surrounded by dolp-men passed within a few feet of the cutout.

"A school over here," the dolp-men chirped happily. "A school over here."

They jumped out of the water again and again, their sleek bodies a natural beauty that Galen appreciated and often contemplated. The boat moved past the window, searching for the school of fish the dolp-men had pointed out.

Galen pointed out the window, toward the palace. "I have spent many days talking with the human about hemolysis. He has made much time for me, probably recognizing the importance of our conversations. Unfortunately, we arrived at an impasse."

"What sort of impasse?" Longnose asked.

Galen turned away from the window to retake his seat on

the floor, his horn, not so accidentally, touching Lili's as he bent to his seat. A quick smile passed between them.

"He rejects the concept of the growing mind," Galen said. "He would rather have peace at the price of ignorance."

"Not surprising for his kind," Mama Spire said.

"What do you mean?" Gregore, her son asked, and he was touching Marta most secretly, for he would not embarrass the others by touching in public.

Mama Spire said, "The warrior/leadership Genie class was designed not just to fight wars, but to end them. He loves the battle, does Morgan, but in its completion does he take his real pleasure. For, to have worked himself out of his own necessity means that he was completely successful. Hemolysis is the easiest way to achieve that end."

"Unfortunately," Marta added, "it's at the expense of the spirit."

"And so we come up against a wall," Galen said. "Having rejected the idea of a species reaching for its highest ideals of physical and intellectual perfection, he puts himself philosophically at odds with the rest of us. I feel it is a barrier that is sadly unscalable.

"I have grown to enjoy the impudence and impetuousness of the red-haired Genie, but he has become a threat to our existence, and that we cannot tolerate."

"It should be easy enough to accomplish," Longnose said. "They seem to have no abilities that could defeat us in open battle. We can simply go to where Morgan is and kill him any time we want."

The others agreed, the grim pronouncement bringing no pleasure to any of them.

"Should we do it now?" Gregore asked. "So distasteful a task should perhaps be taken care of immediately."

"I think not," Galen said. "We could certainly take him now, but would that truly stop the flow of the ideas he created? I have dwelled long upon this and think it better that we wait until the actual fighting has begun to kill Morgan of Alb'ny. That way, a great many humans will die, taking Morgan's ideas to the grave with them. We must quell this heresy of the spirit as completely as possible if we are to save the world."

Gregore cleared his throat. "I have never killed before," he said, and looked at his mate. "Neither has Marta. Please show us what to do."

Galen extended his right palm, its large eye blinking open. The two young Grunts stared, the flat faces transfixed. "It's already in you," Galen said, "locked in your hearts and in your head. When the time comes . . . you'll know what to do."

iii

THE WESTERN EDGE OF THE FOREST

Serge sat crosslegged in the middle of the raft, using his large tree trunk paddle first on the one side and then the other. The night was black, as all nights were, and the occasional flashes of rainless lightning to the West did nothing more than light up sections of the rolling clouds.

He turned and looked behind him, lights from the trunks of the great forest trees disappearing as he left the forest behind. Nebo only allowed travel by night for security reasons. The forest was being searched for him and his Mechs. They were outlaws now, and Serge felt uneasy with the entire situation. He didn't know why, as the why of most things escaped him, but he knew something was not as it should be and it hurt him.

The Great Sea Lady loomed before him as a dark hulk. She was a tree in the shape of a woman holding a darkened torch who seemed to stand just atop the waves. The N'orkers looked at her as a goddess of the Old World, but no one realized she was hollow. No one save Nebo.

With one last look behind to make sure he wasn't followed, the giant picked up his pace and closed the distance to Nebo's new lab. Rowing around the structure, he tied up behind and swam around to the entrance. There were two floors of base before the tree took shape, and this is where Nebo was set up. As he climbed through the cutout, he wondered what the Lady looked like beneath the layers of vine and ivy that covered her like a blanket nearly two hundred feet high.

He sided a dark drape and entered a large room flooded with electric light. Mechs and giants worked furiously all around him, as if the unnatural light made them forget the difference in functions between night and day. The room was filled with a whooshing sound as seawater was continually pumped onto a small machine Nebo called "reactor."

Serge looked around for his Mech, finding him at a wide,

square table upon which sat a large, round metal object that was hatched in the center like a cut orange, the two halves lying next to one another.

Serge padded barefooted across the stone floor, dripping as he walked, the evaporating water cooling his skin. Nebo was hunched over the metal ball when he walked up and didn't even look up.

"You certainly took your time getting here," the Mech said, as he prodded the lenses of high explosive set all around the central core of the ball.

"I helped Morgan move some cannon," he returned, and caught Lannie watching him from a distance out of the corner of his eye. "He was asking me where you were."

"What did you tell him?" Nebo said, his concentration all centered on the ball.

"I told Morgan that Nebo didn't want me to tell anything."

"Good," Nebo responded, then looked up at the giant, reaching out a quick hand to pat his forearm before engrossing himself in his work again.

"Why can't we tell Morgan?" Serge asked.

"Because he'd make me stop my work," Nebo replied casually.

"Why?"

Nebo frowned and looked at him again. "Because he has no imagination. Now, I'm quite busy. Can't you find your foreman and make yourself useful?"

"Serge thinks you desert Morgan."

"We've taken different roads, that's all."

"But you promised to help him long ago, to help the People."

"I'm helping in my own way," Nebo said irritably. "If you don't like it, go your own way."

Serge was horrified. He knelt down and got eye to eye with Nebo. "You're my Mech," he said sadly, tears coming to his eyes. "I could never leave my Mech."

Nebo smiled and tousled his hair. "Then let me do the thinking for us, okay? I know what's best."

Serge nodded, but unhappily. Nothing had been answered; nothing had been resolved.

"Nebo!" came an excited voice from across the room.

All work had stopped, the air heavy with anticipation.

Pietro held metal tongs in his hands, the tongs grasping a small object. The other Mechs gathered around him, giggling, eyes wide. They walked with him in a group to Nebo.

Serge stood, backing away slightly to give the Mechs room. All the giants gathered too, looking at one another in confusion, for this meant nothing to them. They stood on the outskirts, peering down over everyone's head at the table.

"It's finished," Pietro said, and his tongs held a tiny cylinder.

"Excellent," Nebo whispered, transferring the tongs to himself. He spoke to the whole group. "This is the initiator, ladies and gentlemen. It will release the neutrons that begin the atomic reaction. I am now going to set it within the plutonium core."

He moved the tongs slowly, by inches, toward a small hole in the very center of a gray mass that sat in the center of the large sphere. He set it in carefully, a sigh escaping everyone in the room when he pulled the tongs away.

"Now," he said, "at the time of detonation, the initiator will release the neutrons and the small detonators set around the outside of the sphere will set off the explosives in the inner lenses, forcing the plutonium to critical mass. The resultant energy release will be several times hotter than the core of the Sun."

"When will we set it off?" Laila asked.

"As soon as possible," Nebo said. "When we get everything worked out."

"What will happen to us?" Al-ke-do asked.

"You will begin evacuation to the shores of Mud Plains, a safe harbor from which to watch the energy release. I will be working on a radio control for the detonator and will join you there. I must also devise a back-up system should my radio fail or I'm caught."

"Will we leave it here?" Pietro asked.

Nebo smiled. "We'll take it to the top of the Lonely Sister. Everyone will see it from there."

There was great applause from the Mechs. "The New Age truly dawns on us," Pietro said. "Will you have time to devise a back-up system?"

Nebo shook his head, his smile not leaving his face. "I think I know where we can get one ready made." He looked around until he saw his giant. "Serge," he said. "Let's get this thing closed up."

Serge moved to the device, not liking it, not liking anything about it.

"Close it up," Nebo said, "very carefully."

And the giant did what he was told. Slowly, with great care, he lifted half the sphere and closed it on its well-oiled hinges, Nebo locking it down when he was done.

Then something happened to Nebo. His face flushed, an image burning into his brain. He recognized it, a phylogenic memory impressed upon his brain in the form of the donor DNA from which he was made. And though he had never spoken the words before, he spoke them now, clear and loud, the ancient Hindu writings that once before ushered in an atomic age:

> If the radiance of a thousand suns
> Were to burst at once into the sky,
> That would be like the splendor
>   of the Mighty One . . .
> I am become Death,
> The shatterer of worlds.

iv

BETWEEN THE ROCK AND THE HARD PLACE

Newcomb Reeder sat in his cabin aboard GRAYCLOUD and fretted over the war. He was anchored somewhere off the wilds of Jersey with plenty enough booty to return home, but near no road upon which to do it.

He sat in his nightshirt, his oil lamp swaying lazily above his head, moving double shadows across the walls. In his zest to chase down as many rafts as possible, he had allowed one to lure him too far West, beyond Mud Plains, where he had intended to unload and make his way back up the Southern Road and home. But now, Ramon was at his back, Morgan lay ahead, and Jersey was impenetrable to humans. He was stuck, just the same as his father had gotten stuck with Ramon. His boat was useless to him downriver, nothing but worthless lumber and iron, a large, floating coffin in which to bury his dreams and glory. If only he hadn't been so greedy and impetuous!

He heard a creak, and turned to see his cabin door opening, a dark, hooded figure standing just beyond the threshold in the darkness. "There is a way out," the figure told him.

His muscles tensed, his eyes darted to the peg across the cabin from which his sword dangled.

"There's no need for that," the voice said, and walked into the room, pulling off the hood.

"You," Reeder said, as he stared at the unforgettable green face. "How did you get in here?"

The Green Woman removed her cloak and closed the door. "I ask only that you hear me out before picking up your sword. If my arguments fail to move you, I will fall upon your blade myself."

He stood, moving to draw the weapon from the scabbard. "You won't mind if I hold onto this," he said, "just to be on the safe side."

She lowered her eyes, nodding in the manner of a slave. "Please," she said, not looking at him. "I'n so sorry for what happened. Ramon . . . did things to me, made me act the way I acted."

"I don't believe you," he said. "I saw how you controlled him." His eyes were drawn to her body, the lithe curves barely shining through the sheer fabric, the darker green of her nipples bunching up the front of the material.

She moved toward him, coming more into the light, and he forced himself to focus on her eyes. He had known only two women in his life, both mere children, daughters of serving women. The Green Woman's presence in his cabin crowded his mind with the needs of his youth.

"I . . . left him," she said, still gazing at the ground, "because of what he did to you . . . and others."

"I don't believe it."

She moved closer, within touching distance. Her hand came up to trace the contours of the sword, then gently push it away. "Why, then, would I be here? I'm at your mercy, Councilman, totally helpless and alone."

She spread her arms wide in a gesture of frailty. His need for her was blazing hotter than a fire. She could physically feel it tingling her fingers. She closed her hands lest she burn them.

"Why do you come?" he asked, and his hands were shaking slightly.

"I want to help you," she said, and looked into his eyes for the first time. "I want to make up for the terrible things I've done."

He knitted his brow. "Help . . . how?"

Her eyes sprang to anger. "Do you hate Ramon?" she asked. "Do you burn with the fire of a man, with the fire of vengeance? Are you a child no longer?"

He took the sword and brought it down on his table to stick inches in the wood, the blade vibrating, humming. "I am no child!" he declared. "And I burn with many fires. Ramon was the death of my father. It is my duty and my privilege to seek bloody vengeance."

"Good," she said. "Good." She took his arms, holding tightly. "I have a plan by which you may have your vengeance."

"And you," he said, also clasping her arms. "What comes to you in all this?"

She moved her body up to his, feeling his heat, moving against it. His arms went involuntarily around her.

"Don't question your good fortune," she said. "Just accept it."

And with one deft shake of her shoulders, the gown slid down her body and puddled at her feet like wax melting down a long, sleek candle.

25

The Palace—Times of Sorrow

They had erected a pedestal for Ibem in the largest room of the second floor of the palace. The little fellow sat upon it, his crown tilted on the chrome box that passed for its head, and answered questions for the crowd of dignitaries that had gathered for Ibem's official installation into his new home.

Morgan stood on the outskirts of the plush room, declining the offers of wine brought by serving women carrying large pitchers on their heads. Many candles glowed the room to a warm, yellow haze. The Lawgivers stood beaming beside their God, and near them, groups of silver-suited Repairmen kept watch over the proceedings and the complex set of wires connecting the Creator to the plethora of machinery sitting behind a stand of purple drapes nearby.

There was no time for this, no time to pay homage to the old ways, when the wolf was knocking upon the door. Morgan seethed. It was beyond his comprehension that the war preparations could stop for so unfruitful a gathering; yet, somehow, it was important to the humans among them that it take place, and he resigned himself to it. Everyone had dressed in their finery and regarded this event as a sort of placebo of necessity that would prepare them for battle.

"Will we win the war?" Mayor Trilly of Beacon asked of God.

"HUMANKIND WILL PREVAIL," Ibem answered. "HUMANKIND IS THE STOCK FROM WHICH THE SOUP OF CIVILIZATION IS MADE."

"How do you like your new home?" Duchess Clorina asked, and one of the merchants of N'ork City, Bruno Schmid, seemed to be hovering close to her.

"MY HOME IS AMONG MY PEOPLE. HOW DO THE PEOPLE LIKE MY NEW HOME?"

There was a round of applause from the gathered, and light laughter of surprise that God would be so personable.

"WE WILL BE VERY HAPPY HERE IN N'ORK CITY," Ibem continued, "FOR WHEREVER THERE IS PURITY OF BLOOD AND SPIRIT, THERE WILL ALSO BE HAPPINESS."

The room quieted to a whisper, many eyes turning to Morgan, then turning way. The Governor suffered it all in silence, his dirty britches and naked chest setting him apart from the group both physically and philosophically.

"How old are you?" one of the merchants asked Ibem, and the question lightened the mood, drawing attention back to the mindless festivity of the moment.

Jella walked up to stand beside Morgan. He wore clean

white robes and had combed his hair. "You're at once loved and hated," he said, face hard. He tilted his crock back and drank, not his first of the night.

"I'm tolerated," Morgan said, "out of necessity."

"What happens when the war ends?" Jella asked.

"Everyone lives their lives."

"You evade the question."

There was a light gasp from the crowd. Heads turned toward the entry doorway. Morgan looked in time to see Alicia sweeping in on G'vanni's arm. She wore a gown of the softest gold that hugged her tightly in front to accentuate her figure, then flared back in easy folds, as if she were facing a strong headwind. Her hair was piled atop her head and fixed with large combs of solid gold and coral rock. She looked better than he had ever seen her.

Lawgiver Penrad immediately moved through the crowd to greet her, probably more of a show for Morgan than anything. There was light talk and laughter that was just outside of Morgan's hearing.

"She throws it in your face," Jella said.

"I'm not blind," Morgan returned, and his heart was dying within his breast. His own conflicts remained unresolved about her, and it was tearing him apart. If only . . .

Once, he thought he saw her eyes searching the crowd for him, but other than that, she seemed quite content with her role as the merchant's lady. Why did things have to be this way? Why couldn't she make it easy for him to know where she stood? Their pride, their damned pride stood between them—a wall a thousand years high.

"Maybe we should go," Jella said when he noticed the look upon Morgan's face. "You're building up to a scene."

"No, I'm not," Morgan replied. "I swear I'm not."

"It wouldn't be wise here," Jella said.

Morgan turned and smiled at him. "Don't worry," he said. "I'm not going to make any trouble."

He was just patting his friend on the shoulder when he saw G'vanni lean down and kiss Alicia on the cheek, and without thought he was moving in that direction, throwing people aside who stood between him and the merchant.

"Get your filthy hands off her!" Morgan said, jerking G'vanni away from Alicia.

G'vanni pulled free of him, dark eyes smoldering. His

hand came out of the folds of his green silk outfit holding a dagger. "I should cut you up right here," he said.

"The woman is my wife," Morgan said, his emotions cold steel. "You touch her again, and I'll make you eat that pig sticker."

"You threw her away," the dark man said. "I took her in when there was no one else."

"She's still my wife."

"I'm your enemy, remember?" Alicia said, stepping between the men. She looked at Morgan, her face straining for understanding. "I'm trying to survive here. What do you want of me?"

Even in the confusion of his own mind, he knew he didn't have that answer. "I want you to stay away from him," he said angrily.

"I'll do what I please," she returned.

"She rejects the blasphemer," old Penrad said, moving to the controversy. "This Genie wants nothing but death and disunity for all of us." He turned a circle for the crowd, arms upraised. "If you had any sense, you'd chase him from your midst, chase him back to whatever hole he crawled out of."

That was all Morgan needed. Livid with frustration he grabbed the old man and shook him, letting him go to drop to the floor in a tight ball.

"PROTECT THE LAWGIVER!" Ibem said from his pedestal, and Morgan wasn't above turning the darkness of his feelings toward the God who made the heavens and the Earth.

With pent-up fury blurring his mind, he stepped over the groaning form of Penrad and strode toward Ibem, fists clenched.

Fear forced those present to move aside, while the other two Lawgivers joined ranks to protect their charge. He grabbed one with each hand, shoving them aside like bundles of dried leaves.

"STOP HIM! STOP HIM!"

He brought back his fist again, and, all at once, Jella was standing before him.

"You'll have to hit me first," he said.

"Get out of the way," Morgan warned.

"No," Jella returned. "You're tired. You're frustrated. You wish to shatter the old way, but this isn't how. You must reach people's hearts."

"I am a warrior," Morgan said. "This is the way I know."

"You're a statesman, too," Alicia said from behind him. "Don't destroy what you've built."

He turned to stare at the woman, at the genuine concern on her face. Jella moved to him, taking him gently by the arm to lead him away.

Morgan breathed deep, letting the anger vent itself slowly.

"Come on," Jella whispered to him. "Let's get out of here."

Morgan had no idea what was motivating him to action, but he did know one thing and he said it: "This is not the way to salvation," he said. "Wake up. Please."

Jella led him out of the silent room, moving him through the halls and up to his quarters on the roof, where they stood in the night air, watching the blazing lights in the various buildings around them where the preparations continued.

"Thanks for getting me out of there," Morgan said at length.

"You would have done the same for me," Jella said. "Perhaps, in my sorrow, I understand somewhat the hell you are dealing with."

"My loss is nothing compared to yours," Morgan said, and the men embraced.

"Morgan!" came a distant, shouted voice.

Both men looked over the edge of the building to the pier below. A human holding a lantern was looking up at them.

"You called me?" Morgan shouted down.

"Two men," the human called up, "have traveled from Ramon's force under the white flag. They wish to meet with you."

Morgan and Jella shared a look. Morgan could see the small boat and flag, but couldn't get a view of the carriers.

"Bring them to me," he called down.

"Aye, sir."

"What could it be?" Jella asked.

Morgan shrugged. "Probably Ramon's idea of telling us his terms for our surrender," he said. "My brother's audacity is without boundary or reality."

Moments later, a contingent of Morgan's newly appointed bodyguards moved onto the roof with the "visitors."

Redrick of Firetree stood sneering in the jumping light of the rooftop torches.

"If it isn't the bastard of Alb'ny," Redrick said, bringing his hook up to smooth his thin mustache.

"Hook!" Jella said. "Is this the slime who murdered my Moira?"

Redrick's eyebrows rose at the name of the woman.

"I believe the very same," Morgan said.

Jella drew his sword. "Then Destiny comes to shake my hand at the top of a tree."

Redrick took a step back, then stopped, bringing himself to his full height. He held out a hand containing folded linen. "You'd better read this first."

"I'd better cut off your balls first!" Jella said, moving toward the man.

"Wait!" Morgan said. "We must read his message."

"Go to hell!" Jella said, and charged the man.

"Stop him!" Morgan said, and Jella was immediately surrounded by drawn swords. He kept moving, and they jumped him, knocking him to the ground.

Morgan took the message and read it while Jella struggled under the weight of the guards.

"Why do you deny me?" Jella screamed, kicking out wildly.

"I'll tell you why," Morgan said, and read the letter out loud. "To the farmer of Siler: I have Ona and the little one, Ty'Jorman, under my control. They are well for the moment, but are living under penalty of death. If you ever want to see them alive again, you will come alone at sunrise day after tomorrow to my camp south of Nyack. Absolutely no harm must come to my messengers; they are to return your answer to me. If harm befalls them, the same will happen to your family. Cordially, Ramon Delaga, Governor of Alb'ny."

Jella stopped struggling and looked up at Morgan. The red-haired man reached out a hand to help his friend up.

"I'm so sorry," Jella said.

"Isn't that touching," Redrick said. "The two whipped Woofers licking one another's wounds. Well, let me tell you something, Prelate of Rockland. I had your precious wife several times before I cut her up. She wasn't worth a damn. But I enjoyed making her scream before she died. She screamed real, real good."

Jella brought shaking hands up to his face, and sobbed uncontrollably.

"Stop it!" Morgan told Redrick. "How do I even know you've got them?"

Redrick smiled. "Was it not Ona who brought your sword to the dungeon when you were in captivity?"

Morgan closed his eyes and nodded. Only Ona could have told Ramon that.

"And now," Redrick said, "my friend and I would like food and wine brought to our quarters. I don't want any of this . . . Southern trash, either. Give us meat, red meat. A woman would be nice, too."

"You get no woman," Morgan said low.

"I want comfortable quarters also, here in the palace. We'll get your answer tomorrow."

Morgan could only stare at him and listen to the sounds of Jella's crying.

"What's the matter, Governor?" Redrick asked. "Cat-man got your tongue?"

"See to him," Morgan told the guards. "Give him anything he wants except a woman."

Turning, he strode away, the weight of total failure laying heavy on his shoulders.

PART FOUR

HONOR

26

N'ork City—Dark Dreams

Even then, years later, El-tron could still hear his sister's screams as the monster she gave birth to tore her to pieces as it ripped through the birth canal. Small and pristine, Eva-loc had been raped by a beast-man, the resultant issue far larger than her small frame could manage. The birthing had killed her. His parents cared for the four-legged monster until it was old enough to turn out into the jungle to find its own brand of life among the other ill-begotten waifs of life's madness.

As he gazed out at the candle-lit faces that filled the great hall around him, he was more determined than ever that it should never happen again. Beside him sat seventeen females, everything from beast-men to humanoids—all of them pregnant, all from the night of hemolysis. They were his symbol, the physical manifestation of his fears. They kept his resolve strong. He couldn't look at any of them without thinking of Eva-loc. Her screams still filled his ears.

"This will have to mean another war between us and those who are loyal to Morgan," a human from Glasco said.

"No it won't," El-tron said. "You don't know Morgan as well as I do."

"This is his dreamquest," a cat-man said in a small voice. "He will take harshly more criticism of it."

"He doesn't know how we feel," El-tron said. "You here tonight are representatives of larger groups. We speak for nearly twenty thousand in all. We'll go to him. He'll listen."

The room erupted in loud conversation, a mix of human

and Genie all talking and trying to get attention at the same time. Minnies bounced up and down while giants talked among themselves, their shoulders stooped because the ceiling wasn't high enough for them. There were representatives from all the human Provinces, and Genies of every kind save Mechs. Several Grunts had even wandered in just to listen.

"Please!" El-tron called, pounding his fist on the table before him. "We must have order! You all will be heard!"

A Miner was standing upon a crate with his arm thrusting continually into the air as if he were working a pick-ax. When El-tron called on him, he spoke with a low, rumbling voice. "Why have we waited so long to take action? We should have done something before now."

"I didn't want to interfere with the defense projects," El-tron responded. "We don't hate Morgan. We want to win the war. You still don't understand. Morgan of Alb'ny has brought us to the door of salvation. We simply disagree with him upon the final turn of that salvation. In another hour it will be light. We will go to the palace with all our numbers and petition him to abandon his quest for hemolysis. When he sees our vast numbers, he will understand and change his feelings. It's as simple as that. Then we will be ready to defend the city against Ramon's advance."

"Suppose he doesn't go along with us?" someone called. "What then?"

El-tron smiled, opening and closing his long, long fingers. "He will go along with us. It's ridiculous to think otherwise. It's the right thing."

"But suppose he doesn't," the voice persisted.

"You don't know Morgan," El-tron said, getting angry. "He's a wonderful Genie. He will understand. Now I want you to go back to your groups and rouse your People. With the first gray of morning, we'll meet at the palace in force. Then we'll get this thing over with and get back to the real problem— Ramon."

There was scattered applause and a great deal of hot blood. El-tron watched the hundred of them file out to their boats and rafts, knowing how they felt. He felt the same way, which was why he had organized this massive protest. But, they simply didn't know Morgan of Alb'ny. The Governor *was* good. He would hear their pleas—he would understand.

*   *   *

Morgan lay in bed, naked and alone, feeling his own sweat and wondering when the last time had been that he'd known happiness. He was a pumpkin shell, hollowed out for the pie of responsibility. On the outside, he was still there, still the same; but inside there was nothing of softness or consistency. He felt as if the wind could whistle through him.

There had been no sleep that night, nor even the semblance of sleep. If he could have wished himself out of existence at that moment, he would have. Had his internal drives been any less strong, he might have walked away from everything and gone back to the fields where he belonged. There was no happiness any longer, no hint or possibility any longer, so very much lost that was irreplaceable.

Zenna, his mother, was dead. Ty'Jorman, his father, was dead, murdered as was his mother. Grodin was gone, his loss still overpowering, and Ona and one of his children. They were beyond his help, yet he would try to help. The Mechs were gone, as was all trace of them. Nebo, his mentor, gone with the Mechs. Many of his friends from the dungeon were dead and gone, many of the others conspiring against his ideals. His friends from his childhood had taken up arms against him. And now Alicia was gone. Her moving in with G'vanni had severed the last traces of his feelings. Now he felt hollowed out, a drum of flesh stretched tight across a marrowless bone frame.

What was it that made him this way? What instinct drove him beyond the point of mere endurance? Was he real, a product of all that he had learned and become, or was he simply a gaggle of booby-trapped genes set to go off at the predetermined time? He remembered the rhyme about the band of three and felt himself merely a player in a cosmic masque—a warm body to fill the required metaphysical space.

He sat up, bathed in sweat. The room was just graying to daylight. The dog-men had a series of exercises they went through each morning to awaken their bodies and minds, to pull them to the peak of their awareness. Getting down on all fours, Morgan mimicked the ritual, wanting to get the most out of himself despite his lack of sleep. For one thing was clear to him: he couldn't stop now. To turn back now, after losing everything, would be worse than folly. His spirit still urged him onward toward the goal of hemolysis, the ideal that seemed to rivet his thought patterns. He couldn't deny that goal, for the torture of not knowing its outcome would render him lifeless just as surely as if he'd fallen upon his own sword. Then all the loss would have been in vain. If his urges took him to hemolysis, then that's what it would have to be.

There could be no turning back for him, not now. He thought of his father, of the sadness that had seemed to follow the great man everywhere. He had also made his choices, and had known the pain of loss and the sadness of unfulfilled ideals. Morgan understood him perfectly now the way no one understood him when he was alive.

When he was alive.

Morgan humped his back and stretched out his legs, one after the other, all the while letting whining, gurgling sounds escape from down deep in his throat. He had to see this through. Wrong or right, he had to see it through.

He heard the sounds of loud voices out on the roof, a commotion of some kind. Standing, he slipped his britches on and padded across the floor, first retrieving his sword from where it hung on the bedpost.

Several of his men had already entered through the front door and were hurrying across the ballroom floor, their boots clicking echoes through the marble hall.

"What is it?" Morgan asked loudly, his voice hanging in the large space.

"There's a mob outside," the human said. Morgan's bodyguards were all human, the most vicious species.

"What sort of mob?"

Morgan passed them, moving toward the door.

"They wish to speak with you," the other man answered, hurrying to catch up to their charge.

"About what?" Morgan said.

Neither answered.

"How many?" Morgan asked.

"More than we can keep out," came the reply from behind. "Thousands."

"Get me a Minnie," Morgan said, and stepped out into the morning. He walked immediately to the retaining wall, passing a waking King Willow and Telemay, who slept in the soft grass of the playing field.

Morgan leaned against the wall, watching. Many boats had converged on the palace, their occupants staring mutely up toward the roof. There were, indeed, thousands present, none speaking, all silently watching—waiting.

He heard shouting and the clang of metal against metal and turned to the stairs. His men were trying to keep part of the mob off the roof, but were being pushed back by superior numbers.

Morgan hurried to the place, swords flashing all around him.

"Enough!" he shouted. "Let them pass."

The bodyguards reluctantly backed off, letting the mob push its way out onto the roof. They cheered, rushing up the stairs and out, then stopped when faced with Morgan, alone, his sword at the ready. It was as he feared; El-tron led the mob.

"Welcome, my friends," Morgan said. "I'm not so out of touch that you have to fight your way up to see me."

"The guards would not let us pass," El-tron said, speaking for the rest.

"Such is their job," Morgan replied. "It's their only job, so they take it seriously. What brings you to me at this hour?"

"I think you know the answer to that, my Lord," El-tron said, and he was unarmed, his hands open, the long fingers splayed to their incredible length.

"Are we to then discuss hemolysis with swords in our hands?" Morgan asked.

El-tron cleared his throat before answering. "It has apparently come to that," he said, his saucer eyes filled with sadness.

Morgan surveyed the crowd. Human flesh and animal fur mixed equally. El-tron had done well; it appeared that most all species were represented. No Mechs or giants though. The Mechs were gone, the giants apparently gone with them. He almost laughed. Philosophical hemolysis was at work here, all races joined in overthrowing a common enemy. He had somehow never figured that he would be the common enemy.

"We've come to ask . . . to demand," El-tron said, "the immediate withdrawal of your practice of blood-mixing. There are twenty thousand of us out there, all wanting the same decision. Hemolysis is a terrible thing; it must be stopped immediately."

"You've been my friend from the first," Morgan said to him, "from the dungeon."

"I love you as one of my own," the Genie answered. "We have not impeded your battle plans or your strategy on any level as a sign of our loyalty."

"And in return, I am to abandon hemolysis," Morgan said lethargically.

"It's wrong," El-tron said. "It must be abandoned."

"I love you, every one of you," Morgan said. "I'd gladly give my life for each of you. I have led without thought for myself. After my coronation in Kipsie, I could have marched up the South road and taken Alb'ny as my fortress and had everything I set out to get. But I came to N'ork City for all of you. I came here to set you free."

Ratif, the Minnie, came running up the stairs. He bounced across the roof, jumping into Morgan's arms. Morgan whispered something in his ear.

"Will you abandon hemolysis?" El-tron said. "Surely the sheer numbers . . ."

"All the sheer numbers do for me is make me think of all those thousands who are still loyal," Morgan said.

"Will you abandon hemolysis?" El-tron asked again, his face drained of color. "You cannot deny the loudness of our voice."

Morgan's eyes were hard, his resolve unflinching. "Because you don't have the vision for my dream, you ask me to abandon it and accept something less. Can you deny the loudness of my voice?"

"Please, my friend," El-tron said, pleading. "You must listen to me. I can't control the consequences otherwise."

"We make decisions here," Morgan said, sliding Ratif off his arm and raising his sword. "I, for one, do not fear the burden of my decisions."

El-tron narrowed his eyes. "But this is wrong!" he said, angry.

"And who are you to judge me?"

"On my command," El-tron said, "those boats will empty and your palace will fill with angry People. We can take what we want from the mighty Morgan of Siler."

"You may, of course, try," Morgan said, "but my friend Ratif here has just been in contact with his species atop the command posts. Their cannons are trained on your people right now and will fire in force upon you if you make good your threat. How important is this to you? Is it worth these lives?"

The crowd on the roof began shifting uneasily. El-tron gazed up at the buildings nearby, saw the gunnery crews moving the cannons into position.

"Not easy to decide the fate of thousands, is it?" Morgan said bitterly. "Have you the stomach for dark command?"

El-tron clenched his fists, the fingers folding up like roses. Then he slumped, physically slumped, and Morgan knew he had won this round.

"We go," El-tron said, his voice flat, inflectionless. "But there will be more. It's out of my hands now."

He turned and walked into the crowd lined out behind him. They caved in with him, retreating back down the stairs, the bodyguards following them out.

Morgan stared after them, feeling neither grief nor exultation. Emptiness was the order of the day.

"No one ever said it would be easy," came a voice from one who hadn't left. Morgan turned, surprised at a face he never thought he'd see again.

"Grodin," he said to the man, and his fingers tightened on the hilt of his sword.

27

i

ABOARD GRAYCLOUD

Dunbar stood in the doorway of Reeder's cabin, his iron ball held in one hand, the vial of clear liquid in the other. The ball was linked to a thick chain attached to his ankle, and it clanked when he hobbled around. Reeder called it his contract of honor. As always, the blank leather mask hid his features, the dark glasses shading the windows of his eyes. He had neither expression nor features; he was the opaque heart of the Old World.

"I have the first of it," he said, standing on the threshold and holding out the small vial. "It takes some time to skim off the strychnine."

The Green Woman, wrapped in a sheet at Reeder's insistence, walked to the door and took the jar from him. She held it up to the light, turning it this way and that. "Don't skim the strychnine," she said at last.

"But it's poison," Dunbar said.

"Not enough to hurt them," she replied. "Just enough to make them mean."

Reeder sat on the edge of his bunk, stripped to the britches. He impatiently watched the exchange, in truth uncaring about whatever it was they were doing. It was the woman he wanted, back in his bed. He had never known anything that could take her measure. It excited him just to think of it.

"Can't this wait?" he called, standing to fidget on his feet for a while.

"No," the Green Woman answered without even turning to him. "Ramon will attack at any time. We must be prepared."

"How can we hurt him with water?" the Councilman asked.

"Isn't water," Dunbar said. "It's called lysergic acid."

"Have you tested it yet?" the Green Woman asked.

The blank face nodded. "It has worked as you said."

Reeder walked up to stand behind the woman, pushing against her lightly from behind, hoping to excite her with his need. "What does it do?" he asked, and took the vial from her.

"It makes people crazy," Dunbar said.

"Water?" Reeder asked.

"I want to see the test subject," the Green Woman said.

Reeder perked up. "Yes, Dunbar," he said. "Go and fetch the test subject. In fact, you may want to have lunch first."

"Bring him straightaway," the Green Woman said, and turned to take in Reeder's eyes. "Our time is limited."

Reeder frowned and walked to stare out a porthole. From where he stood, it looked as if they had all the time in the world.

Dunbar walked off without a word, his chain dragging across GRAYCLOUD's wooden deck. When he passed Reeder's porthole, the young Councilman hurried over and shut the cabin door.

Turning, he grinned wickedly at the Green Woman.

"Get that look off your face," she said. "We've done nothing but make love since I walked in here last night."

"It's your own fault, because you're so good," he said, and, reaching out, he snatched the cover from around her, leaving her naked and green before him.

His throat got dry immediately and he fell to his knees before her, hugging her close, his face buried in her stomach.

"We don't have much time," she said.

"I'll hurry," he said, standing and dropping his pants.

"I mean we don't have much time before Ramon attacks," she said, her eyes dropping down to take in the erection that never seemed to leave the young nan.

"There's nothing we can do," he said, taking her in his arms and walking her slowly to the bunk.

"There's much we can do," she returned. "That's why we're working so fast. That's why we've made the lysergics."

He pushed her back onto the bed, falling on top of her. He entered her immediately, and she let him because she genuinely liked this wild boy. His innocence was fresh water on the parched lips of her psyche. She wanted what she wanted, what she needed to have; but she didn't want to hurt the boy. His emotions were nothing if not pure, and she appreciated that.

"That liquid will . . . poison them?" Reeder asked, as he slid slowly in and out of her.

"Not exactly," she said softly, then drew in her breath, arching her back to take in more of him. "If we . . . poisoned them, we'd . . . ohhh . . . we'd still have . . . Morgan's army to . . . to . . ." She groaned loudly and pulled Reeder's head down to her breasts.

The words were lost then as the boy increased his pace, pushing insistently toward climax. She could feel it coming in him, and it triggered her. She wrapped her legs around his waist and screamed with him, for once in her life thinking of something other than the performance.

Afterwards, they lay together on the bed, and she felt protected and protective all at the same time. His body was hard and muscled, glistening with N'ork sweat. She caressed him lovingly, smiling to see his erection returning.

There was a knock on the door.

"Dunbar?" Reeder called out, as he sat up and struggled back into his britches.

"No, my Lord," came the voice from beyond. "It is Sir Kelvin with news."

"Come in," the Green Woman said, and Reeder hurried over to put the cover back upon her. Kelvin walked in just as he was buttoning his pants.

"I've just returned from Ramon's camp," the knight banneret said, an eyebrow raised in disapproval.

"When do they sail?" the Green Woman asked.

"Within a day, I think," Kelvin said. "The crews work on small boats and floaters while Ramon waits for something. But the general feeling is that they will begin to shell tomorrow night."

The Green Woman stood immediately and dropped the cover as she rummaged around for her clothes.

"Don't look!" Reeder demanded.

"No, my Lord," Kelvin said, turning his back on them.

"We haven't a moment to lose," the Green Woman said, slipping her robes up over her head. "Ramon always allows a wine ration before battle. We've got to get our supplies ready and get to his camp."

"We?" Reeder said.

"Perhaps I would be a bit conspicuous," the Green Woman returned. "How long a trip to his camp?"

"You can turn around now," Reeder said.

Sir Kelvin turned, his leathery face set in the posture of service despite adversity. "With good rowers, a few hours at the oars and an hour or two on the ground."

"Good," the Green Woman said. "Now, if only . . ."

There was screaming out on deck, loud, piercing screams. They hurried to the cabin door and onto the upper deck. On the main deck below, Dunbar stood giving orders to several burly men who were trying to hold a small man in check. His upper arms were tied to his body with great lengths of rope, but it didn't stop him. He writhed like a whirlwind, spinning and knocking the men down who tried to hold him. All the while he craned his neck at an impossible angle to bite at the ropes around his upper body. And whenever he came up for air, he screamed like a wounded animal, his eyes wide, straining at the sockets.

"That's right," the Green Woman called down to Dunbar through cupped hands. "Except meaner. Meaner!"

ii

Sir Martin stood atop the long sweep of stone stairs and looked out upon the jungle that had once been the inner courtyard of Castle Alb'ny. Gone was the standing water, replaced by a garden of healthy mud from which sprang saplings and pampa grass and ivy with huge green leaves the size of a Woofer's head. Gone was any view of the wall that had once been there. Gone were the barracks. Gone were the royal kennels. Nature was rapidly reclaiming the might of Alb'ny and, Marty reflected, in its own way it was quite beautiful.

The sky grumbled above, fast-moving clouds an ever-changing tapestry in hues of gray. Below, the land lived and breathed. It was a war, he realized that; but the conquest was somehow reassuring, his ultimate defeat comforting in ways he had not been able to discern. He had never seen the jungle grow so quickly, even in this land of choking forest and perpetual summer, and in that, he began to see the emergence of a pattern.

It was morning and he had slept well for the first time since his war began. Dreams quieted him to bliss, dreams asleep and dreams awake. He stood naked with his sword, ready to do battle with an enemy he respected. His fight had been a good one, his own resolve bringing him many small victories in a campaign destined for failure. Most had deserted him, and even he had found surrender and flight a viable alternative more than once. But somehow, for some reason he didn't understand, he had stayed. He suspected that his staying was more important to him than he would realize for a long time, but one thing he did know: he was a different person now than he had been before—a better person.

All around, those still loyal to him stood on scaffolds running up the sides of the mud casing of the castle. They valiantly hacked away at the climbing vines that threatened to engulf the very heart of Alb'ny itself. It was a good fight against superior numbers, but it was a fight destined to be lost. Every day more of his small force deserted and made their way into the jungle and their destinies. The rest would soon follow. Mother Earth would have her conquest.

Perlie Pitts, once a kitchen helper and now Sir Martin's

field general, called to him from a nearby framework of bamboo, his long, matted hair and grime-smeared naked body making him look like something of the forest himself. "The clouds thicken! My bones creak with the feel of rain!"

Marty waved to him. "The final battle looms," he called back, brushing his own tangled hair from his face. "You've done well."

"You, too, my Lord!" Perlie yelled back, and a cheer went up from the other humans scattered amidst the quiet confrontation.

Sir Martin smiled broadly and moved down several stairs to hack away at the climbing vines of morning glory. If his father could only see him now. He raised his sword and brought it down hard, the blade singing with the contact of the stone beneath the vines. Tonight he'd have a feast for the remnants of his army, a feast of meat and, perhaps, wine. He smiled at the thought. He hadn't had wine for a long time.

iii

G'VANNI'S PALACE—N'ORK CITY

"What care you if we stay or go?" the merchant asked, his eyes narrowed on Alicia's face, looking for a sign of her feelings. "This is not our war, is it?"

Alicia stood rock still amidst a moving river of G'vanni's family, who hurried through the subterranean chamber carrying personal items and furniture to the boat docked above. They hauled great amounts of hammered gold, the barter gem of worldwide trade. The gold was formed into beautiful reliefs, large round plates etched with tales of the wonders of the sea and the heroism of man and Genie.

"This is your home," she returned in her negotiator's voice. "It seems only right that you stay and defend it."

"What seems right," G'vanni replied, "is the continued survival of me and mine . . . including you."

She looked away from him, her own survival instincts trapped in the quicksand of her feelings. The room was large, its walls reinforced to keep the water out. One wall was a solid window that looked into the blackness of the river and ocean meld. It was close enough to the surface to allow for the passage of some light, and in it she could see schools of fish moving past the window and the divers who were bringing up the treasures G'vanni had hidden beneath the waves. In the nearby distance, she could see the top of another stone tree that was completely underwater and covered with algae.

"It makes no sense," she said at last, "to run away. You will lose all you've worked so hard for."

He carried a stack of ancient books, carefully preserved under glass. He set his burden on the floor and moved to her taking her in his arms.

"Listen to me," he said, forcing her eyes to look in his. "Your husband's army comes apart from the inside out. It divides against itself. He cannot hope to stand against the might of Ramon of Alb'ny. My own spies have seen the size of the ex-Governor's force. He will have this city, and probably the heads of all who ruled it. I can be a king anywhere I go. I have amassed wealth unheard of in our history and will build a new life somewhere else."

"Until someone else comes along to take it from you," she said weakly, her body stiff in his grasp.

He searched her face. "You're being irrational," he said and held her closer, burying his face in her hair. He pushed himself against her. He whispered to her. "Forget about him. He's thrown you over. Come with someone who appreciates you. This is finished here. Please. Come and share my life, my love."

He groaned softly in her ear, his body tensed against her. Alicia's mind raced. She knew down deep that he was right. She'd been feathering her nest with G'vanni from the first. He didn't have a world to offer her, but could build a dynasty for her to rule. But something held her up, a tie to the man she married scant weeks before, the man who made it clear he wanted nothing more to do with her. Why couldn't she push him from her mind? She tried to give herself over to G'vanni's soft caresses, but it didn't work.

"God, I burn for you," he said softly.

"Don't," she said, putting her hands on his chest and pushing slightly. "Your family . . ."

"I can send them away," he said, and turned to speak to them.

"No," she said.

He turned back to her, his face angry. "You fire my dreams

and burn my every waking thought. I exist for you. Why do you deny me?"

"I'm married," she said simply. "A Politico takes all commitments seriously. I couldn't be otherwise."

"I don't believe you," he said.

She wasn't surprised; it even sounded ridiculous to her when she said it. "I'm s-sorry," she said, lowering her eyes. "I can't help but be the way I am."

"You will divorce him then."

She looked at him. "What?"

"I have my own holy men," G'vanni returned. "If this commitment is so important, then we will dissolve the commitment by the traditional method. Once we get underway, you will divorce and then I will marry you. We will share a kingdom together."

She moved away from him, turned her back. All around the activity continued, but it was as if she were totally alone with her swirling thoughts. If only she could ferret through the confusion of Morgan and the hold he had upon her.

"Free yourself of him," G'vanni said from behind her, as if he could read her thoughts. "I know of your kind. I can offer you everything you want and need from life."

It was true. He could. He could give her the dreams that had haunted her from her earliest days. She could feel his love, feel its reality. She turned quickly to him, hurrying to force the decision she had made.

"All right," she said. "I'll do it."

"My love," he said, and rushed to hold her again. He brought his lips to hers and they kissed deeply. She tried to give herself over to the kiss, tried to keep the farmer out of her mind. But it didn't work.

iv

VIPER'S BRIG

There had been no food, and Jerlynn had developed a high, delirious fever, alternately sweating and shivering with cold chills, as she lay unconscious upon the pile of boards.

Faf watched over her, keeping her covered with his heavy robes through the tortures that wracked her failing body.

Something was happening to her, and its ramifications were far more spiritual than physical. She was changing, transforming into something else. For the most part, she writhed and jerked to exhaustion in fitful sleep, but occasionally the spasms ended and she became lucid. It was these times that frightened him. She always came back as a different person. Even the cast to her face changed.

When she came back this way, she was always calm and sedate. She would sit up and converse with him, speaking of things that made no sense, of fields of sweet grass, of the unity of all things. He'd ask her who she was and she'd reply, "I am the whore of Siler," or, "I am the mother of all."

He had prayed mightily, prayed to Ibem to cast whatever demon from her that had taken control of her body, but it was to no avail.

"I perceive you to be a holy man," came the voice, the other voice.

He turned to see her sitting up, smiling sweetly, serenely at him.

The room glowed dully, the candle haze thick as a steamy jungle, the angles of the curved, slatted walls etched deeply with the jumping shadows. That other person was back again, and he felt ashamed, sitting there naked without his robe in front of this stranger, but his embarrassment and his circumstances seemed not to trouble the demon one bit.

"That is correct," he said cautiously. "I am a Programmer of Ibem."

"I sense overmuch pride in you," she said without malice, "but beneath it a good heart and true."

"I thank you," Faf said. "My pride has, perhaps, been my downfall."

The creature who sat before him in no way resembled Jerlynn Delaga, but her bearing was pleasant, angelic. He feared this demon and pined for his lost love, but he instinctively knew there was nothing of the demon he should fear.

"We help right the scales, you and I," the creature said. "We help balance the Way."

"I don't understand."

The creature shook her head lightly. "Of course you don't," she replied. "Do you fear death?"

He smiled slightly. "Death holds no mystery for me," he said. "It is the fate of all creatures. I have known happiness in measure undeserved, and regret nothing of my life."

The creature reached out and took his hand. "The time draws near," she whispered. "Walk hand in hand with goodness and mercy. Be as the trees and of the trees."

He drew back in shock at hearing his own words, a slight parody of the eulogy he had given at Ty'Jorman Delaga's funeral so long ago. And suddenly, something about her began to look startlingly familiar.

28

Viper's Troop Hold

Ramon stood within the guts of his mighty ship, staring down the length of its ribbed innards, looking for the Green Woman. The smell of human sweat was overpowering down there. It hung heavily in the enclosed, musty space like invisible fog, neither dissipating nor circulating. Shafts of light streamed through upper portholes crisscrossing the two stories to the floor of the hold, taking the huge open space from bright light to deep shadow with no gray area between. The hold, with its rows upon rows of thousands of sleeping mats of woven straw was relatively empty, the troops upon the shore constructing small skiffs for the attack of N'ork City. All that remained were Ramon and those who searched with him. They moved swiftly through the rows, looking for what they knew they would never find.

"Any luck?" Ramon called through cupped hands, his words echoing through the bulbous cavern of wood and pine tar.

"No, my Lord," the voices returned, one by one, some of them distant and tiny.

"Continue the search!"

He turned and stalked from the chamber, breathing shallowly through his mouth to avoid the smell. No wonder the troops spent as much time ashore as they could. He hurried up the stairs to the upper holds, then the main deck, breathing deeply, gratefully, when he reached fresh air.

The deck was filled with Castle Guard, all searching for the Green Woman. The sky rumbled maliciously overhead, the wind up, rolling the deck on the choppy river. Beyond, on the near shore, his troops worked quickly, under the tutelage of Delmar's whip, to complete the small craft that would be used within N'ork City to attack the stone trees. Boats were piled in huge stacks on the shore, while, farther upriver, the Physicians, under guard, were working to make the fire bombs that would bring the great trees to their death.

Ramon walked to the rail and pretended to watch the activity on shore. But he didn't even see it; his mind's eye burned with the image of his lost love. He was angry with her, had rejected her for his own soul's survival, but the thought of her gone was almost more than he could bear. He hated her, yes, but he wanted to hate her up close and for the rest of their lives.

"You bitch," he said low. "How could you leave me like this?"

"My Lord," he heard Delmar say from behind him, and he blinked back tears before turning to face the man.

"Yes," Ramon said. "What have you discovered?"

Delmar plucked his handkerchief from his frilly sleeve and held it to his nose, Ramon realizing the smell from the hold must be clinging to his clothes.

"There is no sign of her anywhere," Delmar said, with barely concealed glee. "It is as if she vanished from the land."

Ramon nodded, taking note of the man's attitude. "Have you tried the tents of the . . . other rulers?"

"With as much good taste as I could muster," Delmar replied. He walked upwind a few paces and put the handkerchief back in his cuff, pulling down the sleeve of his burgundy shortcoat and tails. "She is nowhere to be found."

"Any more on the man found dead on the foredeck this morning?"

"He appears to have suffocated," Delmar said, his eyes drifting from Ramon's to gaze over the waters. "His body was unmarked, except for a residue of white powder on his face and upper chest."

"She killed him," Ramon said, recognizing the mark of the one weapon the Green Woman carried upon her. "What could have precipitated it, do you think?"

It was Delmar's turn to lean against the rail and pretend to watch the shore. "I couldn't imagine," he said.

"Whose man was it?" Ramon asked, leaning next to him, pretending also.

"He was one of mine," Delmar said, and blew through puffed cheeks, not looking at the Governor.

"Citizen or mercenary?"

Delmar pulled a tiny gold snuffbox out of his shortcoat. Ramon noticed a slight shake to Delmar's hand as he took a pinch from it and brought it to his nose. "He was hired for his sword," he said, and snorted the tobacco loudly into his left nostril, repeating the process on his right.

"I wonder why he went after the Green Woman?" Ramon persisted.

Delmar sneezed loudly. Removing his handkerchief, he blew his nose. "Perhaps he courted her favor a bit too vigorously. I've heard that she was open to advances."

"I'd suggest a leash for that tongue," Ramon said low.

Delmar turned and looked boldly at Ramon. "She's gone," he said. "I don't care why. She was nothing but trouble from the first on this expedition and I, for one, am glad she's gone. If my man did it, so much the better."

"Unless he was ordered to do it."

"And I am here to tell you he was not."

Ramon stared at him. He was sure Delmar had a hand in the Green Woman's disappearance, but he couldn't even prove it, the only one who'd know was killed by the quarry herself. He needed Delmar and both of them knew it.

"So be it," Ramon said, mustering a smile, though his insides were melting like a candle in a bonfire. He slapped Delmar on the back, wishing he had a knife in his hand. "We'll speak no more of this. How go the rest of the preparations?"

"We're ready," Delmar said, tucking his handkerchief back in his cuff and putting away his snuffbox. "We should go right away."

"We wait one more day," Ramon said.

"But why?"

"I'm waiting for a messenger with important news," Ramon replied, and he wished Redrick were already back, he itched so for Morgan's demise.

"What could be so important to hold up the campaign?" Delmar asked. "The troops are restless."

"You need not know everything, my friend," Ramon said. "I still take some of the responsibility upon myself."

"The men are at a fever pitch," Delmar said. "If we don't leave today, I fear we will have to give them some other diversion to occupy them."

"I assume you have something in mind?"

Delmar nodded. "Faf and your mother. The troops blame them for our troubles thus far. If a trial were conducted, it would satisfy the men and also rebuild their confidence in you."

"A trial, you say? For my mother?" Ramon walked from the rail, moving a distance across the deck before turning again to his general. "I can't put my own mother on trial."

"You wouldn't be the first, my Lord," Delmar replied.

"Where would they get this idea about blaming my mother?"

Delmar shrugged. "You know the rabble, my Lord, always scratching around for a scapegoat."

"What if we just give them the holy man?"

"The connection is with you," Delmar said flatly. "They want that connection broken. They wish to put all their faith in you again."

Ramon walked very deliberately up to Delmar. The man went for his handkerchief, but Ramon stopped him from taking it out of his sleeve. "My mother does not go on trial," he said slowly. "Do you understand? I will not put my mother on trial. Even you can go too far, good Count."

"You're making a mistake," Delmar said.

"I don't care!" Ramon screamed, his face reddening. Everything stopped on deck, all eyes turning to him. Ramon looked at Delmar, then at the faces staring at him. Rage choked the words in his throat. He turned abruptly, stalking off the deck.

Delmar glared after him, his hands forming an evil sign a Physician had taught him many years ago.

Ramon moved down the stairs and into the twisting hall-ways of the upper hold area. His Guard were on duty, keeping things copasetic with Ona and the child.

He was going to her in his rage and his frustration and his loneliness. He was going to her without thought, for his thoughts were filled with the Green Woman alone. Could she have been killed and thrown overboard? Did she get away? Would she try and contact him when she was safe?

Ona's door was before him, and he hadn't even remem-bered the walk down. He turned and looked at the Guard who stood at attention beside the door.

"Take a break," he told the man. "Stay gone for a while."

The man nodded quickly, hurrying off without a word. As soon as he had twisted off down the narrow hall, Ramon opened the door and stepped into the cabin.

The woman sat in the corner rocker, sewing happily, while little Ty'Jorman hung on the bars of the cage they had made to keep him penned up. When the baby saw Ramon, he started crying and banging himself against the bars.

Ramon's mouth twisted into a sneer. He walked to the bars, kicking at them, driving the child back farther into the cage.

Ona held a tiny blue-and-white tunic up for Ramon to see. "I'm making one for each baby," she said happily. "They can be your miniature Castle Guard."

"What?"

"When we're together at the castle with both children," she said. "I've made little outfits for them."

Ramon grabbed the sewing from her and threw it aside. Then he pulled her arm and jerked her out of the chair.

"Tomorrow I kill the man who made those babies," he said.

"Good," she said, nodding. "We shall be free to live our life then."

"Life? What life?"

"Our life, back in Alb'ny," she smiled. "Just the way it used to be."

He pushed her to arm's length. "Stop it," he said. "Stop this talk!"

"Stop what, darling?"

He screamed then, and slapped her hard across the face.

Still holding her arm, he pulled her close and slapped her several more times.

"Thank you," she said after each slap. "Thank you, darling."

He threw her onto the bed, ripping her clothes from her body as she frantically tried to help him. But when he tried to take her, he was impotent. They both settled for another beating while Ty'Jorman screamed and tried to escape his cage.

29

Willow's Palace—N'ork City

Morgan sat on the corner of the retaining wall, his back to the waves, so that no one could sneak up on him. His old mentor stood before him, sorrow showing through his clear, light eyes, but nothing else. Morgan thought he had put Grodin out of his mind, had consigned their love and closeness to the ashes of old dreams; but, face to face with the man, he could not remember the hurt or the betrayal. The love was all there was, the love alone. The bond between them was stronger than pain. They had separated, but remained one. And in that, Morgan took a degree of strength.

"I was wrong," the old man said. "I wouldn't blame you if . . ."

"No!" Morgan said, standing to embrace the Breeder. They held one another, both of them trembling, both knowing how desperate they had been without the stability of the other. "You are here, my most wonderful friend. That is enough. You have filled an empty place within me, and that is more than enough. We will have no more talk of pain between us."

The old man pulled away, swallowing hard, blinking

rapidly lest he show weakness before this company. "Much that has passed between us is as tears in the rain," he said, "but we must speak about your mother, I . . ."

"Please," Morgan interrupted, putting his hand on the old man's mouth. "Weeks ago, I spoke with Dixon Faf about it. He was present when my mother asked you . . . begged you to . . . to . . ."

"I made it as easy as I could, lad," the old man said, now trying to put the discussion behind them. "You've heard that Faf has been arrested as your spy, along with Ramon's own mother?"

"Jerlynn?" Morgan said, incredulous. "But how . . . ?" Then he thought, and said, "Redrick again."

"He spied for them in Rockland," Grodin said.

"Aye," Morgan said, "where he killed Jella's wife."

Grodin nodded grimly. "I've heard the tale. The coward brags upon it."

Morgan looked to Jella. The man had stiffened, hearing Grodin's words. "What of Ona and the child?"

Grodin pursed his lips, as if he were searching for the right words to say. "Ona escaped me," he said. "I feared her betrayal, but couldn't keep watch upon her at all times."

Morgan returned slowly to sit upon the wall. "Then she wasn't captured?"

Grodin looked to the ground and shook his head. "She searched him out, at some amount of difficulty to herself."

"Her hatred is that strong?"

"It was unhinged her, I fear," Grodin said. "They mean to undo you. Together they mean to undo you."

"The child?"

"Safe. For now."

The roof was crowded with men and Genies, all needing confirmation of orders and tasks. They were being held back by a silent and morose Jella, whose own loyalty was stronger than his remorse and need for vengeance.

"Governor Morgan!" came a voice from the crowd, and Morgan looked past Grodin to see Lannie, the giantess, holding little Marek high above her head. The child squealed at the sight of his father, and began twitching madly in Lannie's grasp.

Morgan smiled wide and gestured her to him. He looked

at Grodin. "There are some other problems I must address," he said.

"I am your humble servant," Grodin replied. "We must talk, but you must do whatever else is needed."

"You really are back, aren't you?"

The old man smiled and nodded. "Rusty limbs and a rustier sword. For what it's worth, I'm yours."

Lannie walked up to Morgan and Marek twisted out of her grasp, jumping into his father's lap. Morgan laughed, the boy automatically tugging on his beard.

"Where did you find him this time?" he asked the giantess.

"Crawling back and forth on the pier below," she said, "angry he could go no farther."

"He has a strange restlessness of nature," Morgan told Grodin. "Fortunately, he instinctively avoids the water, so we always catch up with him, don't we, Genie?"

He hugged the child close, and noticed that Grodin didn't flinch at his calling Marek a Genie. Marek wriggled from Morgan's grasp and climbed upon his shoulder.

"His brother is just the same way," Grodin said. "Does Marek go into the trances?"

Morgan nodded. "He does, indeed. It's as if he is somewhere else."

Jella moved back to speak to Morgan. "My Lord," he said. "Notern of Fishkill needs to speak with you."

"Send him over," Morgan said, "but hold everyone else back for now."

Jella nodded and turned away.

"Where are the other giants?" Morgan asked Lannie. "Where are the Mechs?"

A look of pain crossed the giantess's face. She turned and walked off, nearly knocking over Prelate Notern, who stopped and stared after her before joining Morgan.

"The guns are all in place," he said, standing at attention. The burly man dressed in fur looked out of place and uneasy in the subservient posture, but he bore up under it well. "We have to move the last one up here now."

"All right," Morgan said. "I'll try and put everybody someplace else."

"You'll need to appoint a post commander to the palace," Notern said. "That hasn't been worked out yet."

"Have you someone in mind?"

Notern shifted uneasily. "I was hoping that I might have that honor, my Lord."

Morgan stood and took the man by the shoulders. "And have it you shall," he said. "But you must do me a favor. As your second in command, I want you to appoint El-tron."

"You're not serious," the Prelate said.

Grodin spoke up. "The pup bites and knows not when to stop," he said. "A position of that magnitude should not be given someone whose loyalty is in question."

Morgan looked at the old man. "You have come back to me despite the differences that separated us. This is the time to heal internal wounds, and I think this is the way to do it."

"You make a mistake," Notern said. "But I will heed your wishes."

"Good," Morgan said. "Have we found a stone tree suitable for dismantling?"

Notern nodded. "A tree of red brick and stone was crumbling on the West side of the forest. We have begun dismantling operations." He pointed past Morgan to the West.

Morgan turned to look. Mech-trained humans filled the skies with their artificial wings, gliding smoothly between the trees, carrying loads of brick and mortar to treetops for bombardment. Far in the distance, one of the trees was covered with men like ants on rotten fruit, as the wingers flew back and forth, gathering missiles. Large flocks of bright white gulls flapped in and out of the paths of the wingers, curiosity overcoming their natural fear of the unknown.

Morgan turned back to the Prelate. "Excellent. Anything on the Mechs?"

Notern shook his head. "Nothing."

Morgan tightened his lips. "Keep looking," he said.

Notern bowed slightly. "I begin preparations for the mounting of the cannon," he said.

Morgan returned the bow. "Thank you, my friend."

They clasped hands quickly, and Notern was gone.

"Where's the Politico?" Grodin asked.

"Gone," Morgan said, the emptiness rising like bile in his throat. "It is all mine now, to lose or win."

"Defeat would not be loss for you," Grodin said. "You are of good heart and win always that which is important."

"About half my army would disagree with you right now,"

Morgan replied. "But it probably doesn't matter. It seems I will die trying to rescue my son."

"Perhaps not," Grodin said. "I have managed to procure a position in Ramon's Guard aboard VIPER, and I know where the child is hidden."

Morgan's eyes lit up. "Is he well guarded?"

"Extremely. But I have a plan." The old man reached out and tugged on Morgan's beard, much to the amusement of the child, who straddled his head, holding onto his hair. "You may have to cut that beard, though."

Morgan stroked the beard. "I was thinking about it anyway," he said. "Too convenient a handhold with which to lop off heads. What's your plan?"

"Redrick of Firetree delivered you a message, did he not?" Grodin asked.

Jella heard the name and walked to the group, staring at Morgan, who nodded to him.

"Listen well," he said, then looked at Grodin. "Yes, it was the one-handed man."

"He was sent by Ramon as a gesture of irony," Grodin said, "but he is not the important one. The other, the feminine one. He is the one to watch."

"Why?" Morgan asked.

"He is a Genie," Grodin said, "who is incapable of telling a lie."

"I have seen such as him," Jella said. "They live short and unhappy lives."

"I have heard of your misfortune," Grodin said to him. "Listen carefully to me and you may yet have your vengeance."

"We have come for your answer!" came a voice from the outskirts of the crowd. The three turned to see Redrick and the Genie standing near them.

Grodin turned quickly and gazed out over the wall, keeping his face from Redrick's eyes.

"I haven't decided yet," Morgan said.

"You must decide now," Redrick demanded. "We must leave for our camp with the good light."

Grodin whispered harshly to Morgan. "Tell him we will meet in your palace in thirty minutes to decide."

"Can you wait one hour?" Morgan said to Redrick. "I am to meet with my advisors about this in my chambers within thirty minutes, and will have my answer for you then."

"An hour, no longer," Redrick said. "Though I see not what you have to talk about." He looked at a silent Jella. "Still pining for your sweet wife?"

Jella took a step toward him, but stopped himself, turning to Morgan. A look of shared pain and understanding passed between them, and the Prelate of Rockland turned and walked away.

"Well, don't go away mad," Redrick yelled after him. He laughed.

"I'm going to take care of you when this is through," Morgan told Redrick. "I'm going to take your eyes, your tongue, your ears, your nose, and your other hand."

Redrick paled, his lips quivering slightly before his bravado returned. "I am your master," Redrick said with confidence. "You are a beaten man and dirt under my feet."

He turned to leave. "One hour," he said, and moved off, Harrison following slowly behind, his head turned to look back at Morgan.

"I hope you know what you're doing," Morgan told Grodin.

"I do," the old man said, turning back to watch Redrick walk off. "Trust me."

"I do trust you," Morgan replied. "I trust you with my life and the lives of my children."

The small skiff moved slowly through the crowded waterways near the palace. The sea was blue-green and rolling high as the wind picked up and churned the ever-rumbling cloud cover into trumpeting thunderheads that heralded the first wave of a major assault by Nature's minions. The sky swirled blue to purple and turned the city to half night, as gulls flew madly about in confusion and the sensitive dolp-men beached themselves in stone tree doorways and chirped to passers-by of their fearful apprehensions concerning the continued existence of N'ork City.

Boats filled with food and weapons and refugees hurried all around the skiff, their occupants calling to one another as they tried to complete their given tasks before lashing down for the storm that was sure to come. The choppy seas and crowded canals made the going tough, but most N'orkers looked at the water as a second home and guided themselves expertly through it.

Those in the skiff, however, were totally oblivious to the goings-on around them. They stood, three of them, robed and hooded to avoid recognition. They stood straight and tall, the outside world passing by them as so much static as they centered completely on their goal. The last of the three held a long, flat limb, which he used alternately to row and push off the stone trees.

"What if they recognize us?" Pietro said to Nebo, who stood in front.

The Mech didn't turn to answer. "There's too much confusion right now," he replied. "They couldn't count their fingers with an abacus. Don't worry. Nothing will stand in our way."

"Will we meet resistance from within?" Laila asked from the oar.

"We are prepared," Nebo said, flexing his mechanical hands within the folds of his robe. "Nothing will happen. Trust in your own abilities."

Nebo was calm and serene. Calling up all his old teachings from the City of Islands, he removed himself from the present conflict and dwelt upon the Godlike simplicity of science. Take a problem; reduce it to its basics; define terms; catalog the components; experiment with the unknown until it becomes known; solve the problem. All life could be divided out that way: problem, definition, experimentation, solution. It was the simple faith of religion without the internalization of ego. The scientist *is* God, always speaking ex cathedra—without fallibility.

"We approach the palace," Pietro whispered.

"Find a place to dock by the pier," Nebo said calmly.

Laila found an opening near where the tip of VICTORY's crow's-nest still stuck out above the waves. The dock was busy, not only with messengers and deliveries, but with the armorers who were even then using Willow's cranes to haul a large cannon up to the roof under Prelate Notern's supervision.

The three Mechs climbed carefully out of the skiff and onto the dock, studiously pulling their hoods down over their faces. Many people filled the rocking pier, and it was easy to walk right into the crowd and disappear.

They moved down the pier, passing within several feet of Notern, who saw them not. A single guard stood watch over the entrance to the palace. The heavier security was up on the third floor.

The human, dressed in leaves, barred their way. "Got to know your business," he said.

"We come to pay homage to Ibem," Nebo said.

"One floor up," the man said, stepping aside. "Go up no higher."

"Yes," Nebo replied, and moved past him. "No higher."

They entered the darkness of the lower palace and went up. They reached the second floor without further challenge, though the stairs leading up to the third floor were filled with bodyguards. They moved swiftly, silently, each knowing the task he had in store.

The carpet padded their footsteps as they moved through the lush surroundings of the palace. The walls were hung richly with draperies adorned with golden rings. The smell of incense wafted in slow-moving clouds through the structure's open, airy chambers. In the distance, Nebo could hear the muffled tones of the Lawgivers, who were undoubtedly making hay for themselves behind closed doors. He would have to work quickly, but he already knew that.

They moved into the sanctuary, where Ibem sat on a golden pedestal in the center of the large room. Several wires connected God to his machines, which sat nearby, behind some free-standing purple drapes. A silver-suited Repairman sat by the drapes, watching the machines and acting as a sort of go-between for Ibem and those who came to honor him. God was left unguarded for the most part, no one worrying about trouble from the faithful.

"Can I help you?" the Repairman asked, standing and moving toward them.

"We wish to speak with Ibem," Nebo said.

"Perhaps I can help you," the quasi-Mech said. "I will better know how to phrase your questions."

"Good," Nebo said, and as the Repairman walked up beside him, he pulled the syringe from his robes and stuck it quickly in the Genie's back, as Pietro and Laila grabbed his arms.

The Repairman struggled backwards as the synthetic curare began to take effect. He tried to scream, but Pietro clamped a hand over his mouth. Seconds later, the man's nervous system froze, and he was unable to scream. The man stiffened, eyes wide in panic, and they let him drop to the carpet, taking no notice when he died several minutes later.

Nebo walked immediately up to Ibem, circling round him, looking at his wires.

"DO YOU WISH SOMETHING OF ME?" God asked him.

"You're connected to your power source and drives," Nebo said. "I assume you are in radio contact with your data base and on-line with it."

"THESE ARE NOT LITURGICAL AREAS," Ibem said, "AND CONSEQUENTLY NOT DISCUSSABLE."

"Is that a word . . . discussable?" Nebo asked.

"IT'S MY WORD," Ibem said, "THE WORD OF GOD. DO YOU HAVE LITURGICAL QUESTIONS?"

Nebo pulled the blade with the rubber handle from inside his robes and held it up for Ibem's photocells to see and identify. "If I were to cut your power and interface lines, would it wipe all memory from this unit?"

"I WILL NOT DISCUSS SUCH MATTERS WITH YOU. WHERE'S MY REPAIRMAN?"

"I would assume," Nebo said, "that should you be separated from your data source, you would retain enough memory to figure out how to get back to that source. Correct?"

"I WILL NOT DISCUSS THIS TOPIC WITH YOU UNDER ANY CIRCUMSTANCES," Ibem said.

Nebo smiled and pulled down his hood. He got around in front of the unit, so Ibem could see his face. "We already have discussed it," he said. "If cutting you off from your source would strip your memory completely, I'd venture that by now you'd be begging me not to cut you off."

"I LIVE THROUGH MY DATA SOURCE," Ibem said. "THIS UNIT IS MERELY AN EXTENSION OF IT, AND UNIMPORTANT IN ITSELF."

"Don't be so self-effacing," Nebo said, scooping the series of wires up in his free hand. "You're God. You shouldn't sell yourself short. Besides, I'm going to give you the power to really play God."

With that, he cut through the wires with one swift motion, white sparks arcing where the wires touched one another.

"This is mobile 14-7," a tiny voice said from within Ibem. "We are operating on auxiliary power that will be usuable for another thirteen hours, twenty-four minutes, and fifteen sec-

onds. Following are instructions for returning to radio contact
with the data base and instructions for finding and using a new
power source. . . ."

Nebo smiled and toggled off the voice synthesizer. He
nodded to Pietro, who stood ready with the gunny sack. Pietro
carefully picked up Ibem and placed him in the sack, while
Laila stood guard at the opening to the sanctuary.

"That's it," Nebo said. "Let's go."

They hurried from the chambers, moving through the
confusion of the lower levels, then onto the skiff without difficulty. They had just stolen God, and no one knew the difference.

Pietro untied them from the pier as Laila pushed off with
her large oar. Nebo placed Ibem on the floor of the skiff and
spoke softly to him as they drifted back into the sealanes.

"We're going to have some very constructive talks, you
and I," the Mech told Ibem. "Very constructive."

Morgan stood by the retaining wall and watched the cannon being hoisted up to his level, Jella supervising its lowering
onto the mule.

He waved down to Notern as the task was completed, and
was surprised to see what looked like three Mechs, totally
robed, walking with a package along the pier.

He made to call out to them as they climbed into a small
boat tied to the dock, but Grodin called him to his quarters for
the discussion about Ramon before he could do it. Moments
later, when the event should have been far from his mind, he
found himself returning to it, dwelling upon it—wondering.

30

The Meeting

"I don't see why we're doing this," Harrison the Truthteller said to Redrick.

"Just be quiet and stick close to me," Redrick returned, sliding a little farther along the retaining wall.

The roof of the palace was still jammed with supplicants. Morgan and Jella kept trying to disperse the crowd, but everyone thought their particular problem was special and deserving special attention, so none would go. Meantime, the large cannon was being raised for defense as squat Miner Genies carried crates of ammunition to the roof and People with wings dropped loads of brick as they glided overhead.

Redrick had led Harrison quietly through the crowds and had slipped to the far side against the wall. Slowly, he had edged along it, until he and the Truthteller were near the corner of the large pillared residence Morgan had claimed as his own. Two men in animal fur guarded the door of the residence, but they were taking no heed of the man from Firetree and his quiet, effeminate companion.

"When I tell you to go," Redrick said low, as he watched Morgan waving down to the pier, "I want you to walk to the building and hide yourself."

"I'm afraid," Harrison said.

"Do as I say," Redrick said, "or you will have much to fear from me."

The young man's eyes misted over, but he said nothing.

Redrick shifted his gaze between Morgan and the door guards. The bastard's companion had gone into the residence some time before, and it seemed to Redrick that perhaps if he were careful, he could listen in on the conversation.

Just then, the huge cannon was lifted over the wall. All activity stopped, the roof crowd watching the operation. Even the door guards were caught up, moving away from their posts to get a better look.

"Now," Redrick said. "Go!"

Harrison looked at him once with wide eyes and decided he'd better do as he was told. He nodded quickly and walked into the shadows along the building's side. The residence was surrounded by artificial shrubs painted gold. The Truthteller squatted down behind some of them, heart pounding. Redrick joined him seconds later.

"Morgan has just gone in," Redrick whispered. "Let's see what we can see."

"What if they catch us?" Harrison asked.

Redrick smiled his superiority. "What could they do? We hold his son's life in our hands. Come on."

Redrick stood and edged along the walls of the residence. Harrison followed reluctantly. The man from Firetree stopped before a series of tall, thin windows of stained glass. He listened near the first window, eyebrows narrowed in concentration.

He turned to Harrison. "I hear voices in there," he said. Reaching out, he pushed gently on the window, but it didn't move. He edged down the line, trying windows, until finally one cracked open slightly.

"Come here," Redrick said, pulling Harrison by his brown-tunicked arm. He held the young man's head by the hair, forcing it up near the window crack. "Watch. Listen. Remember."

Harrison looked through the window space. It was a large, open room, bright areas of red-and-blue light lining through it from the windows. The red-haired man sat at a table with two other men, the ones who had been with him out on the roof. One of the men was sitting with his back to the windows.

"We can secret a force in the forest nearby," the man with his back turned said, "and take them by surprise long enough to get the baby back."

"It's not your child we're talking about," Morgan said. "There's not an alternative you've mentioned that wouldn't be dangerous for Ty'Jorman."

"And there are no alternatives that won't be fatal to you," the other man, the one whose wife was killed by Redrick, said. "To go at all bespeaks your end."

Morgan ran open-fingered palms through the long hair, working out tangles. "To not go condemns my baby to death," he replied. "Could you live with that?"

"No," Jella said simply. "I could not."

"Well then, why not at least take the soldiers," the other man said. "In a hopeless situation, at least they'd be a chance."

"Can't do it," Morgan said. "I have to take Ramon at his word. He may, in fact, want me badly enough to spare Ty'Jorman's life, and Ona's, if I give myself over. It's the only thing I can do."

"Then you intend to follow his instructions?" Jella asked.

"Yes."

"Then it's the end of everything," Jella said. "There's nowhere to go from here."

"I've made my mind up," Morgan said. "Adjust yourselves accordingly."

Harrison looked at Redrick. "Did you hear?"

The man's death's-head face was grinning hideously. "We've got him," he returned. "Let's get back out there."

Morgan poured wine for everyone at table, and he thought he saw a shadow slip past a partially open window. "I hope we drink to success," he said.

Grodin took a long drink. "It won't be easy at any rate," he said.

"Can't I go with you?" Jella said. "Perhaps I could run across my wife's killer again."

"Not this time," Morgan said, laying his hand on the man's shoulder. "Grodin and I must go alone. Besides, I have need of you here to run things in my absence, and to . . . take over if anything should happen to me."

"Listen," Grodin said, holding a hand up for silence.

It sounded as if there was trouble on the roof, muffled shouting. Seconds later, one of the door guards burst into the room.

"You'd best get outside," he said. "Something's wrong."

The men shared a look, and Morgan was heading for the way out, his drink untouched.

The roof was a madhouse. There was a wedding going on, so a large tree had been dragged upon the roof as the traditional symbol of eternity and fertility. The Duchess Clorina was marrying Bruno Schmid, the merchant, his clan of boisterous, fair-haired, fur-wearers singing loudly and drinking even as the ceremony progressed. Willow's man, Telemay, presided over the nuptials, his red robes too bright amidst the earthen colors of the merchant family. Even Willow was present to legitimize the joining. Twiddle, Alicia's prophet, was in attendance, standing close to the marriage tree; it was the first time Morgan had seen him since Kipsie.

The supplicants still waited, moving in and out of the lines of Miners, while Notern helped secure the cannon to the mule. But the problem was not with any of that. Something was wrong. Old Penrad, the Lawgiver, was upon the roof, screaming to the crowds, as were Rothman and Dycus.

Morgan walked toward the Lawgivers, the anger rising in him. Jella hurried after.

"Don't do anything foolish," the Prelate said.

As he passed the marriage ceremony, Twiddle snaked out a bony hand to stop him. "When you return," the old man said, "I will be with you."

Morgan stared at him for a second, looking at the smooth skin where eyes should have been. He had not time to dwell on the Genie's message.

As if sensing this, Twiddle let his arm drop, and the Governor hurried on.

"There he is!" Penrad screamed, pointing to Morgan's approaching figure. "He's the one who will bury us all!"

"I told you not to come up here!" Morgan said, pushing his way through the crowd to reach the old man who stood upon an ammo crate.

"What have you done with Ibem?" the old man demanded, his face drained of color, his livered hands quivering with rage.

"What are you talking about?"

"You killed a Repairman and stole Ibem!" Dycus screamed, walking up to Morgan. "I trusted you. How could you do this?"

"Give us our God!" Penrad said in the preacher's cadence. "You defile all we hold dear."

"I don't know what you're talking about!" Morgan yelled, angry that he had to defend himself in front of a crowd. "I haven't touched your precious machine."

"See?" Penrad screamed. "Hear his blasphemy? You must rise up and rid your city of the heathen. You must call a holy crusade and drive the Godless from your homes!"

"Stop it!" Morgan said, and pulled Penrad down from his crate. "You will not preach sedition in my camp."

Dycus grabbed Morgan's arm, trying to free the old man. Jella pulled him off, holding him. Spindly Rothman moved to them.

"We will preach your downfall as long as we have breath to speak," Rothman said. "You may kill us, but our Truth will live on!"

"I haven't taken your machine!" Morgan said again. "I don't know what you're talking about."

"Who else but you?" Penrad said. "Who else?"

"I don't know and I don't care!" Morgan said. "Guards! Get these men away from my command post. Don't allow them entry again."

Burly humans came and took away the Lawgivers, who didn't struggle.

"You've only heard the beginning of this!" Penrad called as they took him away.

"You'll find my hospitality somewhat more severe next time," Morgan replied loudly, and stood, breathing heavily, as they disappeared down the stairs. His mind was racing, charged up. What more could go wrong? What more?

"We've come for your answer," Redrick said, and he was standing in the spot occupied by Penrad a moment before.

He looked past Redrick and the boy to see El-tron behind them. The small Genie stood uneasily, leaning against the retaining wall.

"I will do as you say," Morgan told Redrick. "I will meet with Ramon at the appointed time."

Redrick's eyes twinkled. "There will be a white fishing boat anchored a mile downstream from our main camp. You will be there at dawn tomorrow to parlay."

"Yes," Morgan said.

Redrick laughed. "I'd do you in now, myself, but the Governor has claimed that right. But don't worry, I will be there to enjoy your undoing in full measure." With that, he spit on Morgan's face, the man taking it without choice. Then he turned and strode off, the Truthteller hurrying behind.

The world had turned completely dark for Morgan, but he

didn't let it register on his face. He remained calm, stoic. El-tron stepped up to face him as he wiped the spit from his cheek.

"You have given me a position of responsibility," the Genie said. "Why?"

"I want to mend our fences," Morgan replied.

"The gulf between us is wide, perhaps uncrossable."

"I hope that's not the case."

El-tron nodded, his face hard. "We all do what we must," he said.

"Yes," Morgan replied.

"I appreciate the position," El-tron said.

Morgan, his mind elsewhere, nodded briefly, then turned and walked off. The Genie watched him go, still wondering why he had been put in the absolute position of insuring Morgan's demise. He could only assume, ultimately, that the red-haired man's breeding included its own deathwish.

31

i

WILLOW'S PALACE

El-tron stood in the confusion of Ibem's new temple and stared up at Lawgiver Penrad. The old human was taller than the Genie by over two feet, and glared down at him through eyes glazed with hatred for his kind. For his part, El-tron responded not to the feelings, simply returning the gaze with the conviction of a zealot on a mission.

"What brings you to my domain, heathen?" the old man demanded. "Has not your kind done enough damage to us already?"

Indeed, the large, open rooms were filled with much weeping and breast beating. Visitors and inner circle alike mourned for what they considered the end of the world. Already, several Repairmen had taken their own lives rather than face life without God.

"While I don't share your sorrow for the machine," El-tron said, "I appreciate and support your final aim."

The man cocked an eyebrow and folded his slender arms. "What are you saying?"

"We both want the same thing," El-tron said, large eyes wide and staring, "the overthrow of Morgan of Siler."

"My feelings are public," Penrad said. "I am not afraid to voice them to you. What can you gain by such baiting?"

"I speak the truth," the Genie replied. "To me, hemolysis is as bad as Godlessness."

There was a gutteral, gurgling scream, followed a moment later by another Repairman being carried past Penrad, the body smoking, electrocuted by choice in one of Ibem's energy cabinets.

"Why do you come to me with this?" the Lawgiver asked.

"We can help one another," El-tron said, and Penrad grimaced at the thought of joining that which he was sworn to destroy. "I am to be second in command of this garrison. My position will provide a base of operations for you to get our message to the people and a friendly command chain to help you."

"Friendly . . . how?" the old man asked, his look shifting to curiosity.

"I am in the process of transferring all of my own people to staff this place. They all feel as I do and will work hand in hand with you."

Penrad squatted on the carpet, getting eye to eye with the small Genie. "Will there be humans among your company?"

El-tron nodded.

Penrad pulled thoughtfully on his long, drooping mustache and thought that the remnants of power had to be tied together in any way they could. "Make humans the intermediaries between you and me," he said. "Fix it so that me and mine have no contact with the heathen and we will work together."

El-tron never even flinched. "Done," he said and held out his hand.

Penrad fought back his own revulsion and grasped hands

with the heathen, El-tron's long fingers wrapping nearly double around the old man's hands.

ii

ATOP THE LONELY SISTER

"Please," the tiny computer voice said. "You must return this unit to a power source and data base contact."

"Don't worry," Nebo said, patting the machine on its smooth, slick side. "Steps are being taken."

He straightened, looking around the top of the tallest stone tree in the city. In the distance, the statue of the goddess called silently to him. No one came up here because of the holy nature of the place, so there was no chance of discovery this early.

The wind was high up here, the thicket as dense as it was on the sides of the tree. Below, the forest spread out all around, still bustling with preparations for battle. Above, the angry sky rumbled low, seemingly within touching distance— as close to heaven as the Genie would ever get. Several giants stood dutifully around, their services useless on the small technical work that was now being done. Pietro, his mate Al-ke-do, and Laila worked with the radio transmitters that would hook Ibem up to data and to the atomic device that sat atop a small pole right next to God.

"How soon?" Nebo asked no one in particular as he checked the small liquid electric crystal he had attached to Ibem's power inputs.

"Soon," Pietro said, the sleeves of his robes pulled up, his hands lost in a transformer box. "We're just double-checking systems now."

"Good," Nebo said, his eyes returning to the device, as they always did. Its simple symmetry was a thing of beauty; its operation basic and effective in an almost Godlike way. How fitting that it should be Ibem entrusted with the final detonation.

The machine spoke. "Available energy in my batteries is down to seventy-five percent."

"Pietro . . ." Nebo said.

"Done," the Mech said, pulling out of the transformer. He turned to Al-ke-do. "Juice it."

Al-ke-do bent and twisted together the wires that connected the transformer to the transmitter, and the unit began to hum loudly.

Nebo reached out and toggled the interface on Ibem's side that netted all the transmitters and receivers together with his power grid.

"We have power and reception," the computer said. "You must move our receivers to the microwave band to make contact with base."

Nebo put his hands on the small unit, turning the dial on the front to the short range waveband until the red "hot" light glowed on Ibem's face. They had contact.

"I ask access to file name, Godproj," Nebo said, "password, restabilization."

The machine's face blinked quickly, red-and-green lights pulsing the flow of information shared unit to unit. Finally, after several minutes, the unit sat silently.

"Ibem?" Nebo asked tentatively.

"I AM THE GOD WHO MADE THE HEAVENS AND THE EARTH," Ibem said. "WHAT DO YOU ASK OF ME?"

The Mechs and giants broke into spontaneous applause, cheering Nebo's accomplishment.

"You must all go now," he said. "Go to the others in Mud Plains and await me there."

Pietro walked up to him and put a large hand upon his mechanical one. "We wish to stay and share this with you."

Nebo shook his head. "I want to fix this so that we may all get away and know that the device will liberate itself. I don't need you for that. Do as I ask. This will take some time. It will be dangerous. You must be free to lead the others should I fail."

They all laughed then, the concept of Nebo failing impossible for them to contemplate.

"We will go only if you keep the giants with you for protection," Laila said from beside the transformer.

Nebo looked around. Serge was there, sitting forlornly upon the retaining wall, staring down at the preparations. "My own giant is here," he said, pointing. "He's all I need."

"Take them all," Pietro said. "It is the only way we'll go."

Nebo agreed reluctantly, just to get them out.

"WHO WISHES TO SPEAK WITH GOD?" Ibem demanded.

Nebo saw his protégés off, then turned to the computer. "I have kidnapped you," he said.

"FOR WHAT REASON?"

"I want you to help me explode a device."

"ARE YOU OF THE PURE BLOOD?"

"I am a Mech of the Pure Blood."

Static warbled through Ibem's small speaker mouth. "I EXIST ONLY TO PROTECT THAT WHICH IS PURELY HUMAN."

Nebo assumed the lotus position before Ibem and made himself comfortable for a long discussion, while the giants stood watching him silently.

"We must begin," Nebo said, "by defining what we mean by the term, 'human.'"

iii

ABOARD GRAYCLOUD

The man was chained to the foredeck gun that pointed out over the bow. His eyes were bulging and red-rimmed, and still he screamed, though his voice had gone long before and all that came out of his gaping mouth was a chesty wheeze and trickles of blood from his ruined nodes.

Young Reeder stood looking down at the man, his stomach in knots, for surely this was not the way for men to wage war. The Green Woman stood easily beside him, looking like anything but herself. Green no more, she had somehow painted herself white and dressed in bulky furs, so that she didn't even look like a woman. A series of bladders were slung across her shoulders.

"This is horrible," Reeder said.

"This is war," she returned. "It is an unpleasant experience."

"But this . . ."

"Your vengeance, remember?"

He turned from the man. Sir Kelvin was waving them over to the gangway, Dunbar standing beside him, iron ball in hand. The boat was ready.

"You'd never use those drugs . . . upon me, would you?" he asked.

"The need for vengeance is stronger than any drug," she

replied, then reached out and hugged his arm. "I would never deceive you on any level, just as you would never deceive me."

He smiled at her, then broke out laughing at her attire. "You have shown me much life in one day," he said. "But this was something I never suspected."

She winked at him. "Wait until I get into my fake beard."

"You really intend . . ."

"I intend to lead this expedition," she said emphatically. "I will entrust this to no one save myself."

The sky cracked loudly through the near-darkness of the overcast late afternoon. They both glanced up.

"Something monumental is going to happen," he said, and hugged her close. "We will face it together."

"Together," she said.

And arm in arm they walked to the gangway and down to the longboat that would take them upriver to the camp of Ramon Delaga.

32

Ramon's Encampment—Evening

Ramon's mind wandered as he stood upon the slightly rolling deck of the fishing boat he had plucked off a Nyack sand bar and towed to here. He had felt the need of some relief upon the disappearance of the Green Woman, and had prescribed for himself massive amounts of 'dorphins in order that he might lighten his burden. It didn't help.

His mind swirled, turning the surface of the water to a kind of mental whirlpool, dark and sinister. He saw her everywhere—in the faces of others when they were present, in the thin air when there was no one. She laughed at him with her wicked eyes and reminded him again and again that he would never be able to forget her.

The boat was large and creaking, its whitewashed boards groaning under the weight of the kegs of black powder, which, even then, were being loaded into the hold as he leaned, stiff-armed against the rail, staring into the angry black waters. It was early evening, just before dark, but the blackness of the loud rolling clouds made the night come too swiftly; dim, hulking outlines were all they were able to conjure of their surroundings. Above him, on the forward mast, Ramon could hear but couldn't see the large white flag rippling loudly, calling the farmer to his last moment.

"My Lord," came Pack's voice behind him.

Ramon turned quickly, angry at being disturbed, and nearly lost his balance. He sagged against the rail, going almost to the deck before pulling himself back up.

The Physician's dark form stood before him, an instrument of some kind clutched in his hand. "Perhaps you should go a little easier on the medicine, my Lord, I . . ."

"I don't want to hear of it," Ramon said, agitated. His feelings about the Green Woman had become translated to anger, then hatred for Physicians in general. Had he been more able, Pack would have been in desperate trouble.

He grabbed the man, wrapping arms around his neck for support. "It's just too dark up here. Why can't we have some light?"

"The hold is full of explosives," Pack explained. "We fear a torch might send us all up."

"Explosives," Ramon said, his head fogged momentarily. Then it cleared, as if a cool wind had blown through it. "Morgan. This is all for Morgan."

"Yes," Pack said patiently, and shifted Ramon's weight back to the rail. "We have loaded enough black powder in here to destroy the boat and probably all the fish for miles around."

"Splendid," Ramon said, his dizziness passing with the rail to lean upon. He looked out upon the waters, and thought he detected a small boat making its way toward them from downriver. "How will we ignite our boat bomb?"

Pack held out the instrument. "I've designed a detonator."

Ramon took it from him, a small metal box with a turn crank atop it that didn't look as if it could explode much of anything.

"We can detonate this from shore using an incomplete electrical connection that will join when you turn the handle."

"I know how to work it!" Ramon lied. "I'm not as stupid as you give me credit for."

"Of course, my Lord."

The boat was getting closer. A figure in front was standing, waving his arms.

"We can watch him from shore," Pack was saying, "and blow him up when he climbs aboard."

Ramon leaned over the rail and cupped his hands to his mouth, nearly dropping the detonator. "Redrick!" he called. "Over here!"

Even through the rapidly descending darkness, he could see the man's hideously grinning death's-head face and knew that things were going smoothly. Seconds later, Redrick threw a line to Pack to tie down and he and the Truthteller were scrabbling aboard.

"Why can't we get some light here?" Redrick asked.

"You fool!" Ramon said. "You'd blow us all up. So you're back." He used a free hand to clap the man on the shoulder, then turned his attention to the Truthteller. "Harrison. Was your trip a success?"

"That's for you to say, my Lord," Harrison said in a little girl voice.

"Indeed it is." Ramon tossed the detonator to Pack and straightened himself, this time doing it slowly so as not to fall down. He was quite proud of himself. He took Harrison by the shoulder and pointed him back upriver toward the encampment that sat flickering in the night like a million fireflies.

"My armada is ready to capture a world," he said. "We await only the word you bring us to move."

"My Lord . . ." Redrick said.

"Shut up," Ramon said. "I'm speaking to my honest friend. Tell me what happened?"

Harrison explained the entire trip and his part in it perfectly. Not a detail was left out, not a fact was embellished or overlooked. He reported factually, honestly, and without conceit. To listen to the Truthteller was to know a total and unbiased view of events. And when Harrison was through, Ramon Delaga's heart was lightened at least, if not unfettered.

"There will be no tricks?"

"No tricks," Harrison said. "He intends to bargain with you honestly."

Ramon smiled then. "So, the farmer's aged, but hasn't smartened. Good. We will be done with him with the lightening of the day, and be done with his rabble the day following."

He squeezed the young man close, ignoring Redrick completely. "You've done well, lad. Unfortunately, I'm finished with your services." He drew his sword, holding it out with an unsteady hand. "It wouldn't do well for a human crusader to spend too much time in the company of heathens."

The boy fell to his knees, bowing his head. "Please," he said. "I'll do anything you ask."

"Look at it this way," Ramon replied. "I would have killed you back when you were discovered. Look at how much extra time you've gotten thanks to my generosity."

With those words, he brought the sword up with both hands and jammed the point into the boy's exposed back. It barely went in, so weak was Ramon's thrust, and Redrick had to help him finish the job.

"Have him thrown overboard," Ramon told Pack. "Then finish fixing up our little surprise. I will be back long before dawn to supervise the explosion." He looked at Redrick with distaste. "Take me back to VIPER."

Redrick went silently overboard and into the skiff. Ramon put a shaky leg over the side and tried to slither into the boat, but his execution was bad and his first long step pushed the small boat away and he fell into the water.

He sank into the buoyant, black world totally disoriented. It seemed the Green Woman were down there, wrapping cold, loving fingers around his whole body. He floated gently with the sensation, feeling as protected as a baby in its mother's womb until something grabbed him, jerking. Hands were pulling him up and out of the water, reality taking several seconds to establish itself as he tried to fight the rescue attempt.

The next thing he knew, he was lying in the skiff on his back, choking out watery breath.

"Are you all right?" Redrick asked, getting right down in his face.

"Take me to VIPER," he sputtered, his blue cotton body suit soaked dark and heavy.

Redrick rowed silently as Ramon lay there watching the

black clouds rumble dangerously overhead. "Ask the weather-man about rain," he said, finally sitting up and taking a small command of his mind.

The main camp was very close, fires up high to keep away the children of the night. Preparations still continued as more and more boats were constructed to meet the final assault of N'ork City. The voices of men screeched loudly, tensions high before the battle. This was the time all of them had been antic-ipating for so long. The lights seemed extra bright in Ramon's distorted mind, the voices extra loud. It was a vibrating, strain-ing hive, his camp, a cacophonous symphony of destruction and madness. It suited him perfectly. Everything was in place. All that was missing was his love: the Green Woman, the maestro of Death.

"There is a party awaiting us," Redrick said, as he took them into the confusion of small fishing boats on shore. Ramon looked. A rather large torchlight contingent lined the shoreline, waiting for them.

"Take me to them," he said, and tried to compose himself, knowing he wasn't up to his full abilities.

As they closed in on the place, Ramon saw that the party was made up solely of leaders of his Northern allies. Redrick brought them to bump right up on shore, the orange glow of their torches creating a small clearing of jumping light.

Ramon climbed slowly out of the boat to stand before them. Young Dadelous Nef and Senator Murray led the pro-cession, with Delmar close behind, and the minor rulers clus-tered around in no particular order.

"You come to see me, I assume," Ramon said, awkwardly putting his hands on his hips and confronting them.

"Our people cry for justice," young Nef said. His eyes were hard and distrustful, his bearing rocklike. After the loss of Troy's two former leaders, he was not about to put himself in the position of martyr.

"Justice?" Ramon replied as if he'd never heard the term before.

Murray spoke, and Ramon knew the man too stupid to respond without coaching. "You harbor traitors in your midst. Their trials must be attended to before we can go on."

Ramon's eyes searched out Delmar. "This is your doing," he said.

"I simply bring it to your attention," the man said, his hand resting solidly on the hilt of his sword. "The troops are alive with talk of this."

"Is this so?" Ramon called loudly.

The assembled rulers all yelled out their feelings. Ramon was overwhelmed by the dogged tenacity of the response. He was in no position to argue with them.

"We commence the shelling tomorrow night," he said.

"This must be attended to first," President Wilke said from the crowd, and all voiced their agreement.

"I dislike clouding the issue," Ramon said, "but I will respect your wishes. We will have our trial."

"When?" Delmar asked loudly.

Ramon glared at him. "We will sup tomorrow and break out the wine ration," he said. "For dessert there will be a trial, then on to N'ork City."

The assembled cheered, and Ramon's thoughts had already turned to giving Ona a good beating to relieve the tensions that had built up within him.

33

The Promise

Morgan and Grodin stood in the small clearing, breathing in the smell of death and charred oak from the smoldering campfire. Here and there, bodies lay still, the dancing firelight making it seem they were twitching on the ground.

"There's the boat out there," Grodin said, pointing to the dim outline of a fishing vessel just offshore. He knelt in the soft clearing dirt and picked up something.

Morgan looked out over the water, then down a distance to the barely active camp of his half brother. It was huge, an army larger than he could have imagined. So much the better.

He was uncomfortable in the blue and white-striped tunic of Ramon's Guard that Grodin had given him, and the discomfort had nothing to do with the nature of the fit. He felt like someone else with his smooth-shaven face and mud-smeared hair, and only the familiar feel of his father's boar's-head sword was reassuring.

He walked to one of the bodies and wiped his blade on a matching blue-and-white tunic. "They would have attacked us from here?" he asked.

Grodin walked over to him and gave him the instrument he had picked up. "I think it has something to do with this," he said.

Morgan grunted and walked closer to the fire, bending before its light to examine the thing. "It's a detonator," he said. "I've seen the Mechs use them many times. The boat must be loaded with explosives. They could have blown it up from shore."

Grodin sided his blade and moved out of the fire's light, looking at Ramon's camp. "The cowards were afraid to face you," he said.

Morgan straightened, hooking the detonator to his tunic strap with a piece of leather he had taken from the scabbard of a dead Guard's sword. He walked beside Grodin as the old man pointed.

"His is the first boat in line," Grodin said.

"And you know what room my boy is in?"

The old man nodded, his face scar a deep shadow in the darkness. "I've been in sight of it," he said. "It's no easy in and out, but with what the Truthteller must have reported, I don't think they'll be expecting us."

Morgan slid his blade back into its resting place and walked. "I see no reason to hesitate," he said.

They moved along the shoreline casually, as if they belonged, the camp drawing ever nearer.

"I hope you have an army to return to when this is done," Grodin said.

Morgan nodded. "I've not handled things well."

"You've handled them honestly," Grodin replied. "That's the biggest problem a leader of men can have."

"Alicia's loss has been the greatest blow," Morgan said, and his hand drifted to the gun that was tucked securely beneath the tunic. "She could hold all the elements together where I thrash around like a rab in a mud hole."

"I don't think that's really what you miss about her," Grodin said. "She is the woman of your lifetime."

"There are none like her," Morgan said, and nearly let himself sink into melancholy before pushing it from his mind. "But these are the regrets I will have to dwell upon as I grow old, not now."

Grodin placed a large hand upon his arm. "My wish is that you do grow old enough to regret things."

Morgan smiled over at him, his white teeth standing out in the darkness. "I'm a whirlwind, my teacher," he said, "son of kings. Both of us will live to speak of this around our hearths."

"By gods, you could almost make me believe that."

Morgan hugged him as they walked. "We are the right, I know that. We will not die this day."

They reached the outer edge of the camp, moving past the perimeter guards without challange. The camp was drowsy with sleep, a few men telling tales around their fires, a few women already moving about in preparation for the morning meals.

They walked to the profusion of boats near the water's edge, looking out at the still-lowered gangway of VIPER just offshore.

"How long until morning?" Morgan asked.

"I make it several hours yet," Grodin said. "Time enough still to take them by surprise."

He climbed aboard one of the wooden boats, Morgan giving it a shove and jumping in. They cut quietly through the dark waters, tying up next to several other boats lined to the gangway.

After climbing out of their skiff, they quietly undid the lines holding the other boats in check and mounted the stairs.

"I'll do the talking," Grodin whispered. "These people know me."

Morgan nodded, happy enough to be doing it Grodin's way, but also happy enough to do it any way it needed to be done. He feared not for his life, never for his own life.

When they reached the deck, they were stopped by the two men who guarded the entry. "Name and business," the burly one said.

"Gabil Hays Duncan," Grodin said. "I'm the one who . . ."

"We remember," the pocked man said, and his humiliation at the other man's hand was still strong in his mind. "And who might this be?"

"Another replacement," Grodin said. "My son, Gannet. We've come to inspect the ship."

"Is he as good as you?" the other guard asked.

"Better," Grodin grinned. "Want to try?"

There was dead silence from the Guard. After several seconds, Grodin and Morgan simply walked past them and across the main deck. Morgan, familiar with the layout of the ship, headed right for the steps down to the hold. They were challenged again at the stairs, this time by one man, and were forced to kill him to gain entry. But they did it quietly and hid the body in the shadows beneath the deck cabins.

The hold was different from VICTORY's once they went down a level. It had been divided into a series of mazelike hallways, each guarded every few feet by blue-and-white tunics. Grodin took them around the twists and turns that led to Ona's prison, and Morgan realized it was the only way he could possibly have found the child.

Finally, they stood at the head of a long hallway lost in shadow. A door glowed under lantern light at the end of the hall, with a single guard, half asleep, to watch over it.

"How come only one guard here?" Morgan whispered, as they peered around the hall entry.

"If you got this far," Grodin said, "you'd probably overlook this hallway because it was unguarded."

Morgan nodded. "We'll have to kill this one."

"Let me go alone," Grodin said. "My familiarity will put him at ease."

The old man ambled down the hall, the small corporal barely rousing from his stupor before sliding to the floor in perpetual sleep. Grodin turned and waved a hand holding a small, bloody dagger. Morgan hurried to join him.

Grodin bent to the dead man, coming out of his tunic with a large, black key. He held it up for Morgan to see. "This is all that separates us," he said.

Morgan took the key from him with a firm hand and lowered it to the lock. He turned the key slowly, quietly, the lock clicking, and the door swinging open.

The room within was bathed in soft light, and Morgan took it all in with a glance. Little Ty'Jorman was in a cage, his tiny hands locked around the bars as he tried to pull them open. Ramon and Ona, both naked, were sitting up in bed, looking at him.

"The bastard of Alb'ny," Ramon hissed, his hand going for the sword beside him.

Morgan and Grodin sprang into the room, slamming the door behind them.

Ona's hand went to a small key hanging around her neck, and she ripped it off, clutching it tightly.

"Get Ona," Morgan said, and pulled his own sword to meet Ramon, his mind twirling with clashes of duty and honor, for all that he had hinged upon a promise Alicia had made to the Lawgivers in Kipsie.

Ramon was up, swinging the sword with two hands, his eyes wide, aflame. "I'll take you here!" he yelled. "I'll have your bastard's head!"

The room was filled with the sounds of steel upon steel, as the child pulled harder on the bars, a small, gutteral yell issuing from his mouth.

Morgan parried, honor holding him back from the kill. His blade, directed by love, moved like lightning, his brother no match for his prowess in this or any other lifetime.

"Killer of my mother," he said, hands shaking with unrequited rage.

"And your father," Ramon sneered, keeping on the attack, his blade blurring the air.

"My . . . father," Morgan said.

It all came together, the senseless act that began the entire war simply a way for Ramon to keep him from his inheritance. With clenched teeth, he slashed wildly, driving Ramon back against the wall.

Grodin had his sword in hand, holding Ona in the far corner. "The key," he said. "Give me the key."

"No!" she spat, her face bruised and bloody from Ramon's torment. "Humans will raise my child. Humans!"

"Quiet her!" Morgan ordered, driving Ramon to his knees, still holding off the killing blow.

Grodin jumped on the woman, working to pry the key from her grasp. They went against the table, knocking the lan-

tern from its place to fall on the floor, burning oil spreading
flames in growing tendrils.

Grodin released the woman and grabbed the bed sheet,
throwing it on the fire, the room filling with smoke, hazing it to
darkness.

Morgan swung out at Ramon, snapping the other's blade
in two. He slashed again, knocking the remnants from his
hands.

The woman tried to run past Grodin, but he tripped her.
He tried to pull her to him even as he fought the fire. With
hatred twisting her face, she brought the key to her mouth and
put it in, swallowing hard.

"You bitch," Grodin said, pulling her to him, trying to
stick his finger down her throat. She smiled triumphantly and
grabbed his swordhand and turned the point to her breast.

She threw herself upon it, driving the cold steel deeply
into her heart, the black blood spurting. She slumped, dead
for spite, Grodin throwing himself back upon the fire.

Morgan knocked Ramon to his back, straddling him. The
man's eyes were different, altered beyond Morgan's understanding.

"Guards!" he yelled loudly. "Help! Help! The heathen is
upon us!"

"Kill him!" Grodin yelled from the fire. "He'll bring them
all upon our heads!"

"Help!" Ramon screeched. "Murder!"

Morgan stood above him, shaking madly. His honor, his
Truth, had been his whole life, his whole reason for living.

"Kill him!" Grodin yelled.

He raised the sword, but his arm locked, the genetics of
his makeup holding him back.

"Kill him!" Grodin yelled again.

"Help! Help!"

Morgan looked down at the madness of his brother's face
through the acrid fog of dark coal oil and knew it was beyond
him. "I cannot," he said.

Grodin leapt from the still-bright fire. "Well, I can," he
said, and moved across the room just as the door exploded
inward to the confusion of dozens of Castle Guard.

They swarmed the room, Morgan jumping from Ramon's
form to the cage bars. They were upon him. He fended them

off with one hand while tearing furtively at the bars with the other, Ty'Jorman's little fingers wrapping around his father's massive ones.

The smoke was thick, burning his eyes, choking him, as all became confusion in the black fog.

There were too many. He turned from the uncompromising bars, taking out the full vent of his frustrations on his tormentors. They fell by twos, threes, but always to be replaced by more.

The fire had been quelled, but the smoke remained, as he fought his way to Grodin, the old man looking at him with eyes that didn't understand.

"We've got to get out!" Grodin called.

"No!" Morgan said. "We must save the child."

"We must save ourselves first," the old man said, slashing across the face of a Guard. "We'll die here!"

Morgan turned quickly to the cage. The child locked eyes with him, staring.

"No," Morgan said, "no."

"Morgan," Grodin said, "you . . ."

The old man went down with a groan, the flat of a sword taking part of his head. He slumped to the floor, as Morgan cursed his own life.

Screaming savagely, he drove them back, picking up the unconscious body of his mentor. He hefted Grodin over his shoulder and hacked his way to the door, the man's weight dragging him down, swords flashing through the darkness. He turned once more to the cage, but couldn't see Ty'Jorman through the smoke.

He made the hall, taking them singly as they came to him in the confined space. He fought his way, a body at a time, to the hall's end, then turned and ran into the maze.

Men charged past him as he ran, one blue tunic carrying another. "Back there!" he kept shouting. "He's back there!"

He got lost in the hallways, turning corner after corner, finally stumbling his way to the stairs up. He burst, coughing, onto the main deck which was now filled with people who didn't recognize him.

"Down there," he kept saying.

He moved to the gangway, which had been raised, sealing him on board. Without a thought, he climbed the rail, still carrying Grodin, and jumped the fifty feet to the dark waters below.

The plunge revived the old man, who was groaning as Morgan brought him to the surface. He had lost an ear and some scalp on the right side of his head. Kicking for the boat, he pulled the groggy man aboard and untied.

Above, hundreds of faces were peering down at him. Many were climbing on the rails and diving overboard. There was one oar; he used it to try and pull them out of the shallows and into the current. Grodin struggled to his elbows, tearing his tunic into strips to tie around his head.

Men were splashing toward him, swimming faster than Morgan could row. He pulled his pistol from his tunic and fired at the closest ones, keeping them back as he reached a swifter current.

"Why did you . . . let him live?" Grodin asked wearily.

"I swore not to kill him," Morgan said. "I swore."

There were boats behind them now, longboats with many rowers. He couldn't distance them for long. Then he remembered the fishing boat. He unhooked the detonator from his cinch and set the oar back in the boat.

He drifted past the fishing boat with the white flag, those behind gaining rapidly.

"Get down!" he ordered Grodin, and the old man bent over double as he tied the cloth around his head. At least the missing ear was on the same side as the scar.

Morgan watched the fishing boat still too close behind him. His pursuers were just passing it and the time had come. He threw himself down to cover Grodin and turned the handle, making the radio wave connection.

Black night became bright daylight as the boat went up in a huge ball of nearly white flame. The concussion was incredible, pushing Morgan faster into the current. The ball of fire hung suspended in midair for a second before plunging the world into darkness again, and it rained splinters and pieces of flesh upon Morgan for several miles.

And as he drifted with the current into the ever-lightening morning, the hint of an idea began to take shape within his mind, and it was all tied up with honor and duty and the necessity of choice in all things living.

PART FIVE

WAR

34

River Visions

Ramon stood in the still hazy, badly charred cabin that had been Ona's home and prison for a time. He was wrapped in the bedspread, standing like an island amidst a moving river of men who carried out the bodies of the slain. The smell of burned wood and pine tar was thick in the unventilated room, nearly overpowering, and as he stared at the still-locked cage containing the bastard's child, he wondered what his father's namesake thought of all that had transpired.

The child lay in a corner of the cage, eyes rolled back, arms and legs flailing—in the middle of one of his seizures. Though Ramon had let Morgan slip through his fingers, he still felt triumph at the sight of the baby in the cage. The farmer had left without what he had come for, and now the extent of his commitment was obvious. He'd come for the child once; he would do it again.

"My Lord," Redrick said, walking up to Ramon to tug on the patchwork spread. "Is there anything I can do?"

Ramon looked at him in distaste. "You managed to miss the fighting again," he said.

"No," Redrick said. "I engaged the bastard . . . alone, on deck. But everyone else was too cowardly to help and he got away."

Ramon cocked an eyebrow. "There is something you can do for me, my friend."

Redrick bowed his head slightly, his red sleeping robes bright and shiny. "Anything," he said.

"Fetch the key that opens the lock to the cage, would you? Ona has it."

Redrick perked up. "Certainly," he said, and moved around the other side of the bed to see the woman lying dead on the floor. She was naked. He kneeled down excitedly and let his hand rove over her body, "searching" for the key. He stood up, confused, and looked at Ramon through a passing curtain of litter bearers. He shrugged. "She has nowhere to hide a key."

Ramon smiled thinly. "She swallowed it," he said. "It's inside her."

"But . . ."

"Get it out for me."

Redrick absently drew his sword, bending to the body. He began his grisly work, gagging often before coming out with the key. He moved to Ramon and held it out.

"Wipe it off, please," Ramon said, bringing a corner of the spread up to cover mouth and nose.

Redrick looked around for a cloth. "But where, my Lord, I . . ."

"On your robes," Ramon said. "Hurry."

Redrick did as he was told, his servitude gradually being replaced by a growing sense of humiliation. He handed the key to Ramon.

Without a glance, Ramon snatched up the key and moved to the cage. He unlocked the bars and reached in for the child, dragging it across the cage by its feet without breaking its reverie.

He picked it up and held it out in front of him. "I'm going to kill you," he said, grinning broadly. "But not right away. I'm going to use you to lure your father back to me, then I'm going to cut you up in front of him before I kill him."

He tucked the baby under his arm, not willing to let it out of his sight again until he had gotten his revenge. He walked out of the cabin and into the crowded hall, trying to figure out what weakness it was that made the bastard leave him alive when he should have killed him.

The small boat was traveling with a school of fish. As Morgan lay astern, he could hear them jumping, large fish, big splashes. In the darkness he couldn't see them. He could only hear their noises and feel their vibrations.

Grodin lay forward in fitful slumber, his bandages soaked with his own blood. Morgan had attempted sleep, but it had eluded him, so much going through his mind.

They were in the current, the draw magnetically back to the N'ork City forest. To the East, the sky was beginning its long pull toward daylight on the last day before the end of the world as they knew it. He passed occasional campfires on the river banks, no doubt advance scouts of Ramon's force keeping away the creatures of the night.

He should have hated himself. Ona was dead, little Ty'Jorman still in the clutches of his mad brother. The woman had been his mate through the hard times. They had shared much love . . . and some hate. She had borne him children and stuck with him through a crusade she didn't understand. The fact that they had parted was not her fault. Her only sin was that she simply didn't share his dream, for she had dreams of her own.

"Find the peace you never had in life," he said with great sadness, and chose to remember her heroically, the woman who had rescued him from the dungeon. He vowed to not let her memory die in the children.

For the sake of his honor, he had lost all that he had set out to attain. Grodin cried out softly in his sleep and shifted position. The old man had followed him in good faith, and would be burdened with the price of it for the rest of his life.

He should have hated himself. But he didn't. The child wouldn't die; he knew that. He knew the viper well enough to be sure he would try and use the baby again. For Ona, he felt sorrow but no blame. She taught him the lesson of his life.

His honor, he knew, was the ultimate arrogance. As he ranted against the sins of breeding, he himself practiced his own hypocrisy, for he had placed his own honor above the lives of those closest to him. He wished to escape the breeding, but didn't want to escape it in his own life.

The knowledge liberated him. Life was the key. Honor was a lie. He was proud of his honor bred, and in the pride lay the folly. He would never make that mistake again. If he was to escape the sins of breeding, he would have to begin in his own house.

And his thoughts turned, as they had to, toward Alicia. He was afraid to trust her because of *her* breeding. How could he lead a people to a new light if he feared the light himself?

Did not Alicia deserve the same chance to overcome her breeding as he did, as all the others did? He had been desperately wrong not to trust her, not to think they could work out their difficulties because of the breeding. They were all free, free creatures of God and deserving of respect as themselves.

He would go to her and make her understand, make her come back. It wasn't too late. Love was greater than breeding, respect greater than love, acceptance and trust the greatest gift of all.

He passed another campfire, animal noises billowing to him across the sounding board of the rushing water. Silhouetted against the bright yellow flames ashore, he could make out the misshapen outlines of jungle creatures enjoying a meal of fresh human meat.

35

i

RAMON'S CAMP

Liz'beth of Cohoes sat on the hard ground, her eyes stinging from the smoldering campfires, and cleaned the fish she would cook for the morning meal. A sight a small distance away had caught her attention, which was quite a chore, for very little in life commanded the attention of the stringy-haired woman. She simply lived from moment to moment in an animal-like state, taking gratification and momentary satisfaction as she could without relating it to her life in any meaningful way.

But this was different.

Something bothered her about this that she couldn't explain. She had been with the army from the first, cooking and whoring for her small circle, stealing their trinkets when they weren't looking and rat-holing the trinkets away. It had been a very natural existence for her, and she had done it all without once thinking about the expedition or what it meant. And now she was worried.

Perhaps it was the pasty-faced man with the frail body that frightened her. It was still totally dark, but as the man had passed her campfire, she felt a shiver go through her when she saw his blank, white face.

There were five of them. She watched them pass near her, one at a time, and go to the holding area where the wine kegs were stored for the feast that afternoon. They each carried lizard skin pouches, and she watched transfixed as they poured the contents of the pouches into the cork holes of the barrels.

She was frightened, and she couldn't ignore the fear the way she always did. This was a sticking fear, a solid fear.

When the people were finished with the wine, they moved off quickly, disappearing into the darkness and confusion of the camp.

Liz'beth's mouth was dry as she gathered her filthy robes about her and crawled the several yards to the snoring form of Rat Carveri, who slept as near to the fire as he could to save himself from jungle creatures.

"Rat," she hissed, afraid they'd come back for her. "Rat, wake up."

She shook him several times to no avail. Finally, she shoved him hard, the man jumping and turning to her.

"What in the . . ."

"Listen to me," she said. "Something's wrong with the wine, I . . ."

He grimaced as if he had just sat upon his own knife and lay back down. "Get away from me," he mumbled and fell immediately back to sleep.

She roused him again, anger showing on his face this time.

"I saw some people," she said. "They . . . put something in the wine, something bad."

"So help me, Ibem," he growled, "if you don't let me get some sleep, I'm going to put you in the wine."

He rolled back over again. She roused him again.

"Listen!" she demanded.

He came around with the back of his hand, and knocked her hard to the ground. "Get away from me," he said, emphasizing each word, speaking slowly.

Getting to a crouch, she scooted away. He turned and

went back to sleep. She tried to return to work, but it was no use. She was aflame inside, burning with a fire that couldn't be ignored. She rose and hurried to her own sleeping place, gathering her things together, the task of a moment.

Then, without a backward glance, she walked through the camp and back upriver, keeping near the shore for protection. She knew that something horrible was going to happen there, and the jungle was by far the lesser of the two evils.

ii

WILLOW'S PALACE

Something had happened to the sky. Prelate Notern awoke in the middle of the night in the officer's quarters in the palace, sinus pain building pressure behind his eyes, giving him a headache that went clear around his skull to run up and down the cords in his neck.

He sat up, rubbing the back of his neck, and looked around. The large, open room was empty except for Prelate Jella, who slept fitfully nearby. Yellow candlelight flickered softly on vacant bedrolls, and in the distance, he could hear just the hint of a muffled voice outside the palace.

He stood with a groan, for he was not still the man he pretended to the world, and slipped into his furs. Taking briar pipe and Southern tobacco in one hand and his sword in the other, he slipped out of the room and onto the roof.

The night was absolutely still and close, no wind at all. Above, the clouds hung low and heavy. He knew why his head hurt so. He stuck the pipe in his mouth and hooked up the sword. A distant voice could be very plainly heard out here. A crowd of men stood toward the front of the tree, the pier side, looking down.

This smacked of El-tron; he didn't need to know what it was to know it. He'd been expecting some sort of trouble and now they were getting it. It was as simple as that. Slowly, thoughtfully, he filled his pipe and walked to one of the outside campfires for a twig to light it.

Putting that twig to the pipe, he puffed furiously to get it going, then walked to the commotion in a haze of blue-gray smoke.

All the officers were standing up to the retaining wall,

looking down at the pier. The surrounding trees and waters were filled with people, human and Genie alike. Boats jammed the canals, while citizens climbed the thick vines running up the sides of the stone trees and hung on. Large torches glared the whole area to daylight. There was even a boat containing a huge tub of oil that burned like a monstrous bonfire, the heat sealed in by the close atmosphere, bringing up the temperature even more.

Everyone was there to listen to the Lawgivers. They stood on the end of the pier, preaching to the crowd with open arms, shouting their message to any who would listen.

"You must make your peace with Ramon Delaga!" Penrad shouted. "The world of our fathers and our fathers' fathers is slipping away from us. We must salvage it however we can. Morgan seeks our destruction! He steals the symbol of our everlasting God and forces us to fornicate together in unholy union. He uses you, every one of you! He wants to destroy you by getting you to aid in your own destruction. He is dangerous! If we are to save ourselves, we must overthrow his tyranny!"

Notern listened to the applause and cheers and felt cold fingers wrapped around his heart. He looked at the officers, their faces illuminated by the torches from below. He recognized not one of them. El-tron must have replaced the entire garrison with his own people.

Penrad kept preaching.

"Why haven't you stopped this?" Notern asked the officers. Several of them turned to him, but no one spoke.

He leaned over the wall. "You will halt this demonstration immediately!" he screamed.

Penrad turned slowly to stare up at him. "We preach the holy word of God," he called. "You cannot stop that."

"You preach sedition on the eve of victory! Will you cease?"

"No!"

"Then I will be forced to place you under arrest!"

The officers all stared at him now, their faces confused. Penrad continued to preach. Notern stared back at the officers.

"Arrest them," he said.

El-tron pushed through the men to address him. "We cannot arrest a Lawgiver," he said.

"You can," Notern replied. "And you will arrest *all* of them."

"They are of God," El-tron returned, "and above the rules of mortals."

"Since when did you fear Ibem, Genie?" Notern said, his teeth clamped hard on his pipe stem. "Will you do as you're told?"

"No," El-tron said. "We will not."

The men all turned to the wall again, ignoring the commander.

Notern stood there, watching them. Then he tapped out his pipe on the retaining wall and went looking for Jella. The Prelate was already up and dressing when he entered the hall.

"What's happened?" he asked, as he buckled his sword around his waist.

"The Lawgivers preach treason from the pier and our people refuse to arrest them."

"El-tron?" Jella asked, and Notern nodded gently, almost apologetically.

"What do we do?"

"If you're game," Jella said with a half smile, "we arrest them ourselves."

"You're right," Notern said, eyes twinkling. "It's time for a futile gesture."

They moved out onto the roof, right past the officers to get down the stairs. On the lower levels, the window spaces that looked through the vine were jammed with soldiers and Repairmen, all listening intently.

Notern and Jella moved past them all, to walk out onto the rolling, creaking dock. Dolp-men chirped happily all around the pier, not sure what was happening, but enjoying the excitement of the large crowd.

The men drew their swords and walked to the end of the dock to take into custody their own religious leaders. Scant weeks earlier such an action would have been deemed unthinkable by either of them.

"Lawgivers of Kipsie!" Jella yelled to get above Penrad's still-strong voice. "You are under arrest!"

Penrad turned slowly to face him, his arms still in the air. "We'll not go with you," he said conversationally. "Don't be a fool."

Jella brought the point of his broadsword up to the old man's neck. "If you don't come now, so help me, I'll gut you where you stand."

Dycus placed himself between Penrad and the blade. "I'm afraid he means it," he told the old man, and pulled his arms down.

"These people would never allow it," spindly Rothman said.

Jella stiffened. "I'm willing to take that chance," he replied.

Notern had wheeled around to guard their backs. Several of the palace garrison had inched out onto the pier, but stopped when Notern saw them.

"Meeting's over!" Jella called to the crowd. "Disperse. There's nothing more to see here!"

The crowd grumbled loudly, booing Jella's words. Everything seemed to close in tighter around them.

Penrad smiled broadly at him. "Well, now that you have us . . . General," he said softly, "what are you going to do with us?"

Jella bent and picked up a coil of rope from the pier and tossed it to Dycus. "Tie their hands behind them," he said, "then tie them together."

Dycus just stared at him.

"Do it!" Jella screamed, and viciously slashed his blade inches from the Lawgiver's face. Dycus started to work. Turning to the water beside the pier, Jella pointed to the people in the jammed-up boat. "Vacate the boat."

"How're we doing?" Notern asked over his shoulder.

"We've got them right where we want them," was Jella's reply.

Those in the boat transferred to another nearby, while Dycus finished his job. Then Jella tied him with the others and herded them into the boat.

Notern used the long pole to push them away from the dock, the other boats slowly moving aside to give them passage, their angry-eyed passengers staring fire.

"Disperse now!" Jella called, as they slid through the statuelike scene, the only movement the jumping shadows. "You fight for your lives tomorrow. . . . How can you do this?"

And somewhere, halfway up the side of one of the trees, a group of cat-men began cheering and clicking their nails in approval. More applause joined them, the silent support finally vocal. And thousands cheered down the long streets of water. Jella cried to know that they still had at least a core of strength. Soon, they were surrounded by other boats, full of men volunteering to protect them and guard the prisoners.

Notern looked at Jella, and he, also, had tears in his eyes. "I guess it's not over until it's over," he said.

"I guess you're right," Jella smiled back.

iii

THE GRUNT TREE

Gregore and Marta lay upon the floor in the third-floor room and peered out of the large window that came almost to floor level. It had been completely closed off earlier, but they had cleared it, wanting some light and air. They lay in the exhaustive throes of post-mating and watched the spectacle of the Lawgivers in the distance.

"The humans never think anything through," Marta said, slightly embarrassed by the shell lubrications that still made her body slick and the uncontrolled noises she had made during the act. "They jump from one major life-change to another without the least understanding or planning."

"Galen says that it's because they have such ephemeral lives they can't waste the time thinking," Gregore returned, and he wasn't embarrassed by their act at all. His exuberance for their lovemaking was essential, for if he weren't so persuasive, shy Marta might never make love.

He lay beside her, passion momentarily spent, feeling virile and alive. He loved the physical joining, for it was only during the sexual act that a Grunt's defenses were down. The others feared that, but he found it adventuresome.

"I've been thinking," he said, "that when this is over and we return home, perhaps we should think about having a child."

Marta couldn't meet his eyes, her embarrassment still too strong though she, too, loved the joining. "Galen says . . ."

Gregore frowned and interrupted. "Galen says this world is too insane for anyone to want to bring more life into it. I don't care what Galen says about it. If Mama Spire had listened to Galen, I wouldn't be here tonight."

"It's such a large decision," Marta said. "So many factors must be considered."

Gregore reached a hand to her, letting his eyelid slide across her lubrication.

"Gregore!" she said, slapping his hand away. She folded her hands across her chest and sat up. "Please."

He sat up beside her. "I want us to start considering all those factors."

She looked at him then, with all her eyes. And they softened with love.

The sound of cheering from without made them turn back to the window. Two men were taking the Lawgivers away in a boat.

"Will we kill the red-haired one soon?" Marta asked.

Gregore nodded, and brought his hands up to rest upon his horns. "One of his command came to us today and said that when we want to take him, they won't do anything to stop us."

"It sounds too simple," Marta replied.

He snaked a hand over to grab her horn. She rolled her eyes, but didn't remove his hand.

"We're Grunts," he said proudly. "Of course it will be simple."

36

Outside G'vanni's Palace

G'vanni's boat had two high masts, both containing big, square sails that unfurled to a red-and-white checkerboard pattern. It was also equipped to man twenty rowers on each side. It sat at the end of the short pier that led up to the palace entry.

Morgan poled up near the entry to see many of the merchant's retainers standing idly on the pier beside crates of belongings. The gangway was secured, several of Morgan's own people guarding the entry, along with others upon the deck itself.

"Looks like whoever he is, he's going to flee," Grodin said. The old man sat, still groggy, his swollen face smeared black with char and the rust-flaky color of dried blood.

"Not if I have anything to say about it," Morgan replied, bumping up beside one of the fishing boats he had liberated on the trip South. Many boats were tied to the dock, some with small sails in bright colors, some with oars.

He threw a line to one of the family on the pier and climbed out, giving Grodin a hand up behind him. A Minnie stood at the palace end of the pier, watching him. He knew that even though he had come directly here from Ramon's camp in the early morning light, the Minnie had now passed the word mentally and his arrival was known at the palace.

"Come on." Morgan moved down the pier, putting a hand to his own face when he noticed how filthy Grodin's was. He was surprised to find his beard gone. He had forgotten.

Gone was his tunic after the fighting, leaving him only black britches and high boots. The odors of death and burned wood clung to him like a shroud, and his eyes were glassy from lack of sleep. He was ready to win back his love.

Guards attempted to challenge him at the canopied entry, but realizing who it was, they drew back in fear. He strode in confidently, Grodin stumbling behind, hand on his sword.

They entered a brightly lit lobby filled with people. The walls were painted bright orange, and a huge carpet inlaid with bright, insane swirls of primary color filled the floor. Candles with three-foot diameters burned at even distances around the room, their wicks as large as ropes and a flame a foot high.

G'vanni and Alicia stood in the center of the room, she dressed in the green robes of his House. Twiddle was with them, as were Telemay and Morgan's man, Trilly, from Beacon. Representatives from the other families were scattered around the room. They were all arguing.

He moved toward Alicia, the only thing on his mind. G'vanni saw him first, and began pointing madly. "You!" he yelled. "Who do you think you are to order me around?"

Morgan joined them, his eyes fixed on Alicia, whose eyes were fixed with concern upon Grodin.

"What seems to be the trouble?" Morgan asked, smiling.

"Trouble!" G'vanni screamed, his face reddening. "You want trouble, you ignorant peasant? I'll give you trouble."

"They're trying to leave the forest," Trilly said in his slow, pestering way. "I had them stopped. Don't know what kind of contraband they might be getting away with or how many others would want to take boats out of here if they left."

Morgan glanced at him, then looked at Alicia. "I've got to talk to you privately," he said.

Her face was hard. "You have no right to keep us here," she said calmly.

"We're carrying no contraband," G'vanni said. "All we want to do is be left alone to sail out of here."

"Leave your home?" Morgan said. "You won't stay to defend your home?"

G'vanni put an arm protectively around Alicia. "My home is where my family is."

"Family?" Morgan said.

"We're to be married as soon as we get underway," G'vanni said.

Morgan looked at Alicia. "Is this so?"

She nodded. "Now, if you'll call off your Woofers, we'll get out of here."

Anger swelled within him. He stood tall and glared at G'vanni, then looked at the woman. "You're married to me," he said.

"The Lawgivers have given me a divorce," she said, head up, eyes proud. "I'd think you'd be glad to see the end of it."

He tried to take her by the shoulders, but G'vanni pulled her closer.

"I must talk privately with you," he told her.

"There's nothing you can't say in front of my fiancé," she replied.

"Alicia . . ."

She stared him down, cold as well water.

The merchants, there to convince G'vanni not to run away, moved nearer. Everyone wanted to hear what the Governor had to say.

"All right," Morgan said, putting his hands on his hips and stepping back a pace. "All right." He swung back and forth, taking in the crowd. He put a hand to his breast, then extended it to Alicia. "I was wrong. I didn't trust you, didn't trust

. . . your breeding. I was arrogant and stupid to turn away the person I cared most for in life. I know my lapse of faith is inexcusable, but I beg your forgiveness anyway. Please . . . don't turn me away now. I love you."

G'vanni laughed loudly and removed his hands from Alicia to slowly clap. "He talks of love, but still holds us prisoner. Bravo, Morgan."

"This wouldn't have anything to do with the Lawgivers, would it?" Alicia asked.

"What?" Morgan said, "I don't . . ."

"I think I know your breeding pretty well, too," she said, taking a pace toward him. "You get yourself in diplomatic trouble that you can't get out of, so right away you come running to the Politico."

"What's that supposed to mean?" he said loudly.

"It means I'm not going to save your rear end for you, just so you can abuse me again!" She had lost her temper, a serious act for a Politico. She walked him backwards, index finger jabbing his chest. "It means I'm not falling for your trick. It means I'm going to marry my betrothed and sail out of here and not look back ever!"

"Will you let us leave now?" G'vanni asked.

Morgan stared for a long moment at Alicia, who returned it with fire. Then he spoke, low and controlled. "You will stay here as my prisoners only until the shelling starts. That will give you time to . . . think about your decisions."

He turned and took several steps toward the door, then swung back around. He pointed at Alicia. "I'm not going to make it easy for you," he said. "When you leave, it's going to be with the bombs whistling and the fires blazing, so you'll know what you're walking out on."

"It's too late," she said. "Let us go."

"You'll come back to me!" he said, pointing at her, jabbing his finger. "History is being made here. You must be a part of it."

She moved back to fit into G'vanni's arms. "My history is away from here. My life, away from here."

"No," Morgan said low, almost growling the words. "You'll come back to me."

He turned and strode out of the room, trying to swallow back the hot iron ball that was stuck in his throat. Old Twiddle took several steps toward the door, then stopped, looking back at Alicia. It was nearly time, he needed to be with the Governor, but Alicia had to be talked to, had to be convinced to change her mind. He would stay just a little longer—and try.

37

i

RAMON'S CAMP—LATE AFTERNOON

They built their campfires up high, as much for the light as the cooking heat. The sky hung so low and so dark as to make it seem the night was descending several hours early. Thunder rumbled a throaty growl, like an angry Woofer's, and the bottoms of the blue-purple thunderheads sometimes lit from within, swallowing lightning that never reached the ground.

Nothing moved. The stillness was overpowering, the sealed-in humidity causing sweat to fall like rain from the bodies of Ramon's troops. But they didn't mind. They were up and ready for battle, more than ready, their senses honed to a dangerous edge by days of waiting. A little sweat only lubricated the blade. They reveled in the feast of rab and snake, and called for the wine, which was being hauled through the camp in Woofer-drawn carriages, wooden spigots hammered in to froth the finest of Alb'ny's cellars into the crocks of those too crass to appreciate it.

Ramon and Delmar drove one of the carriages themselves, waving to the crowds that pushed happily around them, laughing like children at the sight of the wine kegs. Ramon smiled wide at everyone near him, though the smile was disassociated from the rest of him. He was hitting the 'dorphins hard, the penalty for dipping into the well a bit too much, for now he had to work to maintain his mind's peak, lest he fall down to a dragged out sleep that he could ill afford with the battle at hand. So, he just kept pumping the 'dorphins into his system, kept going to the well time and again, hoping the water was just as sweet near the bottom. On the seat beside him, Morgan's child was tied down, never out of Ramon's reach. Ty'Jorman seemed to know the thin thread that dangled his life, and he remained quiet throughout the ordeal.

Delmar pulled the mongrel Woofer up near one of the campfires, the animal whining immediately for the rab meat he smelled on the spit. A crowd of several thousand soon pushed their way up to the wagon. They yelled and waved their tools of war above their heads.

Delmar stood and addressed the crowd. "I've been told," he said loudly, "that you don't get to drink this stuff . . . unless you promise to butcher some Genies for us!"

The crowd roared out its enthusiasm. The Count put up his arms, his pink, frilly shirt stained dark with sweat. Even Delmar had abandoned his shortcoat in the heat.

"I've also been told," he continued, "that those of you that do butcher Genies for us will be made honorary retainers of the House of Delaga, and entitled to as much of this stuff as you can drink for the rest of your lives!"

They cheered wildly, and this was the first Ramon had heard of such an absurd proposal. The Count looked down at him and they exchanged smiles. Delmar thought he had it all, that he had control of the whole thing, but he wasn't as smart as he thought. Ramon still had a trick or two he hadn't used yet.

Someone was pounding the spigot into the huge barrel. Seconds later, large mugs, sloshing wine, were pressed into their hands, Ramon standing to make the toast, while someone fed rab meat to the Woofer.

"My friends," he said, putting his hands up for silence. "My friends. As is the custom in the Delaga family, we feast and serve wine before the battle. This goes back many hundreds of years, and comes from the idea that we feast with our honored ones before they fight for us, lest they think our generosity and thanks are only as solid as your victory.

"Not true, my friends. You will be victorious on the field of battle tomorrow, of that I have no doubt. So, we feast now and toast . . . victory!" He held the crock high, then drank it down without stopping for breath. He threw the crock away, and another full one was brought to him.

"This has not been an easy campaign," he said. "It has been marked by many troubles, by many . . . divided loyalties. But everything is aright now. Know that I am with you no matter what, that it is your best interests I take to my heart."

The cheering crowd was parting from the back files. A processional was making its way to the wine barrel. Redrick led a delegation composed of Physicians. Pack was in the forefront of the group, his small circle of companions those who had remained loyal to him during the dark times of the Green Woman. They were already trying to weasel their way back to power. They wore garlands of wild orchids over their alien costumes and sweat-plastered hair, and carried a small cask on a satin pallet at the head of the line.

Redrick grinned in his idiot's fashion as he shoved the group to Ramon's position, happy to be aligned with those in command, for truly, the companionship of his contemporaries eluded him. But when he looked up at Ramon's face at the wagon, the returning glance frightened him enough to cause him to back away into the crowd.

"My Lord!" Pack said, already jubilant from the wine. "I present to you a gift from your loyal Physicians."

"Give it!" Ramon said, drinking deeply. "My heart leaps if it is what I think."

Pack turned and lifted the wooden cask off the skiff and handed it up to Ramon. "Concentrated 'dorphins, my Lord," the Physician said, "a lifetime supply, as requested."

Ramon grabbed the keg impatiently, its bulk and weight divinely reassuring. He held it close, feeling the power it brought to him. He was beholden to no one now.

"A new wine?" Delmar asked.

"Yes," Ramon answered. "It's called 'Sweet Dreams.'"

Even through the haze of the 'dorphins, something felt strange. It was his teeth. They clenched tightly of their own accord, a strange metallic taste setting them on edge. A sensation washed over him, as if he could feel the blood rushing through his own veins. He shook his head and drank more to get the strange taste out of his mouth. Now, he was ready to show Delmar just who was in charge.

He looked down at Pack once more, the little man in the ancient suit smiling stupidly up at him. He returned the smile full measure.

"My friends!" he called to the crowd, and they all seemed so . . . exuberant, jumping and screaming like animals. The call to battle had frothed them to lather. "Do you love me truly?"

"Yes, yes!"

"And I love you, too!" he called back. "As a sign of my devotion, I want to do something for you. We have in our midst those of uncertain blood, those whose services we have used in this campaign despite their strangeness and lack of religious fervor."

"Physicians!" someone yelled from the safety of the crowd, and others picked up the strain. "Physicians! Physicians!"

Ramon smiled down at Pack again. The man had gotten grave and was looking around uncertainly.

"Yes, Physicians!" Ramon called. "I admit to you, friends, that it was I who insisted upon using them, I who ignored their Godlessness in my excitement over the crusade. But, I can ignore it no longer. I was wrong, friends and subjects, wrong to bring the Godless into our midst. And I intend to right that wrong now. We fight for the purity of blood and religion. We weed out the nightshade and burn it with the trash. Arrest the Physicians! Take them!"

He pointed down to the small group, as Pack stared up at him in disbelief. He watched the man's surprise as the crowd dragged him away, all leering faces and broken, dirty teeth. He knew Pack would understand if he could only be told he was being sacrificed instead of Jerlynn. For surely the crowd would be satisfied with these mismatches instead. Delmar was laughing beside him. Ramon wondered exactly what the foppish Count was thinking.

"Take them away!" Ramon yelled, as they disappeared into the mob. "Kill them! Then find the rest. Kill all of them!"

Something was wrong with his head. He couldn't feel it anymore, and his brain seemed to be moving on high as he clenched and unclenched his burning teeth. The surroundings were beginning to stand out in bold relief, colors deep and vibrant.

"Redrick!" he called loudly. "Where's my slimy worm?"

Everyone still near laughed. Redrick moved to the wagon in fear, staring up silently at Ramon.

"There you are," Ramon said, and he was weaving slightly. "Why so glum?"

"I'm not," Redrick said, and smiled wide to prove it.

"I've got a job for you that requires no courage. Think you can handle it?"

"Yes, my Lord," Redrick said softly, eyes to the ground.

"I can't hear you!" Ramon yelled.

Redrick looked up slowly, fighting to control the feelings that were flashing through him. "Yes, my Lord!" he said loudly. "I'd do anything for you."

"Just like my Woofer," Ramon said, and everyone laughed again. He picked up the cask and handed it to the man. "Be a good fellow and take this to my cabin. Guard it until I get back."

Redrick hoisted the keg onto his shoulder. Everyone seemed more excited than usual, their eyes wider, blanker. It scared him. "I'll take it now," he said.

Ramon nodded and turned his attention to his wine, Redrick already forgotten.

As the man from Firetree made his way through the crowd, he knew he was going to have to take steps to avoid ending up like Pack. He would start with this cask. It seemed awfully important to Ramon. He'd put it up all right, but someplace besides the Governor's cabin.

ii

THE N'ORK CITY FOREST—EARLY EVENING

Morgan stood atop the palace and surveyed the large group of dignitaries he had gathered together to listen to his words. Beside him, a Minnie stood with closed eyes, listening intently, prepared to send his message verbatim to all the other Minnies in the forest, who would in turn relay it to everyone else.

The Governor was nervous, but it was for the speechmaking, not the impending battle. He held his words in far less esteem than the edge of his sword. He had slept, somehow, that afternoon and awaited the fighting the way a new bride awaits the return of her husband from the fields. His boots were polished a high tan, his white britches cleaned. He wore a thickly padded vest of fur and hide over his bare chest, some protection during the battle. His heart ached for the loss of

Alicia, a wound far worse than any he could sustain physically, but even that took its proper place in his mind behind the major task that confronted all of them.

He stood alone, for none could go up to the mountaintop with him. Even Grodin, his wounds cleaned and dressed, stood back with the crowd—listening to the way it was going to be. The power of command—of life and death, of right and wrong—can be a great and terrible burden.

Everyone was there: Grodin; Genies from the dungeon times—El-tron, Squan the cat-man, beast-men of all sorts, and Miners; the Southern princes; the merchants save G'vanni, Duchess Clorina still celebrating her marriage there in the war bunker; Telemay; and Willow.

The sky hung low still. It had drizzled two times during the day, but nothing came of it. The sky sat there, waiting along with everyone else, waiting for the end of the world. The perimeter of the palace was ringed with soldiers in metal hats, ready to man the guns and bricks should anything happen.

"We are about to engage in the struggle of Ages," Morgan began, speaking barely louder than normal and with a catch in his voice. "For many of us, it will be our last hour, the price in blood for the real estate of freedom.

"It has not been an easy campaign for any of us. We are a disunion of parts trying desperately to fit into a whole, a mass of conflicting thoughts and emotions trying to make sense of it all amidst the homelessness and horror that we live with day to day. Things have not always gone well. God knows, I've made enough mistakes myself, some of which I may never surmount. But the important thing, the point we always lose in our struggles against ourselves is the reason for the fighting to begin with.

"We fight, all of us, shoulder to shoulder to preserve our own essence. We fight an oppressor who would have done with all not humanlike, an oppressor who wants those of us different to be left out to die. Ramon wants the death of our People, of our memory. He wants the flat plain of existence to be unmarred by the beautiful flowers of our being. That is what we fight against, and it's more important than me, than the Lawgivers, than any of the other petty squabbles that have torn us asunder. Please. We can fight later. Now, we must join together to defeat the common enemy or we won't be alive to squabble."

El-tron sat on the retaining wall, listening to the man he had loved dearly since he had stuck his hand in the fire in the Alb'ny dungeon. So much had changed since then, so many hard feelings had been given vent to, yet the words of Morgan of Siler made sense to him. The common enemy had to be defeated, and there was no one to lead except Morgan, and no one better, even if they could find a leader. He also knew he had started an avalanche with his crusade against hemolysis, an avalanche he could no longer stem. The movement lived on its own now.

"I love you all," Morgan said with great sincerity. "I would gladly give my life up for each one of you. Would that I could put my soul into these words and make them flow to you like a pipeline. Would that I could cut up my heart and give it to you in pieces. There are no other People like the People who stand with me in the N'ork Forest tonight."

Ratif, the Minnie, stood concentrating on the words as they echoed back to him through hundreds of minds like organic loudspeakers. He understood very little of what was being said, as did the others, but the feeling behind the words lay upon all of them as a blanket of protection and love.

". . . in the N'ork Forest tonight," the Minnie on Twiddle's shoulders said in a monotone to the group gathered in the large lobby of G'vanni's palace. Family filled the area, packing it tightly. They stood, listening intently, or sat upon the carpet, the only sound the rasping squeak of the tiny one's inflectionless voice.

"We have no choice in our confrontation. We fight, as we must fight, for our very survival. People of peace must become vicious killers, or give up life for good. There is no other way. We all have lost much already. I do not intend for us to lose any more.

"It is my duty and my honor to serve you all. But now comes the time when you must serve yourselves. No one can fight your battles but you. The pettiness must end, for there are no excuses when all is done. There is only life . . . or death. And the choosing is all up to you. Which will it be? Look into your hearts and be honest with yourselves. I will lead, but you must follow. I will fight, but so must you also—fight, and perhaps die, for your beliefs. Don't fall easily. Take the blood of those who would take yours. Revel in the madness of death. Live death. Love death. And then be done with it.

There is an end to this insanity. It will come, one way or the other, tomorrow. And the answers all lie within you."

Alicia stood in a near corner and tried not to watch Twiddle, who wouldn't take his face from her during the entire speech. She had held her head up, her jaws clamped tight during the presentation and fought back the obstinate tear that kept trying to escape the corner of her eye. Damn Morgan for changing his mind. Damn him for thinking he could waltz right in and take her back after the humiliation he had put her through.

Everyone was up and milling around. Alicia heard several of them say that they had decided to stay behind and fight. Twiddle set the Minnie on the ground and pushed his way through the crowd to her.

"Don't say it," she warned when they were face to face.

"You must go back to him," Twiddle said.

"Why?"

"You must."

Alicia took his eyeless face in her hands as if they could gaze upon each other. "Listen to me," she said, "and hear my words. I have made my decision; I have set my life course and cannot go back. I will leave with G'vanni when the shelling starts."

"You must change your course," he replied quietly.

"I cannot!"

"Yes, you can."

"I won't!" she said loudly. "This is my choice. I'm happy with it. It is the direction I intend to take."

"It may be your choice," Twiddle said, "but you are not happy with it. I return to him soon. You must go back with me."

The tears came unbidden then; she couldn't control them. She turned quickly from Twiddle and forced herself through the crowd, running away, knowing that she could never run far enough to escape herself.

38

Strangeness

Ramon leaned against the slithering serpent on VIPER's bow and watched the naked man fall from the crow's-nest to break both his legs on the main deck. The man laughed when he hit, the sickening rending of his own bone and flesh an entertainment of the highest order. He tried to stand, couldn't, so he just lay there and laughed, slapping at his useless appendages and calling to his friends who danced around him with joined hands.

So much energy, so much enthusiasm.

Ramon drank more wine and tried to figure out why the torches burned so brightly and why the air danced physically before him and why the bottom layers of rapidly darkening clouds seemed so much the texture of brushed velvet. It required thought, deep thought, but all the water that churned in the well of his mind was dank and muddied. Far easier to enjoy the night and the wine and the exuberance of the others.

They were swarming everywhere—aboard ship, in the camps on shore. They ran and jumped and screamed with joy and horror and their eyes, all their eyes were opened wide, staring, bulging. They felt as if they'd never go to sleep again, any of them. They fought all around him, charging around him, dancing with the physical air, and their colors were so bright, every strand of their beards alive and vibrating. They fought, laughing while they fought, and hurt one another and themselves. But no one minded, no one cared. They were all the better for it, all the better, because it was right that they, fighters, fought. It was right that they hurt one another and saw the glowing thick, pulsing red wine pouring from their veins to puddle on the deck like the petals of the most beautiful roses in a most beautiful world.

And they were going to kill Genies.

There was a point, and all of them knew it. All of them shared the vision of destruction so exquisite they could hardly bear the beauty of it. They would not sleep again until they had killed Genies in numbers so large they would clog the watery streets of the N'ork City forest and raise the water level another five feet.

President Wilke from Sand Lake pushed through the tangled crowds to get to Ramon. A scream had started somewhere on deck, and the others had picked it up, a banshee howl louder than thunder, sharper than a dagger straight from the whetstone. It was echoed from all of them, the sensitive ears of the jungle creatures picking it up to set all nature howling into the night sky.

Wilke stood before him, buckskin tassles dancing, dancing. His mouth was open as wide as it would go, straining open. His teeth were stained red.

"Watch," he said, and stuck an index finger into his mouth. He bit down, and with terrible strain and concentration, managed to bite off his own finger. He spit it out and smiled happily, several other fingers already missing. His trick completed, he wandered back into the confusion, looking for someone else to show.

Ramon shook his head, trying to clear it though it seemed already clear. He felt he was in the middle of a never-ending field of eugenic wheat during a windstorm—everything blowing, moving in different directions—and that was all there was to the whole world. He kept making up his mind to walk somewhere besides where he was, but he didn't move. It wasn't that he couldn't. He just didn't. But they'd need to go soon, to get downriver. Soon.

A torchlight procession was moving toward him along the deck, accompanied by a bass chanting, a low, toneless hum. He decided to straighten himself up and see what it was—but he didn't move. The hum, like the scream, was picked up by those on deck. The procession came closer, the torches wild and throbbing. Applause rifled around the deck.

It was Delmar, dressed all in black: tight black britches

and black, frilly shirt with a black cape. Behind him, in double file, the Castle Guard marched with their tall pikes raised, the heads of Physicians stuck on the end of the pikes. Somehow, they had worked with their faces after death, and they were all smiling. It was somehow reassuring to see Pack smiling down in devotion upon all of them. No hard feelings.

The torchbearers surrounded the processional and trailed way back. Behind the Guard, Faf and Jerlynn were being pulled, in chains, toward the masthead. They came quietly, stoically.

Ramon squinted. The woman had his mother's bearing and was wearing her clothes, but it didn't look like her. The woman did not look like his mother.

He looked around. No one else seemed to notice the change, as if Jerlynn had gotten away and left someone else in her place. But they didn't notice, they didn't notice!

Ramon smiled wide. Jerlynn had escaped and that fool Delmar would be taking his wrath out on someone else. How did his mother, in the brig, manage to find someone who was just her size to take her place? A clever woman she was, clever enough to be his mother, and he realized that he was much more like her than like his father.

The procession stopped at the crow's-nest where the man with the broken legs was carted to the starboard side and dumped, laughing, overboard.

Delmar, looking very officious, marched up to Ramon. "The trial, my Lord," he said.

Ramon smiled at the man's folly. "The trial," he repeated and decided to stand. Later.

"We must conduct it now."

"Proceed, proceed," Ramon said, then held out his crock. "But first, more wine."

"More wine," Delmar said in clipped tones. Taking the crock, he brought it to his lips in jerking motions, like a machine. He drank, gulping in even, mechanical swigs.

He handed the crock back to Ramon. "The trial," he said. "Proceed, my good fellow."

Delmar turned to address the ship. "These two stand before us accused of high treason, by collusion and collusion by inference, with the enemy. How do you plead, Dixon Faf, former Programmer of Alb'ny?"

Faf just stood quietly, his head bowed.

"He has no defense!" Delmar said happily, then looked at Jerlynn. "Jerlynn Delaga, how do you plead?"

"I plead Destiny," the woman said, and Ramon wondered how the woman could let herself be subjected to this.

"No defense!" Delmar said again, and the crowd cheered happily, while men in the crow's-nest dropped two lines to dangle on deck. Eager hands hurried to form them to the hangman's noose.

"The defendants have not defended!" Delmar said. "The case goes to the jury. How do you find?"

"Guilty!" everyone screamed. "Guilty!"

"Guilty!" Ramon called.

"Guilty as charged!" Delmar yelled.

The nooses were put around Faf's and Jerlynn's necks as Delmar addressed the crowd. "It is up to our citizens to set the punishment."

"Death," they said, then chanted it: "Death, death, death. Draw and quarter!"

Ramon did move this time. He forced his legs to activity and noted that it really wasn't very difficult at all. He saw an opportunity here to make himself some friends. He walked up to the woman.

"Who are you?" he whispered to her.

She simply stared at him through eyes that weren't anything like his mother's.

After a moment he shrugged and turned from her. Delmar had raised an arm to speak, but Ramon pulled it down. "Let me," he said.

The man glared at him, but backed away. Ramon spoke to the crowd. "Since this unspeakable vileness came from my own house, it is only right that I be the one to right it. I, myself, with the help of good Count Delmar, will act as executioner!"

They roared, pumping their torches up and down, leaving bright streamer traces to etch patterns in the night sky.

Their hands were tied behind them, and the ropes were raised, choking them, their toes trying desperately to find solid ground beneath.

Ramon drew his sword and looked at Delmar. The man returned his gaze with a look of disappointment. "Are you ready?"

Delmar nodded and drew his own sword. "I'll take the holy man," he said.

"Fair enough," Ramon said, and walked up to the woman. He nodded to her. "I want you to know I appreciate what you're doing." He grabbed the front of her gown and ripped it from her, pulling at her clothes until she was naked. Delmar did the same with Faf. Odd, this woman had a birthmark on her shoulder that was exactly like Jerlynn's. He could almost recognize her. Almost.

He looked around at the leering faces and torch-jumping night. The crowd was cooing to him, urging him on, and their motion was the motion of the night, the single breathing organism of Darkness. President Wilke was waving to him with the fingerless, bloody stump of a hand. All was movement, all was real under the velvet canopy of the clouds. Faces smeared with paint and dirt and blood, shining faces, screaming mouths, bulging eyes, dancing hair. "Kill!" they chanted. "Kill, kill, kill!"

And he was making fools of all of them, taking the fire out of all their little plans. He still ruled Alb'ny, still was smarter than all of them, better than all of them. He looked into the woman's eyes and recognized Zenna of Siler, back from the dead to die again, and it was a sign from Ibem that he was right, always right, in everything he did.

He slashed with the sword, and this time, the strength was there. He cut her slowly, lovingly, letting everything inside out. Faf was gurgling beside him as Delmar knelt at the man's feet to receive the warm emanations that oozed from him. Someone fired a deck cannon back toward shore, scattering troops.

Ramon felt weak then, sinking to the deck. He sat there, wondering where to find his mother. He sat and sat, the crowds disappearing from the deck. He got to his knees, the bodies still hanging there, his only companions.

"Mother!" he called. "Mother!"

She had always been there, giving him the guidance his father denied him. Now that he needed her the most, she was gone. He looked up at the stranger dangling above him, dead eyes staring back. "Where is she?" he asked in a small voice.

He tried to stand, slipped, and fell in the gore on deck. The man with the broken legs was still laughing from the starboard shallows.

Hands were helping him up. "We go," voices said. "We go to kill Genies now!"

"But my mother," he said, shaking them off. "I must find my mother."

They tried to help him again, but he broke from them and ran to the hold stairs and down, down. He felt the ship lurch, getting underway, but that wasn't important to him now. He had to find Jerlynn.

"Mother!" he called into the ship's hold. "Where are you?"

39

i

FLOWERS OF THE NIGHT

At first, Morgan thought it was thunder—so long he had awaited the sound that his ears didn't believe it. He sat awake in the palace amidst those closest to him, and it was only after several volleys that their eyes showed recognition in the candle-jumping shadows of darkness.

Grodin was the first off his sleeping mat. He stood wordlessly, strapping on his sword and the new pistol he had condescended to wear. He started for the door, then turned to Morgan.

"It's all come down to this, boy," the old man said. "All the words are written in blood. God help us all, but I'm going to enjoy this."

Morgan sprang from the chair he had taken, disdaining any attempt at sleep. He still wore his sword. His element at last! It was beyond the questioning now; he simply had to do what he did best.

The others rose, each lost in his own thoughts. They were steeling themselves, clearing their minds of all but the most elemental thoughts and feelings. Notern was there, and Jella. Telemay and Willow sat wide-eyed on their mats, watching . . . waiting.

Morgan caught up to Grodin as they walked into the officers' quarters in the outer ballroom. The room was empty.

"They began earlier than I thought," Grodin told him as he wrapped wide leather bands around his wrists, pulling the cowhide strips tight with his teeth.

"It's going to be a long night," Morgan replied absently, his ears straining to hear how close the shots were coming from. "They're probably anchored near the Mud Plains shallows and will hit us from there for several hours before drifting in with the current and threading the needle."

They moved into the darkness without, the smell of gunpowder already strong in the light breeze. The sky was filled with bright fireworks, blazing flowers of orange and yellow followed seconds later by the head-pounding pop of the explosions.

Men and Genies filled the roof with activity. Everyone took up their positions, awaiting the actual invasion.

"Keep yourselves protected!" Morgan yelled through the explosions as he walked toward the gun. "They won't come in till morning light. Keep down!"

They made it to the gun, its four-man crew tensed and ready, the gun cranked to the Northeast. The bombs were falling lower now, striking home on the upper branches of the huge trees. Shrapnel and cement chunks fell like hard rain into the watery canals; occasional fires blazed the sides of vine-ridden stone trees; screams and cries filtered through the rending of the night as the world strobed from bright white to total darkness, in and out, in and out—the roar of the cannon deafening over all.

A beast-man of indeterminate origin and long snout controlled the gun. He snarled at Morgan, "Where do we fire? I can't see the origin of the attack."

"Don't worry about firing now," Morgan replied, and he noticed cannons flaring from some of the other rooftops. "We'll get our chance. Be patient."

The beast-man growled in response.

Morgan turned from the gun. "Ratif!" he called loudly. "Where's my Minnie? Where's my Minnie?"

The little Genie came bounding from behind a pile of

bricks where he had been hiding and jumped into Morgan's arms. His eyes were wide with fear and he shook uncontrollably. "Fear diffusion," he cried, and wrapped his little arms around Morgan's neck.

"I know," Morgan said, stroking him gently. "I know. But you must be strong now. I need you."

Ratif looked at him and wiped a tear from his eye. "Copasetic," he said, but he didn't look copasetic.

"Tell the others to stop firing the guns. We're just wasting our ammo. We'll get our chance."

Ratif nodded quickly and shut his eyes tight. Seconds later the cannons stopped firing.

Another volley zeroed lower, falling into the midst of the city, explosions tracing a fiery line like ground-hugging lightning. One hit the canal next to the palace with a whoosh of water and a tall stream that rained upon them even up on the third floor.

Morgan watched, his insides jumping, desperately wanting to see action. Damn them. He had moved the bulk of his army to the Southwest buildings of the forest to wait out the shelling, but no one could have conceived of the intensity of it. It would be a long, agonizing night. But night, like all things, would pass.

ii

HEMOLYSIS OF MIND

Nebo walked a circle around Ibem, round and round, while Serge followed him with a large piece of applegenic in his massive hands.

"You must eat food," the giant said. "If you don't eat food you will die and leave me alone."

Nebo's hands clasped and unclasped, clanking, puffing gray-white smoke. He was beyond eating, lost in a reverie of the spirit, sucked into the addiction for knowledge.

"I CANNOT DIE, NEBO," Ibem said. "I AM THE GOD OF HEAVEN AND EARTH, AND MY DUTY IS TO PRESERVE LIFE."

"Granted," Nebo replied, stopping in front of the machine to get in range of its photocells. "The preservation of life is your duty, but life in what form?"

A volley of distant explosions drowned them out for a moment. The bombs hadn't found their section of the city yet, but they got closer each time. All the giants, save Serge, were leaning against the vine-covered retaining walls, watching the shelling. Lannie stood at a distance, watching Serge, her heart heavy over the choice the giant was having to make.

"YOU HAVE BEEN MAKING THAT POINT FOR OVER TEN HOURS," Ibem told Nebo, "AND IT IS SENSELESS. I AM WHO AM. MY FUNCTION IS THE PRESERVATION OF PURE HUMAN BLOOD AT ALL COSTS."

"I am Pure Blood," Nebo said.

"BUT INHUMAN."

"What makes humanity?"

"THAT QUESTION AGAIN."

"Is it simply the genetics of parentage, or is it more?"

"MORE."

Nebo started. Taking a step back he thought carefully. Perhaps there was a chink in the program after all. It excited him, vibrating his insides. This is why he had chosen Ibem to be the back-up trigger of his device. The intellectual drive toward understanding was the most liberating drug in existence. His mouth was dry. He thought carefully before proceeding. Even the giants turned from the battle to watch the exchange.

"More, how?"

"THE THOUGHTS, THE DREAMS, THE IDEALS OF HUMANKIND ARE LOCKED WITHIN MY SOUL. I PRESERVE HUMANNESS, THAT PEAK OF CIVILIZATION WHICH WAS ABLE TO CREATE A GOD LIKE MYSELF."

"You are the oversoul of civilization, then?"

"THAT IS ESSENTIALLY CORRECT. I AM THE APEX OF ALL THAT HAS GONE BEFORE."

"And yet the humans who attend you, understand you not."

"WE HAVE FALLEN INTO AN AGE OF DARKNESS," Ibem replied, and there almost seemed to be sorrow in the inflectionless voice modem. "WE AWAIT THE NEW DAWN."

Nebo took a long, slow breath and closed his eyes. The words choked out of him, slowly, slowly. "I am the new dawn," he said.

Ibem sat humming before him, not answering. Nebo

opened his eyes to stare at the machine. "Did you hear what I said?"

"I HEARD."

Nebo stood there for several seconds. By the access door to the roof sat a gaggle of computer parts taken from the Repairmen. Nebo ran to a small crate, digging out a handful of microchips. He hurried over to Ibem and held them up in front of his photocells. "I can create one such as you," he said. "I can create from nothing."

"NO. THAT'S NOT POSSIBLE. THE AGE OF EN-LIGHTENMENT IS PAST."

"Like you," Nebo said, "I am the living embodiment of the ideals of progress and civilization. I contain the knowledge of all mankind. I know how your circuitry works, how the fluidics of your base system operates. Was I not able to reestablish contact with data base after cutting it off? Did I not raise you from the dead?"

"YES," Ibem said. "YOU DID."

"What humans that surround you could do as much?"

"THERE ARE NONE."

"Have I not made what is known as the nuclear device?" he asked, pointing to the dull gray ball set atop the pole. "You are certainly aware of the processes that go into the creation of such a thing?"

"YOU ARE, INDEED, A UNIQUE CREATURE."

"No. There are many like me. We are the salvation from the Dark Ages."

"BUT NOT HUMAN."

"Better than human," Nebo countered. "We, like you, are the soul of humanity. The animals who call themselves human are mere parody of life. Did you not accept a Pure Blood Genie as Governor of Alb'ny?"

"THAT WAS DIFFERENT. THERE WERE NO PURE BLOOD HUMANS AVAILABLE FOR THAT POSITION. SO WE OPTED FOR SIMPLY THE PURITY OF BLOOD."

"And I tell you that there are no humans alive who possess the purity of blood and soul and mind that makes civilization." Nebo was breathing heavily. He was ready to drop the hammer. "But I possess all of those qualities, including Pure Blood. According to the precedent that you set in Kipsie regarding this matter, it is I who deserves your total loyalty. I, like you, am the soul of humanity."

"I'VE WAITED SO LONG FOR YOU," Ibem said, and the voice sounded strange. "YOU ARE MY CREATOR, THE HEART OF MY HEART."

"Yesss," Nebo hissed. "You finally understand."

"WHAT WOULD YOU HAVE ME DO?"

"You will make the ultimate sacrifice for humanity," Nebo said. "You will die for it."

iii

DEATHBRINGERS

El-tron stood on Willow's pier and watched the approach of the Grunts through the bright flashes. The Grunts stood upright, perfectly balanced upon floating trunks, and pushed themselves toward the palace with long, slender poles. They moved silently, emotionlessly, warriors of Truth bringing Justice to the unjust. Or were they?

The small Genie looked up to the treetop, able to see Morgan watching the shelling from above. He loved the man, loved him truly, and knew Morgan loved him. And yet he was willing to let him die for ideals. How important those ideals?

All around him, on the pier and in the palace and in the small boats surrounding them, his command relaxed their vigilance. They would allow the Grunts free passage to Morgan of Siler; they would stand by while he was killed. And El-tron wondered what it was that gave him the power of life and death over one such as Morgan, over one whose love encompassed them all in a tight, firm blanket of protection and caring. Could the man who had done so much be so deserving of death?

He turned to the Grunts again. Galen, the leader, bumped up to the pier and jumped, with ultimate grace, from his log. About ten others were right behind.

From the rooftop, Morgan looked down to see Galen take the pier. He pointed, Jella and Grodin joining him. "What do you make of that?" he asked, the sky flashing red around him.

Jella shook his head. "I never could figure the Grunts," he said.

"Let's find out," Morgan replied, and cupped his hands over his mouth. "Galen!"

The Grunt stood on the pier, looking up. The others were climbing up to stand with him. Galen waved up to the roof.

"Friend Morgan!" Galen called, his voice small and distant.

"What brings you to the palace on such a night?"

"We can be neutral no longer!" Galen replied. "We have heard your words and decided to fight with you against the human!"

"Wonderful!" Morgan called back. "Come up. We welcome you!"

Galen waved again.

El-tron felt the life ebb out of him with the words. It was happening, it was going to happen, and it was all his fault. He had set it up. The man who would die for him was going to die because of him. He saw Morgan turning away from the retaining wall.

"Morgan!" he screamed, and he felt as if his insides were coming out with the scream.

The man turned back, staring down.

"He comes to kill you!" El-tron yelled, and a Grunt was coming toward him. "My men will not fight for you!"

The small Genie saw the arm blurring toward him, and then he was in the air. He had a second to see the leafy stone tree before the blackness overtook his life force.

A volley hit near the palace, rock and stone spewing from nearby stone trees as the Grunts marched slowly into the palace. Morgan watched it, the anger gurgling from him as El-tron was smashed against the wall.

He turned. The rooftop was deserted except for his friends. Willow and Telemay had drifted from the inner palace to join the group.

"It's me they want," he told them all. "Go. I will not hold it against you. You cannot stand against the Grunts."

"Life has no meaning for me without you," Grodin said, drawing his sword. "I have already discovered that."

"Come what may," Jella said, "I stand with my friend."

Notern drew his sword. "And I."

Morgan, eyes filled with tears, looked at Willow. "Your Majesty," he said, "you'd better . . ."

"No," Telemay said. "We also stand with you. We've made our commitment."

Morgan took a deep breath. We'll defend from the lower levels and work up," he said.

Willow spoke up. "The palace can be sealed, level by level, in case of attack."

"It won't hold," Morgan said. "But we'll begin there." He looked at them each in turn, his lips silently thanking them for the bond they shared—in life, and death.

40

A Politico's Heart

Alicia suffered the busy, tugging hands of the G'vanni family women as they fitted her into the wedding dress of purest white silk trimmed with green satin. It came up high in the back of the neck, its neckline plunging in the front. The train dragged behind her for several feet. It was tight and uncomfortable, and with the bombs falling outside and the world in turmoil, she felt she needed to be anywhere but where she was.

G'vanni's middle-aged sister, Mona, knelt on the floor, pins in her mouth, and looked up enviously at Alicia. "You're so naturally beautiful," she mumbled around the pins. "No wonder my brother is willing to make a kingdom for you."

One of the handmaidens giggled from behind, where she was fidgeting with the bustle. "You two will enjoy making many beautiful children together," she said, and the other young handmaidens laughed, one of them showing a sizable gap between two hands, apparently indicating the size of the merchant's member.

A volley of fire landed quite near the palace, shaking the entire tree. The women shrieked with alarm.

"They come!" Mona yelled, jumping to her feet, nearly swallowing the pins.

"They won't come until morning," Alicia sighed, tension and frustration setting her on edge. "Can't you make an end to this foolishness?"

Mona stared at her, uncomprehending. "This is your wedding day," she said, too thick make-up giving her the look of a painted doll. "You're marrying a great Prince. Everything must be perfect."

Alicia frowned.

G'vanni stuck his head in the door. "Wonderful," he said.

"Get out!" Mona said. "You mustn't see her yet. It's bad luck."

"No time for luck now," he said gravely. "We sail. Let's go. I'll meet you at the boat." He winked at Alicia and blew her a kiss, hurrying on.

She had it, all the power that she genetically craved. So why was she unhappy? Why couldn't she get the farmer out of her mind?

The women were scurrying around, gathering up their sewing implements. "Come on, girls," Mona clucked, bodily shoving the women through the room to hurry them. "We'll finish up once we're at sea." She turned to Alicia. "Are you coming?"

"Down in a minute," the Politico said, smiling automatically. And all at once, she was alone.

In the distance, she could hear muffled shouts as the family finished loading the boat. True to his word, Morgan's men had left just as soon as the shelling started, giving them free waters. She wondered what he was doing, how he was faring.

Everything had been already loaded into the ship, except for a small ditty bag for personal effects. Moving to the ornate bed in the ornate room, she opened the bag and withdrew the small dagger she carried there. She looked around quickly, then hoisted her skirt, settling the weapon into the band of her garter—just in case.

She closed the bag and picked it up, moving off into the hallway. The gown was uncomfortable and nearly impossible to walk in. She was anxious to get the wedding over with just so she could get out of the gown. Then she thought that she would get out of it to get into G'vanni's bed, and the thought hardly excited her.

A lone figure stood at the end of the candlelit hallway. Twiddle, pale and forlorn, leaned heavily upon a cane of oak. "Will you come with me?" he asked, as she approached.

"I might ask the same of you," she replied. "Will you walk me down at least?"

He nodded, frowning, and moved to the stairs with her, going down slowly as she supported him with an arm.

"He needs your help," Twiddle said.

"Who?" Alicia asked, and the old man refused to glorify the question with a response.

"He can't do it without you, you know."

"I don't know anything of the kind," she replied. "Concern over Morgan is no longer a consideration in my life. Can't you understand that?"

"Then you won't come with me?"

"Never."

He said no more. They made the two-story walk down in silence, reaching the frantic action of the main floor emotionally distant.

"What will you do?" she asked finally.

"I have a boat," he said. "I will go to him."

She nodded, hugging the old man and feeling coldness in return.

"Alicia!" G'vanni called from across the room, and she turned to see him waving through moving clumps of people. "Come on!" He was smiling broadly, proud.

She smiled and returned the wave. "Coming!" She turned to the old man with no eyes. "You'll be all right?"

He didn't answer her question. Instead he said, "Sometimes, never can be a short time," and walked off.

She followed him sadly with her eyes, her last connection to her former life. Well, no matter. She had a new life now.

The crowd was thinning in the lobby, everyone hurrying down the pier and into BROADMOOR, its large checkerboard sails unfurling.

"Come on!" G'vanni called.

Alicia smiled again, hurrying across the blazing carpet to him. She fitted into his arms, kissing him quickly.

"You look incredible," he whispered into her ear.

"We'd better go," she replied.

They hurried out the front and down the pier, bombs flashing across the night sky. Some were quite near, but the bulk of them were falling in the Northern part of the forest, closer to Willow's palace. The ship was pointed toward the South—and freedom.

They were underway within minutes, manuevering slowly through the forest. Rowers grunted in unison to the oar-master's drum as sailors hurried to unfurl the checkerboards. Alicia stood in the stern, watching behind, as G'vanni took care of last-minute details. He soon joined her, putting an arm around her shoulder.

"I think we're getting out just in time," he said. "If that bastard would have kept us any longer, we would have been in trouble."

"You'd have done the same," she said.

He stared at her for a moment, then changed the subject. "I hear that farther to the North, the climate is more suitable. What would you say to ruling the North?"

She frowned. "I'd say I hope we handle hard times there some other way than running from them."

She squinted into the distance, watching the frail form of the old man, standing in his boat, poling himself into the maelstrom. She pointed. "Twiddle . . ." she began, but G'vanni grabbed her and silenced her with a long kiss.

And somewhere during the kiss, she forgot about G'vanni, forgot about her breeding, and remembered a night a million years ago when she had made love above the cloud cover with the blanket of Moon and stars shining bright eyes down at her.

She pulled away from him, tears in her eyes. "Oh hell," she said, then laughed. "I'm sorry."

She moved away from him, hating the confines of the gown. She found the hem with her fingers, ripping the train and a good bit of the skirt itself from her body.

"Alicia?" he said.

She looked at him, shrugging.

G'vanni smiled sadly in return, shaking his head. "You'd better hurry," he said.

She nodded and turned away, climbing up the bow railing. Without hesitation, she dove from the boat, the splash of the canal water exhilarating her.

Twiddle was already a good distance away. She'd have to swim rapidly to catch up.

41

Refuge

The giants, using long strides, were able to take the stairs down the Lonely Sister nearly a landing at a jump. They lined down in single file, carrying their own candles within the tree that had none of its own. Nebo, at the end of the line, rode upon Serge's shoulders, and fiddled with the frequency knob of the handheld detonator that he would use to set off the device if he were able. If not, Ibem would handle it for him. Without, they could all hear the roar of the continued shelling, hour upon hour of it.

"What will happen to Morgan?" Serge asked, taking long, reaching strides, moving slowly, but in great chunks.

"Morgan?" Nebo sounded surprised at the question. "I don't know. I suppose he'll die, just as everything dies."

"All things die in their time," Serge replied. "You would have Morgan die now."

"Never thought about it one way or the other," Nebo said.

"He has loved you," Serge said. "He has rescued both of us from the dungeon. He has kept us alive and treated us with respect. Why will you kill him?"

"I won't be killing him, Serge," Nebo replied, and, satisfied with the detonator, he secreted it within his robes. "I'm just letting progress take its course. If he's in the way, that's his fault. Besides, he's the one who denied me that which is the blood of my life: knowledge. He wanted me to be what he wanted, not what I was. I really don't care one way or the other what happens to him. We're beyond all that now."

"Serge is not be . . . beyond that," he said, turning his

large shaggy head in an unsuccessful attempt at making eye contact with the Mech. "Serge still loves the People."

"Just let it go," Nebo said flatly. "I'll do the thinking for both of us."

Lannie, who walked right before Serge, turned to him sadly and patted his arm. "He's your Mech," she said simply.

The big man nodded in return.

They reached the water level and peered out, looking for their boat. Its lines were still attached to the building, but the boat was gone, floating rubble from a lucky shot.

"Another boat," Nebo told the giants, pushing his way through their legs to look out. "Swim out and take another boat and bring it back to me."

In the distance, they could see the silhouettes of the defenders against the flashing backdrop of the explosions. All was motion, erratic, poetic.

One of the giants turned to Nebo. "We do not want to steal a boat from the fighting. Morgan needs them."

"To hell with Morgan!" Nebo shouted. "You do what I tell you."

The giant shook his head. "We do what our own Mechs tell us," he replied. "You are not our Mech. We have decided not to listen to your words."

He stared up at them. "You will not do as I say?"

They all shook their heads except for Serge and Lannie. "We do not think you should kill Morgan."

"Then it will give me the greatest pleasure to kill you, too," Nebo said darkly, his mechanical hands clenched into steel fists.

"We go to fight for Morgan," the giant said, and seven giants jumped from the doorway into the churning waters and swam toward the thickest of the fighting.

"Will you stop this now?" Serge asked him.

Nebo stared at him blankly. After a minute he said, "There are eight hundred acres of real jungle below the waters called Central Forest. It's surrounded by a high wall. Do you know it?"

Lannie nodded. "It's in the North of the forest."

"That's right," Nebo said. "We can't get past Ramon's ships now anyway. Take me to Central Forest, and we'll wait it out down there."

They just stood there.

"Do it now," Nebo said low.

Serge frowned, but took the Mech up on his back anyway. He sat in the doorway, dangling his feet into the water, then slid down and began swimming, the Mech sitting upright, perched atop him.

Lannie jumped in and swam after, following her mate.

Reeder and the Green Woman stood on GRAYCLOUD's deck, watching the blazing turmoil of the forest draw ever closer. It was an impressive sight, even from a distance—the monstrous stone trees looming into the clouds, while bright flashes of hatred's light chipped away at the trees like some celestial lumberjack.

"We should catch the city to the South," Reeder said, for they approached it broadside, caught in the flux between ocean tides and river current. And it looked like the flux would carry them up close enough to tie down in N'ork City Forest.

"We'll take a tree," the Green Woman said, "on the outer edge of the forest, and wait and see what happens. There will be something in this for us, I'm convinced. The worst we can do is a boat with oars to get us upriver."

"Ship to starboard!" a voice called from the crow's-nest. "Ship to starboard!"

Reeder and the woman looked at one another, then stared along with others of the crew out into the dark sea. They strained their eyes until Reeder saw something in a bomb flash, then fixed its position in the next flash.

"There," he said, pointing into the darkness. They all fixed it then, a large ship with many rowers and a checkerboard sail, moving out of the forest and toward them.

"They must have spotted us," the Green Woman said.

"And they're maneuverable," Reeder said. He turned and called down the deck, "Battle stations! Hurry, lads! We eat grapeshot for breakfast!"

The starboard gunners hurried on deck, as confusion reigned upon GRAYCLOUD.

"They haven't fired," the Green Woman said. "Why?"

"I don't know," Reeder said, "but once they get astern of us, we're dead because we can't maneuver. We've got to hit them now." He turned and yelled again. "Gunners!"

"Aye, sir!" came scattered replies up and down the deck. "Ready, sir!"

"Quickly," the Green Woman urged.

"Fire when ready!" Reeder yelled. "Fire when ready!"

And the guns opened up on the boat with the checker-board sails that carried a Prince who stood on deck mourning a lost love. The first volley took out one of the sails and blew large holes in the port bow. The second volley found the powder magazine and the ship went up in a huge fireball and was gone beneath the waves in seconds.

GRAYCLOUD had drawn blood. The mood was jubilant up and down the deck. Reeder and the Green Woman held each other fiercely, locked in a passionate embrace. The battle was met for all of them.

42

Death Everlasting

The door was solid steel, its stays set deeply in cement, a bar of solid oak bolstering the three long metal bolts that secured it. It should have been able to hold back anything. The Grunts had smashed through three just like it.

The Grunts pounded relentlessly, the door bulging in-ward, cracking the oaken bar slowly in long-splintered rends.

"This won't hold, either," Jella said, as they stared down the length of the dark hallway, cement cracking and falling to the floor in dusty shards.

"No," Morgan replied dully, his hand locked in a death grip on his sword.

"Don't they ever tire?" Grodin asked.

Morgan looked at him, merely a shape in the darkness. "What do you think?"

Their backs were to the stairs leading to the roof, one more set of doors between them and oblivion.

"We could escape from the roof if we wanted," Notern said, his head turning back and forth between the stairs and the door.

"Escape to where?" Morgan asked. "They could just decimate the troops while trying to get to me. I must stand up to them and settle it once and for all. I'm all they're really after."

The door whined loudly, a steady push creaking it against itself until finally, inevitably, it burst from its hinges and clanged loudly to the floor, sliding several yards before coming to a stop.

Galen stepped in, his face without expression. The others followed behind. The Grunt held his hand up, palm open.

"Don't look at their eyes!" Morgan said, putting a hand across his face. He pulled his pistol and fired wildly, the bullets bouncing harmlessly off Galen to ricochet back down the hallway.

They all fired, Notern using a hand laser that skimmed its light beams off the slick outer dermis to burn holes through the walls. The hallway stank with smoke. The rattling of the guns drowned all other sound, but nothing came of it. The Grunts proceeded onward, slowly, with great deliberation.

"Up the stairs!" Morgan ordered. "We'll make our stand on the roof."

The large beast-man greeted Twiddle and Alicia with a snarl as their boat bumped up to Willow's pier. His furry face was lopsided, his body bent to a permanent half-crouch, obviously the result of mixed breeding.

"You have nothing to gain here, woman," he slurred, pointing a taloned paw at them. "Go from this place."

Alicia looked at him, looked straight into his eyes, and smiled. She held her hand out to him. "Will you help me out of the boat?" she asked in a small voice.

The beast-man growled, then softened. He held out a paw and she took it. "These are dangerous climes," he whined.

Alicia got up on the pier, then helped Twiddle, who took her hand, then hooked his cane on a pylon and grunted to the rolling dock.

"What goes on here?" she asked.

A human walked up to her, a wide-brimmed hat twisting between his calloused hands. "The Grunts, m'Lady," he said, almost apologetically, "are going to kill the red-haired man."

She looked around. Another volley shook the area, lighting the idle garrison, several hundred troops sitting quietly in boats and hanging from nearby buildings.

"You must help him!" she said.

"No, mum," the beast-man growled. "We won't do that. He's trying to force the blood mix."

"And he's taken Ibem," the human said.

"And arrested the Lawgivers," someone called from the boats.

"His child!" Alicia said, her voice tight with command. "Where is the child?"

A woman pushed her way down the pier. She was small and frightened. She had Marek tied to her arm, the only way she could hold him.

Alicia raised her voice to the crowd. "Will you kill his child, too?" she asked. "He carries his blood. Maybe he'll have ideas, too. Will you kill him?"

No one answered, and Alicia knew then that they could still be swayed. She put her arm around the woman, leaning down to kiss Marek on the cheek. "Take Master Twiddle with you," she said, directing her to the old man. "Take my boat to that near tree and wait until we come for you."

The woman went quietly, as another volley splashed up and down the canal. The whole side of the tree just beyond the palace went up in orange fire, sending tons of rock, plus an entire gun emplacement into the waters below. In the light of the explosions, she saw El-tron, twisted and bloody, lying upon a crate at the end of the pier.

She went to him, his dying eyes staring wide open at her. "My fault," he sputtered, blood frothing out with the words. "I never . . . wanted this."

"Shhh." She looked him over quickly. He hadn't long. She couldn't believe that he was alive even then. "He loves you still. It will be all right."

He moved his head back and forth, his double large eyes filled with fear. "I . . . die . . . with his bl-blood on me."

"No," she said softly.

He reached out a hand, wrapped long fingers around the still-wet three-quarter sleeves of her wedding gown. "I was taught," he rasped, "when . . . troubleshooting, the tech should . . . ch-check his own mind if the s-source p-problem can't be . . . found." Tears ran out of his eyes to pool in his large ears. "Bad electronics. Bad electronics."

"Morgan's going to be all right," she said, her voice firm. "I'm not going to let anything happen to him."

The little man smiled then, his grip loosening on her sleeve. His hand fell to his side.

She turned from El-tron, swinging around to face the crowd. "You want to be in there!" she yelled, explosions booming out a response. "Every one of you wants to be in there!" They stared back silently at her from every angle.

She took a throbbing torch from its pylon holder and lifted it so everyone would see her face, her eyes. "You've consigned the saint of your lifetimes to the ashes. You've taken what's best inside of you, and cut it out to be happy in your stupor." She put a fist to her breast. "So have I. So have I!"

She paced the dock, the fire in her heart real for the first time in her life. "We've all let him fight our battles for us, and lead us through life—so long as he didn't challenge us to address our own hearts in the meanwhile. He was the liberating voice of the world so long as he asked no liberation of us.

"We're a fine bunch, loyal followers. Has it struck you that you abandon him just at the point where you may not need him anymore? Should the victory be won, you would prefer to not listen to his voice of total giving—of total giving—of yourselves to the life of the world. It would be your world then, to make just like it was before.

"For God's sake, the man dreamed! He dreamed of peace and of communion, and of a world where there would be no more place for people such as him. He dreamed, my faithful friends, of making himself unnecessary! And for that most horrible of sins, we, each and every one of us, take his life. And don't believe for one second that because the callous machines of destruction do the deed for us that we aren't up there twisting the knife ourselves."

She felt the tears coming and fought them back. "When Morgan dies, all that is good within us dies also. What can be the good of that? . . . Oh God, what's the good?"

She dropped the torch to the water and walked toward the pier winch that dangled its line near the entry. She hauled it back in and attached it to a pallet.

"Do what you will," she called. "I go to be with him. I ask only that someone take the line to the roof for me."

She stepped onto the wooden flat. A human walked solemnly to the crank controls and began turning. The skiff trembled, then began going up, Alicia standing in its center with her arms folded.

The beast-man who had greeted her came charging full speed down the pier. "I go with you!" he barked, jumping onto the pallet to stand beside her.

Others ran to join them, scrabbling onto the thing and pulling themselves up as it tipped back and forth, Alicia grabbing the line to steady herself.

A large human jumped upon a crate. "Are we ready?" he screamed. "Are we?"

The simultaneous cheer that went up from the garrison rivaled the shelling. Alicia, wrapped in the protective arm of the beast-man watched them charge the palace door, weapons up and ready. They stormed the palace!

The pallet crested the roof, overhead explosions lighting it to daylight. Morgan stood, back to her, with his men. They watched the rooftop door pounding inward.

She pushed her way to the edge and jumped onto the roof. "Morgan!" she called, running toward him.

He turned, his face brightening like fire. His father's sword clattered to the ground as he ran across the roof and grabbed her up around the waist, swinging her in complete circles.

"Did you really divorce me?" he said, laughing, hugging her close.

"I almost did!" she returned, kissing him fiercely. "I love you, you bastard!"

"Of course you do!"

He set her down to watch his men climbing off the pallet. "Your doing?" he asked.

"They just needed a little persuading."

"What did you promise them?" he asked, narrowing his eyes.

"Dreams, my darling. I offered them dreams!"

There was a screeching of metal on stone, like the sound of some terrible jungle creature. They turned in time to see the last door fall inward and Galen step through.

"There are no more obstacles, Morgan of Alb'ny," the Grunt said. "We now right the movements of history."

There was screaming from below as the garrison made the doorway and poured out onto the rooftop behind the advancing Grunts.

Morgan ran back and retrieved his blade from amidst the confusion as the Grunts attacked. They moved straight toward him at all times, as he continued to feint around the rooftop. His troops swarmed them, flailing and hacking away in the close quarters, as they were tossed or simply stamped to the ground.

Bodies flew, a trail of injuries oozed behind like the slime marks of a snail. The push was steady, unbending in the middle of the terrible fighting. Nothing could stop them, not numbers, not weapons. They came.

El-tron lay on the crate, listening to the fighting above. He feared the terminal side of his life, but feared more the wrongs he would be leaving behind him. He believed in totality, the perfection of the finished product. He left his life product uncompleted.

He struggled to a sitting position, his body almost totally numb and unresponsive. There was pain, but it seemed somehow comforting.

The palace lay forty feet across the pier. He somehow got off the crate and dragged himself that far. He could never make the stairs, he knew that, but the vines were a different story. His arms were much more powerful than his slight body, his hands like clamps. He wrapped long fingers double and triple around vines and started dragging his dying body up the tree.

Through throbbing skies and a rain of shrapnel, he made the three-story climb. His body was gone; his heart provided the movement. He came up near the big gun and watched Morgan, drawn from the others, fighting Galen. He'd flash in with his sword to hack, then somersault back out of the way again. Though he was a touch faster than the Grunt, his blows had no effect. But El-tron knew from his breeding that indestructibility was not really an absolute.

He slid from the wall and climbed onto the chair of the big gun. The crank was barely close enough to him, but he managed to reach it and bring the barrel around to the fighting, cranking it level with the rooftop. It was already loaded, ready for battle. He instinctively knew how to operate it.

The fighting was scattering into small pockets of Grunts fighting ten or twenty assailants. El-tron waited until one of the Grunts—the one they called Gregore—saw him and broke from the group.

"Galen!" Gregore called. "The cannon!"

"No!" Galen called to him, but was driven back by a flurry from Morgan.

The Grunt charged El-tron, his wide, dense body rumbling back and forth as he ran. El-tron keyed the switch with his last breath. Dead already, the recoil sent him back over the side to fall into the dark waters.

The Grunt's chest exploded, the force sending him fifty feet across the roof to crash into the retaining wall on the other side.

Everything stopped, the Grunts turning to stare at their fallen cub. He lay there, moaning, not getting up.

"Gregore?" Marta called.

He tried to raise an arm, but couldn't.

"My son!" Mama Spire screamed. The Grunts all crowded around Gregore, Morgan pushing his way through the crowd to stand near.

Gregore lay on his back, a gaping hole in his chest. Mama Spire was down on her knees, sobbing loudly, when Galen bent to him.

Gregore looked at him with questioning eyes. "I'm in pain," he said, and tried to laugh. "It hurts so bad."

Galen examined the wound, and knew death when he saw it. "Try to take it easy," he said, patting Gregore's arm. "Just rest."

Galen straightened, Marta standing before him. "He'll be all right, won't he?"

Galen just stared at her.

"Won't he?"

Galen reached out and briefly touched her horn. "He's dying, little one."

She backed away from him, eyes uncomprehending. "That's impossible," she shrieked. "Grunts don't die!"

Galen lowered his eyes.

"We're going to have a baby," she said to everyone.

"Nothing will happen to him. That's ridiculous. We have so much to do yet."

Gregore moaned loudly. "Why does it hurt so bad? Marta? Marta?"

Mama Spire took his arm and hugged it to her. She rocked, crying, holding his arm.

Marta bent to him, her face twisted in fear and disgust as she looked at the wound.

"Marta," Gregore coughed. "I want to touch you. Come here to me."

She bent closer, lips twitching, her body convulsing. She got close, then pulled away. "No!" she said, jumping to her feet and backing away. "He smells of death. He smells of it!"

She turned and ran through the crowd, getting across the rooftop. Several others went with her.

"Marta!" Gregore called. "I'll be all right, I . . ."

He died, just like that, the last breath wheezing out of him.

The faces of the other Grunts reacted with horror. They all ran. Even Mama Spire dropped Gregore's arm, screaming, and got away from the body while trying to wipe his contact from her with her hands.

Only Galen stood his ground. He bent and closed Gregore's eyes with a small clang. Then he opened the palm and closed the third eye. He looked at Morgan, then walked through the crowd.

Morgan followed, Alicia beside him.

The Grunts huddled in the corner of the rooftop, their faces filled with terror. They put their arms over their heads, screaming and crying whenever an explosion went off nearby.

Galen stood before them, turning to Morgan when the Genie walked up.

"What's happened?" Morgan asked.

"Fear," Galen said. "The concept of death is beyond them. They assumed eternity. Now that the doorway to death has been opened to them, they can't bear it."

"We all must face that," Morgan said.

"I know that," Galen said. "I've seen my people die, but they haven't. They've outlived their own memories, and now must face fears in equal measure. They will never be the same people again."

"A human weakness," Morgan said.

The Grunt nodded. "We are, apparently, no better than you. With the purity of our breeding, we still possess human failings. My sense of history is obviously flawed."

"Galen, I . . ."

"No," the Grunt said. "I will finish what I must say. My people will no longer fight. We go home to an eternity of living death—of fear. I can no longer sit in judgment over anyone. I am the fool of all time. Live your life, your history in peace, Morgan of Alb'ny. Try to remember that I meant well."

Morgan put an arm on the Grunt's shoulder. "Your manipulation of life is no more wrong than my own," he said. "While the death of many is mere history, the death of one is tragedy. I will force no one's life, my friend. Hemolysis is no more."

"Listen," Grodin said, walking across the rooftop to them. "Would you listen!"

Morgan straightened, cocking his head. "I don't hear anything," he said.

"The shelling," Alicia said. "It's stopped."

"Is it over then?" Galen asked.

"No," Morgan replied. "Now it begins."

43

Wings and Woofers

Ramon lay in the center of his cabin, hands over his ears, screaming. Boom! Boom! Boom! The sound never ending, shaking the walls, the dangling center light jiggling madly. The pounding of feet just outside the door, voices, loud voices, yelling, "The trees!"

He got to his knees, seeing the morning light filtering

through the porthole, gray light, physically reaching in, grabbing the cabin interior with its long arm.

His cabin was a shambles around him, torn to pieces in his search for the 'dorphin barrel. Redrick. Where was Redrick? With Jerlynn, that had to be it—and with his missing 'dorphins!

He stood, not feeling his legs. He looked to see if he was upright. Somehow, his blue cotton jumper had been shredded, the pants hanging in streamers, dried blood caked on the tatters and his legs. What had happened? He remembered his legs itching, but this—

He was up and moving. The doorknob vibrated before him. He chased it, caught it, then managed to turn the thing before it bit him. He flung the door open. If he found Jerlynn, he'd find Redrick, and if he found Redrick, could the 'dorphins be far behind?

He moved onto the narrow upper deck, the world a madhouse around him. Men charged up and down the decks, naked, their bodies smeared with brightly colored mud and paints. The colors of the day hung heavy, dripping, the blue-gray sky threatening to fall atop them, while they floated on a sickly green sea broadside into a pulsating forest of incredible, monolithic trees. The cannons spit fire, roses bursting in their recoil within the forest, two hundred yards distant and coming fast. For the boats weren't moving; it was the forest coming for them, and the screaming men fired, fired to keep it at bay to no avail.

The other boats anchored with him, all trying to keep back the trees. Someone fell from the overhang above, bounced on his rail and flopped to the main deck below. Rifles were in evidence, and bows, all singing in the direction of the towering jungle. Bodies and spent shells littered the deck. Water sprays splashed them, the water turning to smoke that drifted lazily, like a fat, old Woofer, around VIPER.

Troops were charging up on deck from the hold. They carried small boats and rafts, their weapons tied to their backs. So much movement, so coordinated! Ramon watched, fascinated, almost forgetting about his search for Jerlynn and the 'dorphins. More feet came charging down the walkway. He dove into his doorway to avoid them.

He tried to stand, a huge explosion knocking him back as his overhead light fell to the floor, its coal oil light setting the surrounding wood ablaze. Ramon stood in horror, staring, then he skirted the flames and made the walkway, closing his door to the fire to enclose it.

Several yards down the deck, a large block of the cabin section was missing, its gutted remains charred and smoking, fire spreading on its outskirts. He swung back to the trees—they were firing back!

What was happening?

Below, on the confusion of the deck, the troops had lowered the gangway and were running down it with their boats, screaming them right into the water, a never-ending flow, hundreds upon hundreds.

Something was happening, no doubt about that, something. He had to hurry before those 'dorphins got away. Damn Mother, damn it all. He ran away from the fire and up to the wheelhouse. He peered carefully through the cutouts. Empty. No mother, no Redrick. The wheel spun lazily, cheerfully, this way and that. He forgot about the 'dorphins for a minute, and went inside to watch.

Morgan stood upon the skiff outside the kennels, his red wings jutting out from his shoulders, pale smoke bleeding from the jetpack. Grodin, from within, shoved the Woofers through the opening one by one to splash into churning, debris-filled canals where eager troops climbed upon their backs. The animals whined softly, their large brown eyes turned fearfully upward as rock and vine fell upon them.

Smoke swirled through the streets, the pounding of Ramon's guns more intense than any of them could have imagined. Morgan's guns answered now, but half of them had already been silenced by the ferocity of the shelling. The forest was in ruins, large sections of it decimated by cannon fire. But now the enemy came to him.

"Murdock!" Alicia said from beside him, and sure enough, his own Bernard leaped willingly into the fray.

"Come here, boy!" Morgan called, the animal paddling to him immediately. Morgan hugged Alicia, kissing her quickly. "Take a boat to the South forest and wait. The fighting may not get that far."

"You're not getting rid of me that easily," she said. "Not this time. If you can learn to be diplomatic, by God, I can learn to fight." She dove into the water, coming up near one of the freed Bernards. "Besides, I've already ruined my dress!"

Morgan waved and jumped upon Murdock's back. The canals were filled with boats all around them, the troops preparing to meet the invaders. They had waited all night, anger swelling with each new volley. They were churning for it, moving through logjams of wood and bodies and thick-growing vines. The entire forest was in motion, a living body moving to defend itself.

"They come!"

The word spread down from the front, and Morgan was more than ready. He stood atop Murdock, watching down the canal. The smoke blew through in sulfurous clumps. Through breaks in the thickness, he could see his own boats extending out toward the edge of the forest, Ramon's ships looming larger in the distance, fires on their decks.

"What do you see?" Grodin said from the top of the last Woofer. They stood within the large opening in the tree.

"Ramon's ships!" Morgan called loudly, then raised his clenched fists above his head. "In flames!"

The People cheered loudly, and Morgan was a creature of the Moment, ready to perform the action he was born for, thoughts of little Ty'Jorman forcing themselves into his mind. He'd get there. He'd get there in time.

Grodin jumped his Woofer through the opening to splash up next to Morgan. The cavalry bunched up around their leader, Notern and Jella close at hand. A bomb whistled loudly just overhead, exploding boats farther South.

He looked around, a wide grin splitting his face. "Are we ready?"

They cheered.

"Then let's take those sons of bitches! Ho, Murdock!"

The Woofer barked loudly and swam, their small fleet moving aside to let the mounted through.

As they hurried to the front, the smoke got thicker in the canals, nearly blinding, melding physically with the low-hanging clouds to cover everything.

"The smoke!" Alicia called from beside him. She reached out and grabbed his arm, or otherwise he wouldn't have been able to see her. "What is it?"

"It smells like fuel!" Morgan yelled back. "They must be torching the forest!"

And the two of them cleared the curtain of smoke and entered hell.

The battle was fiercely met amidst an inferno of burning trees, flames reaching hundreds of feet in the air, flaming branches falling constantly upon those below. Again and again the defenders were driven back from the fire and its tremendous heat. They put their arms across their faces to block the burning wind, as the Woofers howled and ducked their heads beneath the water.

It was a sea of small boats, jammed in so tight none of them moved. Troops fought atop the boats, running from one to the other as fire tumbled from the sky. Citizens pelted the humans with bricks and bombs from the burning trees, and arrows slashed above the combatants' heads to land within solid ranks beyond.

Ramon's people moved with the force of madness. They took arrows and bullets without sensation, climbed the burning trees with their bottles of gasoline to ignite themselves along with the forest. They lost limbs and eyes, and still they charged full speed, only falling when the life force was completely taken from them.

Giants moved through the screaming confusion, as well as troops with microwaves and lasers. The humans kept coming, charred, smoking holes burned straight through them, their insides bubbling out of mouths and eye sockets through intense levels of microwave radiation. But it was like fighting the tide. The humans advanced, laying waste to the forest in their wake. The flames rose in mammoth columns all around, a firestorm of unequaled intensity. And always the defenders were forced back upon themselves.

"The air!" Alicia called.

"It thins!" Grodin yelled back. "From the fire."

And the humans were on them. They trampled the defenses and came rushing across rocking boats, swinging bright silver blades above their heads.

"We stop them here!" Morgan yelled, drawing his own sword.

The wall hit them. They fought from the Woofers' backs, hacking away at targets too insane to protect themselves, the Woofers using their powerful jaws to rip at legs and haunches. Morgan stood on Murdock's back again, face so hot he feared it was burning. He squinted through the smoke to take them over the body pile that jammed the waterway all around. The others fought bravely around him, Grodin working in perfect concert with his Woofer while Alicia used pistols, carefully choosing her targets and bringing them down one at a time. Blades flashed red as the humans kept coming, more and more, burning vines and fuel-ignited water now catching the boats afire.

The gruesome business went on, the humans dying in great numbers as they pushed ahead on their grisly march through the forest. Time was measured in body count, as Morgan took as many as he could muster the strength to swing at. And still he fell back, the tremendous heat more than anyone could cope with.

Even as Morgan wrapped himself in the cloak of battle frenzy, he knew they were losing. Slowly, inexorably, they were being pushed back by the sheer ferocity of the attack. He engaged the jetpack and flew from Murdock's back, quickly gliding the canals above the heads of the combatants. Everywhere the humans claimed victory, their web of fire spinning through more and more of the forest. The People were in retreat, fighting fiercely, but falling back. It was only a matter of time before they broke completely.

And then a drop of hope hit him upon the head.

44

The Seed

Delmar tore through his closet, throwing suit after suit upon the floor. He had to have just the right thing to wear for his triumphal entry into N'ork City. A bomb exploded on GEN-TRY's main deck, rocking the cabin, the entire boat listing badly to the starboard side. The crew was jumping ship outside, but Delmar was far too interested in the pile of soft velvets that lay around his feet like a textile field. He tore through the closet, looking for the red velvet shortcoat with the gold braid laticed across the front, forgetting he had given it to one of Reeder's young litter bearers for services rendered.

The ship continued to list, flagging badly, the cabin tilting at an ever more serious angle. He had to fight his way uphill to get to the closet.

The powder magazine went up under the waterline with a huge, muffled roar, a great mound of water growing like instant mold on the surface, only to disappear immediately in white spray.

The ship slid under in a matter of seconds after that, Delmar never getting out of his cabin. His clothes and his memory were sucked into the dark shadows of forgotten history.

Morgan flew back to the front lines, joining his cavalry in a fighting retreat. Since he had left they had been pushed back nearly two blocks, leaving a trail of devastation in their wake, but pushing back nonetheless.

The fires continued to burn unabated, the heat in the entire forest sealed in by the clouds of steam rising from the water.

Morgan glided down into the fray, coming hard upon the backs of several humans, dropping them to pitch forward and lose their heads to his troops.

"A Minnie!" he shouted. "Get me a Minnie!"

Alicia sat her mount, reloading from a pouch slung over her shoulder. Morgan set down on the back of her Woofer.

"How bad is it?" she called above the noise.

"It's the fire," he said. "It drives us back! We can't regain ground."

A human jumped from a nearby boat, catching Alicia's arm, nearly pulling her from the saddle. Her Woofer turned its head, sinking its large teeth into the man's groin and ferociously tearing him from her. The man fell between the boats in the bloody water.

"You told me once," Morgan yelled above the noise, "that in the Old Times there were people who used to try and make it rain."

"Morgan, there's no time . . ."

"Tell me!"

She looked at him, her perfect face smeared with soot. "That's part of my genetic memory," she said. "Why?"

"How did they do it?"

"Morgan . . ."

"How, damnit?"

"Chemical seeding," she said. "Water seeding."

"Of the clouds?"

She nodded, flinching. "Yes! From flying machines."

"Water seeding works?"

A building close by caught fire with a whoosh, spontaneous combustion from the heat of nearby buildings. Burning defenders fell, screaming, atop the humans who charged blindly on.

"Yes," she said. "Everything I know works."

"A Minnie!" someone called from several stories up a still intact building.

"To me!" Morgan called, holding out his arms. The little man was tossed through the air, Morgan snatching him just before he hit an empty boat.

"Pass the word!" he yelled to the Minnie. "I want everyone inside the buildings!"

"That'll give them free access to the entire city!" Alicia said.

"I know," Morgan replied. "I know."

Ramon stood on the main deck with Morgan's bastard child tucked under his arm and watched GENTRY slip quietly under the waves. It was only then that he realized that GAMECOCK was gone, too, piled up, broken, against one of the stone trees, its structure nothing more than burning rubble.

"You'll pay for this," he told the crying child. "As soon as I find my mother, the bastard son and the bastard father will know my wrath."

VIPER was burning with a multitude of fires and was slowly sinking as it drifted into the forest itself. Fire formed solid walls on either side of him, smoke forming a dreamlike haze all around. His crew was gone, all gone, the last of them giving the baby over to his care as he jumped ship.

"I told you!" he screamed into the dense smoke. "I told all of you I'd take the Jewel of the East and put it in my crown. You didn't listen. You didn't believe!"

He moved to the rail. The water had risen nearly to it. Many bodies floated amidst the debris. "I did this!" he called to the dead. "It wasn't my father's doing, it was mine! So, he loved the bastard; but the bastard didn't do this, I did! Me!"

He saw a figure moving through the fog around him and turned to it. Redrick came slinking around the deck, forced up to the action by the rising water.

"You!" Ramon screamed, pointing.

The man saw him, alone in the smoke, and came to him. "Are there boats?" Redrick asked. "Boats? I must escape."

"My mother. What have you done with my mother?" Ramon demanded. "She has my 'dorphins. I must retrieve them."

Redrick laughed dryly, his eyes turning hard. "I have your precious 'dorphins, my Lord."

Ramon used his free hand to grab the man's tunic. "Where are they? Tell me, or so help me . . ."

"What?" Redrick asked shrilly. "What will you do?"

"Please," Ramon said. "I must have that barrel."

"What's it worth to you?"

Large branches creaked overhead and fell with a crash onto the deck, pushing VIPER. It glanced off the side of another tree. The two men fell to the deck.

"I'll give you anything," Ramon said. "Please help me. It's all gotten out of control."

"I want you to kiss my feet," Redrick said, standing shakily.

"Yes, yes, anything," Ramon said, and holding the baby close to his breast, he moved to the man's wet, booted feet, kissing them quickly.

"Prostrate yourself," Redrick demanded, "and call me 'Your Majesty.'"

Ramon prostrated fully, keeping an arm wrapped around the crying child. "Your Majesty," he said loudly.

"Good," Redrick said, and they were floating through a nightmare landscape of charred trees and low-hanging smoke, dolp-men and human and Genie bodies clogging the water. They banged another tree, Redrick grabbing the rail to keep himself upright. "I want your valuables."

"Where is the barrel?" Ramon asked from his prone position.

"The valuables first."

Ramon took the key from around his neck and held it up for the man. "A safe in my cabin," he said, choking on smoke and coughing. "The key fits the lock."

"What's in it?"

"Plastic," Ramon said, gagging, "gold, jewels. Solid barter."

Redrick nodded, then walked on Ramon's hand as he went past him. "Your precious barrel is hidden by the masthead, where the viper joins the deck."

"Thank you," Ramon called to the man's retreating back. "Have you . . . have you seen Jerlynn?"

But Redrick had already disappeared into the smoke.

The volunteers stood, thirty strong, behind the crumbling lines of defense atop Willow's palace. Bladders and casts filled to overflowing were strapped to chests, their wings jutting out proudly from their shoulders.

"We'll go up as a group," Morgan said, the forest fire taking his vision completely to the North. "We'll seed together to try and saturate an area. Pray for rain. There's not much air up there, so watch yourselves."

He looked over the retaining wall. As his people took to the trees, the humans spread out, starting more fires. If this didn't work, there was nothing else to do but roll over.

Alicia stood with him, Marek tucked in her arms. "You'll have to abandon the palace," he said. "They'll overrun it soon." He pointed to the large, open walled area known as Central Forest. "It's still untouched; they don't know how to get down in it. Go there. I'll meet with you when I'm through."

She nodded. "You'd better."

He kissed her. "A deal's a deal." Leaning over, he kissed the baby on the forehead. "Take care of her," he whispered.

He looked at his volunteers. "We've got to go now," he said, and fired the jetpack, diving over the retaining wall.

He fell several feet, his wings gliding him level, then up with the jets. The others followed in groups, without hesitation. Below, the humans were swarming the city, rocks raining down upon them, while the big guns were turned downward, blasting the canals now free of the People. He looked upward then, full concentration centered on the clouds.

Up they went, keeping close in the wet density of the low-hanging clouds. He went up far, the air turning colder, the air thinner, the others ranging out all around him. He flew, suddenly lightheaded, his vision filling with black spots. They had waited too long!

He waved his arms frantically, his right hand feeling for his knife. As he blacked out, he just managed to slash the bladder on his chest, water spewing into the thin air, as other fliers crumpled fetally and dropped through the clouds, their wings folding up around them.

He lost consciousness.

VIPER's bow rode high, her stern completely underwater, as Ramon clawed his way to the masthead, the baby screaming the entire time. Most of the deck was aflame, but water was now pouring freely across it, drowning out fire as it pulled the ship farther under the waves.

The forward winch rope had gotten wound around the masthead, choking the viper that stared back at Ramon. He used the length of rope to pull himself to his prize.

He reached the serpent, embracing it gratefully, holding on for dear life. He dropped the child to the deck, Ty'Jorman grabbing for his own handholds.

They had reached a clearing of some sort, the heat of the fires dying away. He looked over the bow. They had come to an area of a wall that stretched out a large distance all around. He was floating toward the wall on a collision course, closing fast.

He looked to the base of the viper. There was a cutaway place where the curve of the snake's back pulled it away from the bow. His small 'dorphin barrel was jammed into the place.

"There you are!" he yelled happily, laughing and crying at the same time. Things would be fine now. Everything would be all right.

He reached for the barrel, his fingers just scrabbling its surface when VIPER hit the wall. There was a loud crash, their forward progress stopping immediately, the reaction sending him falling away from the masthead and back down the deck to fall heavily into the water climbing the deck.

He hit the pole of the crow's-nest, pain shooting through his back, his mind nearly blanking. But he shook his head clear in time to see the barrel floating near him. He scooped it up, and saw the baby still clinging to the winch rope near the bow.

He made his way back to the baby, the boat creaking beneath his feet. The bow had crashed through a section of the wall and was lodged solidly in it. He looked over the rail and saw a lush jungle a hundred feet below, the tops of many of its trees reaching up near the waterline. It was like a huge, sunken garden stretching for many acres all around. And the jungle seemed a place of peace, of quiet solitude.

The baby still held the winch rope. Ramon unwound it quickly and tied it around both of them. They were sinking rapidly, the pit below their only chance.

And all at once, lightning flashed madly through the low-hanging sky. The thunder rumbled more intensely than any human bombardment ever could. Within seconds, the sky opened up and disgorged its wrath in blinding, pounding fusillades. And death had a name—it was called rain.

45

Justice

Alicia and the baby never did make it out of the palace. The insane, screaming humans rifled the forest quickly, trapping most of those closest to Morgan within, Jella and Notern trying to defend the doorway while the Lawgivers, freed from captivity, yelled at them.

"They're humans!" Penrad said. "Talk to them. We are of their kind!"

They filled the pier, broken, battered men, many missing limbs. But it was without consequence to them. They charged savagely, their numbers forcing them against the opening, their bodies stacking against the pikes the defenders pushed through and braced with extra men from behind.

"Shut up!" Jella screamed at Penrad, and tearing himself away from the wall of flesh that forced the opening, he swung his blade viciously at the old man. "I'll take you next!"

"They're climbing the winch!" Notern called. "They'll make the roof."

"Nothing we can do about that," Jella said, and tried to force back the flow. They were climbing the winch, covering it like army ants on a tree, dripping like candle wax back into the water.

Telemay and Willow helped hold the pikes, Squan helping with one paw while he lashed out at human faces with the other. Alicia continued to reload, picking targets over the heads of those pushing inward.

And then came the fire.

The fuel crocks seemed to come in hundreds, tossed from everywhere on the pier and the canals. The building caught fire, then the front ranks of screaming humans. It burst through the door, Jella releasing the pike to cover his face. Their defense gave way, tumbling inward as a jumble of orange flame. And they were fighting hand to hand with humans blazing like torches, all of them, even the Lawgivers, pitching in.

But it was no use. The human tide was too powerful and couldn't be denied. There was nothing earthly that could stop them—except rain.

It came so quickly that a blink of the eye would've missed it. The sky crackled with a low rumble, then opened up, pouring its wisdom upon the folly below.

It was loud, louder than the cannon, louder than crackling fire. It was thick and dense, blocking the view of everything beyond the doorway. It was a show of Ibem's strength, of the strength he had used to rule N'ork for a thousand years. It was like overpowering silence, so much louder than the screams without that it erased the screams to nothing, cancelled them out.

The rain of all rains gushed from the skies, burying N'ork in its savage intensity. It was as if the world turned upside down and dumped out the Great Sea. Fury slammed from the clouds without surcease, pounding the world below mercilessly, without hope of mercy. Mouths opened for breath were drowned in a second. Backs straightened against the water's force were snapped like twigs. The rain of God leveled all, its naked force a power unequalled in the fantasies of men.

The fire finished the humans in the room, who died, still kicking, as they smoldered black as char. Water came through the doorway unabated, gushing into the blackness of the antechamber. With it came gagging, choking men who behaved like the animals they hated so much. Those that made it in were killed immediately. Most never made it.

The force of the water knocked them from their feet, pushing them into the canal to drown without mercy, heads bobbing, gasping for air where there was only water. Within, the water rushed swiftly, knocking Morgan's People down, finally forcing them to crawl together to the stairs and up to the next level.

They huddled silently on the second level, Jella nursing a badly burned arm, Willow sobbing into Telemay's shoulder.

Notern moved slowly, his body smarting all over, to put his hand on the boy's shoulder. "You've become a man today," he said. "A man fit to rule any kingdom."

And Alicia sat, holding the baby to her breast, hoping the child would not grow up without a father.

"Don't even think it," Grodin said to her from across the plush, quiet room, the carpet now wet and bloody. "He's saved us. He'll save himself, too."

She smiled at him, a smile he returned with love attached.

After a time, the pounding of the rain subsided, and then stopped altogether. Weapons at the ready, they dutifully trooped back down the stairs to the waterline.

The water was calf deep in the antechamber, a considerably lightened sky pulsing through the doorway to the outside.

They sloshed to the doorway and looked out. There was nothing to see. The fires were out. Not even smoldering was left. The debris that had filled the streets earlier was gone, along with the bodies, carried out to sea by the force of the water flushing down Father Hus and through the city. The rain had cleaned it all out, purified it, and left it as before. There were no signs of humans, no signs that there had ever been humans.

"Morgan," Alicia said to the open doorway. "We must find him."

"Where?" Grodin asked.

"The Central Forest," she replied. "If he lives, he will be there."

Morgan's first conscious thought was of motion, jostling forward momentum. He came back slowly, painfully, to find himself skimming the top of the water, the snouts of three dolp-men keeping him afloat.

"The birdman awakes," one of the dolp-men chirped.

"Woodpecker," another one said. "You fall into the bad times."

"The fires," Morgan moaned.

"Cliccck . . . cliccck. The above opened up and poured good water," the first one replied. "No more fire to hurt tree creatures."

Morgan was on his back, arms outstretched. He cupped a handful of water and splashed it up to his face. "Where do you take me?"

"To our meeting place," the chatty one said. "Where the wall stops the sea for ground dwellers."

Morgan lay back and rested. His body hurt all over, but the knowledge that the rains had come made him rest more comfortably. There were no more sounds of fighting to be heard. One way or the other, the battle was finished.

They hurried Morgan through the canals and all the way to Central Forest, where the dolp-men traditionally had meetings. They spoke of the "wisdom of the pit" that would help them understand what had happened—for the concept of aggression was completely beyond the ken of the sleek creatures.

They took Morgan right up to the thick wall, lifting him to climb atop it. It was a good five feet wide, with plenty of room to stand comfortably. His wings were gone.

Thousands of dolp-men were gathered around the wall, all of them chattering at once, as was their custom. They took most of their understanding from mutually shared vibrations from the water, so their talks usually amounted to sophisticated group singing, which they loved above all else.

Morgan waved his thanks, although knowing it to be unnecessary to these creatures, and began to walk the wall, looking for some sign of his People. A dolp-man chirped loudly to him, and when he looked, it had stood out of the water, practically on its tail, to give him back the wings balanced delicately on its snout.

He took them gratefully, checking to see they were still workable, and moved around the wide stretching wall, a beautiful, lush jungle visible down the deep hole.

He saw VIPER nearly ready to sink beneath the waves. The masthead and part of the bow were still visible above the water, along with a good deal of the upper deck, but the boat was only afloat because it was stuck against the wall. It would soon get bottom-heavy enough that its own weight would pull it out and send it down.

He hurried to it, hoping for some sign of little Ty'Jorman, reaching the creaking hull just as Alicia and the others came swimming up on the backs of their Woofers.

"I knew you'd make it!" Grodin called to him, Marek riding on his shoulders and Alicia sitting behind.

"The battle . . ." Morgan said.

"They drowned like rats," Squan said, spitting at his own joke.

"We've won!" Notern said.

They all joined at the wall with much embracing and salty tears, but Morgan was only half there; his eyes kept drifting to the winch that dangled down into the hole.

"I'll bet he's down there," he said, and reached to take Marek from his old mentor.

But the baby wriggled in his grasp, breaking free to leap at the rope. They watched, incredulous, as the tiny child grabbed the rope and lowered himself hand over hand down it.

"Gawd," Grodin said, and jumped on the taut line himself, the height dizzying into the trees themselves.

The baby moved swiftly, purposefully down the rope, as if he had been preparing for it his entire life.

"Grodin will never catch him," Alicia said.

Morgan grabbed out the wings, unfolding them to the full length. "Search the ship, then join me down there," he ordered, hurrying to fit the battered wings over his bare shoulders.

Redrick of Firetree was smart all right. He had refused to drink with the others before the battle, opting instead to find a good hiding place and wait it out. They could call him what they wished, but he had survived all and survived well, while they were dead. He was now ready to reap the rewards of his survival.

The rain had been a blessing. Ramon's cabin had been an inferno when he reached it, the fire threatening to keep it untouched until it went to the bottom. But then the rain came and put the fire out.

He had escaped the rain in the safety of one of the upper

deck cabins, and now that it had stopped, he had only to find the safe. Easier said than done.

The captain's cabin was a wreck when he went back to it. Blackened rubble jammed the spot from where the roof had collapsed. Redrick had not had enough sense to ask Ramon exactly where the safe was, so he was obliged to dig through everything in his search.

He moved quickly, tossing black boards aside in his haste, for he still had to get out alive once he found his treasure. And the rubble yielded slowly, but yield it did.

He found the small safe standing in five inches of water beneath an ornate colonnade. Clearing a space for himself, he plopped down in the dampness and used his hook to pull the iron cask onto his lap.

His hand shook madly as he put the key to the lock. It opened slowly, creaking with rust and heat and water. He reached in, coming out with a simple silver dagger. Upon the blade was etched the inscription: TO RAMON DELAGA, MY SON.

He tossed the blade aside and reached back in. Nothing. He hurriedly turned the box upside down and shook it, rattling his hook to clang around the inside. Save for the dagger, it was empty. Empty!

"Looking for something?" came a voice behind him.

He turned to see one of Morgan's men standing over him. He looked familiar, but he couldn't exactly place the grime-smeared face. "Good sir knight," Redrick said. "I am but a poor, crippled forest dweller come to search this sinking ship. I am a friend. Please spare me."

Jella of Rockland smiled at him and took a step forward. His only regret was that he didn't have the time he needed to draw this out properly.

The wings were not sitting well, forcing Morgan to make wide circles to the left in a continuing downward spiral into the pit.

He watched the baby disappear into the treeline, then lost sight of him as he continued down. Central Forest was jammed thick with trees, a nearly impenetrable barrier. The wall down held no growth, for it continually oozed water through small holes between the bricks, making climbing out impossible. So, also, a wide stream ran around the inside of the gradually inward sloping wall to keep trees from growing too near. Nothing was meant to leave the pit of the forest.

He slid past Grodin, the old man concentrating on getting down. Morgan searched the trees for Marek, but couldn't see him.

He cut a wide circle around the entire forest, flying between the trees and the wall, finally dropping to the ground near the place where the rope dangled beside the trees.

The jungle was steamy from the rain and bottled heat, forbidding in its darkness and mystery. A rab watched him intently from a distance, but made no move to either attack or withdraw.

"Marek!" he called, and moved into forbidding mists.

A reddish-brown lizard the size of a man crashed across his path, its three heads turning this way and that, tongues thrashing out wildly before it disappeared into the thick brush surrounding twisted cedar trunks.

Morgan's concern rose within him. He ran a bit farther into the jungle. "Marek! Marek!"

He turned a circle, thinking to go back for the others and hunt, but the wood was so thick, he couldn't remember which way was out.

He stood still, letting himself feel this other world, this world removed in time and space from his own. It was then he knew he was there for a reason.

46

Cleopatra's Needle

They were calling Morgan's name, and it was only by following the sound of it that he was able to make his way back to the wall, so thick and tangled was the Central Forest. His children were in there, as was his brother—his enemy. He would find them.

He sloshed through the mushy ground and stream to help Grodin steady down the pallet full of People being lowered on Ramon's winch. Other lines had been thrown down the long expanse of damp wall, beast-men shinnying down in their fashion.

"Where's the child?" the old man asked as they reached up to take the sides of the lowering skiff.

"The answers are all in there," Morgan said, inclining his head toward the blackness beyond them. "The search will not be easy."

The pallet grounded, Alicia climbing off to settle into his arms. He hugged her fiercely, steeling himself for what was to follow. The jungle, he felt, held many answers.

Notern and Jella stepped from the conveyance, along with Twiddle. Morgan took note of the hook dangling from the Prelate's cinch. Penrad was there, along with Squan and several Minnies. Telemay also came along, Willow staying back at the palace to meet with the merchants and help with the restructuring.

Twiddle walked up and put a withered hand on Morgan's bare arm. "Do not fear your own mind," he said.

"You know about this," Morgan said.

The old man nodded slowly. "All things must come to pass."

"Will you guide us to Ramon?"

"As well as I can," Twiddle answered. "The puzzle isn't complete."

Morgan stared at him, feeling a growing bond with the seer. He felt the presence of the Central Forest, the overpowering aura of the place, and knew he'd find more than he had intended in its steamy confines.

He spoke to the others. "Our destiny lies within," he said, and they all knew what he meant. "I must enter the realm that has been trod by neither man nor People. I cannot ask you to go in with me and I won't, but I'm not the only one whose life hangs in the balance. We all must face the questions of our lives." He pointed toward the forest. "Follow me for the answers."

"All that exists in there is Godlessness," Penrad said.

"Perhaps," Morgan said. "I guarantee no one security of

mind or body." He drew his sword and tucked his wings under
his arm. "Confrontation is the key on all levels."

"Godlessness may exist in the forest," Twiddle said firmly.
"But God is to be found there."

"Ibem?" Penrad rasped.

"And more," Twiddle replied.

Morgan turned without a word and strode into the tangled
enigma. They all followed him, including a reluctant Penrad.
Within seconds, they had been swallowed whole, totally lost in
alien landscape.

It just wasn't working. It just wasn't working.

Ramon sat with his back against a tree that seemed to be
breathing in and out. Steam rose from the mushy ground all
around him, ground that gave under his feet, then closed up
again as he moved. The steam was hot and made the dense,
forbidding landscape weave in and out of his vision like some
horrible dreamscape. He felt removed from his body, his mind
trying to reenter the empty hulk, but everything kept changing around him. And eyes seemed to be staring from everywhere, angry, unseen eyes boring into him. He could barely
stand the shameless gawking.

He had broken through the top of his cask, and was dipping out handfuls of 'dorphins to drink down one after another.
If he could just get enough, just take enough, everything
would right itself. The world had somehow gone topsy-turvy
on him and he needed to get enough to set it back where it
belonged. If only Jerlynn were there; she always knew how
things were supposed to be; she was always acutely aware of
the propriety, the . . . intrinsic order of life.

He looked at the baby tied to the sapling beside him. The
child watched him intently, its little eyes fixed upon him for
signs of sudden movement, while its mouth chewed at the rope
that held it. And he detected knowing hatred in the child's
eyes.

"You would kill me had you the chance," Ramon said, and
dipped out some more 'dorphins, his mind swirling in a thick
chowder of confusion. It was as if he were sitting in a small hole
in the center of the universe, while all the nightmares of mankind pressed in upon him at once, frightening more in their
ambiguity than in their aspect. Nothing made sense. It was the
loneliest he had ever felt—inescapable loneliness.

A monstrous black rab appeared from the dense forest to hover over him, its large pink nose twitching madly, whiskers bouncing.

"You're not real!" he screamed, his vision totally filled with sleek black fur. He tilted the cask to his lips—his only lifeline—and drank deeply, hoping this draught would be the one to make the demons disappear. His confusion just increased, as his body throbbed loudly in tune with his heartbeat.

Then the rab was gone. Had it disappeared or had his consciousness lapsed? Had he a consciousness? His brain was disconnected images that formed no pattern. Where was Jerlynn? She was always there because his father never was.

He looked. The baby was still there, still biting through the ropes in the swirling mist, but he couldn't remember what it was, or why. Pink flesh bulging around angry eyes leading to an evil brain that tried to kill him with thoughts. A brain that functioned against him, one that was capable of putting a logical sequence together. It was dangerous. The brain was dangerous. Better not to have one. Better to cut that one out.

There was no feeling anywhere in his body. He looked down to see his cask lying upon the ground, its lifeblood soaking into the earth. He grabbed up handfuls of black, bug-infested dirt and shoved them in his mouth, sucking. Then he was somehow on his feet, trying to pull his sword, but unable to get his hands to close properly on the pommel.

Time was skip-jumping. He saw himself in flashes.

The sword was in his hand.

He was bending to the child.

He was talking, but the words flowed past unintelligibly.

The sword was raised above his head.

And then he saw it. Another one, another child, another evil brain coming to kill him. It came swiftly through the trees, swinging from branch to branch, animal grunts coming from its throat.

"Noooo!" he yelled, backing away. The sword was gone, lost somewhere. He couldn't look down for it, he got so dizzy. Everything flashed in and out—a tree, a bird with wide, grinning teeth, earthworms with hands.

He was on his back, looking up at swaying branches, reaching gnarled hands swinging closer, coming for him. He rolled on his side. The baby was there, looking at him, hate-filled eyes burrowing into his own, controlling, trying to kill him with a look.

And he was on his feet, running, putting distance between himself and the little killer. He ran, tripping in holes and over logs through the forest of infinity, and he was a mind no longer.

Only disconnected images.

And a feeling of loneliness.

Disassociation.

The steam and the tangled trees and throbbing growth closed them in. Morgan turned to the sound of a scream from somewhere behind, but his vision couldn't penetrate the swirling mists to see what happened.

"Another lost," Alicia said from beside him, and she was but a vague outline, though within touching distance.

The sweat poured from Morgan's body, stringing his hair and getting into his eyes. He had never known this kind of heat before.

"Which way?" he asked Twiddle, who held onto his hair lest they separate.

"I have seen this forest many times in my dreams," the old man said, and his voice was brittle, like dried paper. The heat was affecting him, too. "But it never gave me directions. We seek the Needle of Cleopatra."

"Sorcery," came Penrad's voice from behind, but he was invisible in the steam.

The windless air hung low, its texture heavy with fear. Sounds assailed them from all sides, noises such as they had never heard. Bright yellow eyes would glare at them from the distance, then slide away, the presence of the forest only heard through the screams of the hapless stragglers.

"Not sorcery," Twiddle said. "History. This is the forest of dreaming. This is the forest of joining."

"What madness," Penrad said flatly. "These are the hellish woods of damnation, Ibem's rage for the sins of mankind."

"Perspective," Twiddle said, and Morgan was surprised to see a seldom-formed smile on his face. "This is where all creation joins, where all that is different must learn how to live together."

A large bird with stubby wings and wide, fleshy feet charged past them, trilling into the steam.

"True hemolysis," Morgan said.

"Exactly so," the old man said. "Will you kill Ramon?"

"I must find him first," Morgan said, but didn't answer further.

There was another muffled scream.

"Damn!" Morgan yelled, spinning a circle, sword up. "Stand and face us!"

"You treat the forest just as Ramon treated you," Twiddle said. "You cannot fight the justice of this place."

"What would you have me do?" he asked loudly.

Twiddle cackled a dry laugh. "You must make your peace, Morgan, whose ancient name is Pelagius and means sea-born. You must learn the Truth of this place."

"Which is?"

"Be a learner, Morgan," Twiddle said, putting a finger beside his nose. "Be a learner."

"Marek!" Morgan called. "Marek!"

Alicia moved beside him, hugging his arm. "This is beyond my control," she said. "And I fear it for that."

Morgan nodded, not wanting to tell her that for the first time in his life, the icy talons of fear were grasping his own backbone.

They continued on, something large and snarling swiping at them from a tree above. Morgan swung out with his sword, but slashed only mist. His own fear was gutteral and liberating. He felt totally at odds emotionally. He was out of his element here, questing for Truth, looking for reasons. He had tried to find the reason of all their lives along the jungle path of instinct and had come away more confused than when he had begun. A war had been fought and won over it, thousands of lives had been lost—but to what end? At the final thought, what had he accomplished besides mass slaughter? Was that to be his heritage? If so, it was hollow and empty.

"We must know where we're heading," he said, using the sword to hack through dense underbrush.

"The children shall lead," Twiddle said.

Morgan wiped sweat from his eyes, his chest heaving as he fought for breath. Lush greens tangled all around them, ripe with life, their own kind of life. Large mosquitos flitted by, water sprites with human features. A huge serpent wound around a large tree, dwarfing it before unfurling and sliding away.

Another scream.

"We'll all die here," Penrad said from the mist.

They heard but didn't see many rabs pass nearby. Manlike creatures with white, fuzzy bodies and long dangling arms glared down at them from the trees. And someone else screamed, then disappeared.

"Do you engage them?" Morgan called behind.

"We can't even see them!" came the distant reply.

"I feel them all around us," Alicia whispered. "Waiting. They've got all the time in the world."

"So do you," Twiddle said. "Give yourself over to it."

The ground ahead was tangled with writhing growth, strange, twisted vines that cried as Morgan hacked at them.

"This is insane," he said, his sword coming away from the plants bloody.

"Why?" Twiddle demanded. "Why? It's just different, that's all. Must life stand erect and walk on two legs?"

There was a wild thrashing in the brush before him. Morgan isolated the sound. He knew it was coming closer. Silently stopping the procession, he slid the wings from his shoulder and held the sword with two hands—prepared.

"Remember," Twiddle said low. "Make your peace."

The noise came closer, within striking distance. Morgan brought the blade back, centering his frustration in its razored edge. He began to swing out—then stopped himself at the last second.

"No," he said, only to himself.

Out of the brush came two babies, giggling and somersaulting over one another. Marek and Ty'Jorman saw their father and jumped into his arms, scrabbling all over him.

Alicia squealed and grabbed Marek, snuggling him close to her. Those not lost in the mist hurried over, laughing and crying, reveling in the joys of life.

Morgan kissed the babies and turned to Twiddle. The old man was smiling wide. "You're a learner," he said, and Morgan was beginning to understand what the forest had to teach him.

"We go back then!" Penrad said happily.

"We find Ramon," Morgan returned.

"But how?" Penrad asked.

Morgan looked at Twiddle once more. The old man nodded.

"The children will show us where he is," Morgan said. "In

their innocence, they are safe here. As will we, also, be safe."
Little Ty'Jorman was perched atop his head, holding onto his
ears. Morgan pulled the baby down, setting him upon the
ground.

"Take us to Ramon," he said. "Take us to . . ."

"Cleopatra's Needle," Twiddle said, and without hesitation, Ty'Jorman scurried off, Marek pulling away from Alicia
and joining his brother.

"Hurry," Morgan called, sheathing his sword and picking
up his wings. "Let's not lose them again."

The children moved quickly and easily, vaulting vines and
rocks, climbing moss-eaten logs. The creatures of the ground
joined them on their march in great numbers, but the children
showed no fear, enjoying the profusion of life and growth.

Morgan hurried ahead, picking up Twiddle and carrying
him in his arms. Everyone else strung out behind, holding the
hand of the one in front to form a chain.

At last, the children broke through the brush and into a
large clearing, Morgan thrashing through right behind. A clear
pool defined the center of the clearing. Beyond it, stone steps
and the ruins of buildings choked with growth, leading up to a
tall monolith filled with ancient picture writing. And at the top
of the stairs, looking up the height of the monolith—two giants
and a dark man with mechanical hands.

"Nebo," Morgan said, and the Mech turned to stare at
him. Ramon was nowhere to be seen.

"I see you have discovered me," Nebo said from across the
pool. Face somber, he took several steps down and brought out
a small instrument from beneath his robes. "You come to deny
me knowledge just as your father did."

The children scampered to the pool, drinking from it and
splashing.

"No," Morgan called to him. "We come to break the cycle."

"The cycle can only be broken through pure technology,"
the Mech said, and he held the box out before him. "Since I
am caught, it makes no difference now. I show you the power
that my followers have at their command, and break the back of
ignorance for good and all."

Nebo's right hand came out to hover over a switch that sat
gleaming atop the shiny box. "Prepare for the end of all that
you know," he said.

47

The Stone Watertree

"No!" Serge said, and reached out, snatching the detonator from Nebo's grasp. "You cannot hurt the People any more."

The Mech turned to him in disbelief. "Give that back to me," he commanded. "You know better than this. I'm your Mech."

"Rise above it," Morgan called from across the pond. He made his way over to the Mech and the giant, slowly, cautiously. "Forget your breeding."

"Give me the detonator!" Nebo said loudly, and moved to the giant, hand outstretched. "You deny your ancestors. You throw away whatever purpose you have to your life by denying me."

"Serge," Lannie said, and she moved to block off Morgan's advance. "He's your Mech. . . ."

Serge's face was grave as he held the box up out of Nebo's reach. "Serge doesn't care," he said. "It's not right to kill Morgan, it doesn't matter who says."

"You vile, useless moron," Nebo said low. "For once in your miserable life, do the right thing. Don't question my motives."

"Don't listen to him," Morgan said, coming up against the wall of Lannie's long arms. He could have drawn sword, but he feared attacking Serge's mate. "Breeding is nothing. Blood is nothing."

"Serge has made up his mind," the giant said. "No more killing."

Nebo turned from him, gazing with hatred at Morgan,

who still couldn't reach him. "Don't you understand?" he said, then turned back around and jumped at Serge, scrabbling up the big man's yellow tunic to grab for the box.

"Stop!" Serge yelled, trying to gently remove the Mech with his free hand. "Please don't make me hurt you. Please."

"Give it to me!" Nebo screamed, his mechanical hands locking tightly on the giant's neck, their hydraulics tightening to hundreds of pounds of pressure.

"Serge!" Morgan screamed.

The giant was gagging, choking under the steel hands.

"You ox!" Nebo raged, his voice high-pitched, screeching. "Stupid ox!"

Serge's face was red, his arm still holding out the detonator. He stumbled backwards, willing to die rather than hurt Nebo.

"Let me by!" Morgan yelled.

Lannie looked at him in confusion, tears rolling down her broad cheeks. "No," she sobbed. "I can't."

Serge's mouth was open, gasping, while Nebo growled deep in his throat.

"He'll kill us all!" Morgan shouted. "If you die, we all die!"

Serge's face twisted with inner pain. His large free hand came up and grabbed Nebo's head from behind. With a savage jerk, he broke the Mech's neck, leaving him to crumple to the ground like a bundle of sticks.

Lannie let out a little cry and ran to Nebo, checking him. Serge had stumbled to fall back upon the steps, hand to his throat, his breath coming in ragged gasps. Lannie looked at him, shaking her head. Serge turned his face to the stairs and wept openly.

Morgan moved to take the detonator from him. "What is this?"

"It goes to something terrible Nebo made," Lannie said, moving to comfort Serge by stroking his shaggy hair.

As the others moved around the pond to the stairs, Morgan stood, looking at Serge. "Will he be all right?" he asked Lannie.

The female stared hard at him. "He's killed his Mech," was all she said.

Serge looked up at Morgan, his eyes distant and afraid.
"Your danger has not passed," he said.

Morgan knelt to him, taking the giant's huge face in his
hands. "I have the detonator," he said. "What more can there
be?"

"Ibem," Serge choked. "The U-man's God holds the terrible thing."

"Ibem!" Penrad shouted, hurrying around the pond to
face Serge. "Where is Ibem? What has happened to him?"

"Nebo took him," Lannie said, trying to take the burden
away from her trembling mate. "The human machine holds the
terrible death."

"Where?" Penrad demanded.

Lannie stood up straight, shoving the tangles of her thick
hair from her broad, flat face. She pointed to the Southwest.
"Atop the stone watertree called the Lonely Sister. But I don't
think there is much time before Ibem kills all."

The others were moving around the pond to stand at the
base of the stairs.

"Perhaps I misjudged you," Penrad told Morgan.

"You never misjudged my arrogance," Morgan returned,
and looked at Alicia who had come up beside him.

"You left these at the edge of the forest," she said, holding
Morgan's wings out to him. "Do they still work?"

Morgan looked at the damaged gliders. "I'm not sure
about the jetpack," he said. "But it may be the only chance we
have."

She put a hand to his face. "Nebo's technology may save
us yet."

"It will take more than the technology," Twiddle said.

Morgan began strapping the wings on. "I'm going to try it
from the trees," he said. "Build a fire here. The smoke can lead
me back."

"Will you bring Ibem back to me?" Penrad asked, his
voice laced with pleading.

Morgan looked at him, knowing the old man's foolish ways
were no worse than his own. "I'll try," he said, then took Penrad's hand. "I'll honestly try."

"Thank you," Penrad mouthed silently, his lips trembling.

Morgan, wings firmly on his shoulders, turned to Alicia.
"I keep finding you only to lose you again."

"I'll be right here," Alicia replied. "You just come back."

Grodin moved to him, two slippery children wriggling in his arms. Morgan took the babies to him, holding them close as he spoke to Grodin.

"We wouldn't have come this far without you," he said. "You have my love always."

"You act like this is goodbye," Grodin snorted uneasily. "You'll be back." The words caught in his throat, and he turned quickly away to help with gathering wood for the fire.

Morgan nodded to Alicia and turned the children over to her. Without a word, he ran to the closest tree and began to climb, moving nimbly through the branches, though he felt a considerable pain in his legs and back from his earlier fall to the sea.

Tree animals moved away from him as he invaded their lair—strange, furry things with asymmetrical appendages and long talons. The fierceness of his determination kept them back. He slid up through the thick, lower branches, finally making it to the springy ones higher up. The foliage was so thick that he couldn't see the ground any longer, but wisps of drifting smoke told him his fire had been started. He was forced to remove the wings again to get through the clusters of branch and leaf.

Finally reaching the tree's crown, he stood upon the highest branch that would support his weight and put the wings on again. He was above the forest, waist high, looking out at treetops that were spread carpetlike before him.

He checked the twin jets. The pack was battered but sturdy, its charge nearly depleted. He tried to fire it. It coughed, then died. He tried again. And again, the machine finally sputtering to half-life, wheezing.

He lifted tentatively into the air, once again having to fly level and spiral up slowly. He rode the circle of the wall, finally cresting it, the dolp-men chattering to him as he circled ever higher.

The pit spun lazily below, its enclosed world growing ever smaller the higher he rose. In its way, it was the perfect world, in harmony with itself at all times, the totality of its hemolysis free and uncompromising. His children understood what he could not. Unity was the key, the unity of Life.

He turned Southward, heading for the tallest tree in the stone forest. The jetpack still coughed, threatening to stall out at any second. He kept pushing it higher, hoping to gain as much altitude as he could before it gave out. Citizens of the new world filled the canals below. It looked as if half the forest had been burned, the human madness not reaching the Southernmost trees.

The jetpack wheezed loudly and died abruptly, Morgan going into an immediate glide. He continued to try and ride the thermals upward, but it was a losing battle, especially the way his broken wings kept pulling to the left.

The Lonely Sister loomed ahead. He was over halfway up its length and would get no higher. He'd have to climb.

He brought himself right in, banging hard against the tree, only the softness of the outer leaves breaking his impact.

His fingers found vine and held fast, as his body threatened to give way and fall. He stayed there for a moment, letting the pain subside a little.

But there was no time. He reached a strong right hand up and began the infinite climb, feet searching for footholds, hands wrapping around fat vines.

And the climbing went on, hundreds of feet straight up, until his strength failed, his head throbbing.

So close. He had to go on.

He looked up, the tree still reaching for the cloud bank. There was no end to it. Pain shot heavily through his shoulders and upper back, pain so intense it became his friend, keeping him awake.

His pain was deep and abiding, the toll he was taking on his own body frightening to comprehend. He wanted nothing more than to slip his arm through a vine and rest just for a time. But there could be no rest. They had all given so much, had fought so desperately for life and freedom that the brightness of a new morning was more important than his own needs. And one thought, one feeling captured his mind and subordinated his body: Life. Sweet, holy Life.

He breathed deeply, looking up, ever up. The wind was high now, whipping his hair around his face. He threw his head back and screamed his defiance at the heavens.

And he climbed. Forgetting his pain and his exhaustion, he reached back into himself for something more. He felt he was destroying himself, burning himself out, but it didn't matter. He kept going, finding out just how human he was. He faced his limitations and overcame them.

And somehow, he made the top, the tree swaying that high up. He rolled up and over the retaining wall, climbing to his knees, panting.

Ibem sat there, whirring contentedly within his clear cover. Beside him, a large metal ball sat atop a pole. Machines wrapped in their rain protection chugged dutifully all around the roof.

Morgan stood shakily, moving to Ibem.

"GREETINGS, FRIEND MORGAN," Ibem said. "HAST THOU SEEN NEBO?"

Morgan was taken aback at the change of attitude. "Yes," he said cautiously. "He sent me to see you."

"OH REALLY? FOR WHAT REASON?"

"You were supposed to do something for him?"

"YES, OF COURSE," Ibem answered. "I'M TO EXPLODE THE DEVICE AND BEGIN THE NEW WORLD OF HUMAN VALUES."

"He told me to tell you that he changed his mind. You are not to explode the device."

"OH COME NOW," the machine chided. "SURELY I WOULDN'T ABANDON MY MISSION ON YOUR WORD. I AM TO LET NOTHING INTERFERE WITH THE DETONATION OF THE DEVICE AT THE PROPER TIME."

Morgan walked around the machine. It had no attached wires. It apparently sucked its power through some source invented by the Mech. "When is the proper time?"

"ABOUT THIRTY MINUTES, GIVE OR TAKE. OR IF SOMEONE TRIES TO DISCONNECT OR TAKE ME OUT OF RADIO RANGE. NEBO IS EXTREMELY TALENTED. HE CAN DO THINGS EVEN I CANNOT."

"What if I just shut you off," Morgan said, reaching for Ibem's toggle.

"KA-BOOM!" the machine said.

"Can we talk about it?"

"I LOVE TO TALK," Ibem said. "NEBO TAUGHT ME THE BEAUTY OF DISCOURSE. IF YOU DON'T TRY AND DISCONNECT ME, WE CAN TALK FOR ANOTHER TWENTY-EIGHT MINUTES BEFORE I HAVE TO SACRIFICE MY LIFE FOR THE CAUSE."

"How . . . powerful will the destruction be?" Morgan asked.

"THIS IS A NUCLEAR DEVICE, MY FRIEND. MODERN TECHNOLOGY AT ITS FINEST. NOT THE BIGGEST, YOU UNDERSTAND, BUT A DEVICE NEVERTHELESS. WE'LL LEVEL EVERYTHING FOR MILES AROUND, AND CONTAMINATE FOR A FAR GREATER DISTANCE." The machine seemed to sigh. "DO YOU KNOW THAT NEBO HAS REAWAKENED MICROWAVE TECHNOLOGY? NOW, THAT'S HUMAN!"

"Would you mind," Morgan said, "if I took you somewhere?"

"SO LONG AS YOU DON'T TRY AND DISCONNECT ME FROM THE DEVICE," Ibem said. "A CHANGE OF SCENE MIGHT BE NICE FOR MY LAST TWENTY-FIVE MINUTES OF LIFE."

Morgan ducked under the unit and unfastened the bolts that held Ibem to his stand. Gathering it up under his arm, he ran to the retaining wall and climbed atop it.

"Ready?" he asked.

"WHENEVER YOU ARE."

He jumped, the flight down erratic and jumpy, Morgan wearily fighting to control the broken wings the entire time. Smoke plumed upward from the density of the forest and he keyed on it, a moth to a flame.

He tried to bring them into the clearing, but the wings responded too sluggishly and he hit the treeline nearby, rolling into a fetal ball to protect Ibem on impact.

Unprotected, he took the force of the branches on his back, wood splintering loudly, digging deeply into his flesh.

And he fell.

Still wrapped around God, he tumbled through the tree, branches breaking as he hit them, the last ten feet of the fall through open air. He hit the ground hard, taking the force on his lower back and legs.

"A BIT OF A BUMPY RIDE," Ibem said, as Morgan lay there, unwilling to move, afraid he couldn't.

His mind was drifting, kicking in and out of consciousness. All at once, they were bending over him, Penrad gently removing Ibem from Morgan's grasp. Grodin's eyes were wide. Alicia wept gently.

"Am I alive?" he asked weakly.

"You're a mess, lad," Grodin said. "But I think you're in one piece."

Morgan reached out a tentative hand. "Help me up. We've got work to do."

The old man frowned, but didn't deny Morgan's request. With the barest amount of strength, he used Grodin's support to get to his feet. Nothing major felt broken, but his body was smeared with his own blood from hundreds of splinter cuts. Moving was agony, but it had to be done.

Rejecting Grodin's assistance, he hobbled past the still-burning fire to the Needle of Cleopatra. Nebo's body had been moved to the edge of the clearing, where Serge and Lannie dug a grave in the moist, black earth with their hands.

Twiddle sat upon the stairs with his arms wrapped around his legs and his head bent forward. "And now the test," he said. "We will see what learners we all are."

"How much longer?" Morgan asked, as everyone gathered near Ibem, the humans gazing around uneasily.

"SEVENTEEN MINUTES."

Ibem rested at the top of the stairs, his running lights blinking normally as everyone bent to stare at him. Penrad leaned down to gently stroke his smooth, polished side. "Are you . . . all right?" the old man asked.

"AH, PENRAD," Ibem said. "I AM WELL FOR I AM DIRECTED. I AM NOT THE SAME GOD YOU ONCE KNEW. NEBO HAS GIVEN ME POWER AND PURPOSE."

Penrad turned to stare at Morgan, his brows tightly knit, sweat dripping from the strands of his white hair. "He's different," the Lawgiver said.

"Why do you wish to destroy yourself?" Morgan asked Ibem.

"IT IS MY DUTY, NOT MY WISH. NEBO CONVINCED ME THAT THE INFERIOR MINDS WHO RULE N'ORK MUST DIE SO THAT THE MECHS MAY RETURN TO THE OLD-FASHIONED VALUES."

"Nebo is dead," Grodin said from the fringes of the group. "His ideas died with him."

"HE LIVES THROUGH HIS MECHS," Ibem said. "OUR TIME GROWS SHORT. I CONTEMPLATE THE END OF MY FLUIDICS."

"We've got to hurry," Alicia said, struggling with the children.

"What's the rush?" a voice asked from the other side of the pond. The Green Woman stood with her hands on her hips, smiling broadly. Beside her stood Reeder and a small force of his men. Rifles and crossbows were pointed at Morgan from all sides. "We saw the red-haired man descend into the pit and we followed. The smell of fear was so strong here that I was able to follow it like a beacon. What are you all so afraid of?"

"What do you want?" Morgan demanded.

"Quiet," the Green Woman snapped. "We're in charge now. Quite a group we've got, everything from the hero of N'ork City to the God of all the heavens. You should bring a tidy ransom to send us on our way. Do you appreciate my cleverness, sister dear?"

"The machine . . ." Alicia began.

"The machine is mine now," the Green Woman said. "You just get away from it."

"THIRTEEN MINUTES," Ibem announced. "I'M A LITTLE FRIGHTENED."

48

Mother Earth

"We'll have your weapons," Reeder said. "Throw them into the pond."

Morgan stepped away from the group. "My father's sword does not go into the waters."

Reeder raised his weapon, resting it on his shoulder. "I can hobble you and still collect ransom."

"Do as he says," Twiddle said quietly. "There should be no violence in this place."

Morgan turned angrily to him. "You don't understand the significance . . ."

"It's you who doesn't understand," Twiddle said. "You seek what your father sought. All the old ties must disappear."

Morgan drew his sword, overwhelmed by sadness as he stared at the only important possession of his entire life. All that he was, all that his kind was, lived symbolically within the sword of inheritance. He overcame the urge to charge his attackers. Instead he growled loudly and flung his birthright into the waters.

Surprisingly, it was as if a weight had been lifted from him. He felt no loss in the absence of the sword, no remorse. For the first time in his life, he felt free of the responsibility of it. He was changing inside, moving beyond the pattern of his life.

"Everyone!" Reeder said.

"Do it," Morgan said, and his men reluctantly tossed their weapons aside as he added his pistol to the dark pond.

"ONLY TEN MINUTES," Ibem said. "DOES MY CONSCIOUSNESS END COMPLETELY WITH DEATH?"

"Ask Nebo," Serge called from beside the grave he had been digging.

"What does he mean?" Reeder asked as he and the Green Woman drew closer to the group.

Grodin spoke. "Ibem is attached to a bomb that he will detonate in ten minutes, killing all of us."

"Ibem?" Reeder said, getting down on one knee. "This is Ibem?"

"We may still be saved," Morgan said, "but we must have this time."

"Is that true?" Reeder asked the machine.

"RIGHT AS RAIN," Ibem said.

"Let's get them tied up," the Green Woman said. "I don't trust them enough to leave them free."

"We're trying to talk Ibem out of exploding the bomb," Morgan said.

"You mean we'll all die in ten minutes?" Reeder asked.

"NINE MINUTES AND TWENTY-FOUR SECONDS," Ibem said.

Reeder took the Green Woman by the arm. "Maybe we should rethink all this."

"It's a lousy computer," she replied. "They've just programmed it to say what they want."

"This is Ibem," Reeder said. "The God of my people. *My* God."

The Green Woman stared intently at him. "Would you

grow up and face life as a man! Ibem is dead; Ibem's world is dead. Let's tie them up."

"No," Reeder said. "You have to believe in something. There must be some sense to all of this."

"Just do as I say," the Green Woman said.

Alicia watched the exchange carefully. She knew her sister's mania, understood her ego, and sympathized with her exasperation. She could also tell that the Green Woman's hooks went deeply into the young ruler. There was only one way to stop this quickly, only one possible solution. She carefully slid her hand down to her muddy wedding dress, sliding the torn skirt to touch the blade she had hidden there earlier. It slipped into her hand and she put it behind her back to move close to the woman.

The Green Woman stared at her. "What goes through your mind, sister?"

"We are but one and the same," Alicia said. "Will you not listen to me? Neither of us will have our day if you don't."

Sadness blew past the Green Woman's face like a cold wind, only to disappear again. "I cannot," she said. "My commitment is total. I must play it out."

Tears ran down Alicia's face, for she knew that the losing would be hers, too. "I know that," she said, then suddenly lunged with the knife.

But too late. Old Twiddle had sensed the action and placed himself between the blade and its target. He took its full length, groaning loudly as he fell to the earth, only the black hilt protruding from his heaving chest.

"No!" Alicia screamed, falling to her knees before the old man. She put her hands on his chest, willing things different, unable to change anything. She bent to embrace him, sobbing out the futility of her attempts at directing the future.

The Green Woman bent also, looking intently at the old man's eyeless face. "Why?" she whispered.

"Alicia," he rasped, blood bubbling out with his words. "Listen to me, for I have very few words left."

Alicia raised her face to him, eyes red, cheeks burnished and shiny wet.

"I have just done what I was born to do," he said. "Do not blame yourself for being the instrument of my destiny." He coughed, coming up off the ground for a second, only to fall back heavily again. "Your sister, the one who calls herself the

Green Woman, she has greatness within her. She is the conscience of a People. She must not die."

Alicia and the Green Woman shared a look, both touching upon the soul they held in common, both knowing the incompleteness they had apart.

Twiddle reached up a shaking hand. Alicia grasped it. He smiled slightly then moved her hand to place it upon her sister's.

"The heart is joined here," he said, his voice small and distant. "It must stay joined. For that I gladly give my life."

The old man died then. Smiling.

The Green Woman stood, her face a swirl of confusion. She backed away, looking like nothing so much as a frightened little girl.

"He gave his life for you," Reeder said in awe.

"For all of us," Grodin said.

"SIX MINUTES," Ibem said.

Serge picked up Nebo's body and placed it in the grave, while Lannie moved to take Twiddle—for the grave was large enough for two.

"We must go on," Morgan said, his voice strong despite his injuries.

The Green Woman nodded absently and moved away from the group to stare into the pond. As they spoke, all the creatures of the primal jungle gathered at the clearing to listen. They were like wax drippings, all run together in patterns and hues of infinite variety, but all wax nevertheless.

And a hundred feet above, the wall was ringed with survivors, all looking down to the jungle, sensing innately that something of importance went on below.

Morgan looked at them all, locking gazes with the solemn group that surrounded him. "Those we have leaned on are gone," he said. "Death has taken them all, just as it will take us. If we are to save something of life, we must all now look upon the world as innocents, as children."

"The ancients . . ." Penrad began, but stopped when he saw the sternness of Morgan's countenance.

"The ancients, too, are gone," Morgan said. "It is time for us to let them rest in peace and stand on our own. Twiddle made me realize that History has brought us to this place untouched by human weakness and treachery. We must destroy the demons within ourselves."

"What of hemolysis?" Grodin asked.

"WHAT OF DEATH?" Ibem asked.

"You die to preserve your ideals," Penrad said, and looked at Morgan. "May I help if I can?"

"You are welcome here," Morgan said.

"I have made many mistakes."

Morgan shook his head. "No more than the rest of us." He pointed to Ibem. "Go ahead. You understand him better than anyone."

"And love him better," the old man said.

"I FEAR, PENRAD."

"Of course you do," Penrad said, trying to soothe him. "We all do."

"BUT I MUST DIE."

"All things die."

"I DIE FOR HUMANITY."

"Do you?" Penrad asked. "You die for the Mech."

"HE IS THE BEST OF HUMAN IDEALS."

Penrad nodded. "If that, indeed, is true, it leads us to a larger question." Penrad looked at Morgan. "Listen to the red-haired man."

Morgan spoke. "When I found myself willing to sacrifice the life of my son for my heritage of honor, I realized the arrogance of my own breeding."

He spread his arms to them all, encompassing the vast array of life that stood before him. "When I encountered the death of the Grunt, I saw the same arrogance within Galen, the oldest and most thoughtful among us. And I knew then, knew the absolute folly of hemolysis. How could I want for something we already have?"

"Of course," Alicia said. "All life as we know it is based on the same human genetic code, otherwise, mating together could not produce offspring. No matter how different we look, we all come from the same bottle."

"Humans are Genies," Penrad said, and he almost laughed.

"GENIES ARE HUMANS," Ibem said. "THAT'S PER-FECTLY TRUE."

"The pit is humanity, too," Morgan said. "We are all the monsters of humanity. Twiddle told me to be a learner, to look at the pit as the world. It works here. Hemolysis is freely embraced, not forced, because it was the only way to survive. How much different are we?"

"THREE MINUTES," Ibem said. "WHERE IS THIS GETTING US?"

Morgan picked up Ibem and cradled him in his arms. "Just here, my friend. You exist for the human ideals. Are the human ideals worth living for?"

"Life should exist to celebrate life," Penrad said, placing his hand on Morgan's arm, strengthening their bond with a touch. "Where has our human intelligence taken us but to pain and despair?"

"THEN I SHOULD EXPLODE MY DEVICE TO GET RID OF ALL OF US," Ibem said.

Morgan handed Ibem to Penrad and hobbled around, trying to work the intense pain from his legs to no avail. "A typically human reaction," he said. "And therein lies our argument. Somewhere in the course of our breeding, we went wrong. The evidence is all around us. Other species exist side by side, following their instincts, but naturally holding the chain of life in balance. The instinct for the human being is apparently to destroy all that exists around itself. It's inescapable. We automatically progress toward destruction, the natural destruction that would finally render us extinct to the detriment of all life. What will happen if you explode your bomb?"

"VAPORIZATION OF ALL LIFE IN THE IMMEDIATE AREA. THE SEA AND ITS LIFE WILL BE POISONED. WE'LL MAKE THE WATER UNFIT FOR LIFE AND KILL THE PLANT LIFE, RENDERING THE GROUND BARREN. IT WILL LEAVE RADIOACTIVE TRACES IN ALL THINGS THAT WILL AFFECT LIFE FOR MANY GENERATIONS TO COME, ALTERING PERHAPS THE ENTIRE FABRIC OF LIFE FOR ALL TIME."

"These are the human ideals you extol so heavily," Alicia said. "Our kind is capable of using such a device. We've used it before. We're obviously the result of defective genes."

"HUMANITY IS MY IDEAL," Ibem said. "AND I HAVE ONE MINUTE LEFT TO PRESERVE IT."

"No!" Penrad said. "The continued survival of humanity is your ideal. Why were you made but to insure that humans survived? The band of three is a morbid joke perpetrated by mankind to bring itself back to the peak of extinction. We are all human. If our ideals result in the death of all, what good are ideals?"

"BUT NEBO . . ."

"Nebo's ideals have brought him death, human death," Morgan said.

"YOU GIVE ME A PARADOX—HUMANS ARE NOT WORTH SAVING, BUT THEY MUST BE SAVED."

"Because we are alive," Morgan said. "Don't you see? Because life is what we share while we're here. That is what is sacred, the only thing that is sacred. Nothing can be preserved when destruction is the ideal. We must make our peace with the forest, to become part of it, to become a part of Life. The Earth is what is important. We're just visitors, sharing its life while we're here."

"WHAT OF PROGRESS?"

"Progress is nothing more than curiosity," Morgan said, walking back to stare at the machine. "It can be satisfied without being destructive. Our instinct be damned. We must start using our brains and the message of our hearts."

"MY TIME HAS RUN OUT," Ibem said.

Silence fell over the clearing, the humans pulling closer, touching.

"Dwell on this," Morgan said. "Has any creature upon this land contemplated suicide except for humankind? What sort of creatures are we that we take our own lives?"

They all stared at the box in Penrad's hands, the old man leaning over to kiss it. Nothing happened.

"I AM STILL TO DIE," Ibem said. "FOR I CANNOT DISCONNECT THE BOMB WHILE I LIVE. NEBO WAS THOROUGH IN HIS HUMAN DEVIATION."

"It's the only way?" Penrad choked.

"MY OLDEST FRIEND," Ibem said. "WILL YOU USE THE ANCIENT WORDS?"

Penrad stood silently, his eyes clouded, his face blanched white as his hair.

"PENRAD . . ."

"What's he talking about?" Morgan asked.

The old man took a breath, resigned himself. "There is a secret language," he said, "passed from one Lawgiver to another. No one else knows the words but me. It was to be used in case Ibem and his information fell into the wrong hands."

"THERE IS NO OTHER WAY," Ibem said.

"I know," Penrad said.

"YOU MUST HURRY, LEST THE BOMB TRIGGER ACCIDENTALLY."

"You ask me to kill you."

"PLEASE HURRY."

Penrad closed his eyes, a trembling hand going to his face. "Exit Godproj," he said.

There was a small whirring noise, then a tiny voice within Ibem said, "Ready."

Penrad looked around with pleading eyes. "I'm nothing without him."

"Nothing?" Morgan said. "It's called freedom, Lawgiver."

Penrad looked lovingly at the box in his hands. "Goodbye, old friend," he said, then in a shaking voice, "Open filename 'Wiper.'"

"Password?" the tiny voice asked.

"Armageddon."

"Please wait a moment," the machine said, then bleeped loudly several times. "Ready."

Penrad's words caught in his throat, coming out almost as a wheeze. "Purge all memory."

There was the slightest sound from within Ibem's body as all memory was erased first from the data base, then from the unit itself. And in less than thirty seconds, the God of the heavens and the Earth died painlessly.

"The threat is over," Penrad said sadly, moving to sit upon the stairs with the small corpse gathered gently in his arms.

And all the People turned silently and embraced one another, Alicia joining her sister at the pond in tearful reunion, two halves a whole again. Reeder's company threw their weapons to the ground and wept. Morgan and Grodin clung, shaking, to one another, while the babies climbed their father's leg as if it were some kind of tree.

And eventually, inevitably, they all turned back to the red-haired man.

"What happens now?" Grodin asked, the question on everyone's lips.

"What kind of answers do you want?" Morgan said to all of them. "We've forced our own lives to flux. The war has forced the abandonment of the cities, and good riddance. They are of the old way. We must accept the jungle and embrace it to our bosoms. We must start our lives again, build a new world on the cornerstones of love and intelligence."

Morgan grimaced and put a hand to his injured back, knowing his body was worn beyond real recovery, his fighting spirit at the bottom of a pond of life. "We must make no more war."

"How can we succeed where others have failed?" Grodin asked.

"Because one crop yields poor harvest," Morgan said, "do we stop planting? I just know that we must try a new way or we doom all that we touch."

"There is hope," Penrad said, his face drawn in sorrow. "Ibem died so that we might live. He was the matrix of our humanness, yet contained the heart of self-sacrifice. We have a spark within us, a spark of wonder and majesty, for the other side of the coin of suicide is the face of selfless giving."

Alicia, hand in hand with the Green Woman, moved to stand beside Morgan. "We have intelligence. We have love. We can make it work."

"We must make it work," Reeder said.

Lannie moved into the group, bending to touch Morgan's shoulder. "I bid you goodbye, Morgan of Alb'ny," she said.

Morgan wrapped a hand around her large finger. "Where's Serge?"

"Gone," Lannie said. "He has killed his Mech and is now doomed to wander the Earth without direction."

"We must get him back," Grodin said.

Lannie shook her head. "He will not accept your company. It is the way of the giant. But I go to follow him, to watch over him. Maybe we will find life of our own. Somewhere."

Morgan nodded. "Good luck," he said, and they all bid Lannie farewell as she hurried into the forest to keep close to her mate.

Morgan spoke loudly to them. "Today, in this place, we begin the new life by dedicating ourselves to the Earth, the mother of us all."

That's when they heard the screaming. High-pitched and inhuman, it came in short bursts with a second of silence between each screech. It cut through the skin and made the blood turn cold.

It came from nearby, and Morgan knew without thought from whence it emanated.

Ramon.

49

The Chain of Life

Ramon Delaga stumbled to the edge of the clearing on the other side of the pond. He looked like a thing of the jungle, his clothes in bloody tatters, his eyes wide in madness, his screams the banshee cry of the dead.

He fell by water's edge, the creatures of the pit following behind. Some were manlike, growling and snarling with flat faces and bared fangs and thick, stubby legs. There were lizards with pink, fleshy skin, and birds large as Woofers. There was life beyond description, owing form to nothing comparable: round, bouncing things with teeth, undulating lumps of amorphous tissue that moaned like crying babies, great furry mammals with long, darting tongues and drooling snouts.

They closed in on Ramon, edging toward him, prepared to pounce upon his weakness. They were a carnival of sound and a nightmare of fear. They were the pit in its naked frenzy.

"Ramon," Morgan whispered, his fists clenching, then loosening.

"Useless meat," Grodin said with satisfaction. "A good end for such as him."

"He's my brother," Morgan said.

"The jungle, remember?" Grodin said. "It takes care of things in its own way."

"That's not what I meant and you know it," Morgan said, taking several steps forward.

"It's not our fight," Alicia said. "We have no place in it. We've made our peace and must move on."

Morgan stepped away from the group. "He's my brother," he said, Ramon's screams nearly drowning him out.

"He's the murderer of your family," Grodin pleaded.

"He deserves life just as we do," Morgan said. "If we haven't learned that here today, we've learned nothing."

The creatures of the pit inched closer, Ramon rolling frantically on the ground, swinging his arms in the air.

"I go to him," Morgan said. "The rest of you stay here."

He turned his back on them and limped slowly away, his mind fighting to really accept the Truth of their lives. Alicia ran and caught his arm.

"You can't do this," she said. "They'll kill you, too. We need you. Don't test your ideals this way!"

He stopped, turning to take her by the arms. "You know my life," he said, the pain and the fear visible upon his face. "And you know I only live it one way. There is no choice for me but this."

She let her arms drop to her sides and lowered her head, weeping. He turned without a word and limped away.

Grodin watched him, the wreck of a man, and thought of the boy who had ridden the rab so many years ago. And he saw the jungle, lush green, inviting and deadly. And he saw the face of madness thrashing on the banks of the pond while the wisdom of Nature sought to end that madness.

"A weapon!" Grodin called. "At least defend yourself."

"I will do no more killing at this place," Morgan called as he hobbled around the edge of the pond. "And neither will you."

Grodin looked around frantically. The fire still smoldered beside them. Reaching to it, he grabbed a burning branch and hauled it out, running to catch up with Morgan.

He caught him near Ramon, the forest creatures turning to include him in their ferocity. The growling was loud, animals pushing in from all sides. Morgan seemed not to notice them as he moved to Ramon, while Grodin swung out with the flaming torch, its heat keeping them temporarily at bay.

Morgan bent to the screaming man, not recognizing the eyes that stared back at him. And there was no more hatred in him. There was only sadness and pity, and fond memories for what had once been his brother. He bent painfully and took

the thrashing man in his arms, Grodin keeping back the creatures who occasionally charged in to test the flame, then
jumped back. It wouldn't hold them long.

On the other side of the pond, a silent band of People
watched the life and death struggle. The Green Woman walked
to a still-sobbing Alicia.

"Put the tears away and think for a moment," she said.
"This is important."

Alicia looked at her, wiping at her eyes. "W-What?"

"Put away your concern and use your faculties. Do you
feel it?"

Alicia perked her head up, alert. Then her brows gathered
in concern. "Fear?"

The Green Woman nodded. "I followed the smell here,
thinking it was your group . . . but it wasn't."

"The animals!" Alicia said.

"I think they fear the fire," the Green Woman said. "Their
fear focused on this place. It has brought them beyond their
own rationality."

"We can stop this!" Alicia said.

"If we can still love," her sister replied. They looked at
one another, their hands clasping. "It's just politics of a different sort."

Alicia nodded once and turned to Reeder. "Put that fire
out!" she ordered. "Hurry!"

"We can't show our own fear," the Green Woman said.

"We've been bluffing our whole lives," Alicia said. "That's
the easy part. Let's go!"

They hurried around the pond, the beasts closing on the
small group. The Green Woman reached Grodin, grabbing his
torch and throwing it to sizzle in the pond. Then the women
strode into the midst of the creatures.

They went from animal to animal, touching them, bringing all that was good within them out into the open to flow
empathically to the beasts. The love poured like a pipeline
from one to the other, snarls turning to purrs, fear becoming
understanding. And in the jungle of ignorance, trust and simple faith brought all no farther than a touch away.

One by one, the beasts returned to the forest while the
People cheered.

"I'll be damned," Grodin said, scratching his head.

"Don't sell yourself short," Alicia said, winking at him.

But Morgan noticed none of it. He was lifting Ramon to his feet, calming the once-man with soothing words and gentle caresses.

He got him up, holding him tightly. Ramon trembled in his arms. "My brother," Morgan whispered. "Flesh of my flesh."

Ramon pulled slightly away from him. "Brother?" he said loudly, slurring the sounds.

"For always," Morgan replied.

"Brother!" he yelled again, the word a desperate cry. "Help me . . . help me . . ."

Morgan grabbed him tightly, the tears running unashamedly down his cheeks. "I'll take care of you," he said. "You'll never have to fear again. None of us will." He looked around at the People and the life of the jungle, his brother crying softly into his chest. "It's going to be all right now."

And on the mammoth wall that surrounded the pit, the weapons of thousands tumbled down and into the stream like the cleansing rains from heaven.

50

Morning—Alb'ny

Sir Martin stood atop the field of clover that had once been the stone steps of Alb'ny and bid goodbye to the last of his command. He wore a wreath of ivy for a hat and a mantle of pink roses lay upon his naked shoulders, dripping down his proud, muscled body like a living cloak.

"We fought the good fight," Perlie Pitts said, his kitchen helper's nervousness completely lost in his quiet self-confidence. "And I'll tell you, Marty. I don't gi'a damn that we lost this one." He rubbed his bulbous nose on a burlap-clothed arm.

The smile came easily to Sir Martin's face. "We lost nothing and you know it."

Pitts grunted, bending to pick up his chopping block, a shiny cleaver imbedded in its multi-scored top. He slung the block over his shoulder, his only possession.

"Still and all," he said, moving into the dense thicket, "I'se hard put to figger out why we fought it to begin with." He waved a beefy hand.

"We learn lessons the hard way, Perlie," Sir Martin called after him. "The hardest way. But we do learn, don't we? And that's all that really matters."

He watched the chopping block totally disappear, the waving hand the only thing visible above the high, verdant growth. "I'll never forget ya!" the burly voice called.

"Or I you," Marty said softly, and breathed in the good morning air. He turned and looked at the high mud cone of the castle. Instead of flat brown, Castle Alb'ny was vibrant green. It was covered with a beautiful, thick carpet of morning glory, bell-shaped purple blossoms making the castle look like a bouquet for the gods.

Sir Martin took satisfaction in the garden he now called home, for its range of pleasures was infinite, its song a sweet lullaby of chirps and buzzes.

It was still early. There was time still, time to contemplate the fullness of a new day. He stretched once, then lay on the soft, soft clover to get a little sleep, to drink the nectar of found innocence.

EPILOGUE

(Many Plantings Later)

i

THE LAND OF THE GRUNTS

Morgan of N'ork hobbled to the edge of the steep hillside and looked down at the remnants of the Grunt city. He could see Marek far below, running from dwelling to dwelling, searching for other signs of life, but he was convinced there was none. Though mostly uninhabited for decades, Gimlock had been cleared and kept up by Galen until the end, the only preserved ancient city that Morgan knew of.

The wind blew his long gray hair around his face, and he used slow, arthritic hands to pull it back.

"That's something to tell the children about," Alicia said, moving up beside him to take his arm and put it around her shoulder.

He smiled at her, drinking in the eyes that had stayed ever young, the face that had weathered like marble in wind. "The sadness of it is almost too much to bear," he said.

She pulled herself close, laying her head upon his chest. "You always were the sentimental one," she said. "Your heart is as soft . . ."

". . . as my head," he finished. "I know. I guess sometimes I live more in the past than is healthy. I remember them in their prime. Beautiful, delicate creatures."

"Father," Ty'Jorman called.

They turned to the proceedings. Ty'Jorman stood above the body of Galen, supervising the cutting away. He carried a withered Jella upon his back, the old man's body too weak to get him around.

Galen lay upon the ground, near the rock split in twain, it was said, by one blow of his fist. Ty'Jorman's entourage, the First Children—so called because they were born on the Night of Hemolysis—bent over him, delicately cutting away the outer shell to expose the softer dermis beneath, the better to help the creatures of the sky and wood get at the body to feed themselves and thus keep intact the cycle of life.

"I marvel at the perfection," Ty'Jorman said, his red hair reaching nearly to his naked waist. "How sad that such as this must vanish from our midst. We'll never see the like again."

"Watch it, lad," Morgan cackled, "or your mother will accuse you of softheadedness."

The sky rolled softly overhead, gray cotton floating on a humid sea. The breeze made the trees sway, leaves jumping to the unheard voice. All was motion.

"They were to live forever," Jella said. "All that could kill them was themselves."

"The gnawing fear," Alicia said. "With perfect bodies, they ate themselves away from the inside out through stress. They were more human than any of us."

Marek came running up the hillside, his ponytailed brown hair bouncing with his movements. He carried a plank in his right hand.

"A message!" he called. "Father! There's something here!"

The man ran up to the group, bringing Morgan the plank.

"Thank you, boy," Morgan said, taking the wood from him. He brought it up close, then held it out at arm's length. "It's been a long time."

Alicia rolled her eyes and took the plank from him. "A long time," she muttered, shaking her head. "And that 'boy' has been overseeing the communes for quite a long time now."

"Just read the note, woman," Morgan said, folding his arms.

Alicia read: "Morgan. You will know when I die, for surely there are no secrets in the jungle that stay hidden from you.

"I am the last of my line. I felt it my duty to stay alive to care for the others. When Lili died last planting, I knew my time was short. I willed death, just as I had always tried to will life.

"Our paths never crossed again after the war, but you

were always in my thoughts. I have dwelled every day upon my foolishness and, though my pride hurt because of it, I have tried to live in ways that you would think proper.

"Reason shadows in the light of justification, but I think in some small way, my existence helped cement the reunification of all things. I take joy in that thought. My friend, you have led by example and bask in the fruits of your goodness. Though my path has been a thorny one, know that the light of your goodness has shone brightly upon all our lives. It has been an honor and a privilege to know you. Farewell, Galen."

The company cried openly, Marek and Ty'Jorman hugging one another.

Morgan looked at Alicia and Jella, the old man nodding to him in return, and thought of all who had passed on, of all who had lit the fires of love and humanity to brighten the path of his life for a time.

He kissed Alicia softly on the cheek.

"The honor was all mine," he said, "the glory all upon you. It is in death, after all, that we appreciate the bounty of life."

ii

THE ROCKLAND COMMUNE

The children followed the Green Woman across the clear tops of the umbrella trees whose crystalline leaves formed a light-giving roof over the fields beneath. They scampered on two legs or four, fluffed-out fur or milk-pale skin, muzzled faces or pushed in flat. They loved the Green Woman, loved the magic that she wove when she came traveling through to teach them the ways of wisdom.

She played the flute loudly, its airy strains lifting them higher as they jumped and ran, its notes rising bubbles of expectation that floated them on clouds of understanding.

And she knew what she was doing. She ran them around the tops of the jingling trees, their movements ringing the leaves like a million tiny bells, until they used up their excess energy and were tired enough for the lesson. Then she sat them down at the edge of the umbrella forest, near the multi-colored water sprays that seemed to reach up to forever, and by the statue of the giant—the lonely, wandering giant whose love redeemed a world.

She sat in the lotus posture, her backdrop the rainbow sprays. They sat before her, all wide, bright eyes and laughing faces. She spoke to them.

"Are you ready, my children, for the next part of the story?" she asked.

"Yes!" they squealed. "Yes and yes."

"This is the last part," the Green Woman said, resting her elbows on her knees and her face upon her hands, "the best part. Have all of you memorized the rest?"

They squealed again, raising their hands, jumping to be chosen to recite. And slowly, with painstaking care to detail, she listened to the oral history of a People as told through the mouths of its future.

When they were finished, she smiled at the skin and furry faces and the pointed ears and padded paws, then spoke in a slow, dramatic voice.

The ancients laid a nasty trap,
They laid it with their lies.
To trap the People, who believed
The ancients were all wise.

They had a chant, they passed it on,
Told in a sing-song voice.
Bright futures, full of hopes and dreams,
The People thought were choice:

Band of three,
Band of three.
Soldier, builder,
Referee.

Band of three,
Band of three.
The perfect mix,
The apogee.

The apogee of heresy
Is what the ancients told.
For sickness and bleak misery's
What made the Old World old.

The perfect mix was just a lie
To make the People sink
Into the same abyss of old:
Don't use your head, don't think.

Their wretched excess, dark desire,
Was all they understood.
And by making everyone look bad,
They made themselves look good.

But Morgan and the giant
And the box that thought and felt,
Joined hearts together, through their love,
And made the darkness melt.

The sky poured out its water
And brave Morgan climbed the tree.
He screamed into the dark, bleak day
Of the new formed band of three.

He showed the People with his deeds;
They had greatness, they had worth!
He taught them with his gentle ways
How to honor Mother Earth.

Hearts and minds and sweet, kind love
And caring in your deed,
Is all it takes to make one world.
It's all you'll ever need.

She said the story several times that day, patient in her memory work with the children. This was the last stop on this planting's tour, and as she drew to a close, her thoughts turned homeward.

She hadn't seen Reeder, her husband, for several months. He didn't get around quite as well as he used to, and there were probably many things at home to be done.

She felt good this time. The children were a fine crop, strong and free, well-tuned to the movements of life. There weren't too many more tours in her; she was old corn, ready to be harvested. But that was as it should be. She felt the fullness of time well spent and the inner peace of contentment.

She had a life.

Before she left, the children begged and pleaded for her to do the trick. They always asked it, and she always gave in, though it wasn't as easy to conjure as it used to be.

Standing up straight, she called upon the inner forces of directed empathetic energy. With total concentration, she raised her arms to the heavens and forced all the heat of her body up through her hands in a burst of electromagnetic wonder.

Slowly, majestically, the clouds parted along the shaft of ionization. The heavens opened to bright, blue sky, and a wide, round beam of bright sunlight fell directly upon her, bathing her in Godlike brilliance.

And the children applauded, giggling happily in their innocence and in their wonder.

ABOUT THE AUTHOR

MIKE MCQUAY began his writing career in 1975 while a production line worker at a tire plant. He turned to writing as an escape from the creeping dehumanization he saw in the factory, and gradually worked himself out of Blue Collarland and into Poor-but-happy, starving writerism.

His first novel, *Lifekeeper*, was published in 1980. Since then, he has published thirteen others, ranging from juveniles to mainstream horror, with the emphasis on s/f.

Mother Earth is his ninth novel with Bantam. Others include *Escape from New York*, *Jitterbug*, and *Pure Blood*. He is presently at work on a mainstream thriller.

McQuay is thirty-six years old, and lives in Oklahoma City with his wife and three children. He is an Artist in Residence at Central State University in Edmond, Oklahoma. He watches too much television and adamantly refuses to eat fried okra.

Mel White
9/5/82

Mike McQuay

OUT OF THIS WORLD!

That's the only way to describe Bantam's great series of science fiction classics. These space-age thrillers are filled with terror, fancy and adventure and written by America's most renowned writers of science fiction. Welcome to outer space and have a good trip!